Shae,
Much

Beautifully Brutal

By Nicole Edwards

The Alluring Indulgence Series

Kaleb

Zane

Travis

Holidays with the Walker Brothers

Ethan

Braydon

Sawyer

Brendon

The Club Destiny Series

Conviction

Temptation

Addicted

Seduction

Infatuation

Captivated

Devotion

Perception

Entrusted

Adored

The Dead Heat Ranch Series

Boots Optional

Betting on Grace

Overnight Love

The Devil's Bend Series

Chasing Dreams

Vanishing Dreams

By Nicole Edwards (cont.)

Sniper 1 Security
Wait for Morning

Southern Boy Mafia
Beautifully Brutal

Standalone Novels
A Million Tiny Pieces

Writing as Timberlyn Scott
Unhinged

Unraveling

Chaos

Beautifully **Brutal**

Southern Boy Mafia
Book 1

Nicole Edwards

SL Independent Publishing, LLC

PO Box 806
Hutto, Texas 78634
www.slipublishing.com

Cover Image: © kho | 123rf.com (18628943)
Cover Design: © Nicole Edwards Limited
Editing: Blue Otter Editing www.BlueOtterEditing.com

ISBN (ebook): 978-1-939786-46-3
ISBN (print): 978-1-939786-45-6

Table of Contents

Dedication 8
Chapter One 10
Chapter Two 24
Chapter Three 33
Chapter Four 39
Chapter Five 50
Chapter Six 65
Chapter Seven 76
Chapter Eight 88
Chapter Nine 97
Chapter Ten 105
Chapter Eleven 119
Chapter Twelve 132
Chapter Thirteen 140
Chapter Fourteen 153
Chapter Fifteen 164
Chapter Sixteen 173
Chapter Seventeen 182
Chapter Eighteen 188
Chapter Nineteen 193
Chapter Twenty 200
Chapter Twenty-One 213
Chapter Twenty-Two 218
Chapter Twenty-Three 223
Chapter Twenty-Four 230
Chapter Twenty-Five 235
Chapter Twenty-Six 239
Chapter Twenty-Seven 246
Chapter Twenty-Eight 250
Chapter Twenty-Nine 261
Chapter Thirty 270
Chapter Thirty-One 275
Chapter Thirty-Two 279

Chapter Thirty-Three 285
Chapter Thirty-Four 290
Chapter Thirty-Five 295
Chapter Thirty-Six 298
Chapter Thirty-Seven 304
Chapter Thirty-Eight 311
Chapter Thirty-Nine 318
Chapter Forty 322
Chapter Forty-One 326
Chapter Forty-Two 335
Chapter Forty-Three 338
Chapter Forty-Four 347
Chapter Forty-Five 354
Chapter Forty-Six 359
Chapter Forty-Seven 363
Chapter Forty-Eight 367
Chapter Forty-Nine 371
Chapter Fifty 376
Chapter Fifty-One 378
Chapter Fifty-Two 385
Chapter Fifty-Three 395
Chapter Fifty-Four 404
Chapter Fifty-Five 409
Epilogue 412
Acknowledgments 416

Dedication

This book is dedicated to my soul mate, Colt Edwards.

It's hard to believe this is book #29. I couldn't have made it this far without you.

Note from the author:

The Southern Boy Mafia series is a spin off from the Sniper 1 Security series. It can be read without reading the Sniper 1 Security series, however, if you'd like to read more about the Kogans and the Trexlers, you should certainly check them out.

I've been known to cross my series over so that you can keep up with the characters from other stories, but the intent is always to keep them separate so they can be read independently.

Enjoy!

Much love,

Nicole Edwards

BREAKDOWN OF THE ADORITES

As with a lot of first books within a series, there is a lot of groundwork to establish. Below is an outline of the families within this series.

THE ADORITES

Parents: Samuel and Genevieve
Children: Maximillian (29), Brent (27), Ashlynn (26), Aidan (26), Victor (24), Madison (22)

THE KOGANS (from Sniper 1 Security)

Parents: Casper and Elizabeth
Children: Conner (33), Hunter (31), Trace (28), Courtney (26)
Grandchildren: Shelby (Conner's daughter)

THE TREXLERS (from Sniper 1 Security)

Parents: Bryce and Emily
Children: Ryan/RT (33), Colby (31), Clay (28), Marissa (26), Austin (24)

BRYCE'S YOUNGER BROTHER'S FAMILY:

Parents: TJ (Bryce's younger brother) and Stephanie
Children: Tanner (25), Kira (24), Evan (23), Dominic (22)

Chapter One

It starts the same as it ends.
Beautifully brutal.

Twenty-four months ago

Maximillian Adorite studied the woman strolling toward him, curious as to why she had graced him with her presence tonight of all nights.

Coincidence?

No. Couldn't be.

Max didn't believe in coincidence.

Despite his interest in who she was and why she was there, on the very night when a potential shit storm was brewing around him, he found himself transfixed by her, something that didn't usually happen to him.

Not like this.

In his world, women were a dime a dozen. He credited that to the wealth and danger that surrounded him. Women liked bad boys, and Max's reputation definitely qualified him for that list. Then again, the women he shared his time with usually figured that out the morning after, when he—politely, if he had been interested enough to catch her name—asked them to leave.

However, this dark-haired beauty … the one with the most striking eyes he'd ever seen—they literally glowed white—was so intriguing he'd found himself watching her for most of the night. But that was all he'd done. Because this woman wasn't the type who would warm his sheets for only a few hours. He knew that instantly, and since he wasn't interested in anything more than a couple of hours, he had fought the urge to introduce himself.

Then again, she knew who he was. He was the very reason she was there, or so he'd been told. It'd been his idea to offer the invitation so he could get more information on her, see her in action. This woman … she was his enemy, and Max was interested in keeping her close, getting to know more about her to determine if she was the threat he'd been told she was.

Not that he was all too worried about what she did or didn't want from him. Or vice versa.

He could sense by her nearness that she was a distraction he definitely didn't need. Especially tonight. Seeing as he was the host of this party—or what appeared to be a party from the outside looking in and was, in fact, the announcement of a transfer of power—she was a temptation he should avoid but one he couldn't bring himself to stray too far from. And here she was, successfully keeping him from his other guests, yet he couldn't muster an ounce of regret.

"And you are?" he asked innocuously, holding his hand out to greet her when she approached.

"Courtney Kogan," she replied firmly, a hint of defiance in her raspy tone, in the subtle way she tilted her chin as she spoke. "But I suppose you already knew that."

A battle of wills.

Very intriguing.

With his hand still hovering between them, he waited for her to slide her fingers against his palm. Never taking his eyes off her face, his gaze locked with hers, Max allowed his brain to process her touch, his body hardening instantly. Bringing her fingers to his lips, he kissed her knuckles softly, inhaling the subtle yet sexy scent of her perfume, something warm and exotic—much like her—with a hint of jasmine and amber wood drifting toward him. Intoxicating.

"Nice to meet you, Courtney Kogan."

Max hadn't needed the formal introduction, however; he still would've recognized the name, known who she was, who she worked for, and why she was there, but he kept his expression masked.

"Don't be so sure of that," she said, a throaty drawl accompanying her words while her satisfied grin hinted at something darker, far more dangerous than what he'd expected from her. From a distance, Courtney had appeared sweet, perhaps a little shy even, but up close, she was anything but.

There was a glimmer of determination in her white-gray eyes, the kohl liner making her look slightly intimidating and a little older than the twenty-four years he knew her to be. The daring smirk on her glossy lips and a hint of a blush on her high, delicate cheekbones contradicted that steely resolve, though.

No, this woman wasn't sweet or shy. She was a contradiction. A dangerous one if he had to guess.

Max knew all about dark and dangerous. It was his life. He was the son of Samuel and Genevieve Adorite, and Max's world was entrenched in the dark and dirty underworld that his parents had proudly built around them.

Southern Boy Mafia, they called them.

Max wasn't one to put labels on himself or his family, but he couldn't deny the fact that, by definition, that was exactly what they were. Mafia.

No, there weren't any Italian roots in his family, nor were they tied to any of the five families directly, didn't have any involvement with the Cosa Nostra, either, but they were, in fact, connected. *Even without those direct ties, they were extremely powerful, more so than most people realized, which had brought them to the attention of some of the most formidable families in the world.*

His father, Samuel, was the leader of the Adorite family—known to all as the boss. Before him had been Max's grandfather, Floyd, and before him, Max's great-grandfather, Andrew. And so on and so forth. Throughout time, control of their extremely profitable businesses had remained within the family, transferring to the eldest male child, although their organization, spanning the vast state of Texas, was made up of much more than that.

Max had recently moved into the position of underboss, a rank within the hierarchy that had been set out for him from the beginning. At least until he would take over the entire organization from his father. Until recently, the second-in-command position had been held by Samuel's younger brother, Nick. However, since Nick's stroke three months ago, which had resulted in Max's uncle being partially paralyzed and suffering from immense neurological damage leaving him unable to make decisions critical to his position, Max had taken over. As had always been the intention.

At twenty-seven, Max was now the second most powerful man in their organization. Despite the number, Max certainly didn't feel young. In fact, he felt decades older, thanks to the toll this world had taken on him.

Not that he spent his days worried about his next birthday or the chain of command or that the media had dubbed them the Southern Boy Mafia sometime in the late sixties. Business was business, and it just so happened that their family dabbled in plenty of money-making opportunities.

Were they legal? Some of them, sure. Others, no. But that was the way of the world.

Max's respect for his father and the family ran far and wide, and he'd been born into a life that would forever be based on a strict structure, so Max had fallen into the position as was expected of him, which he took very seriously.

As for his three brothers, Brent, Victor, and Aidan, as well as his two sisters, Ashlynn and Madison, they were all involved in the family business in one way or another, or, as in Victor's and Madison's case, they were finishing school before they devoted themselves fully. Both of Max's youngest siblings were currently in law school. Although the rest of them had all handled their own aspect of the organization as they'd seen fit since the day they'd each turned twenty-one, they still reported directly to Max, always had, even before this change. Not that he was certain what they were doing most of the time, but he made a valiant effort to keep up with them when he could.

The one thing he knew with utmost certainty was that people feared him, feared what his family was capable of. And rightfully so. With the help of his right-hand man, Leyton Matheson, Max fully intended to carry on the business, as well as the family name.

But right here, right now, with this woman in the sparkling silver gown that accentuated her perfect curves—the kind of curves a man could easily grab hold of—he wasn't worried about business or family, or even money, for that matter.

He was curious as to what her game was.

"And why do you say that?" he probed, amused and intrigued in equal measure.

"No reason," she stated off-handedly, her gaze sliding down to his mouth briefly before breaking away completely. "I should let you get back to your guests. I merely wanted to thank you for inviting me."

Max nodded, once again studying her. She was an enigma. Her body language was saying things her luscious lips weren't, but he could tell with this particular woman, her brain called all the shots. If he had to guess, she didn't listen much to what her body wanted. Something else that fascinated him where she was concerned.

"I look forward to seeing you later," he declared. It wasn't a request, and by the way that her iridescent gaze slammed back to his, she recognized that.

"For your sake, Mr. Adorite, I hope you're comfortable with disappointment then." With that, she turned and took two steps in the opposite direction, glancing back at him over her bare shoulder as she said, "Because as far as you and I are concerned, that's all I have to offer you."

Another challenge. He liked that about her, as well.

Max watched her go, admiring the sleek lines of her curvy, petite body, the smooth, golden skin of her back, which was completely bare in that halter dress, the generous flare of her hips…

He wondered if she was as soft to the touch as she appeared.

Yes, Courtney Kogan was a decadent temptation, one he hadn't allowed himself in quite some time.

And Max found himself craving more of her.

He kept his eye on her as she slipped into the crowd, mingling with some of his high-profile guests, including a state senator, a couple of local judges, an overabundance of his own organization, along with, yes, a few of his enemies. What was the saying? Keep your friends close but your enemies closer? That was one he took to heart.

Max glanced to his side when a large body appeared in his peripheral vision.

"Anything you need, sir?" Leyton asked, his keen eyes scanning the room as he stood beside Max.

"I've got some preliminary information, but I want you to find out what you can on her," Max instructed, nodding his head toward Courtney. "Everything you can."

"Yes, sir."

With Leyton's help and some more personal inquiry, by the end of the night, Max fully intended to know more about Miss Kogan.

A lot more.

□»«□»«□»«□

"Max! Oh, God! We… Max! We can't do this." Courtney knew her denial sounded lame, especially since she was breathless, moaning, and clutching Max to her, giving in to the wonder that was his mouth.

The man could kiss, she'd give him that.

Although this… She wasn't sure this was classified as a mere kiss.

No, the way he crushed her between his impressive body and the wall, his rock-hard cock pressed against her belly, his muscular thigh grinding against her sex, his strong hands cupping her head, his determined tongue delving into her mouth…

No. This wasn't a kiss.

This was a claiming.

And Courtney was giving in to the intoxicating pleasure although she knew she shouldn't. Hell, she still wasn't entirely sure how she'd gotten to this point, making out in an empty hallway, plastered to the wall by the glorious weight of this man.

For the better part of the night, she'd kept a safe distance between herself and Maximillian Andrew Adorite and thought—apparently in error—that she'd managed to stay off his radar. But then, after she'd mingled a couple of hours with the people closest to him and had a few glasses of champagne, he'd asked her to dance. Which, now that she thought about it, had led to this heated make-out session.

Oh, God!

"Max," she said breathlessly. "Please, I…" What the hell was she trying to say?

Another moan escaped her.

If he kept doing that, she was going to come.

"You want this as much as I do," he groaned as his mouth trailed down her neck, the smooth skin of his clean-shaven jaw brushing against her cheek, his warm lips leaving a path of fire in their wake. He smelled good, like musk and man and … sex.

Sliding her fingers into the silky dark hair at the back of his head, Courtney pulled him closer, holding him to her, while his big, strong hand slid over her shoulder, drifted down her bare back, toward the curve of her waist and then farther, coming to rest briefly on her hip. He squeezed her gently before gliding his palm over her ass and down the back of her thigh.

His touch was exquisite. Powerful, determined. And she found herself defenseless against the onslaught of desire that sizzled in her veins, setting every nerve ending on fire.

When he lifted her thigh to his hip, bent his knees slightly, and adjusted their positions so that she was no longer riding his thigh, Courtney thought she would detonate. Now, she was…

"Max!" The erotic grind of his thick, rigid cock against her clit nearly sent her over the edge. When his mouth returned to hers, his teeth nipping her lower lip before sucking on it, the pleasure-pain had her hovering on the brink of orgasm.

Oh, God, yes!

Never once in her twenty-four years had she had a reaction to anyone like this. That all-encompassing need, the desperate, almost painful ache to be surrounded by him, filled by him. She'd always been daring and wild, but underneath that reckless exterior, Courtney's decisions were carefully thought out.

This wasn't what she'd consider careful.

Making out—in plain sight of anyone who cared to take a trip down this hallway—with Maximillian Adorite, the oldest child of Samuel David Adorite, the official crime boss of the Adorite family, otherwise known as the Southern Boy Mafia. More accurately, she was making out with the oldest son, the heir to the throne, so to speak, of one of the wealthiest—not to mention deadliest—families in Texas.

Technically, Max's status had just been upgraded, and Courtney was now lip-locked with the recently instated underboss, something she couldn't lose sight of, no matter how good his mouth was.

Max.

The same man who was making his power known tonight to those who would be working with him going forward—not to mention to her*, although this particular expression of power was an entirely different type of conversation.*

The changing of the guard, as her father had referred to it, was the reason for this party, the sole explanation as to why she was there to gather information for the client who'd hired Sniper 1 Security, her family's business.

Oh, God! Why me?

"Max." Courtney could hardly speak, the pleasure robbing her of her common sense, making her want things she was usually smart enough to resist.

"Stay with me tonight," Max insisted, his head lifting, his sparkling honey-gold eyes meeting hers as he released her leg and brought his large palms up to cup her face. His thumbs gently skimmed her cheeks as he held her head firmly between his hands once again.

He was so big, so broad, so … there.

At six foot, Max's presence was felt as well as seen, the power that radiated from him palpable. He made her feel feminine, almost delicate, and definitely smaller than her five foot four inches. So much smaller.

Aside from how hot he made her, there was so much about the man she should fear, including who and what he was, but she couldn't seem to keep her hands off him.

Trying to fight the desire, to listen to the warning bells clanging in her head, Courtney shook her head, swallowed hard.

"I can see it in your eyes, Courtney." The rough, deep tenor of his voice resonated along her nerve endings, making her ache for him. "You want to stay with me. You want to feel me inside you, to feel me against you, skin to skin."

Again, she shook her head. It was a lie, but one she was sticking to. She did *want him,* did *want to feel him inside her, to sweep her fingers along his naked flesh and touch the rock-hard body beneath the expensive tuxedo while he fucked her into a mind-numbing euphoria.*

But that was stupid.

That *was reckless.*

Max's thumbs pressed against her chin, his palms cupping her jaw, fingers splayed along the back of her neck, as he tilted her head so that she had no choice but to look up into his eyes. Her body succumbed to the ecstasy of his touch as he pressed against her, his hard, muscular thigh once again sliding between her legs, grinding against her pussy, waves of pleasure crashing inside her, intensifying until she could hardly breathe for wanting this man.

Thankfully, she had an ounce of common sense left.

"No." She made sure there was no mistaking her adamant denial that time.

And just as she had hoped he would, Max released her, slowly stepping back, but his piercing gaze still pinned her in place.

"I'll never force you, Courtney. But I will *have you. Make no mistake, I will have you in my bed, where you'll be beggin' me to make you come. It* will *happen."*

Courtney swallowed hard. She hated him. Hated what he did to her. Hated how much she wanted him, despite knowing better. Hated that, when it came to him, her body seemed to be making all the decisions.

But more importantly, Courtney hated him for the man he was.

Despite the lavish exterior—mocha-brown hair and glowing gold eyes, a sexy body, and exquisite mouth—Courtney knew exactly who this man was beneath it all. No matter how attractive or polished he looked on the outside, Max wasn't the man he appeared to be.

He was evil. Pure and simple. A killer.

And her mission was to get information on him and his family, the transfer of power, the businesses that they ran … not to get into his bed. Yet here she was, battling with her conscience, weighing the difference between right and wrong, good and bad.

Righting her dress and sliding her hand over her hair in an effort to tame it, Courtney stood straight and squared her shoulders. "Tell yourself whatever you have to in order to sleep at night, Mr. Adorite. But *make no mistake*," she said, throwing his words back at him, "it will never happen."

To her surprise, Max didn't argue, but the smirk that flirted with the corners of his mouth said more than words.

"Good night, Mr. Adorite," she told him, turning and walking away without looking back.

As she headed back to the ballroom, where the party was still going strong, Courtney felt his eyes penetrating her, the same as they'd done for most of the night. She inhaled deeply, trying to regain her composure.

That man…

Damn it.

Fighting the urge to turn back and run into his arms, Courtney rounded the corner, grateful that no one was there to see her loss of equanimity as she leaned her back against the wall, her breaths coming in shallow and rushed. Her body was on fire, her insides melting from the pleasure his touch had promised.

How had she gotten herself into this position? How in the hell had she allowed herself to be seduced by Maximillian Adorite? A freaking gangster.

Get a hold of yourself.

Taking a long, deep breath, then exhaling slowly, she stood straight once more, refusing to let him win this round.

Walking away from Max was the smart choice. Her only choice. And as her breathing returned to normal, she made up her mind to do just that.

Not that she thought Max was giving up. He was the type of man who got exactly what he wanted. And she understood that she presented a challenge to him. One that he would likely conquer eventually, but Courtney knew she had to walk away. And stay away.

Easier said than done.

Exhaling deeply, Courtney ignored the unnerving feeling that slammed into her … the one that told her, without a doubt, she was on a collision course that she couldn't repave, one that would end, based on what she'd just experienced tonight, either beautiful or brutal.

Then again, based on what she knew of the man, she was more inclined to believe it'd be beautifully brutal.

And part of her was anxious to find out.

The reckless part.

Chapter Two

He still wanted her...
That would never change.

Present day
March 3rd

"She the one?"

Max dared to turn his gaze toward the tall blonde moving slowly across the room. Although *gliding* would probably be a better way of describing her catlike grace. The woman was…

Well, she was vicious. That's what she was.

Nice to look at, sure. Evil incarnate, definitely. Not to mention spoiled and vindictive.

And Max had absolutely no interest in her, aside from appreciating her beauty from afar, admiring the political power that her family was affiliated with, but even that didn't do much for him. His biggest issue with that woman was that the two of them weren't on the same page regarding how things were supposed to work.

In Max's world, he called the shots. All of them.

It'd been two years since he'd taken over as underboss, and during that time, he'd proven himself, proven that he could run the family business, do what needed to be done. Yet that woman seemed to think she had some sort of power over him. It didn't matter that he wasn't physically attracted to her in the least, nor did he want to spend any extra time in her presence; she was disillusioned in her beliefs to the contrary.

Then again, with the current situation he found himself in, it wasn't all that surprising that Angelica Winslow believed otherwise. He knew that she'd been put up to it, coerced by her grandfather and Max's own father to pursue a business arrangement that Max couldn't seem to wrap his head around but knew better than to brush off.

However, yes, she was the one he'd been talking to his younger brother Brent about earlier that morning.

"Yeah," Max confirmed. "You'd be smart to stay far, far away from that one."

Max had never been the kind to give that sort of advice, but he couldn't help himself. If Brent wanted to take a chance with a viper like her, more power to him. Truth was, if Brent would step up to the plate, Max's life would be that much easier.

If Max's brother—hell, any of the three—would figure out what the fuck it was they wanted to do at all, Max would possibly be able to catch his breath. But until that happened, his focus had to remain on keeping his family's businesses running smoothly. Luckily, his two sisters were capable of pulling their own weight, so at least he had that.

"She doesn't *look* evil," Brent commented frankly, sipping his champagne and tucking one hand into the pocket of his slacks. It was a wonder Brent had bothered to dress up for the party. Max's brother had traded his preferred black Stetson and Wrangler jeans for a tuxedo at Max's insistence.

"They never do," Max grumbled under his breath, his thoughts immediately drifting back to the one woman he'd spent the better part of two fucking years wanting with an unrivaled passion. A woman who no other woman could ever hold a candle to.

The very woman he expected to show up tonight.

"You've got guests coming your way, sir," the assertive voice in his ear said.

"You need to take off." Max nodded to his brother, a blatant dismissal that Brent didn't argue with as he cast a curious glance over his shoulder before heading in the opposite direction.

Max turned toward the closed doors of the elaborate ballroom, where he'd been hosting parties for the last couple of years, waiting to see which of the many guests on his extensive list had arrived. The moment the doors opened and *she* stepped into view, his heartbeat slowed, as did his breathing. It was an automatic, predatory response, one that he'd honed over the last two years. It was his body's way of arming for the battle he knew would come. The battle that fired him up and made his body ache for her.

Courtney Kogan.

Fuck, she looked good enough to eat.

He instantly knew that she had worn that dress to torment him. He loved the way the black strapless number hugged her curves, accentuating her narrow waist, her beautiful tits, and the toned muscles in her arms and shoulders. But he knew that the flirty skirt that caressed her mid-thigh wasn't just to draw his eyes to her superb legs. No, that skirt was hiding her weapon, the one she kept strapped to her thigh at all times.

When the four guests neared, Max didn't take his eyes off her.

"Courtney," he greeted assuredly, willing her to meet his gaze.

"Max." The way she said his name, so cold and emotionless, only made his dick twitch, but he didn't allow his expression to change. Instead, he admired the blush that bloomed on her chest and carried up to her cheeks. That was something he loved about her, how easily she responded to him, even though she didn't want to. She continued speaking as he admired her sexy mouth. "You've met Ryan Trexler. This is Trace Kogan, and this is Ryan's sister, Marissa."

Yes, Max knew Ryan Trexler, better known to most as RT. In fact, Max knew Ryan's entire family, as well as the Kogans. It was his business to know about people he suspected of snooping into his organization. With that in mind, the crew at Sniper 1 Security was one he kept his eyes on at all times. Hence the reason they were there.

And tonight, the mere fact that RT was pretending to be Courtney's date, escorting her to Max's house, would've gotten him killed if it weren't for the fact that Max knew the man was gay. Yes, RT's preference for men was the only reason he was still breathing.

"Very nice to see you again," Max said, smiling as he cast a brief glance at RT's sister, politely shaking Marissa's hand.

"Likewise," Marissa replied in kind.

"Thank you again for the invitation," RT said, his eyes searching the room.

Max looked directly at RT when he spoke. "Well, I'd say that I'm happy to see you again, but I'd be lying. However, I do hope you manage to enjoy yourselves tonight," Max stated dismissively, his eyes traveling over Courtney once again before stopping on her face. "As for you, I hope you'll save at least one dance for me."

Courtney didn't respond, at least not with words. Max pretended not to care, not to be overwhelmed with the urge to pull her against him and claim her mouth, forcing her to face this thing between them. This thing she'd been running from for two fucking years. It wasn't the chase that bothered him. Max was all for working for what he wanted, but with Courtney, his willpower came into play. Or lack thereof. The very fact that she could shatter his control bothered him more than anything.

Max watched until Courtney disappeared into the crowd, her friends following close behind.

Touching the earpiece that traveled down into his shirt, Max said, "Leyton. I want eyes on those four at all times. Also, have someone outside. I'm sure there are others."

"Yes, sir," came the gruff agreement from his head of security. "We've got eyes on the three at the perimeter of the house."

"Good. As for these four, don't let them leave this room."

"On it, sir."

For the next hour, Max managed to keep from seeking Courtney out, but it wasn't easy. Mingling with guests, listening to stories he'd heard a half dozen times already while anticipating seeing her, wasn't exactly what he'd consider an enjoyable evening, but it was part of the job. At least the former was.

As he made his way across the room to the bar, Leyton approached, leaning his head in and speaking quietly. "Sir, we've got someone at the door. He's insistin' he talk to you. Says his name is Barry Thompson."

Max lifted his head and met Leyton's unwavering gaze. "Have someone bring him in. Hold him somewhere, I don't care where, just don't let him into this room."

"Yes, sir."

Approaching the bar, Max nodded to the bartender, who stopped what he was doing and proceeded to make Max's drink. As Max stood there, waiting, he turned to scan the room when Courtney approached. He watched as she fiddled with the diamond pendant on her necklace.

She was naïve if she didn't think he was on to her. He knew about the transmitters those four were wearing. He'd known the moment they'd stepped through his doors. But as he waited to hear what she had to say, he pretended not to notice that he now had an audience listening to their conversation.

"Hey, Max. Sounds like there's someone tryin' to crash your party," Courtney offered casually—*too* casually—her eyes never coming to rest on his face.

He hated that she did that. That she wouldn't look him in the eye when she spoke to him. If she'd been anyone else, he would've considered it a sign of disrespect. With her … he knew that wasn't the case. No, with Courtney, he knew her inability to look him in the eye when she had something to say didn't have anything to do with respect but was more of a self-preservation mechanism.

She wanted him.

And it was eating her alive.

"It's bein' handled," Max confirmed, reaching to take the tumbler the bartender set on the bar behind him. Turning back to face her, he followed with, "Tell your boys to stand down."

She did look at him then, glancing over at him from behind the silky fall of her dark brown hair. Her exotic white-gray eyes slid over his face as she swallowed hard. "As long as you can promise he won't get anywhere near Marissa."

"You've got my word on that," Max assured her, never looking away, willing her to see him. *Really* see him.

Unfortunately, she was the one to break the eye contact.

Taking a sip of his cognac, Max studied Courtney, taking in her elegance, the sexy way she carried herself, and most importantly, the way she pretended he wasn't standing less than a foot away from her.

He wanted to tell her that tonight wasn't about Marissa Trexler. Not entirely, anyway. But he kept that little tidbit to himself. No sense in handing over his own agenda when it wasn't necessary to accomplish his goal.

He knew that the Sniper 1 Security team was dealing with an internal issue, one that happened to bleed over into Max's organization to a degree, which was why he fully intended to put that to bed tonight. Their enemy, Dan Duchein—the man Courtney and her cohorts were there to find—had at one point been someone who'd proven himself useful to Max. Until recently.

Ever since the asshole had gone off the reservation and started hunting down Ms. Trexler in an attempt to silence her completely, Max had been watching him closely. He'd known what the guy was doing, who he was after. Hell, he even knew why. It didn't bother Max that the man was attempting to silence what he thought to be a threat to his livelihood. No, Max actually respected him for that. But he didn't approve of the way the guy was going about it.

It was one thing to silence those who could cause a ripple in the financial pond of a corporation, something else entirely to lay the blame elsewhere while doing so. Max fully believed in owning the reason behind the reaction, not opting for the cowardly way out.

Max stood motionless, staring at the beautiful woman he'd spent countless hours getting to know personally—and intimately—when she glared back at him. Neither of them said anything, but nothing really needed to be said. There was a wealth of conversation going on without the need to cloud it with words.

Despite her denial, Courtney still wanted him.

And he still wanted her.

"If you'll excuse me," Courtney said softly before turning.

Max reached for her arm, stopping her before she could retreat. "I want to talk to you."

Courtney glanced down at his hand on her arm, then her gaze lifted to meet his once more. "I've said everything I need to say."

He leaned in closer, and her hand instantly went to the pendant, clearly cutting the transmission so no one else would hear him. "You're wrong about that. There are plenty of things left to be said between us."

Max released her, watching as she walked away, not willing to play this game with her here. Too many eyes on them, too many people who didn't need to see the emotion Max was unable to disguise. Courtney meant something to him. Hell, she meant *everything* to him. And based on experience, Max knew that his enemies, those who thought they could take him down or disrupt his business, wouldn't shy away from using her against him.

It wasn't until he noticed RT and Trace speaking to the man Max had been expecting to show up that he realized the games had begun.

Special Agent Dan Duchein had arrived.
Which meant the real party was about to begin.

Chapter Three

A weakness…
Those were easy to resist, right?

Courtney forced herself to walk away from Max, reminding herself—again—of the reason she was there tonight. It certainly wasn't to steal glances at him from across the room or battle the jealousy that coursed through her when she saw him talking to other women. She was the one who had broken it off with him nearly a year ago, which meant she had absolutely no right to be jealous.

No right to him at all, in fact.

It wasn't easy, pretending not to want him, but then again, it never had been easy to walk away from the one man she wanted more than she wanted anything else.

For the past two years, since the very first time she'd given in to Max, making out with him in a hallway in this very house, she'd felt as though she were living in a modern-day version of Romeo and Juliet. Her family, a group of elite security advisors, spent their lives protecting people, saving them from dangerous situations, handling their every protection need in some cases. As for Max's family … they were gangsters fueled by money and power, and they'd stop at nothing to get what they wanted.

She and Max were from two very different worlds.

And it'd taken every ounce of willpower she had to stay away from him, but somehow Courtney had managed for the last year. She'd used her best friend, Marissa, as an excuse, wanting to focus all of her extra energy on bringing her back home after their families had started stashing Marissa in safe houses across the US in order to keep her safe from the man who was hell-bent on kidnapping—or worse, killing—her.

How well did that work for you?

Ignoring the prickly voice in her head, she forced her attention on the mission. Z was waiting at the rear entrance of the lavish ballroom for Courtney to deliver Marissa to him. They needed to get their principal out of there, and that was Courtney's one and only job at the moment, ensuring Marissa made it safely from point A to point B.

There were voices sounding in her earpiece. Excited, eager voices. Trace. RT. Z. The determination in their tone spurred her into action as she made her way across the room, coming to assist.

"Well, look there. It's none other than Special Agent Dan Duchein. Didn't know you had an invite to this party."

Courtney noted the urgency in her brother's voice. Apparently their guest of honor had arrived and set his sights on Marissa, as they'd expected him to.

"We need to get her out of here." That had to be Duchein. He sounded almost frantic. Impatient.

Trace's voice broadcasted in her ear again. "Her?"

"Marissa Trexler," Duchein snarled. "The woman behind you?"

Courtney continued walking while waiting to hear what Duchein's excuse would be. He didn't disappoint.

"I'm here on official business. We got some intel that this is a setup. You've walked her right into a trap. The Adorites won't let her leave here alive."

Courtney rolled her eyes. If that'd been the case, Max would've had Marissa eliminated before they stepped foot *in* the house. He wasn't the type to delay the inevitable if he felt it would benefit his cause.

"Ask him where his backup is." RT's voice came through loud and clear, but Courtney had yet to locate where her team leader was.

As she continued to listen to the conversation, she moved closer, squeezing between the other guests lingering in the ballroom.

"Where's your backup?" Trace asked.

"Two stationed at the front, two at the back."

"If they are, they're invisible." Conner's rough grumble resounded in Courtney's ear. Her oldest brother was stationed outside, keeping an eye on things with Z, one of Sniper 1's tenured operators, along with RT's brother, Colby.

"I'm taking her into protective custody, Kogan. Nothing you can do to stop me."

A chill washed over her when Courtney heard her brother's answering growl. "Over my dead fucking body."

"This isn't your call. She's in danger, and you're putting her there."

"You're the only danger to her, Duchein."

"What the fuck are you talkin' about?"

Yep, definitely guilty. Duchein's defensive counterpoint had come out far too quickly.

"I'm on your six," Courtney said, smiling sweetly as she squeezed past another couple standing directly behind Marissa. "I'm escorting Marissa to Z."

"Confirmed," Z responded in her ear.

The conversation between Trace and Duchein continued, but Courtney tuned them out, focusing solely on getting her best friend to safety. Peering around Marissa, Courtney saw Z standing at one of the sets of doors leading out onto the terrace. Gripping Marissa's wrist firmly, Courtney led her to Z, not releasing her until Z had her.

"I've got Marissa. Conner's with us. Escorting her out." Z's monotone drawl was in stereo—she heard him speak directly in front of her, and it echoed in her earpiece.

Nodding her head, she turned as they disappeared outside. "I'm on my way back to you," Courtney told Trace.

Courtney noticed people were beginning to focus on the heated squabble, other guests now circling the men arguing as they watched the verbal spar. She knew they needed to find somewhere private to deal with this issue. And fast.

"Gentlemen," Courtney said, injecting as much saccharin in her tone as she could, "why don't we take this somewhere with a little more privacy. Our gracious host has offered his office." It was a lie, but she figured it was a safe one. She knew without a doubt that Max did not want this to take place in public.

"After you," Trace told Duchein, signaling for him to lead the way.

Unfortunately, it didn't appear that Duchein was worried about other eyes watching them because he didn't move. That blatant disrespect for Max sent warning bells clanging. If the man knew what was best for him, he wouldn't cross the one man who *would* eliminate him right here, right now, witnesses be damned.

"Where is she?" Duchein barked. "Where is Marissa Trexler?"

"*Who*?"

The sound of Max's voice had Courtney's entire body going on high alert. The venom dripping from the single word told her that he'd passed the point of calm. And when he placed his hand at the small of her back, she sucked in a breath. His touch had always done that to her, and clearly she wasn't as immune to him as she'd hoped.

No one replied to Max, and when he spoke again, there wasn't an ounce of request in his tone. "Gentlemen, either we relocate this conversation to my office or things are about to get real ugly."

"Lead the way, Mr. Adorite," RT stated in response.

Courtney had no choice but to walk when Max pressed her forward, the warmth of his hand searing her back. Those sensations she'd worked so hard to stop thinking about once again rioted inside her. Unfortunately, and despite knowing what was best for her, Courtney feared her body would always belong to Max. No other man would ever be able to touch her the way he did.

As Courtney walked close to their gracious host, she heard him when he leaned over and spoke to RT. "If anything happens to her, I'll kill you myself."

Courtney rolled her eyes, knowing Max was referring to her. From the moment she had met him, he'd been the protective, possessive type. At no point during their entire relationship had she ever given him the idea that she needed him to take care of her, but he apparently had never noticed.

Without looking at either of them, she said to RT, "He always had an issue with me knowin' how to protect myself. It's one of the reasons our relationship never worked out."

Not the main reason, but one of the many.

Courtney picked up the pace, heading directly to Max's office. She needed to get this over with and get far away from this man before she did something really, really stupid.

Like give in to him again, because no matter what she tried to tell herself, Maximillian Adorite had always—*always*—been her weakness.

Chapter Four

No more games… Dead man walking.

Max followed closely behind Courtney as she stepped into his office. He nodded to the two armed bodyguards as he walked by them, signaling for them to follow him inside. This evening hadn't gone quite as he had anticipated. The events thus far had pushed him past the point of furious, despite the fact he'd been the one to set this in motion.

Regardless, he was done playing games with these people. It was time to put an end to this shit once and for all. He would allow RT and Trace to get the answers they were looking for—if they could do so timely and without bullshit—but he wouldn't be much more gracious than that.

"Where is she?"

Max turned to face Duchein, noticing his usually calm façade had slipped, his face splotchy and red, his anger evident. No, the ATF agent hadn't managed to get his hands on the woman he was seeking, but Max hadn't intended for him to when he'd offered the invitation for tonight.

Although he'd known that this would happen, his motives had been not at all altruistic. That wasn't Max's style. If anyone believed him to be one of the good guys, they didn't know him. At all.

He could've easily resolved this by putting a bullet in Duchein's head long before now, and his men would've disposed of his body, never to be seen or heard from again, yet here they were. Duchein's chest puffed up as though he actually had any sort of authority with his government job and his fancy-ass title.

Remaining close to Courtney, Max tilted his chin toward the doors, and the two men stationed there closed them, flipping the lock.

No one took a seat.

"Where is *who*?" Courtney said in response to Duchein's question.

Peering over at her, Max fought the surge of lust that ricocheted inside him at the resonance of her sweet voice and the cocky look on her beautiful face. She sounded oblivious to what was going on, but he knew better. The woman knew how to play a man well.

Too well.

"Marissa Trexler," Duchein sneered.

Courtney glanced at her brother. "I thought she was with you."

RT turned to Trace. "I thought she was with you."

Trace shrugged. "I thought she was with you."

Max was quickly growing tired of this fucking game. These guys—the ones who considered themselves the *good* guys—might have their own way of doing things, but here, in Max's house, he called the shots.

"Question is, what do you really want with Ms. Trexler?" Max asked, his tone hard, firm.

"She's … uh… We're… That's none of your goddamn business."

Really?

Max sighed.

Here was a man Max had done business with for quite some time. A smart man. A powerful man. Also a thief, a liar, and a cheat. One who provided Max with confiscated guns that were in the hands of the US government, and the bastard was going to talk to him like he was a piece of shit on his shoe?

No.

Not going to happen.

Rather than retaliate by killing the man instantly, Max continued to stare at him. He'd successfully honed his patience, learned not to react. It had served him well over the years, and it had earned him a shit load of respect.

From smart men. Men unlike Dan Duchein.

Max kept his voice calm yet deadly when he said, "No? Considering this is my house, my fucking party, I'd say it's exactly my business."

"I don't answer to any of you," Duchein retorted hotly. "Don't forget who I am. Who I work for. Trust me, you'll regret double-crossing me."

"Double-crossing? Is that what you call this? Seemed more to me like biting the hand that feeds you," Max imparted. God, he hated this little shithead, but he had to admit, the guy had served his purpose over the years. "Now, we can settle this like men or you can take your chances with my boys." Max nodded to the two gunmen flanking the exit. "Either way, we're going to get a few answers before you go."

"I have nothing to say. To anyone."

What happened next ripped every ounce of Max's well-honed patience to shreds in an instant.

The world around him slowed, everything centering on Duchein when the man reached out, wrapping his thick fingers around Courtney's slender arm and wrenching her toward him. Caught off guard, she stumbled but righted herself as Duchein slammed her body against his, her back to his front, as his right arm rose, his gun aimed directly at Courtney's temple.

Courtney's stunned gaze slammed into Max's, and right then and there, something snapped inside of him. Something colder and darker than anything he'd ever known before, something that he knew he would never be able to get back again, but he couldn't bring himself to care.

Time seemed to slow even more as Duchein shifted toward the door, and that was when Max slipped his gun out of his waistband and aimed it at Duchein's head. Trace and RT, as well as Max's guards, followed suit. The sound of weapons being cocked resounded in the room.

Max felt an internal shift, and the growl that came out was reflective of the beast roaring inside of him. The one that told him to kill the fucker who'd dared to touch the woman who meant more to him than his own fucking heartbeat. It'd been Duchein's last mistake. Max would make damn sure of that. "Let. Her. Go."

"Let me out of this room and I'll do that," Duchein countered, as though he had a chance in hell of walking out of there alive.

Max decided to placate him for the time being. "Open the door for him."

His guards moved to the doors, opening them as they kept their attention locked on Duchein and Courtney, following every movement while Duchein backed them toward the exit.

Max fought the red haze that blurred his vision. "Duchein, I'm gonna make myself very, very clear. You better listen to every single word. You hurt her in any way, I'll gun you down myself and put a bullet in your face. Feel me?" Truth was, Max would prefer to gut the fucker and watch him bleed out while suffering for as long as Max could keep him alive.

Duchein nodded as he continued to back out of the room. When he got to the door, Duchein released Courtney. As she toppled forward, Max reached for her, just as she pulled her little .38 from beneath her dress.

Relishing the thought of killing Duchein slowly, Max called out. "Hey, Duchein! You can run, but I can guarantee I will find you. And when I do…"

"Goin' somewhere?"

Max clenched his teeth in anticipation when he realized his night wasn't over yet, his chance for immediate revenge not out of his grasp. One of the other good guys—the big bastard who'd come with RT to talk last week—placed his gigantic hand in the center of Duchein's chest and forced him back into the room. More of RT's people followed behind the giant, including Marissa Trexler.

A reunion took place as Trace claimed his woman. Max turned his attention to Courtney. She didn't look at all fazed by what had happened, which didn't surprise him. She was, without a doubt, one fierce woman. Then again, how could she not be, considering the world she'd grown up in?

The world that had molded her into who she was, the same as Max's world had molded him.

Good versus evil.

Max reined his thoughts back in. "I guess the night's not over yet, huh?"

Knowing things were about to get really ugly, Max repositioned himself, pulling Courtney behind him. She did surprise him then when she didn't put up a fight, which likely meant she wasn't as unaffected as she pretended to be. The possessive beast inside him roared once again, desperate to claim her. To show her that, yes, she did belong to him.

RT interrupted Max's thoughts when he said, "So, why don't we try this again."

Duchein didn't look at all happy.

"What do you want with Marissa Trexler?" Max ground out as his patience slipped another notch. He wasn't interested in having a chat over fucking tea. It was time they got this shit over with.

"To take her into protective custody," Duchein stated firmly.

"That's horseshit," the big guy—Z—declared.

"Do you even know who I am?"

The smartass answer that followed came from none other than Courtney's brother Trace. "I've got this one. I think I've answered it before. A prick in a suit. That's the right answer?"

Duchein snarled.

Max saw the instant Trace decided to take charge. A sideways glance at Z, who then reached for Marissa, and then Trace was stalking toward Duchein. It was an almost casual move, one Max actually admired.

And when Trace gripped the front of Duchein's shirt and yanked him closer, Max admired him all the more. "I'm fucking tired of the bullshit, asshole. Either you answer the questions or I'm gonna assume I know them already."

"What do you think you know?" Duchein growled in response.

This was the part where Max had to be careful. It was one thing for Sniper 1 Security to want to protect their own. But it damn sure wouldn't be at Max's expense. He had a business to run, and Duchein—although he didn't realize it yet—was about to become an example to all the others whom Max did business with. He wouldn't sit by and allow Duchein to share details of his organization's dealings. There were partners to protect, some very powerful men who respected Max and trusted him with their livelihoods, not to mention, Max had his own reputation to protect. He certainly hadn't made it this far because he'd tolerated bullshit from men like Duchein. Quite the opposite.

Trace lifted his gun and trained it on Duchein's forehead. Max didn't worry that Trace would shoot the guy. Sure, Trace was capable of capping him, but he knew that was the difference between Max and the good guys. They had a sliver of conscience that would step in and stop what had to be done.

Max did not.

He'd already taken stock of the situation, understood where RT and his crew stood. They were willing to protect Marissa at any cost. In any normal circumstance, Max might've reconsidered his options, but he didn't fear what they would do to him. They wanted to be rid of Duchein as much as Max did.

Trace growled, his face close to Duchein's. "That you're a greedy fucking bastard. That you're sellin' confiscated guns, and when the media got a little too close to the truth, you panicked, taking out an innocent journalist and trying to kill Marissa. That sound about right?"

Duchein's jaw clamped shut.

Smart bastard.

Of course, as Max expected, Trace continued, and he let him.

"So, during this war of yours for the past year, we lost one of our best agents, another took a bullet from one of your hired guns, and Marissa has lived through hell trying to hide from you. All because you wanted her silenced."

Duchein's eyes darted over to Max. "She knows too much. She can bring us all down."

Exactly what Max had been anticipating. Duchein wasn't going to go down alone, but Max had known that about him all along. One of the reasons Max had made sure to have eyes on Duchein since the stupid asshole had approached him in the beginning, offering his "services." Duchein was fueled by greed and the need for power.

Max was not. He had both.

"Who's us?" Max asked innocently.

"That's bullshit. Don't you dare pin this shit on me," Duchein snapped.

Max heard the big guy—Z—relay instructions into his earpiece, and the door at the back of Max's office opened. Never allowing an unknown to come from behind him, Max shifted so that his back was to the wall and so that Courtney was still behind him. It put him directly in line with Duchein's profile. A perfect shot.

"Recognize him?" RT asked. "The guy used to work for you, right? But then you sent him to us. Asked him to try to get some inside information."

It was the mole that the Sniper 1 boys had in their midst.

"Mr. Rhames, you have anything you wanna say?" RT asked.

"He's the one I work for," Isaac said.

Max rolled his eyes. These people. Seriously. Sure, the guy had a gun pointed at his head, but he seemed awfully eager to tell the truth. As though that was going to save him. Had it been someone in his own organization, the fucker would've already been buzzard food in one of Max's many landfills.

"Bring the other one in," RT insisted.

Max nodded at the guards near the door. Once the door was opened, Leyton joined them, holding their surprise visitor at gunpoint.

"Gotta name?" RT asked.

"That's the guy from the mall," Courtney commented from behind Max, her hand resting on his arm. "The one who tried to grab Marissa."

"Barry Thompson," the guy mumbled.

"Who do you work for, Mr. Thompson?" Max questioned. He already knew the answer to that, but he figured what the fuck. These people were in search of answers, he might as well help them out a little.

"This asshole," Thompson declared, nodding toward Duchein.

"And what is it that you do for him?" RT asked.

"He hired me to snatch the girl."

"Which girl?" Trace asked.

"Marissa Trexler. He told me that Mr. Adorite was blackmailing him and he had to produce the girl or he was as good as dead."

That was his cue.

"Well, he got one thing right," Max disclosed gruffly. Without hesitation, Max lifted his trusty 9mm, aimed, and fired one bullet perfectly into Duchein's skull, brain matter and blood spattering all over Trace, who was still holding the man up by the shirt.

Silence. That was all that could be heard after the muted gunshot.

Time to get back to the party. Turning his attention to RT, Max asked, "You get the reassurance you needed?"

The dead guy dropped like a stone when Trace released his shirt. Max didn't look away from RT.

"What reassurance is that?" Trace questioned harshly.

"That I'm not after your girl," Max replied casually.

"No? That's not what Duchein said," Trace said coldly. "According to your *business partner*, you set us up. Lured Marissa here to take her out."

Business partner. Right.

"I heard what he said," Max retorted. "I hear every fucking thing that goes on. Don't forget that."

RT stepped closer, coming to stand directly in front of Max. "We're takin' you at your word. This is over."

"She's never been an issue for me." Max glanced over at Marissa. "I assure you, the threat to her is gone."

"Why'd you kill him?" Barry asked.

Well, that was easy. "Because he touched what belongs to me."

Max didn't need to tell them that he'd intended to kill Duchein all along because he didn't trust him, because the man had betrayed him. That wasn't the only reason Max had put a bullet in his skull tonight. The main reason was that the stupid fucker had dared to touch what was his. Any man who thought he could lay his hand on Courtney and get away with it had better think again.

"Thank you for inviting us to your lovely party," Courtney said sardonically, drawing Max's attention to her. "But I think we're gonna call it a night."

"Courtney."

In a move that Max actually found amusing, Courtney merely lifted her hand, waving it behind her head without turning back. "Good to see you, Max. Let's not do this again sometime."

Max fought a grin as he followed the others to the door.

"What about me?" Barry asked as they passed.

"Oh, we're gonna have us a little chat," Max told him. "Don't you worry."

"What about that one?" Dean, another of Max's employees, asked, nodding toward the back of the room.

Max paused briefly, turning to glance at their mole. He pretended to consider that for a moment and smiled to himself when RT called out, "We're done with him. If you don't mind, we'll let you take out the trash."

"My pleasure," Max said, turning back around and heading to the door. "But not tonight. I've got a party to get back to. Y'all find those two shitheads some accommodations for the night," he instructed his employees, holstering his gun beneath his jacket, adjusting his tie, and returning to the party.

The night hadn't been a complete loss.

At least not for him. He couldn't say the same for Duchein.

Chapter Five

Sometimes it's easier to give in to temptation.

Twenty-three months ago

I want to see you.

The text came through at four thirty-three in the afternoon, surprising Courtney. She stared at her phone, wondering who would be texting her considering her work left her with little time for a social life. She knew it wasn't her best friend, Marissa, and Courtney didn't have many other friends who sent her random texts, either. She hadn't dated anyone in the last four months, so definitely not a man from her past.

Rather than answer it, she pushed her phone away and turned her attention back to the computer monitor. She was halfway through rereading the first paragraph for the third time when her phone buzzed again.

Tonight.

Without giving the phone anything more than a cursory glance, Courtney tried to focus on the article before her. She was reading up on Maximillian Adorite and the Southern Boy Mafia, attempting to get as much information as she could to provide to her father. The party she'd attended at Max's home just three short weeks ago hadn't been quite the haven for gathering details that she'd hoped it would be. The only thing she'd really learned was that the man could kiss like no other, his hands made her body burn, and he could set her on fire with merely a heated glance.

Not quite the information her father was probably seeking, nor was it anything she intended to share.

Though she'd gone to the party with good intentions, at every turn, Courtney had been met by one, if not more, of Max's intimidating bodyguards. There was no doubt about it, the Southern Boy Mafia had their hands in some serious shit, but they protected their privacy with a hell of a lot of muscle. Never had she been allowed into any part of the house that could possibly have given her a chance to dig deeper. The plan, no doubt.

My place. Seven o'clock. I'll make dinner.

Okay, so now her curiosity was piqued. She didn't know many people who offered to cook her dinner.

Grabbing her phone, she replied with:

Who is this?

A good two minutes passed, and Courtney figured someone had gotten the wrong number, texting her in error, but then another message came through, and the instant she read the screen, her heart slammed against her ribs.

Max. I take that as a yes. You remember the address. See you at seven.

A smile tipped the corners of her lips, although she tried to disregard the anticipation that stirred in her belly.

How did you get my number?

Courtney waited patiently for his response, but it never came.

Glancing around the near-empty office, she hated that she was looking forward to seeing Max. Sure, jumping at the opportunity to possibly snoop into Max's affairs was a no-brainer, but she knew her heated reaction was more than that. She didn't get giddy over a job. A little excited, maybe. But definitely not the riot of butterflies that had erupted in her core at the thought of seeing Max again.

Telling herself that she was only going because he was a job, Courtney grabbed her purse from her desk drawer, tossed her cell phone inside, and then snatched her laptop before heading out.

Luckily, no one was there to ask where she was going. Nor was anyone there to question why she had a grin the size of Texas plastered on her face.

After going home to shower and change, Courtney arrived at Max's at seven o'clock on the dot. For some reason, she got the impression that Max wasn't the type who would appreciate her being late. Based on what she'd seen and the information she'd retrieved, he was in control of everything in his life, and the last thing she wanted to do was piss him off so early in the game. If she did that, she ran the risk of not being able to complete the job, and that wasn't an option. She'd never failed on the job before, and she certainly had no intention of starting now.

After getting past security at the gated entrance, she pulled up to the front of Max's beautiful house, parking her beloved Camaro close to the door. Before she was on the porch, the door opened and a white-haired older man stepped out, a smile on his aging face.

"Miss Kogan. Such a pleasure to see you again."

Courtney tried to remember meeting him. He looked incredibly familiar to her. It would've had to have been at the party, but for the life of her, she couldn't place him or his name.

"Mr. Adorite would like to know if you're armed. So I'll simply ask, because I'd lose my hands if I tried to frisk you," he said kindly, a glimmer in his dark brown eyes.

And then his name came to her. Walter. Yes, that was it.

Walter Smythe, seventy years of age, five foot six inches (or he had been in his prime years), one hundred thirty pounds. Employed by the Adorites for the past thirty-eight years, Walter had initially been Samuel and Genevieve's butler, but then when Max moved out of the Adorite family home at the age of twenty, Walter had gone with him. From what she had read, Genevieve—although married—had a penchant for younger men, and looking at the white-haired elderly man standing before her, Courtney knew he didn't quite fit the bill.

Remembering his question, she responded with, "Yes, Walter, I'm armed. I'm always armed."

Walter's smile brightened his face, surprising her with its potency. She hadn't expected quite that reaction considering the last—and only—time she'd been there a few weeks earlier, she'd had hell arguing with another man she'd encountered after informing that not-so-nice gentleman that she would not be handing over her weapon.

"Very well, Miss Kogan. Right this way." Walter turned, and Courtney fell into step behind him, winding her way through the enormous mansion that belonged to Max.

She knew, based on her research, that he was the owner of the vast property that had been featured in several prominent Dallas magazines, although no one had ever been granted an in-depth tour, likely because Max had too much to hide. Other than quite a few ladies—most of them supermodel beautiful—that he'd been pictured with over the last few years, Courtney also knew that the twenty-seven-year-old multimillionaire was single and had never been married nor did he have any children. There were a number of security personnel who lived on the premises, but only two actually lived in the big house. The rest resided in another house on the property.

When Walter stopped inside the kitchen, after he shared a quick look with the formidable man alone in the oversized room, he motioned for her to precede him, and the instant she laid eyes on Max, standing at the wide island, opening a bottle of wine, her mouth went dry.

The last time she'd seen Max, he'd been the best-looking man at the party, dressed in a tailored tuxedo, with his silky brown hair and mesmerizing golden eyes. That man wasn't there tonight. No, this Max was wearing a black button-down shirt, the sleeves rolled up to reveal thick, muscular forearms dusted with dark hair, the top button unhooked, making him appear far more casual, relaxed. Her eyes gravitated to his hands, and a shiver danced along her spine as she remembered the way they'd felt on her body.

"I'm glad you could make it," Max said, the deep baritone of his voice breaking through her thoughts.

"I wasn't given much of a choice," she told him as she stepped farther into the kitchen, coming to a stop on the opposite side of the island from him. Even from there, she could feel the electricity spark between them.

For a moment, the two of them simply stood there, staring back at one another. His eyes never left hers, and for the first time in as long as she could remember, Courtney had the urge to look away. The man was intimidating, and that was saying something because she wasn't intimidated easily. But the way he looked at her... There was something in his gaze, something that stole her breath and told her to run far and fast.

This man was dangerous; there was no doubt about that.

Max held out the bottle for her to see and she smiled. Nineteen ninety-two Screaming Eagle Cabernet.

Not surprising.

She smiled. "Difficult to get your hands on that one," she said, grateful for the ability to look away from him.

"It helps to know people." Max tilted the bottle and poured the rich red wine into two glasses. He nodded toward the doorway. "Food's ready."

Courtney retrieved the glass he handed her, taking a sip and doing her best to avoid his heated gaze.

Well, at this point, she knew she wouldn't be disappointed with the evening, merely for the fact she was drinking one of the best wines she'd ever tasted.

Rather than leading her into the next room, Max walked around the island, his hand sliding to her lower back as he urged her forward. A warm, sexy musk permeated from him, sending a tingle of awareness deep into her core. Heat infused her entire body from the brush of his fingers, the warmth seeping through the thin, silk sheath dress she'd opted to wear tonight. Based on Max's choice for evening wear, she'd made a wise choice to dress up. His expensive black slacks and Italian loafers reflected his wealth.

But the man himself exuded so much confidence and power he could've been naked and she'd still have been slightly intimidated by him.

They arrived in a dimly lit dining room outfitted with a table that seated at least twenty. A large crystal vase holding lilies, white roses, and an abundance of greenery that overflowed the sides was the centerpiece of the monstrous, dark wood table. Two places on the end closest to the kitchen had been set, the plates filled with food.

Max pulled her chair out and waited for her to take a seat before helping her closer to the table. He then lowered himself into the chair at the end, putting him dangerously close to her.

"Did you make this?" she asked, taking stock of the contents on her plate. Not only did the steak look and smell divine, the entire meal—aside from the steak, there was roasted asparagus and mashed potatoes—looked as though it should've been on the cover of a culinary magazine.

"I happen to enjoy cooking," he informed her, sipping his wine as he watched her.

Not a quality she would've expected from a man like Max, but something that certainly intrigued her.

"I try to steer clear of the kitchen," she told him truthfully. "Cooking is not my strong suit."

Max set his glass on the table and picked up his fork and knife. "What is *your strong suit?"*

Courtney felt more heat infuse her face. The question hadn't been at all sexual, but her thoughts instantly retreated to the last time she'd seen him, to the way she'd nearly come apart in his arms.

"I'm fairly good with a gun," she finally told him, cutting her steak before taking a bite.

"Doesn't surprise me," he said gruffly.

After chewing, she peered up, realizing Max was still watching her.

"How is it?"

Courtney took a sip of wine.

"Likely the best I've ever had," she found herself saying.

Max's lips curved upward. This time there was definitely something inherently sexual in his wicked gaze.

And the sad part … something inherently sexual inside her responded in kind.

□»«□»«□»«□

Max hadn't expected Courtney to come tonight. To his house, that was.

When he'd finally given in to the urge to contact her, he'd fully anticipated a rebuttal.

Then again, he knew what she was after, so offering the invitation had been a gamble of sorts. To see her or not to see her? It had been a question that had plagued him for three weeks, to the point he couldn't take it any longer. His thoughts hadn't veered far from her since the moment he'd met her, and now that she was there with him, he had to wonder why he'd taken so long.

The instant she'd stepped into his kitchen, wearing that sexy bronze dress and the fuck-me heels, her long, dark hair hanging over her shoulders and her bright gray eyes flashing with heat, he'd been flooded with memories of her kiss, her touch, and the sweet moans he'd wrought from her when they'd consumed one another in the hallway. He'd replayed that scene over and over again in his head for weeks, trying to determine whether or not it'd been real, wondering if her touch, her taste, could've really been as magnificent as he remembered.

He'd only been left wondering for a second once he laid eyes on her again. She was everything he remembered and then some.

There was certainly curiosity in her nearly colorless eyes, but there was more than that. There was heat and intrigue and … lust. The woman might've been there on a job, but she was just as interested in the chemical reaction between them as he was.

Somehow he managed to eat his meal, watching her while he did, anticipating the questions he sensed she wanted to ask.

"From what I've read about you," Courtney prompted as she wiped her mouth with a linen napkin, "it sounds like you're rather close to your family."

"Is there a question in there somewhere?" he countered, smiling back at her.

"So that's how you want to play?" she asked.

Max placed his silverware on his plate and retrieved his wineglass. "I prefer the direct approach."

"I can see that," she mumbled softly. "So are you? Close with your family?"

"What do you consider close?"

Courtney glared back at him, which only amused him.

"We're close," he said simply. "And you? Are you close to yours?"

"Very," she answered readily.

"You have more of an extended family, correct?"

"I see you've done some checking up on me, have you?"

"Of course." He didn't see any reason to lie to her.

"Yes, it's rather extended. But I'm sure you're familiar with that. If I'm not mistaken, there's no blood relation between you and some of those you're closest to."

Max liked her. He liked how straightforward she was, how she spoke her mind. It was refreshing, even though he knew she had an ulterior motive.

The two of them continued to eat. Thankfully the questions lulled for a little while; however, the silence that ensued wasn't awkward. Max found it rather comfortable to sit with her, neither of them having to speak just for the sake of filling the silence.

Once they were finished, he cleared away their dinner dishes and returned to the table with more wine, tossing out an off-the-cuff question as he did. "Where'd you go to college?"

Casually sitting in his chair, he crossed one ankle over the opposite knee and regarded her while he waited for a response. She appeared unfazed by his curiosity.

"Texas State. Two years and then I'd had enough. I came home, went to work for my father."

"So, you had an interest in security?"

"Something like that," she said with a cheeky grin.

Little did Courtney Kogan know, but Max had an entire dossier devoted to her. He knew everything there was to know about her, from the last guy she'd dated and how long that had lasted, her blood type, the results of her last physical. He likely knew more about her than she did about herself, right down to the minute she was born and the fact that her mother had had an emergency C-section, three weeks prior to her due date, and her father had been on an op at the time, not making it home until Courtney was almost a full day old.

In Max's world, he knew better than to trust anyone. She might believe he was merely interested in her on a physical level—and that was true, he was—but Max was also attempting to keep her close. If she wanted information, he'd make sure she received it. But only the details he wanted her to have.

"What about you?" she inquired. "Where'd you go to college?"

"I didn't," he informed her.

"You just worked your way up in the organization?"

"Organization?" he asked, grinning. "What is it that you think I do?"

"Land development," she replied without missing a beat. "And one of your brothers is in the waste management business."

Well, she was right on those counts. That was the basis of his family's business. At least from the outside looking in.

"Don't forget the nightclubs," he offered.

"Right. How could I have forgotten? Devil's Playground, is it?"

"That's one of them," he told her. There were several others in the Dallas area, along with one in Vegas and another in New York, but he didn't bother to share that information. If she was curious, she'd ask.

"So, like I said, you just worked your way up?"

Max smirked. He liked that she thought she had the upper hand. He knew what information she had on him; some of it had actually been strategically planted. "It's not difficult to move up in a world you were born into," he told her. "But I suspect you're familiar with the concept."

Courtney nodded, holding her wineglass close to her lips. "So you're not just a businessman?" She took another sip of wine, and he watched her throat work as she swallowed. He wanted to put his lips on the slender column of her neck.

"I never said that," he answered quickly.

"No, but you alluded to it."

"I never allude to anything, Courtney."

"No?"

"No," he assured her. "Direct is definitely my preferred approach."

Max noticed the challenge in her gaze, and it turned him on. The air crackled; electrical impulses made his heart rate speed up, his dick throb. His reaction to her wasn't unheard of because, since the dawn of time, men had been attracted to beautiful women. But this… This was potent, powerful, impossible to ignore, and Max wasn't interested in playing games. He wanted her, and he fully intended to show her what she was getting herself into by being with him, even if she thought she was the one interrogating him.

He stood and held out his hand for her to take. When she placed her delicate fingers in his palm, he helped her to her feet. Taking the two wineglasses, he set them on the cabinet behind him, then turned to face her.

Her eyes widened as he closed the distance between them, backing her up until her ass bumped the table.

"As amused as I am by this conversation," he told her with a slight grin, "I'm gonna kiss you now, Courtney."

He paused briefly to see if she would refute him, but she didn't. When her gaze dropped to his mouth and she nodded her head ever so subtly, Max's dick twitched, thickened.

Cupping her face, he grazed her lips with his thumbs, forcing her mouth open as he leaned in. The way her breath hitched as his mouth hovered precariously close to hers only made his dick harder. She wanted him; there was no doubt about that. The powerful physical reaction they'd had to one another a few weeks ago hadn't dimmed. If anything, it had intensified.

Unable to resist any longer, Max licked his way into her mouth, her tongue meeting his, tentative at first, but then the fire he remembered ignited, and Courtney was kissing him back with fervor. He took another step closer, pressing his rigid cock against her belly, wanting her to feel what she did to him.

"Touch me, Courtney," he commanded gruffly, speaking the words against her sweet, luscious mouth.

He felt her shift, her hands hesitantly sliding up his chest. Her breathing was labored, her eyes locked with his as he allowed his body to acclimate to her touch. It was just as he remembered. Cataclysmic. Every one of his senses went on high alert, anticipation steadily growing until the ache was so fucking strong he knew he wouldn't be able to keep from taking her right there on the goddamn table.

Sliding his hands down her body, he gripped her hips and lifted her, setting her on the surface and coming to stand between her thighs. Her legs widened, the short skirt of her dress riding higher on her tanned thighs. While her hands rested on his chest, he peered down, admiring the way her nipples puckered beneath the thin bronze silk that covered her. The dress was little more than a nightgown, and Max fucking loved it.

He could see the outline of her gun secured to her thigh beneath her dress, and he slowly slid it from the tiny lace holster, setting it on the table beside her before flattening his palms on her thighs, lifting his gaze to hers as he caressed her smooth skin.

"I've dreamed of touching you again," he told her. "Hell, I've even fantasized about laying you out right here on this table and feasting on you while you beg me to make you come."

Her breath hitched again.

"Is that what you want, Courtney?"

Her hooded gaze never separated from his as her lips parted ever so slightly. "Yes."

"Tell me again," he ordered.

Her throat worked as she swallowed, her hands easing down his torso, coming to a stop over his, which were still resting on her silky thighs. She moved his hands higher, forcing the silk of her dress up more. "Yes," she whispered. "This is what I want."

That time her words held more conviction, as did the way she aggressively forced his hands between her legs.

Max slid one finger beneath the thin barrier of her panties as he kissed her again. She hissed in a breath when he dipped between her slick folds, stimulating her clit. She was so damn hot, and her soft, sexy moans encouraged him.

The kiss went nuclear, her legs spreading, her ankles pressing against the backs of his thighs while her fingers found the back of his head, lacing in his hair as she pulled him closer. Lips and tongues dueled as he used his free hand to slide the thin straps of her dress off her smooth shoulders. She shrugged out of them, baring her perky tits as he cupped one in his big hand, fondling her nipple between his thumb and forefinger, watching it harden more. Max hovered over her, forcing her to her back on the table. He kissed his way down to her breast, licking and sucking her nipple while he fingered her, slipping inside her warm, wet heat, fucking her with one finger, then two.

"You're wet for me," he mumbled. "You like this." It wasn't a question, and he didn't expect a response.

Her back bowed, and he devoured her tit, sucking hard as she cried out, her hips bucking upward, her cunt grinding against his hand. Unable to resist tasting more of her, he switched, laving her other nipple with his tongue before nipping it with his teeth and sucking it into his mouth.

"So fucking beautiful," he groaned, releasing her nipple and trailing his mouth lower.

Max pushed her dress up, the silk ringing her middle and leaving most of her sinfully delicious body bared to his hungry gaze. Dropping into the chair, he pulled her panties to the side and buried his tongue in her pussy, licking her as she cried out, begging him not to stop, pleading for him to make her come.

She was so fucking hot, so damn responsive, Max wasn't sure either of them would survive this, but he damn sure had no intention of stopping until she'd come in his mouth, until she'd given herself over to him completely.

He impaled her with two fingers, twisting his hand around, buried deep inside her as he sucked her clit between his lips. It only took him a second to locate the spot he was seeking, and as he rubbed, Courtney's cries grew louder.

"Max!"

Doubling his efforts, he flicked her clit with his tongue, then began relentlessly fucking her with his fingers until her pussy clamped down on his hand.

"Oh, God! Max!"

Max didn't intend to go any further tonight, satisfied with how she ignited, coming apart at the seams. For now, anyway. Considering he found so much pleasure in making her come with his tongue and his fingers, he forced himself to refrain from taking her right there on the table. As much as he wanted to plunge deep into her, fucking her until she didn't know her own name, he knew he had to take things slow.

And slow in his world, as she had just found out, was definitely a relative term.

Chapter Six

Her mental state?
It'd be best not to assess it right now.

Present day
March 3rd

Courtney stormed into her house, flipping on lights as she went, deliberately making as much noise as possible. She couldn't ignore the frustration that had built inside her after the events of the night.

Why the hell had she thought she could waltz right up to Max, confront him for the sake of an op, and not be affected by him? It wasn't as though she'd ever been successful at it before. So why had she thought tonight would be any different?

She wasn't sure she would ever have the answers to those questions, nor did she intend to ponder them, either. Trying to figure out this crazy reaction she had to that man was an incredible waste of time, and she'd done enough of that over the past two years.

It was just a damn good thing she wasn't alone, or there was no telling how she would've opted to release that pent-up anxiety. She'd never been the type to hold back her emotions, and Max was her sore spot. Her Achilles' heel. Always had been.

Courtney sighed, refusing to think about him anymore.

Kicking off her heels, sending them both flying into the wall beneath the breakfast bar, she pulled her gun from the lace holster on her thigh, checked it as she always did, and set it on the counter with her cell phone.

"Can I get you somethin' to drink?" Courtney asked RT when he followed her inside, closing the door behind him.

"Sure."

Courtney caught his incredibly cautious tone but chose to ignore it. During the drive back to the compound—the appropriate description for the large amount of gated land her family occupied with several houses spread throughout—neither of them had said anything. Not one single word. It'd been the most peace she'd had all night, despite all the thoughts of Max that continued to batter her brain.

Not that she could necessarily blame RT for walking on eggshells. She was on edge, and by choosing to keep her company, he was directly in her path of destruction. A place he probably didn't want to be on a good day.

And today certainly wasn't a good day.

"You okay?" RT asked, a hint of concern in his gravelly voice.

Well, looked like the blessed silence was about to come to an end.

Pity.

"Of course," she lied.

Courtney doubted she would ever be okay again, but as much as she liked the guy, RT wasn't the one she would choose to share her innermost secrets with. Seemed she didn't have anyone to do that with these days. It wasn't easy to tell the people she was closest to that she'd fallen in love with the devil and had spent the last year of her life trying to find her soul, trying to forget the dark world she'd succumbed to. They wouldn't understand. She didn't even understand it herself.

"Talk to me," he demanded, the squeal of wood against wood sounding from behind her as he pulled a chair out from her kitchen table and proceeded to drop into it.

"Nothin' to talk about." She retrieved a bottle of vodka from her freezer, along with two tumblers, two shot glasses, and a can of 7-Up. Hip checking the refrigerator door closed, she carried her loot to the table and set it down in front of RT.

"What's goin' on between you and Max Adorite?"

And there it was. The question she'd been expecting all night.

Hell, she'd thought she would be peppered with questions from more than just him after the debacle at Max's. If it hadn't been for the fact that Courtney's best friend was safe and sound, and likely in Trace's bed about now, Courtney knew her brother would've been standing right alongside RT, interrogating her about Max until her ears bled.

"Nothin'." And that really was the truth.

There hadn't been anything between her and Max for nearly a year. Eleven months, one week and three days, to be exact. Not that she'd been counting, but during that time Courtney had managed to stay far, far away from him. There for a while, she'd actually thought she might be at a point where she could move on, but that hadn't been the case. Sometimes she wondered whether she ever would.

"Try again," RT stated, reaching for the bottle of vodka and the two shot glasses, ignoring the 7-Up entirely.

Worked for her.

"Nothin' to tell. I know him."

"Intimately?"

Courtney lowered herself into the chair opposite RT, watching while he unscrewed the lid from the bottle and poured the clear liquid.

"Yes," she finally said. "I know him intimately. But it's been over for a long time."

"How long?" he asked, raising his gaze to meet hers.

"Not long enough," she muttered.

When he pushed one of the shot glasses toward her, Courtney drew it closer.

Lifting the glass, she watched RT. Neither of them looked away as they both downed their shots. As the vodka left a tingling burn down her throat, Courtney put the glass back on the table, easing it closer to RT for a refill.

He obliged and they repeated the process.

"How'd you end up meeting him?"

"An op." Courtney nodded toward the bottle, signaling for him to refill the glass. "If you remember, two years ago, Max's uncle had a stroke, which left him incapable of fulfilling his duty within the organization. The Adorite family came together to show their support when Max took over as underboss. That move advanced him to the second most powerful position within the family." She'd originally been sent to the Adorites to get intel when the power exchange had occurred, and had she acted as the professional she prided herself on being, none of this would've ever happened.

"A sanctioned SBM op?"

Courtney nodded, downing the next shot RT had poured her, once again returning the shot glass for another as the heat from the liquor seared her all the way down to the pit of her stomach. She welcomed the distraction. The last thing she needed was to spend any more time thinking about Max.

"Who assigned it? My father? Or yours?"

"Mine," she told him.

"Who was the client?" he inquired, his face reflecting none of the interest she heard in his tone.

Courtney shrugged. "That's more your job than mine. Asking who and why is not in my job description. I simply did as I was instructed, hoping to get all the facts I could and relay them to Casper."

Casper Kogan, Courtney's father, had been keeping tabs on the Southern Boy Mafia for an undisclosed client when the news had come in regarding the change within the mafia family's hierarchy. Duty to the client, as well as curiosity, she suspected, had driven Casper to assign Courtney to go in and see what details she could get. Purely informational and, according to her father, completely off the radar.

"Why you?" he asked, staring back at her.

Courtney glared at him. For all intents and purposes, RT was her boss. He was the next in line to take over Sniper 1 Security alongside her brother Hunter and had been playing the part for the last year. That didn't mean she would tolerate the condescension in his tone. "Why *not* me?"

"I didn't mean it like that," RT said, defending his obvious misstatement. "However, had it been my decision, I wouldn't have sent someone quite so…"

Courtney's eyebrows lifted, daring him to finish that statement.

"Tempting. That's what I was gonna say, Courtney. Don't get all up in arms. No one is sayin' you're not good at your job. You're an exceptional security consultant, bodyguard, whatever you wanna call yourself. I just think it would've made more sense to send in Hunter or even Clay."

"They didn't have the required … skills to get the job done," Courtney informed him, tilting her head to the side.

"Or Casper didn't want me findin' out," RT mumbled, pulling her empty shot glass back over to his side of the table.

Courtney lifted her eyebrows in question.

RT shook his head as though clearing his thoughts. "So you went in, attempted to breach the walls of his organization, and the two of you started what? Dating?"

Courtney wasn't even relatively close to being comfortable with the direction this conversation was heading—at least not where her personal life was concerned—so she changed the subject. "You tell me what's goin' on between you and Z first. Then I'll be happy to tell you my deepest, darkest secrets."

RT's gaze bored into her, his crystal-blue eyes flickering as she'd seen on more than one occasion when Z's name was mentioned. She knew that he didn't want to talk about Z or the feelings he'd evidently developed for the guy over the years.

"Nothin' to tell."

Exactly.

Courtney smiled. "Then we're even," she stated, nodding her head toward the shot glasses. "Let's drink."

For the next few minutes, neither of them said anything, both downing one shot after another until RT set the bottle aside and leaned forward. His expression turned serious.

Ryan Trexler was like a brother to her. The Trexlers, like family. Since Casper Kogan and Bryce Trexler had created Sniper 1 Security some thirty-odd years ago, their lives had become entwined. And when Casper and Bryce had started their own families, those families had become interlaced. Since Courtney had grown up around the entire Trexler family, RT's sister Marissa being her best friend, Courtney expected RT—the oldest of the Trexler children—to care about what happened to her, about how she felt, but she really wasn't in a talkative mood.

She'd prefer to take the alcohol to her bedroom, down enough shots to block out all thought, and then crawl beneath the blankets. It wasn't an indulgence she gave herself over to often, but tonight of all nights, Courtney felt she deserved the mental break.

"You okay with what went down tonight?"

Courtney knew he was referring to Max killing the ATF agent. Truth was, she wasn't sure how she felt about that. "If you're askin' whether or not I'll lose sleep over it, the answer's no."

Her concern was more about her mental state and the fact that she'd felt a strange detachment to the situation, likely due to the things she'd seen during the year she'd spent with Max. Throughout the ordeal in his office tonight, Courtney had been more worried about keeping Max safe, making sure the tables didn't turn on him. The fact that Duchein was going to die at Max's hand—because she'd known that was what it was coming down to—had been the least of her concerns. Caring about what happened to Max only pissed her the fuck off. Max was a big boy; he could take care of himself.

He'd informed her of that on more than one occasion.

But more importantly, Courtney was going to have to give some serious thought to her own intentions. Had Max not killed that asshole, Courtney couldn't say that she wouldn't have. And she wasn't sure exactly what her motivation would've been. Trace and RT had had the situation under control at all times. Even when Duchein had grabbed her, she'd known they wouldn't allow him to take her. Sure, Duchein was a threat, and he'd needed to be eliminated, but they had enough dirt on him to put him in prison. He didn't have to die.

But he had.

Before RT could say anything else, Courtney's cell phone chimed.

She was up and walking across the kitchen before she realized she'd moved. A wave of dizziness swept over her, letting her know she was a little on the tipsy side. How many shots had she had? Three? Four? Seven?

Squinting down at the screen, Courtney frowned when she saw who it was.

Punching the talk button, she put the phone to her ear. "What do you want?"

"Let me through the gate."

"No."

"Courtney."

God, she hated the way he said her name. It was so … sexual.

"Let me through."

Sighing, Courtney hung up the phone and then hit the icon for the program to allow her to see who was at the main gate of the family compound. Sure enough, it was Max. More accurately, it was Max's phantom-black Dodge Charger SRT Hellcat idling at the gate, waiting for her to grant him entry.

"Damn it."

"What's wrong?" RT questioned.

Hitting the button to allow Max through the security gate, Courtney resigned herself to having to deal with him. She hadn't been naïve enough to believe he would just leave her alone. It was never that simple for her.

"Nothing," she lied. "Max is here."

RT's golden eyebrows lifted as he pushed to his feet. "Courtney, you need to stay away from—"

Courtney put her hand up, effectively halting RT's brotherly advice. "Don't. Don't tell me what I need to do. I'm twenty-six years old. I know what's good for me, and I know how to make my own decisions."

"I just—"

"I know," Courtney stated, lowering her voice. "I know you care about me. But I know what I'm doin'."

RT simply watched her, and she wondered whether he was assessing her state of mind.

A car door closed outside, interrupting their stare down.

"I guess that's my cue to go."

Courtney wanted to tell him to stay, to be there as a buffer between her and Max, but she didn't.

She blamed the liquor.

But as she'd told him, she was a big girl, and she certainly knew how to take care of herself.

"Are you good to drive?" she questioned.

RT smirked. "I live on the property. It's a one-minute drive."

"I know, but still. I—"

"You sure you'll be okay?" he interrupted as he moved closer, his tone full of concern.

Watching him carefully, Courtney remembered that Max would be knocking on her door any second. No, she didn't think she'd be okay, but it wasn't as though she could tell RT that. He would think she meant physically, and that was the farthest thing from her mind. In that sense, she was probably safer with Max than anyone else. But emotionally… That was an entirely different story.

"I'll be fine." She prayed she'd be fine. Prayed like hell she'd be able to resist Max. And, unfortunately, her weakness for him had nothing—absolutely *nothing*—to do with the liquor.

RT's hand was on the doorknob when the knock sounded. Sucking in a deep breath, she nodded to RT when he shot her a dubious look over his shoulder. He pulled open the door, and Courtney didn't budge from where she stood a few feet away. Her eyes instantly drifted to Max, gliding over him from head to toe.

God, he looked so fucking good.

He'd changed out of the tux and into faded jeans and a black polo. Despite the black leather jacket he had on, Courtney could still see every hard angle of his body, from his sculpted chest to his muscular thighs.

Why? Why the hell did she do this to herself?

"Good night," RT said, nodding at Max as he stepped outside.

The two men shared a look, and Courtney could practically hear the threats they were silently sending one another. RT was warning Max, and Max was assuring him that she was fine, all without either of them saying a word.

Men.

Max walked in, his eyes on RT until the door closed, leaving the two of them alone in her living room. And then he turned that penetrating stare back on her.

That was when Courtney realized her shitty night had just gotten worse, and no amount of liquor was going to help.

Didn't mean she wasn't going to give it the good ol' college try.

Chapter Seven

A gangster does have a heart.
Who would've thought?

When the door to Courtney's house opened, Max immediately took in the scene before him. RT was standing there, still wearing the tux he'd donned at the party, his blond hair mussed as though he'd been…

Fuck no. Max wouldn't go there.

Likely RT had been running a frustrated hand through his hair for most of the night. That was one of RT's tells. Something Max had noticed about him from the first time they'd met.

So, upon seeing RT's disheveled state, Max had tamped down his initial anger. He reminded himself that, one, RT was climbing the ladder within the ranks of Sniper 1 Security and had every right to ensure Courtney got home safely, and two, the guy was gay and nothing would've happened between him and Courtney.

Nothing.

Granted, the acceptance wasn't easy, especially when Max's gaze strayed past RT, landing on the woman responsible for messing with Max's head for longer than he cared to admit. She was so *fucking* beautiful, standing there with her hand cocked on her hip, her shoes off, her short dress showcasing her incredible legs, her creamy shoulders bare…

No, not fucking easy to resort to the calm he typically managed to cloak himself in. Then again, she was probably one of the only people who could so easily push his buttons.

"Why are you here?" she questioned when they were alone, turning and heading toward the kitchen with a heavy sigh. He smiled when she paused, reaching for her gun and carrying it with her.

Max watched her walk away, noticed the slight sway of her magnificent ass. His hands itched to touch her, to hold her, to draw her beneath him while he claimed her with his own body. A torrent of memories flooded his mind, memories of those days when she'd been his.

He forced them away, refusing to stray from his reason for being there.

A quick glance around the room told Max that not much had changed over the last year. Courtney still had the black-and-white pictures of Marilyn Monroe decorating her living room, along with the giant television, mounted on the wall over the fireplace—which, oddly enough, had never been used to warm the house and was actually lined with tiers of candles, a decoration Max didn't quite understand. On his left, there was the same black suede sofa that they'd rolled around on during that one night she'd brought him back there, and yes, there on the bar that separated the living room from the kitchen was the crystal bowl that held Courtney's guilty pleasure—M&Ms.

Not much had changed, not much at all.

As she approached the table, placing her gun within reach, he noticed the bottle of vodka.

Great.

Just what he *didn't* need tonight.

Courtney was a wildcat without liquor, but when she was inebriated, she tended to get incredibly feisty. And not necessarily in a good way.

"I wanted to check on you," he told her honestly.

He'd spent the rest of the evening thinking about little else other than her. After what had happened with Duchein—after Max had *killed* the bastard—he'd had the overwhelming urge to go to her, to see how she was doing, to make sure she was processing what had happened, dealing with it rather than shoving it aside as she'd been known to do. He knew firsthand that watching someone die wasn't easy, especially for someone like Courtney, someone with a conscience.

Courtney spun around, her gaze slamming into his.

"Check on *me*? Why the hell would you wanna do that?"

Because it was an excuse to see her. But that wasn't what Max told her. "I wanted to make sure you were all right."

Courtney huffed as she returned to pouring the vodka into a glass, adding 7-Up from a can sitting on the table. Max's gaze instantly strayed to the extra glass, and his frustration rose again.

She tossed him a glare over her shoulder. "Oh, you're referrin' to when you blew some guy's brains out in the middle of your office? Don't you have a dead body to clean up or somethin'?"

He didn't say a word. His rule was that he'd never own up to anything. He didn't feel safe anywhere that wasn't home, never knew when someone was trying to trap him. And of all people, Max wasn't delusional enough to believe Courtney wouldn't turn on him with the right motivation. Ultimately, she was one of the good guys. And that was why they never had been able to find a middle ground. It was more difficult than it appeared considering they were at opposite ends of the spectrum—middle ground was just too far away for either of them.

Not to mention, arguing with Courtney was moot. Max knew from experience that she would never let up, which was why he'd given up long ago.

"Oh, right. You have people for that," she continued, turning to face him again before taking a sip from her glass. "I'd offer you a drink, but then you might think you can stay."

"I'm gonna stay," he informed her.

Courtney's eyes narrowed on him, and Max's body instinctively reacted, hardening instantaneously.

"You're *not* gonna stay," she retorted, her tone clipped. "Not today, not tomorrow. Not ever."

Max shrugged out of his leather jacket, folding it across the arm of the sofa as he moved closer.

"I'm serious, Max," Courtney said, her eyes widening as she backed up until her ass hit the table. "You're not stayin'. RT'll be watchin' my house until you leave. It's not an option."

Max continued to stalk her slowly until he was standing only a few inches away from her. Unable to resist, he cupped her face in his hands, enjoying the silky smoothness of her skin against his palms.

Damn, how he'd missed her. It'd been damn near a full year since the last time he'd touched her, since the last time he'd made love to her. Although touching her now … it was as though not a minute had passed since that fateful day.

"I'm stayin'," he said softly.

Courtney shook her head, opened her mouth, but then snapped it closed. She wanted to argue; it was evident in the lines that creased her forehead.

Leaning forward, Max tested the waters, allowing his lips to brush hers lightly. Even that was nearly more than he could handle. It'd been too damn long since he'd touched her, tasted her, *loved* her. And fuck if he didn't want to do it all again. Right here. Right fucking now.

"Max, please," Courtney pleaded quietly. "*Please* don't do this."

"Do what?" he questioned roughly, pulling back and allowing his eyes to slide over her beautiful face, down the slender column of her neck, where he noticed the rapid thump of her pulse.

"We're through," she stated, her tone holding a hint of conviction.

"So you've said." In fact, Courtney had told him they were over many times during the year they'd been together. And for the year that followed, right up until this very moment, Max had thought about her every single day, about the way she'd ended things so abruptly the last time. Didn't matter that he'd called her bluff and that had technically been the reason they'd gone their separate ways.

Had it not been for the crazy shit he had to deal with on a daily basis, he might've actually taken the time to play her games. But there was another problem with that. He was fucking tired of playing, which was the only reason he'd allowed her to walk away then.

And that was the real reason he was there tonight. He wanted to know whether or not this was truly over. For him, it wasn't. There wasn't a chance in hell that he'd ever be able to get over her. Probably not in his lifetime. But that didn't mean that moving forward wasn't possible. With or without her.

If she didn't want him, he'd move on. He had business arrangements dangling in the wind, one in particular that was entirely dependent on where he stood with Courtney.

"Tell me you want me to leave, Courtney. Tell me to go, and I'll never darken your doorstep again. You'll never have to see me."

Max could see the surprise in Courtney's eyes, in the way her throat worked when she swallowed hard. He'd never made her that promise, never told her that he'd willingly let her go, although he'd spent the last year staying away from her. He'd had eyes on her the entire time; he knew every single move she'd made during those months. He knew for a fact that Courtney had never brought another man home with her, nor had she ever gone home with a man. Had she made that choice, Max wasn't sure how things would be at this moment, but more than likely, there'd be another dead asshole buried six feet under.

The point was, she hadn't.

"Tell me that's what you want, and I'll do it, Courtney. But know this … if you send me away this time…" Max took a deep breath, exhaled. "I won't come back. Whatever this is between us, it'll never die, never go away completely, and we'll both have to live out the rest of our lives with the decision that you make right here. Tonight."

"I want…"

The pause that followed stole the air from the room.

"What? What do you want?" he implored quietly, his thumbs gently brushing her cheeks before he trailed his hands down her neck, over her shoulders. A tremor ran through her, and he paused, taking the glass from her hand and setting it on the table. "It's all up to you."

"I can't do this," she answered, her voice so faint he hardly heard her. "I can't be with you."

"I've heard that before, but you're a grown woman, Courtney. There's nothin' stoppin' you."

Max noticed the instant the fire returned to her eyes, brightening them with a flame fueled by lust and need.

And denial.

"Are you fucking serious right now?" she exclaimed, her palms flattening on his chest as she tried to push him away.

He didn't budge, refusing to give her any space. This decision had to be made tonight.

"Deadly," he answered.

"Do you *know* who you are?" she asked, her voice pitched higher than before. "For that matter, do you know who *I* am?"

Max lifted one eyebrow. He figured the questions were rhetorical. That or she was more intoxicated than he thought.

"You killed a man tonight, Max. You didn't even blink when you shot him. In. The. Head."

He wasn't going to deny her statement, but he wasn't going to cop to it, either. She might be questioning who he was, but he knew exactly. He wasn't a good man, a noble man. His conscience wasn't ringed with worry or concern. He lived his life by one rule … live to see tomorrow. Sometimes, that was the only thing he *could* do.

"Do you love me, Max?"

Her question surprised him but only because Courtney had never brought up the subject of love before. Not in all the time they'd been together. Yes, he loved her. He loved her more than anyone or anything in the fucking world. He loved her enough to lay down his life for her. But he'd never told her that. There was only so much power he could relinquish, and admitting that he loved her was more than his quota allowed.

So rather than tell her as much, he said, "That seems irrelevant at the moment."

"No! It's not irrelevant, Max. It's… Fuck."

Courtney tried to maneuver past him, but Max held his ground, not budging an inch. "Don't walk away from me," he ground out. "Tell me what you want, Courtney. What. Do. You. Want?"

When she didn't speak, Max gave in to his craving for her. He cupped her face in his hands again and crushed his mouth to hers, tasting her defiance. And then she was kissing him back as she'd always done. A brutal mating of tongues, lips, teeth. Her arms went around his waist, beneath his shirt, her fingernails digging into his back as she pulled him closer. There was nothing gentle about this, but there never usually was.

No, what he and Courtney had was combustible. Hot. Erotic. Intense. And no matter how long they were apart, that need, that desperate craving he had for her, and she for him, never seemed to abate. But as with anything, there was only so much pressure that could be contained before the lid was blown sky high, and that was the exact point they'd reached.

Max shifted, shoving her against the wall as he crushed his body to hers, grinding his cock at the juncture of her thighs as he desperately tried to touch every part of her with every part of him. They devoured one another, teeth clashing, tongues mating. When she forced her hands between their bodies, reaching for the button on his jeans, jerking it loose, Max sucked in a breath.

She wasn't tender as she sucked on his tongue, bit his lip, roughly attempted to pull his cock free. Within seconds, she had his dick in her hands, her smooth fingers gripping him firmly.

Aww, fuck.

She was … heaven.

Her hands … *fucking* spectacular.

He'd missed her touch. He'd missed *her*. He needed to be inside her, to bury himself in the deepest parts of her.

Without hesitation, he lifted her dress, ripping her panties from her body as he thrust his hips forward, grinding his cock into her hand.

"Condom," she groaned against his lips, biting him again, this time harder than before.

During their time together, they'd stopped using condoms, trusting one another implicitly, but now … a year later… He wasn't going to argue because the only thing he could think about was fucking her against the wall, claiming her once again.

"Pocket," he told her, sliding his hands into her hair and jerking her head back. "Put it on me, Courtney."

Courtney's eyes locked with his as she reached into his pocket with her free hand, retrieving the condom he'd placed there for this very reason. He released her head, wrapping his hand around hers, forcing her to jerk his cock more insistently. Within seconds, she'd ripped open the foil with her teeth, and together they rolled the latex over him, her touch making his cock pulse and throb.

Once he was sheathed, he adjusted their positions, lifting her leg as he guided himself to her entrance. Her eyes never left his as he pushed forward, forcing his cock past the tight muscles that instantly clenched around him.

"Fuck." She felt so good. "Tight, Courtney. God, baby. So fucking…" *Good.* Hot and wet and … *his.*

Slamming his mouth over hers, Max kissed her, driving his tongue inside as she kissed him back. Her hands drifted up to his hair, pulling violently as he fucked her against her kitchen wall. His hips drove forward, forcing his cock deep into her slick pussy. Her body gripped him, pulled him deeper.

So goddamn tight.

"*Max.* Yes. God, yes!"

He loved when she said his name, crying out for him, begging him for more, just as she did now. He didn't let up, relentlessly fucking her hard. Lifting her from the floor, using the wall to brace her, Max changed the angle, pumping his hips, burying himself deeper, deeper still.

He wasn't going to last, but neither was she. The way her hands fisted in his hair, sending blinding shards of pain down his spine, her tongue dueling with his, he knew she was close.

Her mouth separated from his as she threw her head back, hitting the wall behind her as she cried out his name again and again and again.

"Harder," she pleaded. "Fuck me harder, Max!"

Max thrust his hips forward, burying himself deep, retreating and slamming into her over and over. She moved, her hands falling to his shoulders as she fought to hold on to him. Her body gripped him, her fingernails digging into his biceps.

"Come for me, Courtney. Aww, fuck," he breathed against her ear. "Fucking come for me, love."

Her body gripped him like a vice, wrapping him in mind-blowing pleasure as she cried out his name.

His release barreled down on him.

He slammed into her once, twice, and then he let go, coming deep inside her, holding her to him, his lips on the curve of her neck as he bit back the words he'd wanted to say to her for so long.

I love you.

Although true, he couldn't break that part of himself open. It wasn't safe.

She wasn't safe. Not only because of who her family was, the hellfire that they could rain down on him and likely were planning in the future, but also because of his enemies. Courtney's life would be in imminent danger if anyone found out what she meant to him. And he couldn't allow that to happen. Not yet. Not with things still so volatile between them.

Neither of them moved, remaining right where they were until his limbs steadied, his breaths returned to normal. When he regained his composure, Max lowered her feet to the floor and pulled his semihard dick out of her. He removed the condom, then deposited it in the trash bin before tucking himself into his jeans and fixing his clothes, never taking his eyes off her. He could see her mind working, but for the life of him, he didn't know what she was going to say.

When he tried to kiss her again, Courtney turned her head, avoiding his mouth.

And he knew.

He fucking knew.

Max cupped her head, forcing her to look up at him. "Tell me," he growled. "Tell me to leave and never come back. That's your only choice, because if you don't, Courtney…" He took a deep breath. "If you don't, I'm gonna carry you to your bedroom and fuck you again and again. All goddamned night."

Another shiver raced through her, but Max didn't see an ounce of trepidation.

He'd never detected any sort of fear from Courtney. She never backed down, and he loved that about her. She knew him, understood him. More so than anyone else. But in the same sense, she was as fucking stubborn as they came. Yet she never was able to give him a good excuse as to why she continued to push him away.

Other than they came from different worlds, and that was something Max couldn't deny.

Courtney's gaze locked with his, her teeth scraping over her bottom lip.

And the next thing she said nearly leveled him.

"I want you to leave, Max. I never want to see you again."

Releasing her, Max took one step back, his heart slamming against his ribs. With a subtle nod, he backed up another step. His brain was trying to process the words, although his heart already had.

"I'll leave," he said, his voice rougher than he expected.

For a fraction of a second, Max was sure he saw indecision in Courtney's eyes, but it disappeared just as quickly. He knew he hadn't imagined it, but he had to force himself to believe he had. This was what she wanted. And he was too fucking tired to continue playing this game with her.

Retrieving his jacket, Max didn't bother putting it on. He forced his feet to move as he made his way to the door. With his hand on the knob, he didn't turn back to look at her when he spoke. "Things are about to change for me, Courtney. Major things. But I want you to know, no matter what happens, if you ever need me, I'll be there. You just have to call."

With that, Max took the shattered remains of his heart and walked out the door without looking back.

Chapter Eight

Glorified babysitter...
Seriously? Again?

The following day
March 4th

"Have a seat," Casper stated when Courtney walked into her father's office the following morning. "You look like hell."

"Thanks," she told him coarsely. She felt like hell. The hangover she was nursing did little to brighten her mood, and the fact that her father had summoned her into the office so early in the morning wasn't helping, either.

"RT told me how things went down last night."

Courtney nodded. She had no intention of getting into a conversation with Casper or anyone else regarding the details of the night before. She would fill out the required paperwork, as she always did, but other than that, she wasn't in the mood to chat it up.

Casper retrieved a file folder from the drawer of his desk and set it in front of him.

"I've got an assignment for you."

Courtney raised her eyebrows in question. This was good news. She would jump at the opportunity to do something other than spend the next few days or weeks or, hell, even months, thinking about everything that had transpired last night. And she wasn't referring to the op, either.

"Wealthy hotel owner in California. Needs a bodyguard for his daughter."

Courtney tilted her head and looked at her father in disbelief. "Are you serious? I'm gonna be a glorified babysitter?"

She could tell by the look in her father's eyes that he couldn't deny that statement. And when he couldn't tell her what she wanted to hear, he usually kept quiet.

"Damn it, Dad. Why? Why can't you send me anywhere else? Hell, I'll be happy to volunteer to take on the cheating spouse cases. But shit, I don't want to be some rich girl's wet nurse."

"He insisted on a female," Casper stated. "You're all we've got right now."

"You need to work on that," she told him frankly. "Hire some more women. This place is overrun with testosterone as it is."

"Do you want the case or not?" His tone held a hint of frustration.

Fuck. Why not? It would get her out of Texas, away from the lure of Max. Since she knew his family rarely made national news, at least she could keep herself safeguarded from the goings-on in his world.

"I'll take it," she told him, pushing to her feet and snatching the file from the desk. "When do I leave?"

She briefly flipped through the papers, then abruptly closed it, staring back at him.

"Today. Let Kira know when you need the jet," Casper told her. "She'll make sure to have it ready."

Realizing her father hadn't mentioned Max one single time, Courtney figured it was time to high-tail it out of there before he remembered to.

"I'll see you when I see you," she told him, reaching for the knob on the door.

"Stop by and see your mother before you go," Casper instructed, coming to stand at her side before she could get the door open.

"Will do," she replied, leaning into him when he kissed her forehead. "Love you, Daddy."

Opening the door, she turned back and smiled at him. Despite the fact she was being used as an overpaid, certainly overqualified babysitter, she still loved her father, still respected the hell out of him for all that he'd built for himself.

"Love you, too, baby girl."

Closing the door behind her, she made a beeline for the front desk.

"Hey, Jay," she greeted their receptionist. "Get someone to man the phones and I'll buy you coffee."

"Have I told you how much I love you?" Jayden Brooks replied, grabbing the phone and punching a button, her pixie-cut, strawberry-blonde hair—a recent change that Courtney adored—falling into place beautifully after she spun around. "I'm takin' a break. You got the phones? You're awesome. Thanks, Dom."

Less than a minute later, Courtney and Jayden were riding down the elevator to the bottom floor of their office building.

Standing beside the tall, statuesque woman made Courtney feel short. Jayden was always put together, wearing heels that boosted her into the six-foot range. It was no secret that, besides being otherworldly beautiful, Jayden was the glue that held their office together. Not to mention, she was also well loved by the entire staff. She was as much family as the rest of them, having been with the Sniper 1 team for the last seven years, ever since Jayden had strolled in off the street at the ripe young age of eighteen, looking for a job.

"Hey, Lee, where's Ally?" Courtney asked the barista, referring to the shop's owner.

"Writing," he said with a smile. "You know how she gets. If the words flow, she doesn't emerge for a while."

"Right. Good for her." Courtney passed the kid a twenty and told him to keep the change.

"Where're you off to?" Jayden inquired after they got their coffee from the counter and took a seat in the nearly empty place.

Courtney glanced around, taking stock of the few customers who were there. An older man was on his cell phone, his eyes glued to his iPad, while a young woman sipped her coffee and stared at an open textbook on the table in front of her.

"Cali," she said, meeting Jayden's curious light green gaze. "Looks like I'll be babysittin' the rich and famous."

Jayden frowned.

"No, it's good, really," Courtney said before her friend could get defensive on her behalf.

"Anyone we know?" she questioned.

Courtney smiled. "Think rich, snotty, reality show reject."

Jayden's smile widened.

"Someone's gotta do it, right?" Courtney chuckled, spinning her cup in her hands.

"I guess. Not sure why it's you, though." Without missing a beat, Jayden moved right on to another subject. "How's Marissa?"

Courtney remembered the events of the night before. "She's…" She sighed heavily. "Free. Finally."

It was hard to believe that after a year of being on the run, her best friend was finally free from the shit storm that had derailed her life. And to think it'd been as simple as RT going to Max, interrogating him a little for information, then garnering an invite to a party. Had Courtney sucked it up, gone to Max herself, it would've been over a long time ago.

She kept her attention trained on the paper cup as the guilt churned in her belly.

"Are she and Trace…?"

Courtney nodded. "They're happily in love," she confirmed.

"That's good. That's real good."

"How are you?" Courtney asked, looking at Jayden again. "How's that guy you were seein'? Tom?"

"Tony. He's an asshole," Jayden said with a grin. "I'm not seein' him anymore."

Courtney and Jayden had become friends over the last few years, spending time drinking coffee or wine, having dinner, hanging out. Sometimes the two of them, more often than not—before the chaos of the past year—with Marissa. Girl stuff. It was a friendship that had been born of what little free time they had, but she found spending time with the woman to be easy. Effortless.

They were a lot alike in many ways. In fact, they were both in love with men they knew they couldn't have. For Courtney, it had always been Max. For Jayden … well, it wasn't quite so simple. She'd been in love with Courtney's oldest brother, Conner, for as long as Courtney could remember.

The fact that Conner had been married hadn't made Jayden's infatuation with him exactly appropriate. And Conner's wife being brutally murdered right outside the Sniper 1 office eighteen months ago had only made things more difficult. Jayden was a fixer, the type of woman who wanted to help however she could, but they all knew there was no fixing Conner. He'd lost his high school sweetheart, the mother of his child. Based on the downward spiral he was consumed by, it didn't appear that anyone had the ability to fix him.

Thankfully, Jayden had never put her life on hold for him, but she'd also never fallen head over heels in love with anyone else, either.

"Well, when I get back, we'll go out. Find us a coupla hot guys to take home and use for a night. How's that sound?"

Jayden blushed. "How long's the assignment? I could use a hot guy right about now."

"Who knows? Casper didn't say. I'm sure it'll be a few weeks. In the meantime, keep your eyes open. There're always hot guys traipsing in and out of the office. Maybe you can snag one of them."

Jayden laughed. "Not likely, but I'll certainly keep my eyes open."

After draining what was left of her lukewarm coffee, Courtney got to her feet. "I need to go home and pack. Kira's gonna have the jet ready for me today."

"Well, you be careful. And call me if you get bored. You know I'm here if you need someone to talk to."

"Will do," Courtney said, hugging Jayden. "And do me a favor. Keep an eye on Marissa. She's safe now, but make sure she's doin' okay. She needs a friend. Especially while I'm gone."

"Absolutely," Jayden responded with a huge grin. "Be safe."

Forty-five minutes later, Courtney was walking into her parents' house, calling for her mother.

"In here," Liz responded loudly.

Courtney ventured into her father's office to find her mother sitting at his massive desk, her eyes glued to the laptop in front of her.

"Your dad told me you've been assigned," Liz said with a smile, closing the lid on the laptop and giving Courtney her full attention.

Flopping down into the chair across from her mother, she nodded. "Looks that way."

"And I heard things went well last night?"

Her mother had phrased it as a question, which meant she wanted details. Details Courtney had no intention of sharing with her. Or anyone, for that matter. "Yep," she answered simply. "Marissa's safe."

"Are *you* okay?" Liz questioned, leaning forward and resting her forearms on the desk. "Something botherin' you?"

Courtney shook her head. "I'm good. Just ready for an assignment, I guess."

"This one'll be interesting," Liz said. "At least it sounds like it. You'll get another chance to see how the … extremely wealthy live."

Courtney knew her mother meant something else. Her family was extremely wealthy, but they were nothing like the rich and famous she'd been assigned to before. Liz likely meant snobbish, entitled, or spoiled. Not that it mattered; the assignment wasn't going to be interesting. It was going to be a pain in the ass, but Courtney didn't say as much.

Liz handled the accounting for Sniper 1 Security. She was very much the reason the company had done so well over the years, but she admittedly didn't care for the details of the assignments.

Fidgeting slightly, Courtney felt the need to get up and head out before her mother had a chance to interrogate her about last night. Clearly no one had shared the details of what had gone down at Max's house, and she didn't want to be the one to tell them. Hell, if she were lucky, no one would tell them, and her mom would never be the wiser.

Right. Like that would ever happen.

Until then, she figured she would put as much distance between them as possible. Starting now.

Getting to her feet, Courtney smiled. "I've gotta go pack. Kira's gettin' the jet ready for me."

Liz nodded and stood, walking around the desk and hugging Courtney tightly. "If you need to talk, I'm here."

"I know, Mom," she said softly, letting her mother's strength seep into her. Over the last two years, she'd put a little distance between herself and her parents. In the beginning, it'd been because of her relationship with Max and the fact that she hadn't understood her feelings for him. Since then, she'd simply felt like an outsider. Her time with Max had changed her in so many ways.

"I love you," Liz said, releasing her and taking a step back.

"I love you, too," Courtney replied.

"Call me when you land. Let me know you're all right."

Courtney nodded, then turned away before her mother could see the emotion brewing in her eyes.

With that, Courtney ventured back out into the brisk morning air. It was time to move on with her life, and she decided to embrace this situation, to accept it for what it was. It was an opportunity to start over, to completely rid herself of all thoughts of Max.

And when she returned, whenever that might be, she'd be ready to move on.

At least that was her intention, anyway.

Chapter Nine

Drunk enough? Hmm... No, not yet.

Present day
March 4th

Max didn't try to hide the fact that he was three sheets to the wind when Angelica arrived at his house that evening. Nor did he pretend that he wanted to see her. He'd merely called her over so they could hash out the details of their upcoming nuptials. He'd met with Artemis earlier in the day, agreeing to his terms for the land.

By marrying Angelica, Max would soon take possession of nearly seventeen thousand acres of ranch land along the US-Mexico border. It wasn't that Max couldn't afford to purchase the land, but the senator refused to sell it outright for various reasons. Exactly how the proposition had come about, Max was still looking into, but from what his father had said, Artemis Winslow had approached him with a suggested arrangement that would benefit both the Adorites as well as Artemis—financially as well as organizationally. The downside, now that Max had agreed—he would have to marry Artemis's granddaughter, Angelica.

Just the thought of marrying her had him tossing back the rest of his drink and marching back to the nearly empty bottle for a refill.

After the shit day he'd had, it'd seemed appropriate that he got shitfaced and had to face the wicked witch. Seeing her would only bring another downturn in his mood, and after last night with Courtney, walking away from her… Max didn't think it could get much worse.

Hence the reason he'd been drinking for the last few hours, trying to numb the pain that had taken up residence in his chest.

I want you to leave, Max. I never want to see you again.

He could still hear her words, and every time they replayed in his head, he fought the urge to punch something.

"Sir?" Leyton called from the doorway. "She's here."

Max nodded but didn't say a word.

As though walking away from Courtney hadn't been hard enough, now he had to plan a fucking wedding.

Fucking married.

A hell of a business arrangement, wasn't it?

Angelica's heels clicked on the hardwood floors of his living room when she entered the room, the sound making his back teeth hurt. He downed more scotch, eyeing her as she moved toward him. She reminded him of a jungle cat on the prowl, ready to claim her mate. The thought made his stomach turn.

"I'm so glad you called," she said sweetly, closing the distance between them, clearly oblivious to the fact he didn't want her anywhere near him.

Max purposely put space between them. He damn sure didn't want her touching him. After his encounter with Courtney … Max wasn't sure he'd be able to let another woman touch him ever again.

"Sit," he ordered. "Somethin' to drink?"

"No, I'm good, thank you." Angelica moved to the sofa, her eyes trained on him as she elegantly took a seat. "I thought maybe you'd offer me dinner."

"Not tonight," he told her.

"Somethin' wrong?" she asked, her blue eyes fixed on him.

Max busied himself by pouring another drink, then moving to the floor-to-ceiling windows that overlooked the pool. "Nothin' you need to worry about," he said, slurring some of his words.

"I heard that you accepted my grandfather's proposal," Angelica said sweetly.

Max nodded.

"Well, since you've so generously agreed to marry me in order to strengthen your organization, I'd like to think that by becoming your wife, I'm entitled to hear your problems."

"Entitled?" Max snorted. "You really don't get how this works, do you?"

"Explain it to me, then," she said, her tone turning icy.

Keeping his back to her, Max gritted his teeth. "Maybe you should explain it to *me*, Angelica. What is it you're gettin' outta this deal? That's somethin' I haven't figured out yet. Here you are, a good girl, allowin' your grandfather to pimp you out?"

"He's not pimping me out," Angelica countered.

"No? Seems that it'd be a helluva lot simpler if I just paid him the fourteen million that the land is worth and we went our separate ways. Instead, good ol' Artemis insists that I marry his granddaughter. Sounds like pimpin' to me, sweetheart."

Through the glass, Max could see Angelica's hands fisted at her sides. He was met with silence, so he glanced over his shoulder. She was looking at her feet, not bothering to answer, which raised his hackles a little. When he was in a better frame of mind, he needed to seriously give that some more thought.

But not tonight. He didn't want to think tonight. Or feel.

Hell, the only thing he wanted to do was drink until he fell down. And if he no longer hurt at that point, he'd consider the night a success.

"It's the right thing to do," Angelica finally said, drawing his attention back to her. "Our marriage will benefit both of our families. With your political pull, he'll continue to hold his office. With him giving you the land, you'll expand your business. And if things go well, maybe we'll be able to find what we're both lookin' for."

"Which is?" he asked with a snort.

"Love. Happiness."

Max laughed. "It's business. Plain and simple."

"Business. Right. It's all about the land with you, isn't it?" Angelica said snidely, clearly offended by his remark.

Max nodded.

"Keep in mind, I wield some power of my own," Angelica snapped.

"Is that right?" he slurred. "You still haven't told me what you're gettin' out of this deal."

"Protection," she said quickly, her eyes widening as though she'd said something she hadn't meant to.

"Protection?" he questioned. "Who do you need protection from?"

"My grandfather's a powerful man. He has enemies. If I'm your wife, he won't have to worry about me anymore."

Max lifted his eyebrows. Was she fucking serious? And she thought it was a good idea to marry him for that bullshit reason? He didn't buy it. Something was off, and he wanted to know what it was, but his brain was too fuzzy to deal with her at the moment.

"Well, it looks like we all get what we want, then don't we?" he murmured.

"If, by that, you mean we'll have babies together, grow old together, then yes, we'll all get what we want."

He snorted again. He damn sure wasn't having babies with this woman. Hell, he didn't want his dick anywhere near her.

Rather than turn to face her, he kept his attention on the exterior of the house, watching the water ripple as it cascaded from the hot tub down into the pool, the lights beneath the water shifting from blue to red.

His mind attempted to drift back to a different day, a different woman, but before that memory took root, he felt Angelica's hands on his back. He instantly stiffened, a chill racing down his spine, and it wasn't a comfortable one. Gritting his teeth together, he fought the urge to pull away.

"This can be a good thing, Max," Angelica said softly.

Her perfume assaulted his sinuses, making him instantly nauseous. There wasn't anything subtle about the woman, not her demeanor, not her sense of fashion, and certainly not her taste in perfume. He hated it.

"Don't wear that shit again," he told her.

"What?" she asked incredulously, her hands falling to her sides.

"That perfume. It's hideous. Don't wear it around me again."

Angelica huffed but didn't move away. "You've had too much to drink, Max."

He was thinking he hadn't had nearly enough, but he kept his mouth shut.

"If you'll keep your mind open to the possibilities, I think we'll have a happy life together." Her arms came around him, her hands sliding over his stomach.

Why did it sound as though she were still trying to sell him on the deal? Hadn't he told her it was done?

Max wrenched out of her grasp and headed for the liquor once more. "What fucking part of this do you not get? It's business," he told her bluntly. "Don't think this is some fucked-up fairy tale. We're not havin' babies. Hell, I don't even wanna have sex with you."

"Max!"

He spun around, meeting the shocked expression on Angelica's face. She looked as though he'd slapped her, and he couldn't even bring himself to give a shit.

"When's the weddin' date?" he questioned. "I need to know the logistics so I can show up when expected."

She studied him momentarily and then took a deep breath. "I think we should do an engagement announcement," she said, her tone chipper once again.

Had the woman not heard anything he'd said?

"We'll have the *Dallas Morning News* do an article on us. After all, we need this to look real. I'm thinkin' a June wedding would be appropriate. It's the perfect season."

Perfect? For what? His life sentence without the possibility of parole?

There wasn't anything perfect about it. It was all bullshit.

Max turned back to the windows, keeping his eyes on her reflection in the glass. He didn't want her to get too close. It wasn't that he completely disliked her, but he couldn't bear the touch of another woman. Not yet, anyway.

"My grandfather has some connections. We'll book the venue of our choice. Do you have any place in mind?"

"I honestly don't give a fuck," he said harshly. "Like I said, I just need the details once they're finalized."

"Why'd you call me over here, Max?" Angelica questioned softly, a trace of hurt in her tone.

He turned to face her. Studying her for a moment, he finished off the rest of his drink before setting the empty glass on the table with a loud clank. Trying to pretend he wasn't wasted, he glared at her. There were two Angelicas staring back at him. He found it sadistically amusing. As though one weren't enough.

"To make sure you understand this is strictly business. Nothin' more. We won't be sleepin' together, you won't be in my bed, and you won't be cookin' my meals or pretendin' to be the good wife. There's a contract involved, and I'll follow it to the letter, but know that it'll never be about love. I wanted you to look me in the eye and tell me that you understand that." Stumbling once but quickly righting himself, he moved toward her. "I'm not lookin' for love or sex or a family. It's a mutual agreement. Nothin' more."

"I think you're drunk."

"There's no *thinkin'* about it, darlin'. I'm wasted." And yet it still wasn't enough. "But it doesn't mean I don't know what I'm talkin' about."

"Max." Angelica crooned his name, her hand coming to rest on his arm. "If you give us a chance, I think you'll find that I'm not as evil as you want me to be. I also believe, in time, you could actually come to love me."

Max wrapped his hands around her scrawny arms, jerking her forward and bringing his forehead down to hers. "I'm not in the market for love," he barked. "Do you understand that?" The rage that boiled in his gut intensified. "Not with you, not with anyone. And as long as you can wrap your fucking mind around that concept, this'll work just fine. If not, then I suggest you reconsider before it's too late."

Releasing her, Max headed toward the stairs, staggering again but managing to keep upright.

"Leyton!" he called, glancing around in an attempt to locate his bodyguard.

"Yes, sir?" Leyton responded instantly, coming to stand just a few feet away. Max had no idea where he'd come from, but he was glad he was there.

"Show her out."

"Yes, sir. Do you need anything else, sir?"

Max started up the stairs, an ache in his chest nearly sending him to his knees. "Yes, but not even *you* can get that for me."

There was only one thing he wanted. But no one could bring Courtney back to him, and unfortunately, he had to figure out a way to come to terms with that.

Or die trying.

Chapter Ten

Impulsive? Her?
Okay, maybe a little bit.

Twenty-two months ago

The intimate Italian restaurant Max had taken Courtney to had been magnificent. Not only was the food incredible, but the entire outing had been far more romantic than she'd thought it would be. To be honest, it'd been exactly as a date should've been, though she hadn't anticipated that with Max. Perhaps that was because he had an entourage of security following them, she didn't really know. Or possibly because there were several patrons, as well as the owner of the restaurant, who wanted to bestow their high praises on him. It was like a scene directly out of The Godfather.

She'd been hesitant to go with Max when he had called and made the offer, but as the evening was coming to a close, she was glad she'd accepted. It'd given her a chance to watch Max, the way he interacted with others, the way others interacted with him. Throughout the meal, she'd even managed to get a few answers to her questions, although he had perfected the art of dodging more than he actually answered.

Now, as they arrived back at his home, where she'd insisted they meet prior to going out, she was trying to come up with an excuse to simply get in her car and go home before the inevitable happened.

This thing between them, the chemistry … it was already smoking, threatening to set off the fire alarms, and the longer she was with him, the more she wanted him, the more she craved his smile, his kiss, his touch. It was a recipe for disaster, and she was hard-pressed to ignore it.

Which was ultimately the problem.

A solid month had gone by since the last time she'd seen him, the night he'd cooked her dinner and then given her the most explosive orgasm of her entire life right on his dining room table. She hadn't had to avoid him, because Max had done a good job of that himself. Although they had talked on the phone a few times, shared some rather sexy text conversations on top of that, she hadn't seen him until tonight. Needless to say, the anticipation had been building.

Leyton pulled the Cadillac CTS through the main gates and headed toward the house. She was hoping he would pull up next to her Camaro and she'd be able to avoid going inside Max's house altogether and just be on her merry way, but to her dismay, he pulled around to the back of the house and parked in the garage, the door closing silently behind them.

Max exited, holding out his hand for her, and she took it, scooting toward him and climbing out behind him. By the time Max closed the door, she realized they were alone in the garage. Although garage was a slight understatement for the monstrous room that housed at least seven cars and not a single tool. The floor was tiled with travertine, the walls painted a rich brown and made to look like leather. Or hell, maybe that was leather.

With her hand still encased in Max's, she followed him into the house, where he went directly toward a set of stairs.

"I should—"

"No, you shouldn't," he interrupted, stopping on the first step and turning to face her.

Courtney wanted to argue, but she couldn't find the words. He stole her breath with just a look. The man was temptation personified, and Courtney never did have the ability to fight her impulsive nature around him.

Before she could come up with something to say, he continued, "You should stay with me tonight."

Courtney knew she should refuse. It wasn't going to benefit either of them if she stayed. Well, other than possibly explosive sex.

The heat in his golden gaze spoke of promises and orgasms, and her traitorous body found a way to overrule her common sense. The next thing she knew, they were stepping into a beautifully decorated bedroom on the second floor.

Max's bedroom.

Another room that looked as though it should be pictured in a magazine with its oversized masculine furniture, dark hardwood floors, rich silk bedding—black and maroon, which matched the large rug on the floor. On the far side of the room was a monstrous stone fireplace that was the focal point of one entire wall. She found it interesting that there wasn't a television in sight, but considering all she knew about Max, she assumed there was one hidden somewhere for when he needed it.

A tray containing a decanter of what she assumed was brandy, considering Max's preference for the stuff, along with two crystal tumblers sat on a table near a set of French doors that were standing wide open.

Max released her hand and moved toward the liquor while Courtney made her way out onto the balcony. The night air was warm and humid, but the light breeze coming through the wide space was refreshing. It did little to cool her off but managed to calm her rioting nerves somewhat.

When he joined her a moment later, Max handed her a glass and then leaned against a column to her right, his eyes on her.

"It's beautiful up here," she told him as she peered out over the acres of land and trees before her. In the distance, she could see a pond with the moonlight bouncing off the water.

Max didn't respond, but she hadn't needed him to. Sipping from her glass, she did her best not to think about him or the fact that her body temperature continued to rise with each passing second. There was no doubt in her mind what would transpire between them tonight, but somewhere deep down, she knew there was a reason she should go.

Getting close to Max wasn't in her best interest. At least not like this.

She'd managed to get little to no information on the man in the past few weeks, settling on taking a few small jobs that kept her close to home while she anticipated the opportunity to see him again.

It was one thing to dig for information, but Courtney knew that patience was a virtue when it came to getting that level of detail from a man like Max. If she had come on too strong, he would've pushed her away. And if she had tried to avoid him, the chances of her getting anything at all were nil. So she was caught between a rock and a hard place.

And she was hoping that hard place would soon be Max's warm body, as fucked up as that might sound.

Several minutes passed before Max came to stand behind her. He took her glass from her and placed it on the balcony's ledge, and then his strong hands were on her shoulders.

Courtney trembled, his mere touch threatening to make her knees buckle. She'd dreamed of him touching her again, of her being able to do the same. She wanted to know how his hard body felt against her palms; she wanted to see more of him, taste all of him.

Max turned her to face him, his big hands cupping her jaw as he seemed to enjoy doing while he stared down at her.

"I can't stop thinkin' about you," he told her, the raspy rumble of his voice rattling her nerves delightfully, making her insides tingle with awareness.

"Me, either," she whispered back, her eyes roaming over his face, taking him all in, his dark eyebrows, his perfect nose and smooth cheeks, those full lips, and his square jaw. The man was too handsome for words.

Devastatingly beautiful, she'd have to say, which was a total contradiction to the man's soul.

"I'm gonna touch you, Courtney. And I'm not gonna stop."

Courtney nodded. She wanted that. She wanted it more than she wanted oxygen or water or… Hell, she wanted it more than she wanted anything.

When his hands caressed her bare arms, his lips pressing gently against hers, holding back just enough to keep her wanting more, Courtney thought she would spontaneously combust. Even the slightest touch made her body quiver, and she ached to feel him touch her in other places, intimate places. She wanted his mouth on her the way he'd done the last time.

He was going so slowly. Too slowly. She wanted to feel him everywhere.

Leaning up on her toes, she met his mouth with hers, desperate to taste him. When she coaxed her tongue into his mouth, she tasted the brandy as well as the dark promises of dirty, raunchy sex and glorious orgasms. This man knew his way around a woman's body, and hers was ready for his perusal.

The kiss lingered, slowly at first, but the heat between them intensified. His hands moved over her arms, her shoulders, her neck. He never stopped touching her, leaving a trail of warmth over her sensitive skin. And then he was reaching behind her, lowering the zipper on her dress, and pushing the material down her body until it pooled around her ankles. Stepping out of her heels, she grabbed his head and pulled him down to her, unwilling to release his lips.

A rough groan escaped him when she tugged on his hair, anxious to get closer. She wanted him to take her into his room and throw her down on the bed and have his wicked way with her, but Max had other ideas.

"Let me look at you," he mumbled against her mouth.

Reluctantly, Courtney pulled back, her hands gripping the rail of the balcony at her back, which thrust her breasts forward. Her nipples hardened as Max's eyes traveled the length of her body, ever so slowly. His fingertips grazed her collarbone and the slope of her breasts. He deftly unhooked the front clasp of her strapless bra, allowing the black lace to flutter to the ground.

A moan escaped her when he cupped each breast, kneading them firmly, sending electric pulses firing straight to her clit. The man had fantastic hands. Warm, big, and surprisingly smooth.

Her eyes followed his movement as he leaned down and sucked one nipple into his mouth. Arching her back, she attempted to get closer, aching for more. He continued to give both nipples his full attention, and when he went to his knees before her, Courtney could hardly breathe.

His fingers drifted down her sides, curved beneath the band of her panties as he tugged them down her hips, leaving her completely naked standing outside on his balcony. It was a rush being where anyone could see them. The erotic element only made her body burn hotter.

At twenty-four, Courtney had been with only three men in her life, and none of them had been even remotely as skilled at the art of seduction as the gorgeous man kneeling before her.

"Spread your legs," Max demanded.

Her body instantly responded. She widened her stance, watching as his eyes raked over her most intimate place, his fingers smoothly caressing her sensitive flesh as he separated her slick folds. Her breath caught in her throat; a moan rumbled up from her chest as he licked her.

"Max," she whispered, releasing the railing and gripping his thick, dark hair, holding him to her as he ravished her with his mouth.

There was no way she would survive a night with him. No way would she live to see tomorrow, because he would surely kill her with pleasure. And for the first time in all her life, Courtney was ready to hand over every ounce of herself to someone else. To him.

And for one night … this night … Courtney was going to give herself over to Max without thinking about the repercussions. Tomorrow she would find a way to put the pieces back together once he shattered her world completely, which, undoubtedly, he would do.

Even if that wasn't in his plan.

□»«□»«□»«□

Max couldn't hold back any longer. He needed to bury himself inside of Courtney's wet heat, to feel her body grip him, to lose himself in her arms while he fucked them both to another plane of existence.

For nearly a month, he'd fought the urge, punished himself for wanting to lose himself in a woman who could so quickly bring down his family should she get too close. The only pleasure he'd found was with his own hand, and that hadn't been even remotely enough.

Pushing to his feet, he glided his hands over her glorious curves. "Don't move," he instructed.

Taking his drink, which he'd set down beside hers, Max moved to one of the chairs and set it on the small table. Turning to face her, he slowly undid his slacks, freeing his cock. Slowly stroking himself, he carefully took a seat, adjusting himself accordingly. While he teased his erection, he continued to look at her, to drink her in, to allow himself a few minutes to breathe before he took her hard and fast. When it came to Courtney, he knew the moment would be explosive, and he welcomed it, but he wanted to relish the sight of her for a little while longer.

"Max." The way she whispered his name, her gaze lingered between his legs briefly before lifting to meet his again, her naked body trembled slightly made his cock jump.

Placing his glass on the table beside him, he released his cock from his slacks, continuing to eye her as he stroked himself slowly. He needed to feel her lush lips wrapped around his dick, sucking him deep into the furnace of her mouth.

"Come here," he said, his voice rough and raspy with need.

He was hanging by a thread, desperate for her, aching for her, but he continued to torture himself because he knew the pleasure he'd find when they finally came together would forever change him. It wasn't something he took lightly considering the consequences of his actions and what that could mean for his family and his organization, but Max couldn't bring himself to listen to reason.

He wanted her.

All of her.

Courtney released the railing, taking one step closer, then another until she was standing in front of him.

He brushed his thumb over the swollen head of his cock. "I want to feel your lips on me. I want to fuck your sweet mouth, Courtney."

Her hooded gaze lowered as she slowly went to her knees before him. He didn't release his shaft as she knelt, needing to apply just the right amount of pain to keep him from going too far.

"Open your mouth for me," he instructed. When she did, he slid his fingers into her silky hair, pulling her head closer. With his eyes glued to her mouth, he tapped the swollen head against her lips. The warmth of her breath against the sensitive area sent a chill racing down his spine.

He urged her forward, tightening his grip on her hair and tilting her head so that he could feed his cock into her mouth. Her eyes closed, and a sexy moan escaped her as she laved him with her tongue. With trembling hands, Max pushed deeper into her mouth, forcing her to take him all the way to the root. Her lips closed around his shaft, her tongue gliding over him, and he never took his eyes off her.

He controlled the pace for a minute, maybe two, loving the way she sucked him, licked him, teased him. His muscles tightened as the pleasure accosted him.

Giving her free rein, he dropped his hands to his sides. "Suck me, Courtney. All of me."

Christ, it felt so damn good, the way her mouth worked him. She knew exactly the amount of pressure to apply with both her hand and her lips as she alternated between stroking him and sucking him. He kept his eyes on her fingers wrapped around the thick shaft, thinking about all the things he wanted to do to her. All the crazy, wicked ways he intended to make her come for him.

Not tonight, though.

Tonight was an introduction to his world. He'd anticipated this moment, tested his own patience even. And now that she was there, he intended to take full advantage by making her need for him grow as great as the need he had for her.

"Ahh, fuck," he groaned, unable to hold back. He thrust both hands into her hair, tugging hard as his hips drove forward, his cock tunneling in and out of her mouth. "So good. I've imagined you on your knees, thought about what it would feel like to fuck your mouth, to watch you take my dick, but nothing compares to this."

Max tried to relax, reveling in the pleasure as she cupped his balls with her free hand. The coolness of her fingers against his hot skin had him damn near seeing stars.

When the sensation became too intense, the need to come nearly taking over, Max stilled her head by pulling her hair roughly. Her gaze flew up to meet his as he took his dick from her mouth and helped her to her feet.

Without even attempting to be gentle, he launched to his feet, gripped her hips, and lifted her so that she was forced to wrap her arms and legs around his body. He then carried her inside to his bed, where he laid her out before him, never taking his eyes off her. She was perfect. Her smooth, tan skin glowed, her sex glistened as she spread her legs for him, beckoning him toward her with her eyes.

Drawing from his dwindling pool of patience, Max managed to undress as he observed her.

"Touch yourself," he ordered. "I want to watch."

Her hand drifted down over her belly, her slender fingers sliding over her mound, before she slipped one finger into herself, her back arching off the bed, her eyes glowing in the dimly lit room.

Courtney Kogan was by far the most exquisitely beautiful woman he'd ever laid eyes on, and Max had been with beautiful women before. But there was something about her that was different. He couldn't quite put his finger on what that was, but he intended to find out. Until then, he wanted to lose himself in her body, to make her scream and beg as she climaxed. He wanted her as addicted to him as he seemed to be to her.

Gripping his cock and stroking slowly, he retrieved a condom from the bedside table, but he didn't put it on. Crawling between her splayed thighs, he dropped the condom on the bed as he leaned over her.

"Touch me," he ordered.

When her hands roamed over his torso, Max claimed her mouth and pressed his cock between her thighs, his body coming down atop hers, their lips never separating.

They were like teenagers, grinding, groaning, eager to get closer but managing to hold back just long enough to make the ache nearly unbearable. When it was too much, he fumbled for the condom he'd tossed on the bed as her nails scraped over his skin, her body writhing beneath him in an attempt to get closer.

"Max."

He loved the way she said his name.

"Tell me, Court. Tell me what you want."

Kneeling between her thighs, he sheathed himself with the condom and then resumed his position above her.

"Tell me," he growled, wanting to hear her say it.

"Fuck me," she said firmly, her eyes locking with his.

It was a battle of wills. She was trying to gain the upper hand, and that spurred him on like nothing else. This wasn't a meek, timid woman who would allow him to pleasure her the way he wanted. No, Max sensed that Courtney knew what she wanted and knew how to go about getting it.

And he damn well intended to give it to her.

He brushed the head of his cock through her slit, teasing her clit and then gliding lower. He lined up with her entrance and pushed inside.

Fuck.

She was tight … so goddamn tight. He met her gaze, looking for signs that he was hurting her, but there were none. He inched deeper, holding his breath as her body gripped him almost painfully.

"Need more," she whispered.

Max pushed his hips forward, but he stopped before he was lodged all the way, wanting to make her beg him.

Her nails dug into his ass as she tried to pull him closer.

Crushing his mouth to hers, Max plunged forward, her muscles clasping him as he worked his cock deeper into her until, finally, he was buried to the hilt.

Courtney cried out, and he swallowed the sound, his tongue licking into her mouth. He gave her a moment so that her body could acclimate to him being inside her. And when her legs wrapped around him, he knew she was ready.

"God, you feel good," he said against her lips, continuing to kiss her as he pumped his hips, filling her, retreating, only to fill her completely again. She was so tight, so fucking wet, her body gripped him, strangling his dick with pleasure.

Courtney's mouth pulled back from his, and she stared up at him. The raspy words that came next made his dick throb. "Fuck. Me. And don't stop until we both can't breathe."

Max separated their upper bodies, kneeling between her thighs. He braced one of his hands on the headboard, the other around her hip and lifted her slightly off the bed, pulling out and then slamming into her. He held her tightly, the bed rocking with every movement as he pounded into her to the point he figured the headboard would shatter, but he couldn't stop.

Her eyes were closed, her head thrown back, her hands on his thighs, nails biting into his skin as he fucked her harder, faster, harder, faster until sweat beaded on his skin and the room was filled with her cries of pleasure and his answering grunts.

It was brutal and beautiful at the same time, and Max never wanted it to end, but his balls were drawing up tight to his body, the initial tingle starting at the base of his spine, a warning that he was going to come and he was going to fucking come hard.

Releasing her hip, Max grabbed the back of her knee, folding her leg toward her and changing the angle. He drove down into her, his hips over hers as his cock tunneled in and out of her pussy while she begged and pleaded, crying out for more until he knew he wouldn't last much longer.

"Max! Oh, fuck! Fuck. Fuck. Fuck!" Her nails scored his skin as her body tightened, her cunt clasping his dick painfully hard, sending pleasure coursing through his veins as he attempted to hold back but found himself inevitably losing the battle.

"Yes! God, yes! Max, make me come!" Courtney screamed, the most beautiful sound he'd ever heard as she came apart beneath him, and only then did he let himself go, his release battering him until there wasn't an ounce of strength left in his entire body.

He collapsed beside her. The scent of hot, sweaty sex drifted on the breeze coming in through the open doors as they fought to breathe. And when they finally came down from the sexual high, after he tossed the condom in the bathroom receptacle and cleaned up, Max pulled Courtney into his arms and held her, refusing to let her go. Only when her breaths evened out and she was sleeping soundly against him did he give in to the exhaustion that overwhelmed him.

Despite the peace that filled him while he dreamed about her, Max's world would forever be changed when he woke up to find her gone from his bed, a tiny slip of paper on the pillow she'd been sleeping on that read Thanks for the orgasms *the only thing keeping him company.*

She was a wildcat, there was no doubt about it. And based on the note, she thought she had the upper hand. He looked forward to showing her that wasn't the case.

A smile tipped the corners of his lips as he lay there remembering the night before. It was then that Max accepted Courtney's challenge. Because, above all else, that was exactly what she was, and he damn sure intended to conquer her.

Staring into the bright, empty room, Max vowed to make her his before it was all over.

Chapter Eleven

Ever had one of those days when you should've just stayed in bed?

Present day
Seven weeks later
April 24th

Courtney made her way into the Sniper 1 Security office a little after eight in the morning, dragging ass and clutching a cup of coffee.

She was what one would likely consider a social coffee drinker mostly, but this morning, she had needed the caffeine and had stopped at Percolation—the small shop in the Sniper 1 building—before heading up.

She'd been up late the night before, having returned from her most recent assignment, pulling bodyguard duty for a spoiled little rich girl whose daddy—the owner of a chain of fancy hotels—had felt it necessary to hire a high-priced, not to mention armed, babysitter to keep an eye on his sweet baby girl. Yes, he'd actually referred to her as such.

There wasn't a single thing sweet about that girl.

For the last month and a half, Courtney had spent her time watching the girl immerse herself in meaningless sex, recreational drugs, and whatever else struck her fancy as she lived up to the bad-girl image the press had of her. Not that Courtney had cared what the pretentious little brat did. It wasn't her job to care. She'd been there to protect her, which she'd done until the girl's father had pulled the plug, refusing to do anything more when the snobby brat had ended up in jail for driving while intoxicated after evading Courtney at one of the ritzy L.A. nightclubs they had frequented.

Truth was, Courtney was glad it was over.

But morning had come too quickly, as far as she was concerned. Especially when she was running on only three hours of sleep, having finally passed out after crawling into her own bed trying to drown out thoughts of the one man she'd been running from for longer than she cared to think about.

Max.

It'd been just over seven weeks since she'd last seen him. Fifty-one long, painful days of babysitting, where the only positive was her inability to spend too much time thinking about her personal life when she had to be working. Unfortunately, that was the part she missed now that she was home, because the second the Sniper 1 Security private jet had landed back on Texas soil, she'd missed Max immensely.

She'd felt as though someone had taken a sledgehammer to her heart the instant she'd walked into her house, her eyes traveling to the kitchen, to the wall where she and Max had…

The point was, her heart ached, her head ached, her body ached. Every piece of her was broken, shattered, yet she knew that life had to go on. She had to put one foot in front of the other because this was her choice. She wasn't going to roll around in self-pity when she'd been the one to send Max on his way.

Courtney had known all along that it wouldn't work. *They* wouldn't work, no matter how much her heart wished it were possible.

"Mornin'," Jayden greeted when Courtney walked through the main door and into the lavishly decorated waiting area for their clients. The polished wood walls and gleaming marble floors looked exactly the same as when she'd left.

"Mornin'," she grumbled in return.

"Glad you're back," Jayden said.

Lifting her gaze, she met her friend's inquisitive green eyes. Courtney hated shutting her out, but that was what she'd been doing ever since they'd met for coffee before she'd left. She'd been shutting everyone out. Turned out that taking off to California hadn't been as simple as she'd thought it would be, especially not after the word got out about her involvement with Max. Once that'd happened, her family had practically blown up her cell phone with calls and texts. Most of which she'd ignored.

Unfortunately, she hadn't been able to ignore her brother Trace when he and Marissa had flown out to California just to visit. Right, because that had been fun. Turned out, Trace wasn't willing to let her off the hook. He'd given her hell about her relationship with Max—despite the fact that Courtney assured him it was in the past. The man was like a dog with a bone, unwilling to let go until he was satisfied with the way things ended. Marissa, as always, had proven her friendship, standing up for her and gently talking Trace back from the ledge.

She'd been none too subtly informed that she was lucky it had been him and not their father who'd come to visit. Courtney couldn't argue with that point.

Luckily, she'd been fourteen hundred miles away, sheltered by the crappy assignment her father had sent her on, and hadn't had to deal with her father's wrath at the time.

Work had been her only focus, the only way she could keep moving forward. For weeks on end, she had felt as though she were held together by a fine thread, one that threatened to snap, and now, as she returned to her normal routine, the last thing she needed was to see sympathy in Jayden's eyes.

"Thanks. Nice to be back."

"So, how was it?" Jayden inquired. "With … you know who."

They'd agreed not to speak the rich girl's name around the office, not wanting to draw attention to the assignment, because, had the girl's father not been a friend of Bryce's, there was no doubt they'd have turned it down. Instead, Courtney had drawn the short straw, it had seemed.

"As expected," Courtney replied, continuing to move slowly toward the hall that led back to the main part of the office.

"One of these days, you're gonna give me all the dirty details," Jayden told her sternly.

Thankfully, the phone rang, and Jayden was distracted, which allowed Courtney the perfect opportunity to disappear. Rather than linger and risk a million questions, she made a beeline for her desk, hoping no one else would be in the room where several of the agents, herself included, worked on the rare occasions they had to come into the office. She was only there to complete the official paperwork on the last assignment and to find out where they were going to send her next.

"Courtney! My office. Now!"

Shit.

Courtney stopped abruptly, taking a deep breath and releasing it. She'd known this was going to happen, so she shouldn't have been surprised. She only wished she'd had a little time to get herself together, to acclimate once again to the day-to-day at Sniper 1, but unfortunately, that wasn't the case. Reversing her course, she walked down the narrow hallway to her father's office. Casper sat at his desk, his beefy arms crossed over his thick chest as he glowered at her.

She took a moment to peruse his features, realizing that the man she hadn't seen in nearly two months still looked the same, just as formidable as ever. His graying hair was still short, his white-gray eyes, so like her own, were still intense. And focused on her.

"Yes?" she asked, pretending not to have any idea why he'd called her into his office first thing.

"Shut the door."

Damn it.

She closed the door, taking another deep, calming breath before turning to face her father once again.

"Now sit."

Courtney bristled at the command, but she did as instructed. She'd never been the type to argue with her parents. However, she'd never been one to talk openly with them about relationships, either, and she knew without a doubt that Casper wanted to discuss her involvement with Max Adorite. There was no way she could continue to put that conversation off.

Apparently, as she'd learned from Trace, RT hadn't been the one to share the details of Courtney's involvement with the mafia underboss, which was how she'd managed to get out of town prior to enduring her father's tirade. However, Trace hadn't had an issue sharing the information, and thus, her father had been trying to get her to talk since the jet had landed in California.

It was a topic of conversation she'd managed to avoid, but that had been easier to do when she'd been several states away while her father was back here in Texas. Not so easy anymore.

Unfortunately.

She could see his irritation written clearly across his handsome face.

Once she was in her seat, she set her coffee cup on the table beside her and folded her arms across her chest, mirroring her father's position. "Yes?"

"What the hell happened Wednesday night?"

Courtney cocked an eyebrow, a wave of relief washing over her. So he didn't want to talk about Max. He wanted to know about her last assignment.

Considering that for a moment, she watched her father. She had no idea what RT had told Casper after Courtney had called to inform him of the change in plans thanks to the girl's arrest, but she damn sure wasn't going to supply additional information if Casper didn't already know.

"How'd that girl get behind the wheel of a car in the first place?" her father asked, as straightforward as ever.

"No idea," she told him, crossing one leg over the other and feigning a casualness she didn't feel. Technically, she knew exactly how it had happened and had actually watched it all play out. Didn't mean her father would be happy with her explanation, so she decided to water down the details. "As usual, we were in the VIP room at the club. She said she had to go to the bathroom. I didn't feel it was necessary to hold her hand. After ten minutes, I went to check on her. She was gone."

"Do you realize what this will do to our reputation?"

"Steph's already on it," Courtney told him, referring to Stephanie Trexler, the public relations genius who'd managed to keep Sniper 1 Security out of the hot seat on more than one occasion. "And it's not like her father's gonna have much to say. He doesn't want the news of his daughter's upcoming stint in rehab to become public information."

Casper sighed but didn't say anything, which surprised Courtney. They simply sat there, staring at one another while Courtney wondered what was going through her father's mind.

"She was a brat, huh?" he finally questioned, his face softening somewhat.

"Very much so."

Casper nodded but again remained quiet. He appeared to be regarding her, likely questioning her state of mind. Not wanting him to think too long on that, she prayed he would get on with it. Just when she was going to ask a question of her own, he spoke.

"Do you have another assignment lined up?"

"Don't know yet. I'm supposed to meet with RT in a bit." Although Courtney was used to receiving her assignments from her older brother Hunter, it seemed her brother had disappeared into thin air, handling some off-the-books mission overseas. What that really meant was her brother was running hard and fast from the woman he loved, the woman who'd stood him up at the altar a few years back, the same woman who was supposed to reappear any day now.

"Good. I need you to do something for me."

Courtney did not like the sound of that. Her father didn't usually assign her missions—even the rich girl assignment had surprised her—and when he did, they tended to be of a more personal nature. She was good at infiltrating, and he had come to rely on her for that. Especially when…

"I'm not sure if you're familiar with Senator Artemis Winslow."

"Not really, no," she told him.

Casper leaned back in his chair. "Looks like the good senator is digging his heels into the dark underworld."

The hair on the back of Courtney's neck stood on end. That particular expression was how her father chose to talk about the mafia. Namely the Adorite family.

Surely he wasn't about to…

"Based on the news, it appears that Artemis's granddaughter, Angelica, is about to wed into the Adorite family."

Courtney's lungs seized up, all of the oxygen in the room instantly disappearing, making it impossible to draw in a breath as she anticipated what he was about to say.

"On June sixth, Angelica Winslow is set to marry Maximillian Adorite. I need to know what the angle is. What's Artemis getting out of this deal? And I need to know before they say their vows."

Her father continued to talk, but the only thing Courtney heard was a roaring in her ears. Her mind drifted back to the last night she'd seen Max, to the last thing he'd said to her before he'd walked out on her at her request.

Things are about to change for me, Courtney. Major things. But I want you to know, no matter what happens, if you ever need me, I'll be there. You just have to call.

Max was getting married?

Oh, God.

"Courtney?"

Courtney brought her father's face into focus, trying to recall what he'd just said, but she couldn't.

"Do you think you can do that?"

"Why?" she questioned, the word tumbling out of her mouth.

Casper's thick eyebrows formed a V as he frowned back at her. "Why *what*?"

"Why do you care if the senator's granddaughter gets married?"

"It's not me who cares," he told her simply, but Courtney didn't buy it. She could see that same interested look on her father's face that she'd seen before. There might very well be a client interested in the Southern Boy Mafia, but Casper was curious for his own reasons. She just didn't know what they were.

She knew she wasn't supposed to ask questions. There were certain jobs they did for the government that were off the record, so to speak. And when it came to the Adorites, she figured some power-wielding desk jockey in a tacky suit wanted specific details, especially if there was a well-known Texas senator now involved.

"Is this gonna be an issue for you?" Casper paused. "Considering?"

Courtney didn't respond. She couldn't. The thick silence lingered between them, making it even harder to breathe.

"Is somethin' goin' on with you and Max Adorite? Beyond the job I originally assigned you?" he finally asked.

Courtney shook her head. That was the honest-to-God truth. After the last time he'd come to her house, when they'd…

She was *not* going to revisit that particular memory again.

"That's not the story I was told," Casper countered, surprising her.

Squaring her shoulders, Courtney tried to pull herself together. "Well, I don't know what story you were told."

"Don't play games with me, Courtney."

"Dad…" Taking another deep breath, Courtney resigned herself to telling him as little as possible. Her objective was to get out of his office as quickly as she could, and the longer she put up resistance, the longer he would glare at her. "I met Max two years ago. On the op that *you* sent me on. To collect information when Max took over as second-in-command of the SBM. I provided what little information I managed to get. That's it."

"So you're *not* involved with him?"

"No." *Not anymore.*

She ignored the pang in her chest, the bottomless echo that continued to shake her when she thought about Max walking away. Never before had his exit been quite so … final.

"Courtney…" Casper thrust his hand through his graying hair, his gaze softening somewhat. "If there was something between you and Max…"

Finally grasping her resolve, Courtney faced her father head on. "I just told you I wasn't seeing him. If you need information, I can get it for you." It wasn't the retort she should've come up with, but it was an automatic reaction.

She loved her parents. They'd always stood by her and her three brothers, supported them, loved them, encouraged them. But being that she was the only girl, Courtney had spent a good portion of her life dealing with the testosterone that ruled her house. At twenty-six, she didn't need her father supervising her life or telling her who she could or could not spend her time with. And certainly not when it came to business.

She was an enforcer, an agent. As good as, if not better than, any of the men who worked there. She'd never failed, with the exception of infiltrating the SBM and the spoiled little rich girl, and even then, she didn't consider the last one a failure. That girl… Well, if Courtney were completely honest, she'd needed help. Serious, professional help. The fact that Courtney was the one who'd called the cops, tipping them off to the drunk rich girl leaving the parking lot of the club, proved that the op hadn't been a failure; it had, in Courtney's opinion, been an intervention. Not that she intended to tell anyone that.

"You understand how dangerous this is?" Casper asked. "*Max* is dangerous. His *father* is dangerous. His entire family is—"

Pushing to her feet, Courtney stared back at her father, interrupting before he could continue. "I'm well aware of that. And I told you, I can do this."

Casper's facial expression didn't change, but it rarely did. The man was the master at masking his emotions, and sometimes Courtney wished she was capable of the same. But she wasn't built that way. Unfortunately, she was an open book, which she knew was the only reason her father continued to push her.

"I need more information this time," he told her. "Real information, Courtney. I want to know what he's workin' on, who he's workin' with, where and when the guns and the drugs are being moved. What part Artemis intends to play in all of that. I don't give a shit about anything but that."

Courtney nodded. She understood completely.

"I've got things to do," she told him.

When she reached the door, her father spoke again. "Courtney, I know what it's like to be in love. When I was much younger, before I ever met your mother, there was…"

Courtney waited, staring at the door. Her father had never spoken quite so candidly about his own life, especially not about anything before he'd met Courtney's mother.

"I know it can hurt at times," he continued. "But you have to know that sometimes it's best to move on, to forget the past."

A surge of emotion came up her throat, threatening to choke her. She didn't turn around, didn't look at her father. "Just so we're clear, I've never *been* in love."

With that lie hanging in the air, Courtney stormed out of his office and made a beeline for the restroom. It was time she pulled herself together, because no matter what, she wasn't going to let Max continue to haunt her. No matter what she thought she wanted, Courtney knew there were only three things that were true:

Their paths should've never crossed.

Their lives should've never mingled.

And most importantly, she should've never given him her heart.

But as with anything, life continued to move on, regardless of the devastation and destruction obscuring the path. She simply needed to move on with her life.

Chapter Twelve

Same shit … different day.

"Mr. Adorite, you have a visitor," Leyton relayed when opening the door to Max's office and sticking his head inside.

Max could hear the sound of the club below, the booming bass rumbling into the room as his head of security stared back at him. He didn't mind the noise so much, but on busy nights, he rarely got the solitude he found when he hid out at the club during the week, and tonight proved to be no different.

Max lifted his eyebrow in question.

"Ms. Winslow. She says it's important."

Shit.

"Bring her in." Max shoved the file folder he'd been reviewing into the top drawer and got to his feet at the same time the blonde sauntered into his office.

"Max," she crooned as she moved across the room toward him, an unnecessary amount of sway in her narrow hips. As always, Angelica Winslow was dressed impressively, her highlighted blonde hair perfectly styled, makeup flawless, nails a blood red, and she'd ditched the atrocious perfume, opting for something … less offensive.

She looked every bit the viper Max knew her to be, despite the sweet innocence she still attempted to portray.

"Angelica," he replied, accepting her hug when she approached. For the past couple of months, she'd been trying to schmooze her way into his life. Not that it had worked, but she seemed to believe they were making progress, so Max hadn't bothered to tell her any different.

It was just easier that way.

Of course, that simple, polite gesture wasn't taken as such by Angelica. She proceeded to draw her claws over Max's neck, her smile venomous as she stared back at him.

"It's so good to see you," she said softly, seductively. "Pretty soon I won't have to go so long without seeing you. I'll be waking up in your bed every morning."

Max ignored her statement. Unfortunately, she was right. About part of it, anyway. In a little more than a month, they would be married; however, he'd be damned if she'd be spending even one single night in his bed. It wasn't going to work that way.

He'd made a grave mistake in the last few weeks. He'd vowed to stay away from her, never wanting to feel her hands on him, but then one night, he'd plied himself with enough liquor that he'd given in to his baser urges, suited up, and fucked her. From behind.

Right on his living room sofa, Max had fucked Angelica senseless. The entire time he'd pretended she was Courtney, pretended she was the woman he loved. When it was over that first time, he'd yelled at her, demanded her to go away, angry more with himself than anything. Not that she'd listened. Angelica had seemingly made it her mission to get closer to him.

Since then, he'd found himself taking out his sexual frustrations on her, although he had been extremely careful each and every time, using his own condoms, unwilling to let Angelica do something so stupid as to get pregnant just to get her way. He wouldn't put it past her. Hell, he wouldn't put anything past her.

He hated her with a growing passion, despised the sound of her voice, the touch of her hands, yet he had continued to give in, desperate to get past this devastating ache that had taken up residence in his chest. Not once had he fucked her without protection and never unless she was fully clothed and he was too. Never in his bedroom, either, but Angelica didn't seem to mind. He didn't even think she'd noticed that he refused to look at her when he fucked her, preferring to take her from behind so he could pretend she was someone else.

Although it was strictly business, the poisonous woman who'd been working to get her claws into him seemed to believe at some point he would eventually change his mind.

That wasn't going to happen.

Angelica was the type of woman any right-minded man would want to steer clear of. Then again, Max wasn't in his right mind these days. For weeks on end, he'd immersed himself in business, focusing on the increase in shipments coming from Mexico, along with the land deals he had in the works, as well as the nightclubs that had needed his attention.

After the FBI's raid nearly a year ago, on Devil's Playground and a couple of the strip clubs he owned, he'd been forced to shut down for a while. He hadn't spent a minute in jail, although the assistant US attorney had tried his damnedest to make the charges stick. It hadn't taken long for that to clear thanks to his family's endless connections, but it had required some extra effort to get business back to full capacity, and only in recent months had Max seen a shift into the black.

"Can I get you somethin' to drink?" Max offered, taking Angelica's wrists and removing her hands from his neck.

"I'll take a scotch. Neat."

Max motioned Leyton to retrieve the drink. He then urged Angelica toward the leather sofa. When she took a seat, he opted to sit opposite her.

"You said it was important," Max relayed, hoping to get this over with and send Angelica on her way.

"My grandfather asked me to speak to you."

Max sighed. Artemis Winslow was quickly becoming a serious pain in Max's ass. For some reason, the man believed that he was the one calling the shots, as though Max were some sort of dancing monkey he could order around. Oddly, the man was becoming more persistent after every incident that occurred between Max and Angelica, and he had a sneaking suspicion that she was holding more of the reins than they were telling him.

"About?"

"The wedding."

Oh, hell. "What about it?"

"He'd like to move the date up."

Max lifted an eyebrow. Angelica might be used to lying her way through life, getting what she wanted because people were either too stupid to notice or they merely didn't have the balls to stand up to her, but Max wasn't falling for it.

"Is that so?"

"Yes."

"So June isn't soon enough?" he asked as Leyton delivered the drink, informing Max that he would be waiting outside.

Angelica shifted, her prim posture never wavering as she retrieved the glass. "Doesn't appear that way. I tried to tell him that these things take time, but he wants to move forward now."

To ensure Max didn't back out, no doubt.

Max didn't share his thought with Angelica. "And when would *he* like to see this take place?"

"May sixteenth."

How very convenient.

He'd recently received an invitation to a wedding scheduled for that very day, the nuptials of Trace Kogan and Marissa Trexler. Being the glutton for punishment that he was these days, Max had actually RSVP'd, asking his sister Ashlynn to accompany him, something Angelica hadn't been at all happy about. His choice to attend had been a completely selfish decision. The need to see Courtney again, even from a distance, had been more than he could bear.

"That date doesn't work for me," he told her, meeting her gaze.

Her blue eyes burned, her sweet façade slipping as she stared back at him. "You need to make it work for you."

Max pushed to his feet. "No. I don't."

He wasn't going to sit there and argue with her. He'd done enough of that for the past few weeks, trying to acclimate to Hurricane Angelica coming in and stirring shit up in a world that was already filled with plenty of chaos.

She slammed the glass on the table and stood.

"Don't you dare walk away from me, Maximillian."

Christ, he hated when she called him that.

Max slowly pivoted on his heel, dipping his hands into his pockets as he stared back at her. "In case you haven't noticed," he told her sharply, "you don't call the shots. That's not how this works."

Angelica moved toward him, her eyes narrowed, her red lips pursed. "You're wrong. I call *all* the shots."

Max barked out a disbelieving laugh, only pissing her off more.

Angelica glared at him, pointing a red-tipped finger in his direction. "You forget who my grandfather is."

"Oh, trust me, I remember," he snapped.

"He's got more power than you'll ever dream of having," Angelica spat. "And if you expect our families to work together, then you'll need to come over to my way of thinking."

Max considered her words for a moment. Locking his eyes with hers, he followed with, "It's not happening."

Angelica huffed. "I hate you."

"Then why the hell did you agree to this in the first fucking place?" he roared, turning away from her.

"Why wouldn't I?" she hissed. "An opportunity to marry into the notorious Adorite family. It's every girl's dream."

Max hated the sarcasm, but he understood what Angelica was saying. He also knew—even though he truly believed she was using him and his family for her own ulterior motives—that there was a hint of truth in her statement, which was why he'd steered clear of this issue for as long as he could. The thought of an arranged marriage to Artemis's granddaughter didn't sit well with him, but there were opportunities that would come along with it. Not only the land. There were other things that could very well launch Max's organization into an entirely different playing field, offering them significantly more territory to control, some that his family had longed to get their hands on, but also giving them a political stronghold that they could use as leverage in other aspects of their businesses. Max would admit, he was intrigued by the idea but, at the same time, put off.

He didn't want to get married.

Not to this woman, anyway.

Her grandfather was the senator of the great state of Texas, a very powerful man, who, should Max keep their business options open, could be a tremendous asset to his organization. It had actually been Artemis's idea for his granddaughter to marry into Max's family, and engineered into a worthwhile plan by Max's father, Samuel. Max was merely a byproduct of the grand scheme. Or so everyone believed.

However, he wasn't stupid. The underhanded senator, and likely Angelica, was hoping to get a hand in Max's business ventures, and by inserting himself—indirectly—into Max's world, the other man felt as though he might be able to take control. Made sense based on the true nature of the US government, always wanting a little more control, always needing a little more power, never feeling the need to abide by the law.

Little did Artemis know, but Max had absolutely no intention of releasing even an ounce of his control. But the more thought he'd given to the suggestion, the more beneficial it had seemed. For him.

Before Max could say anything more, the door to his office opened and in walked…

"Sir. We…" Leyton's eyes cut to Angelica briefly. "We have an incident that needs your attention."

"Have Brent handle it," Max instructed.

"Sir, it can only be handled by you."

Max tried not to let his confusion show. He couldn't think of a single thing that his younger brother couldn't handle, but he took the opportunity for what it was.

"You need to go," he informed Angelica, moving back to his desk. "We're not changin' the date. You can let your grandfather know, or I'll be glad to call him myself. Your choice."

Angelica snarled at him. "We're not done with this conversation."

"We most certainly are." Max glanced up at Leyton. "Have someone take Angelica home."

"Yes, sir."

Leyton spoke into the microphone on his shirt as he escorted a very pissed off Angelica out of Max's office. When he returned a moment later, Max stared back at him, waiting for him to tell him what was so goddamn important that he had to be…

"Sir. Courtney Kogan just arrived at the door."

…interrupted.

Yes, that would certainly be a good reason.

Son. Of. A. Bitch.

Chapter Thirteen

If only work could always be this entertaining.

Twenty months ago

Meet me at the club.

Courtney glared at the phone screen, a strange concoction of anger and desire raging inside her. Rather than give in to the longing that had seemingly taken control of her entire fucking life for the past four months, Courtney responded with:

No.

Tossing the phone onto the cushion beside her, she turned her attention back to the television.

She'd come home from work eager to sleep but found herself too wired. So, she'd made popcorn, grabbed her always handy bowl of M&Ms, the television remote, a glass of wine, and flopped onto the couch after putting on her pajamas.

Just as she got interested in the show again, her phone buzzed.

It wasn't a request.

Tempted to throw her phone through the plate-glass window, she didn't bother to pick it up. She wasn't giving in to Max's demands, no matter what her body wanted.

For the past four freaking months, she'd spent endless hours with the man, a majority of those naked with him buried balls deep inside her. They spent more time fucking than they did anything else, and now, she found herself ensconced in his world, seeing the nasty side and hating herself more and more each day because she couldn't seem to find a way out. Actually, truth was, she wasn't looking for a way out, and that concerned her deeply.

She didn't have a problem with their physical relationship because she happened to enjoy the way Max fucked her. And she didn't necessarily have to like him to enjoy the pleasure he could give her. But in the past couple of weeks, she'd noticed a change in him. Something was obviously going down, and he was keeping her on the outside as he'd always done, despite her every effort to infiltrate his organization.

And that was the very reason she needed to stay away from him. He was a job, pure and simple. This thing between them, it would never go anywhere, because he didn't trust her, and she'd given him no reason to.

As of late, she'd started talking to Max's security team, trying to see if they'd be willing to open up. She didn't usually make much progress, but she was getting closer to a few of them. Eventually, she prayed, one of them would give in and tell her what she needed to know.

Granted, Leyton seemed to be on to her plan and had warned her off, telling her that Max would kill anyone who betrayed him. She'd only briefly considered this but hadn't heeded it. As far as she was concerned, Max would do what he needed to do. As would she. If she could get someone to give her information, Max didn't ever have to know. And that was what she was working on, keeping it from him and still accomplishing her goal.

There was no doubt about it, though, their physical relationship had taken precedence over the job, and Courtney didn't have the strength, nor the desire, to end it. Never in her life had she met a man like Max, a man who knew his way around a woman's body so effortlessly. He could practically make her come with just the heated look in his eyes.

But that wasn't all there was between them. When they were alone, she saw a different side to him. A softer side. Max would kill for her, lay down his life for her. Although they didn't speak of feelings, they were there, silently swirling around them, bringing them closer, holding them together, making them both stronger.

But it was time for her to put her foot down. She wasn't getting any further with her investigation, yet she found herself deeper and deeper under Max's spell. Not a place she wanted to be. If she wasn't careful, before long, she'd wind up in a situation she wouldn't be able to get herself out of. Since that wasn't an option, because she refused to live in the dark underworld that he lived in, Courtney needed to put some distance between them.

If you're not at the club in half an hour, I'm coming to you.

Shit.

It wasn't the first time he'd threatened to show up at her house. Since she lived in a compound with the rest of her family—a group that fought against everything that Max stood for—that was a risk she wasn't willing to take. And she knew that Max didn't bluff. If he said he was going to do something, he would do it.

Grabbing the phone, she typed out a response.

Fine. I'll see you in an hour.

Courtney threw the phone on the couch and then trudged to her bedroom to change clothes, all the while reminding herself just how much she hated Max.

An hour and fifteen minutes later, she arrived at the club. Rather than wait in the line that wrapped around the building, she waltzed right up to the bouncer—an immensely sexy black man they called Rock—and smiled.

"Good evening, Ms. Kogan. Mr. Adorite is expecting you."

Of course he was.

She was allowed through the door as Rock spoke into the mic on his shirt, informing whomever that she was making her way inside.

Devil's Playground was a wildly popular Dallas nightclub. Although the bouncers were strict with the rules of the house, she knew that there was quite a bit of illegal activity that went on there. Aside from the booze—the only legal substance in the place—that flowed like water, there was an abundance of drugs and sex that came into play on a nightly basis.

Though the club was boasted as a high-class establishment and even managed to appear that way to the unsuspecting eye, Courtney wasn't oblivious to the whores who trolled inside, many of whom were actually entangled in Max's organization. Not that he laid claim to them, but it hadn't taken long for Courtney to get the gist of Max's so-called land development business. It was a front for all the illegal activities he ran—including guns, racketeering, drugs, and, yes, whores. The only thing she hadn't been able to firmly tie him to was the drugs. At least not yet.

"Ms. Kogan."

When Courtney reached the end of the hallway that would lead to the open floor of the club, she looked up to see Leyton waiting for her. She rolled her eyes at him but then allowed him to usher her through the back hallway, then up the staircase that led to Max's private office.

"He's waiting," Leyton informed her, opening the door and allowing her inside before closing it behind her.

"An hour, huh?" Max asked, not looking up from the paper he was reading at his desk.

Courtney didn't respond immediately. She set her clutch—which contained her phone and her gun—on the small side table and walked to the window that overlooked the club, watching the strobe lights flash on the mass of people down below. She knew that the people could see her if they happened to glance up. Although the glass was bulletproof, it wasn't mirrored or tinted to keep outsiders from seeing in. According to Max, he liked it that way. She sensed that was the voyeur in him returning the favor. There was no doubt about it, the man had some serious sexual kinks.

When Max didn't say anything after several minutes, she moved to the black leather sofa and flopped down with a huff. She expected Max to at least look at her, but he didn't. He stayed focused on whatever it was he was doing, which irritated the shit out of her.

"Why'd you summon me?" she questioned, her irritation getting the best of her.

"Come here," he commanded, still not looking up.

Courtney inhaled sharply at the rough tone of his voice. She'd heard that before. Max was the type of man who expected people to jump when he snapped his fingers. In recent weeks, Courtney had stopped jumping, and she knew it was only pissing him off, but she couldn't seem to help herself. She wasn't trying to be recalcitrant, she was merely trying to remind Max that she wasn't one of his whores. She wasn't at his beck and call.

"Over here. Now," he growled, his gaze lifting to meet hers.

His eyes widened when he took in her appearance, and a chill danced down her spine. She'd selected the outfit just for him, figuring if he could play hard ball, so could she. A strange flutter erupted in her belly as she saw the heat in his golden eyes. Sure, he was pissed, but he was also turned on. Why that pleased her, she had no idea, but the next thing she knew, she was walking over to his desk.

Max placed his hand on her thigh, sliding it upward. "You're not wearing your gun."

Courtney shook her head. "But don't worry, I've got it."

The outfit she'd opted to wear left little to the imagination, which meant that the S&W lightweight sub-compact .380 ACP pistol couldn't possibly be hidden beneath her skirt.

"Panties off," he instructed.

Courtney gave him a go-to-hell glare.

He didn't seem at all intimidated, but she was, especially when his eyes narrowed. She lifted the short black skirt and slid her fingers into the band of her panties, pushing them down her legs and working them over the knee-high boots she wore. She reached down and retrieved them, placing them on his desk.

"Sit down."

Looking around, she tried to figure out where he wanted her to sit. "Where?"

Max rolled his chair back and nodded toward his desk. Courtney looked at him, confused.

"Sit. Down," he snarled.

Realizing he wanted her to sit on *his desk, she stepped in front of him and then perched her ass on the edge. His glare pretty much singed her, and she knew he wasn't in the mood to be pushed, so she hefted herself up onto the desk, facing him.*

He rolled closer. "Feet on the arms of the chair," he instructed, crossing his muscular arms over his chest, the bunch of his biceps visible beneath the short sleeves of his polo.

It didn't take her long to realize what direction this was headed. For a fraction of a second, she thought that she should've been appalled that he'd expect her to put herself on display for him, but the desire that infused her erased all concern. Her traitorous body did as he asked, and she slowly lifted each foot, placing the toes of her boots on the arms of his chair, which left her in a rather precarious situation, her legs spread wide, the short, flowing skirt doing little to cover her.

Not that it mattered, because when his next command came, Courtney knew her vulnerability was exactly what he was after.

And angry at him or not, she was powerless to resist him.

□»«□»«□»«□

"Lift your skirt," Max demanded, his body coiled tightly as he watched Courtney get comfortable on his desk.

She was tempted to defy his every command; he had sensed it from the second she'd stepped through the office door. Hell, he'd known since she'd denied his initial request.

But he wasn't in the mood.

As it was, he was having a damn hard time keeping his hands off her. More so when he'd noticed what she was wearing.

The short black skirt was just long enough to cover her ass, and the silky black halter barely covered her breasts, the sides peeking out from the flimsy material. Most of her midriff was bare, as was her back. He was beginning to wonder why she'd even bothered with clothes at all, for as little as they covered her.

But the boots… Those were a nice touch. Black leather with four-inch heels… Yeah, he wanted to see her in nothing but the fucking boots.

Had he allowed his need to take over, he would've already fucked her twice in the few minutes she'd been standing in his office. He was that wound up, and it wasn't entirely her fault, but she was his release. She was the only good thing in his world at the moment, and he needed her. Needed her with a desperation he didn't understand.

So, keeping his hands to himself was the only way he could keep her safe from him at the moment.

Max's gaze traveled between her splayed thighs, admiring the silky-smooth golden skin she revealed. It wasn't enough, but it was a start.

"Either lift the skirt or I'm gonna rip it off you," he told her roughly, keeping his arms firmly pinned across his chest.

Courtney slowly lifted the short black skirt, revealing her beautiful bare pussy to him. He drank in the sight of her spread out before him. He wished she was naked—wearing only the boots—but he knew better than to do that here. Anyone could walk in at any given moment. Not that he'd give a shit, but he was trying to think about Courtney.

For the last couple of months, he'd pushed her limits, further and further each time they were together, but she wasn't quite ready for all he wanted from her. So, he was trying to take things slow, ease her into it gradually.

"What's wrong, Max?" Courtney asked, holding her skirt to her waist as he admired her petal-soft folds, glistening with her desire.

Oh, yes, she was wet for him. He knew this turned her on as much as it did him, which was part of the reason he continued to push her. But he mostly did it for selfish reasons. He needed her; he needed the solace she provided him, even if she didn't realize what she gave him. It wasn't as though he'd shared that with her, nor did he have any intention of doing so.

"Nothing," he responded, meeting her gaze.

"Talk to me," she said, her glossy mouth tempting him. He wanted to order her to her knees at his feet, to make her take his dick in her mouth, to blow his mind with the sweet suction of her lips.

But he didn't.

Not yet.

"This isn't about me," he told her.

"It's always about you," she snapped.

He regarded her for a moment. She was pissed at him, but that wasn't unusual, either. Their relationship was … complicated.

From the first time he'd made her come on his dining room table, Max hadn't been able to get enough of her. She knew it, too.

Unfortunately, there were times that she got too inquisitive for her own good, and he'd had to resort to sex to get her to back off. Otherwise, he would be forced to kill his own men for betraying him. As it was, she was asking too many questions, making friendships with the men who worked for him. She was getting in over her head, but she didn't seem to care.

Getting her to back off required too much effort.

He much preferred the sex.

Sure, he was insatiable, didn't think he'd ever get enough of her, but the fact of the matter was, he was using sex to keep her from going too far.

He knew what she was after, knew everything she'd figured out thus far, and some of it concerned him, but he was beginning to be blinded by his emotions, something that'd never happened to him before. What he felt for Courtney was vastly different than anything he'd ever felt for another woman. And he'd known that from the instant he'd met her. With every encounter since then, his need for her had only intensified.

"Spread yourself for me," he instructed.

He didn't want to talk about himself, didn't want to talk about the shit day he'd had. Didn't want Courtney finding out that he'd fucking killed two fucking people just a few short hours ago. He'd executed them in their own kitchen, watched their blood splatter across the pristine white surface, and he'd walked away completely unscathed.

That was what happened to people who crossed him, people who didn't follow through with their promises. Although he had people who would do his dirty work for him, there were times when handling the situation himself was the only way to get the point across.

But their deaths didn't bother him. Not in the least. And sure, sometimes he worried about the fact that he didn't feel anything. Not when it came to taking a life.

When it came to Courtney, that was the only time he did feel. And he'd started to crave that, to crave her like a drug, always wanting more, needing more.

His eyes slid down between her thighs as she used her fingers to separate the slick folds of her beautiful pussy.

"You're wet," he told her.

"Yes."

"Because you like showing me your pussy?" he asked, not looking up at her face.

"Yes."

Reaching into the desk drawer in front of him, Max retrieved the item he'd purchased for this specific occasion. He took his time removing it from the plastic packaging.

He held up the thick dildo for her to take.

She leaned forward, taking it from him, and he noticed the slight tremble in her hands.

"Scared?" he asked.

"No," she said assertively.

"Good. Now I want to watch you fuck yourself."

Her sharp intake of breath made his cock thicken more. He was hard as fucking stone, aching to be buried in her warm body, but he held himself back. His need was too great, and he didn't want to hurt her.

Max placed his hands on her feet, gently squeezing the leather that encased her ankles as he watched her take the large blue dildo and slide it through her slit. Her juices coated the end of the toy as she began teasing herself.

"Push it inside," he commanded. "Fuck yourself with it."

She shifted, propping herself up with her other hand before inserting the tip of the dildo in her pussy.

Max watched the head disappear as she gasped.

"You like that?" he asked, eager to whip out his dick and stroke it, but he refrained.

"Not as much as I like to feel you inside me," she said breathlessly, continuing to force the toy deeper.

Max bit his tongue as she began to fuck herself in earnest, driving the toy into her pussy, the wet sounds echoing in the otherwise silent room.

"Max," she cried out.

"Make yourself come, Courtney. Make yourself come all over my fucking desk."

She continued to fuck herself, but he sensed that she was holding back.

Reaching for the toy, he got to his feet. When the chair moved out of her reach, she held her legs high, still open to him. He took one of her feet and planted it on his chest, the other falling to the side, offering him an enticing view of the toy sliding in and out of her slick pussy.

Max stared down at her delicious cunt as he fucked her with the toy. He wasn't gentle, driving it in hard, then retreating, at the same time his dick throbbed, pressing against the zipper of his slacks, frantic for the feel of her slick, smooth walls gripping him.

He was punishing himself, denying himself the pleasure because he didn't fucking deserve her. But he couldn't bring himself to walk away. He fucking needed her.

"Oh, God, Max. I'm… Fuck. I'm gonna come!"

Max plunged the silicone toy into her cunt, over and over, fucking her harder until she fell back onto her elbows, her cries of pleasure bouncing off the glass windows.

"Fuck yes, Courtney. Come for me, baby."

Her legs tensed, her pussy clamping onto the toy, nearly pulling it from his grasp as she screamed his name. Max tore the toy from her pussy, tossing it to the side as he leaned down, hefting her legs over his shoulders while he lapped at her sweetness, licking her as she trembled on his desk. Only when she came again, this time in his fucking mouth, did he give her a moment's peace.

Not that he intended for that to last long. He had a hell of a penance to pay, and he was serving his time by indulging in Courtney's pleasure. Not to mention, the night was still young.

Chapter Fourteen

When he says he wants to talk …
don't believe him.

Present day
April 24th

Courtney knew that showing up at Max's nightclub—aptly named Devil's Playground—was a risk, but it was one she had to take. Considering she didn't know how else to get on his radar—something she never thought she'd willingly do again—this had been her only option. Even then, she wasn't sure if he was there tonight, but she kept her fingers crossed as she stepped through the doors and down the dark hallway that led to the club proper.

"Have you been here before?" Jayden asked excitedly, walking beside Courtney.

After Casper had laid out her assignment, Courtney had known exactly what needed to be done, and since she'd promised Jayden a night out on the town when she was back, it had been a way to kill two birds with one stone. And it gave her a reason not to have to be alone with Max, should the opportunity arise.

She hoped it didn't, but she had every intention of getting him to notice that she was back.

"A few times," she told her friend. "You?"

"Nope. First time," Jayden answered.

"Brace yourself."

The sounds of the club reverberated off the narrow walls, the sensual thump of the bass infusing Courtney's blood. The visual stimuli came next as they walked into the multi-floor, cavernous space. Above them, along the outer walls, were hundreds of scantily clad bodies lined up around metal railings, while down on the main floor, hundreds more.

They were packed tonight.

"This is hot," Jayden said, a wide smile on her pretty face.

"Come on, let's get a drink."

It took some time to venture over to one of the many bars, but they finally managed, squeezing through the hordes of writhing bodies. The musky scent of sweat and sex mixed with the sharp odor of cigarettes and booze, making Courtney's head throb. It didn't help that the music was so loud she could hardly hear herself think.

They stood beside the bar, waiting their turn while they surveyed the crowd.

Ten minutes had passed before the bar cleared enough for them to approach, and when they did, two men standing close by offered to buy their drinks. Courtney considered the repercussions of the evening should Max actually be there and find her accepting a drink from a stranger. And just as quickly, she blew it off. Max was getting married, so why the hell would he care if she was being hit on by another man?

"What'll it be, doll?" the dark-haired man, who had introduced himself as Jordan, asked, his dark eyes raking over Jayden slowly.

Jordan and Jayden. Now that was a serious tongue twister.

Jayden smiled, a seductive tilt of her lips. "Jack and Coke."

"And for you?" Jordan's blond friend, Michael, asked Courtney directly.

"Fireball and RumChata," she said, trying not to look around when she felt eyes on her.

Michael's lips twisted, and Courtney knew what was coming. There were two different names she'd heard for that particular drink: cum shot or cinnamon toast crunch. She wondered which he would request.

"Jack and Coke and a Cinnamon Toast Crunch for the ladies," Michael requested when the bartender made his way down to their end of the bar. "And two Coronas."

He'd picked the sweet route. Nice.

Rather than agree, the bartender met Courtney's gaze and then nodded his head toward something over her shoulder.

She turned, coming face to chest with… "Leyton."

Shit.

"Mr. Adorite would like to see you in his office," the massive man informed her, leaning in so that she could hear him.

Well, that answered the question of whether or not Max was there.

When Leyton stood to his full height again, she met his celadon-green eyes. "I'm not here to see him, but thanks for the offer," she lied.

Getting close to Max *was* the plan, but Courtney knew she had to play it safe. If she seemed overeager, he'd know what she was there for. After all, things hadn't gone well the last time they'd seen one another.

Leyton didn't budge, peering down at her with a frown on his handsome face. "You know I can't go back and tell him that."

"Is there a problem?" Michael asked, inserting himself closer to Courtney as though he knew her well.

Luckily, Jayden and Jordan were deep in conversation a few feet away. "It's fine," she told him. "Just an old acquaintance of mine. He was just … leaving."

Turning her back on Leyton, she pretended to give Michael her full attention while trying to ignore the bodyguard now fuming behind her.

"Courtney," Leyton drawled out, leaning in closer.

Michael's eyes lifted to Leyton's, a predatory gleam in his blue eyes.

Knowing the situation could only get worse, Courtney placed a hand on Michael's arm. "I'll be right back. Don't go anywhere."

Turning to face Leyton, she glared at him, slapped her hand on his arm, and pulled him toward a fairly empty corner. Courtney weighed her options as she squeezed by a couple making out against the wall. She could go with Leyton, pretend she was put out that Max was showing his hand, or she could refuse to go, which would only incite Max's anger and likely bring him down to the floor.

She decided to go with option two.

"Honestly, I'm not here to see Max," she told him. "And I don't want to bother him, so do us both a favor and pretend I'm not here."

"Too late," Leyton told her. "Boss already knows you're here."

"Damn it," she exclaimed. "Why'd you go and do that?"

"If you didn't want Max up in your business, why'd you come here, Courtney?" His tone reflected his frustration, but based on the cool expression on his face, they could've been talking about the weather for all anyone knew.

"I'm here with my friend," Courtney explained. "Girls' night."

"And the guy who's eye fucking you from the bar?" Leyton questioned harshly.

"Don't know him, but he seems like a nice guy," she said, glancing over her shoulder and offering Michael a wave and a smile.

"He's a nice dead guy if Max sees you with him, Courtney."

Yeah, well…

"I didn't come to argue; I didn't come to see Max. So if you don't mind, I'm just gonna go back to the bar and mind my own business."

Without waiting for a response, Courtney returned to the bar, standing beside Michael but making sure not to touch him. Leyton hadn't been exaggerating when he'd said that Michael was as good as dead if Max saw him touching her. Regardless of whether or not Max cared about her, he'd always considered her a possession. And Max Adorite didn't share. At all.

The bartender chose that moment to bring their drinks. In an attempt to save Michael some bodily harm, Courtney placed two twenties down, but he refused to take it. Without looking behind her, she knew that Leyton was instructing him not to take her money.

Rather than argue, she slipped the bills back into her purse and turned to survey the crowd.

Pretending Leyton wasn't still hovering behind her, Courtney focused her attention on Michael. It was too loud to actually have a conversation, so she simply smiled and took a sip of her drink. His gaze continued to bounce between her and the big guy standing less than a foot away.

Leyton Matheson, all six foot four inches of him, was a menacing man. Handsome with his dirty-blond hair, bright green eyes, and chiseled jaw, he had an air of danger about him. Then again, he was Max's head enforcer, so that seemed logical.

Didn't mean that Courtney was going to allow him to intimidate her.

"Ignore him," she told Michael, having to yell for him to hear her.

"He's just gonna come down here," Leyton explained, stepping closer.

Courtney peered up at him over her shoulder. "I'm sure he's got more important things to deal with," she replied. "Doesn't he have a wedding to plan or somethin'?"

The moment the words were out of her mouth, she knew they sounded childish and petty, but truth was, she couldn't help it. As soon as she'd learned that Max was getting married, Courtney had punished herself by digging up as much detail as she could. Pictures of the happy couple, articles regarding their pending nuptials, interviews showing how content the two of them were… That little dirt-digging session had ended with Courtney puking her guts up and fighting off tears.

Your own fault.

Yes, or so her subconscious continued to remind her.

"He'd call it off in a minute if you'd take him back," Leyton stated, his mouth close to her ear.

Courtney's eyes widened as she looked up at him. "So, he doesn't…?" *Love her?* She couldn't bring herself to say the words aloud.

"Sometimes he has to do things, Courtney. Even you should know that."

For whatever reason, that didn't make her feel any better.

"You wanna dance?" Michael asked, clearly frustrated by her having a conversation with Leyton.

Turning to face him, she shook her head. "Not yet. Give me a few minutes?"

Unfortunately, Jayden had other plans, and Courtney looked up in time to see her friend following Jordan out to the dance floor.

Crap.

"I'll take it from here."

Courtney heard Max's gravelly voice before she saw him, and her body reacted instinctually, her respiration slowing, her heartbeat speeding up.

The next thing she knew, Leyton was gone, and Max was standing in his place. Courtney's mouth went dry; her palms began to sweat as she stared up into his golden eyes.

"Why are you here?" he asked, moving impossibly close to her.

She figured that was because it was hard to hear with the music, the bass, and the conversation taking place around her, but even then, she found herself wanting to get away. To protect herself from what this man was capable of doing to her.

"Can't a girl enjoy the nightlife without having a reason? Maybe I like to dance," she countered.

"So why aren't you then?" he snarled, nodding toward Michael.

"Thirsty," she said simply, holding her drink up for him to see.

"Do you two know each other?" Michael asked, leaning in close to Courtney, his hand resting on her shoulder.

Aww, hell.

Max's gaze instantly zeroed in on the spot where Michael touched her, and she felt the anger bubbling up from inside him.

She quickly shrugged Michael's hand off, turning to face Max fully. "Don't. Don't do this here."

As though planned, the song that was playing faded away, and in its place came a much slower, much sexier beat. Without asking her, Max reached for her drink, taking it from her and setting it on the bar before he took her hand in his.

His touch sent electrical impulses firing up her arm, through her body, and ending in a deep, sensual throb between her legs.

When common sense returned and she tried to pull her hand from his, Max tightened his grip as he led her into the mass of bodies. Once they were situated with the others, he jerked her up against him, grinding his hips against hers.

"Put your arms around my neck," he ordered, his voice harsh and loud in her ear. "And if you want that asshole to walk out of here in one piece, you won't so much as look his way."

All thought fled, and Courtney found herself doing as he asked, ringing his neck with her hands, inhaling the seductive, intoxicating scent of him.

Their bodies began a slow, sensual grind, touching from chest to knee. Max's hand slid down her back, then down farther, firmly cupping her ass as he roughly jerked her against him.

"You shouldn't be here," he warned, anger dripping from his words.

"I didn't come to see you."

His head pulled back slightly, far enough that he could look into her eyes, and Courtney knew he saw the lie for what it was. How could he not? She was eagerly pressing against him, wanting to absorb him into her skin, to hold him there for eternity. Anything to fill that emptiness inside her, the one that had tripled in size every time she walked away from him.

"Liar."

Courtney swallowed hard, mesmerized by the golden glow of his eyes, intensified by the strobe and colored lights flashing around them. They were repeatedly pitched into darkness only to be lit up again. But Courtney didn't need the light to see the intensity in his gaze. She could *feel* it.

Max's erection dug into her hip as he ground himself against her, squeezing her ass as he kept her body aligned with his. She could hardly breathe for wanting him, but she knew that was stupid.

He was…

Reality broke through the haze of lust, and Courtney pushed him, forcing him away from her as she took a cautious step back, their gazes still locked.

"You're getting married," she bit out.

Max didn't respond, but she saw the fury that warred inside him. He took her hand and pulled her, forcing her to follow him across the floor.

"Max! Stop!" she yelled, but it was useless; he wasn't listening to her.

When they reached a set of doors, manned by two big guys, she knew she should turn around, run the other way as fast as she could because being alone with Max was only going to prove to be disastrous. For both of them.

"I can't leave my friend," she told him abruptly, making one last-ditch effort to pull away from him.

"Find her friend," Max ordered one of the men. "Don't let her out of your sight."

"Yes, sir," the bigger of the two men said dutifully.

He didn't release his hold on her wrist as the two men pushed open the doors and allowed them through. The chaotic noise coming from the club was muted when the doors closed behind them. She expected him to take her up the set of stairs on her right, the one that led to his office, but he didn't. He kept a firm grip on her arm and led her down the hall, deeper into the bowels of the building until they reached another set of doors.

"Where are we going?" she asked, once again trying to pull away.

"My penthouse," he snapped.

"But you don't live here," she retorted.

"Consider it my home away from home."

"Why did I never know about this place?" she asked, trying to understand how they'd dated for a solid year, come to the club on more than one occasion, yet she'd never been invited to his *home away from home*.

"It was … recently acquired," he informed her, his tone gruff.

Courtney followed in silence as they walked through a narrow tunnel that seemed to be endless, and she realized they were leaving the nightclub and heading into another building entirely. They ended up in front of another door, this one locked. Max entered a code into the panel on the wall, along with his fingerprint, and the lock disengaged.

Once through the door, things got interesting.

Gone were the concrete walls and floor, and in their place was an elegantly furnished area with a glass table topped with a giant flowering plant, and plush black carpeting laid out before a chrome-trimmed elevator. There was only one button on the wall, as well as inside the elevator.

Once they were sealed inside the steel box, Courtney tried not to fidget, refusing to look at Max although that was easier said than done since the walls of the elevator were all mirrored.

Max ushered her out when the doors opened, and they were greeted by another mammoth in a suit, this one clearly armed to the teeth. He was standing in a hallway, watching a monitor that appeared to show him a view into the elevator as well as the lobby area on the bottom floor.

The lone door in the hall was open, and Max urged her forward, his hand on the small of her back once again.

It was then that Courtney knew they weren't just there for a simple conversation.

Chapter Fifteen

What he wouldn't give for a view like this all the time.

It was all Max could do to keep from pulling Courtney into his arms and crushing his mouth to hers. He'd been stupid for dancing with her, feeling her body moving with his, her fingers caressing his neck, the warmth between her legs against his thigh, but he'd had no choice.

Either that or he would've strangled the fucker who'd put his hand on her as though he actually had a right to touch her. The instant Max had seen her talking to the other guy, he'd been blinded by rage, ready to pull out his gun and kill the bastard where he stood.

"Why didn't we go to your office?" she asked now, glancing around the penthouse.

"This gives us more privacy," he told her simply, making his way to the wet bar, trying to calm himself. He needed a drink, something to take the edge off, because the instant he'd learned that Courtney was in the club, he'd been close to losing it. It'd only gotten worse when he'd realized she hadn't been alone.

"We don't need privacy," she insisted.

Max didn't bother to argue with her as he proceeded pouring their drinks.

Courtney strolled through the open living area, moving to the wall of windows that overlooked the city. Beyond the glass, blanketed in inky darkness was the Bank of America Plaza building, outlined in green, along with the Renaissance Tower, with its well-known X of lights. Just behind those was the uniquely designed I.M. Pei's Fountain Place, which Max actually found more intriguing during the day than at night.

The building he now occupied was actually the home of numerous companies that conducted their business in the bustling city. It hadn't been easy—at least not until the owner had realized who he was up against—but Max had managed to convince the man to sell him the top three floors for his personal use. He'd converted two of them to office space—merely a front for his land business—and the top floor to his own private retreat.

Not that he was ever there. He'd never brought anyone back to the penthouse—certainly not Angelica—and only used it on the rare occasion he was conducting business late into the night. However, it'd been designed with Courtney in mind, proof that he'd never be over her, never be able to completely let her go.

The entire space was monochrome—the black, white, and metal décor expensive—with enough furniture to make it feel lived in but not so much that Max felt claustrophobic. He'd had a Jacuzzi tub installed in the bathroom because he knew how much she'd enjoyed using the one in his house. He'd even gone so far as to purchase several framed images of Marilyn Monroe, including one that was autographed, costing him nearly forty grand. He still remembered their conversation.

"What's with the fascination with Marilyn Monroe?" he asked her.

Courtney glanced up at the framed photos above her couch.

She shrugged. "She's … real. There's something about her. You can see it in her eyes. It's almost as though she's haunted but happy. As though she's come to terms with who she really is. I guess I admire that."

When she'd told him that, he'd seen that same haunted look in her eyes, and he'd wondered whether he was the reason it'd been there.

"This is … nice," Courtney said when Max handed her the drink. Her eyes drifted to the far wall, where the pictures were hung.

He watched as her mouth opened slightly, realization dawning. Yes, he'd done this for her, hoping that one day he'd have her back where she belonged. With him.

"I thought you'd like it," he said, backing away from her before he did something stupid, like kiss her.

"I still don't understand why you brought me here."

Max sipped the whiskey, his eyes on Courtney's face. Lowering the glass, he admired her beautiful, soft features. She was still just as lovely as the last time he'd seen her, perhaps more so. And fuck if he didn't miss her.

"The question is why are *you* here, Courtney? What are you after now?"

Courtney stiffened, as he had expected. He wasn't gullible enough to believe she'd come to him *for* him, and certainly not for girls' night with her friend. She was after something, and he simply wanted to know what. If she'd merely been out for a night on the town, he imagined the last place she would've willingly gone was his club.

This game of hers was tiring, but he'd initially started out playing it two years ago, so he figured he could continue the ruse. Because, despite what Courtney might want to believe, this thing between them had started off as a means for her to find her way into his organization, but it had turned into something much, much more than that. Had he not been willing, she never would've made it into his world.

"I hear congratulations are in order," Courtney said acrimoniously as she moved away from him, circling around behind one of the white leather sofas, her fingers trailing over the top of the cushions.

Max didn't respond.

"I didn't figure you for the type to fall for a blonde."

"I could say the same about you," he disputed.

She inhaled sharply but didn't meet his gaze.

He wasn't going to rise to her bait. If she wanted to confront him head on, he'd be more than happy to oblige her, but this tiptoeing around bullshit was quickly boring him.

When she turned back to the window, holding her glass close as she stared out at the scenic view, he was reminded of a time much like this one. Only then, the view she'd been peering out at had been his swimming pool, not quite as interesting as the one now.

However, his view—of her—had been equally stunning.

"Have a seat, Courtney," Max encouraged, forcing himself to stop watching her as he moved to the black sectional that filled the space. Without waiting for her to join him, he lowered himself to the buttery soft leather, getting comfortable with one arm on the armrest, crossing his ankle over the opposite knee.

He wasn't sure he'd ever actually sat in that particular room in his house. He looked around, taking it in. No, it was just another room that went unoccupied. Most of his time was spent in his office, the kitchen, or, when he was sleeping, in his bedroom. The ballroom was used for parties, the dining room for family gatherings. But never this room. Hell, he could still smell the new leather from the sofa.

She joined him a minute later, only she didn't sit next to him. There was an entire cushion between them, but that didn't surprise him. For a moment, he simply watched her, caught up in her and unable to look away. Never in his life had he had this sort of reaction to a woman. Where being in the same room with her was enough. Having her close, hearing her breathe. Max could've simply sat there in silence for hours just so he could observe her.

But that time wasn't available to him anymore. He needed to understand more about her, such as her reasons for coming here.

He'd been pleasantly surprised when she showed up at his door, but after the way she'd slipped out on him the other morning, he'd been reluctant to let her in. Nevertheless, here they were, and the silence was beginning to irritate him.

Presuming she wasn't going to out-and-out tell him what he wanted to know—why she was there—he figured casual conversation would be the easier route.

"Tell me something," he prompted.

"What's that?"

Pretending to think a little longer, he took a sip of his drink. "You went to work for your father, but you never said that's what you wanted to do. When you were younger, what did you want to be when you grew up?" he asked, eyeing her carefully.

She visibly relaxed, easing back into the cushion as she stared down at the glass in her hand.

"The CIA," she said softly, a small smile forming. "I always dreamed of being in the CIA. I wanted to go on missions, to infiltrate terrorist networks and draw out the bad guys."

Max chuckled. "So you followed your dream?"

"Not necessarily," she replied, glancing over at him. "My father has always treated me with kid gloves. Although none of my brothers would ever take the babysitting jobs forced on me, they seem to expect me to smile and nod when they're offered."

"Why do you think that is?" he inquired.

"At first, I thought it was because I was a woman. But I've proven myself time and time again, and I refuse to believe that my father is sexist. I'm reliable, focused, not to mention good with a gun," she said with a smirk. "The only thing that makes sense is that I'm my father's daughter. He doesn't quite know how to let me go, let me be what I was meant to be."

"But he assigned this mission to you," he told her frankly, watching her closely.

Courtney's eyes lifted to his, but she didn't respond. She knew as well as he did that this was an undercover assignment, a way for her to dig into the Adorite family, to learn more about the Southern Boy Mafia. He didn't know who their client was, who wanted dirt on him, but Max knew it could be a number of people. From the government to his enemies, or hell, even one of the five families could be looking into them, assessing them.

Not that he thought the latter would've reached out to a group of elite security advisors, but he never underestimated anyone.

"I'm not supposed to be here," Courtney said, her voice soft, uncertain.

Max dropped his foot to the floor, leaned forward, and placed his empty glass on the table.

"Then why are you here?" he asked.

The silence lingered for longer than Max cared for, but Courtney's response finally came, and it was exactly what he'd been hoping to hear.

"Because I can't stay away." She swallowed hard. "I can't stay away from you, Max."

Tears glistened in her eyes, and his heart melted a little more. They'd only known each other for two and a half months, but during that time, they'd grown closer, despite her consistent need to put distance between them. Ever since the night he'd fucked her, she'd been standoffish, coming up with excuses as to why she couldn't see him and not giving in. It was beginning to wear on him, and he had to wonder what she was up to.

But then she'd shown up on his doorstep today, unannounced. And now she was sitting so close he could smell her sweetness, see the dark gray flecks in her nearly colorless eyes, hear the way her breaths were becoming uneven.

"Come here," he ordered, his voice low, unwavering.

Courtney mirrored his actions, placing her glass on the table before scooting closer.

When she was within arm's reach, he lifted his hands to her face, grazing his thumbs over her smooth cheeks while she eyed him speculatively.

"I don't want you to stay away," he told her.

Taking his time, Max leaned in, his mouth hovering so close to hers he could feel her breath against his lips. When he finally leaned far enough to kiss her, he settled his mouth over hers gently, waiting for her to give in to him.

And just like that, their worlds collided, much as they had that night in the hallway when he'd been so taken by this woman that he hadn't cared where they were. He'd needed her, wanted to be inside her, to bury himself so fucking deep she wouldn't be able to run from him.

"Max." The husky way she said his name had his cock throbbing.

Pulling her onto his lap, Max settled her so that she was straddling him. Their mouths never separated, their tongues seeking, devouring. Unable to resist, he slid his palms up her thighs, pushing her short skirt higher, until he gripped her hips beneath. He jerked her forward, pressing his aching cock against her, grinding until the pleasure was so intense he thought he would come in his jeans like a fucking schoolboy.

"Oh, God, Max. Please," she pleaded.

"Please what?" he asked as her mouth trailed over his jaw, his neck.

Working his thumb over the thin fabric of her panties, Max found her clit. He pressed, circled his thumb until she was begging him for more. He wanted to make her come, to make her cry out his name. And then, he wanted to bury himself inside her and fuck her until neither of them knew which way was up.

For long minutes, Max continued to tease her, sliding his thumb beneath her panties, feeling her slick heat against his skin while he kissed her, their tongues mating.

It was too much. He'd held out for too long.

Growling, he pulled back, peering up at her. Neither of them said anything, but words weren't needed. She knew what he wanted, the same as he knew what she needed.

Without thinking about the consequences of their actions, Max freed his cock from his slacks, forced her panties to the side, and eased his cock inside her. And right there, in the middle of his living room, on the never-sat-on-before sofa, Max lost himself in her, fucking her sweetly, gently. She rode his cock until they were both breathless, moaning. And when she came, her mouth crushed to his, her moans muffled by his lips, he let himself go.

Max forced himself from the memory, realizing that Courtney was standing there staring at him. Rather than face the curiosity in her gaze, he turned away from her, maneuvered back around to the end of the sofa, and sat down.

"Sit down, Courtney," he ordered her. "It's time we have a talk."

Chapter Sixteen

Crazy is as crazy does.

Leyton Matheson moved with purpose along the outer wall of the club, keeping an eye on things as was his position tonight. Now that Max was safely locked away in his penthouse and Leyton had handed Angelica off to Dane to ensure she made it home safely, he could breathe a little easier. At least for a little while.

Making his way up the stairs, he forced his way through the people lingering over every inch of real estate they had to offer. After doing a quick check on the VIP room, Leyton slipped down the back stairs before returning to the floor once more. He spotted a couple arguing in a corner, so he made his way over. It only took a minute to calm them both, threatening to throw them out on their asses if they caused a scene, and then he was once again keeping to the perimeter, scanning the room for other issues.

"Sir, we have a problem."

So apparently breathing easier wasn't on his list of things to do tonight.

Rolling his eyes because he had a good idea what that problem was, Leyton moved toward the exit doors that his boss had slipped through ten minutes earlier.

Yep, just as he'd thought.

"Angelica," Leyton greeted when he approached the two guards being berated by the uptight woman who'd recently become a fixture in Max's world. He glanced over at Felix and Darius, a silent question in his eyes as he tried to figure out what had happened to Dane, but they both shrugged.

"Where is he?" she yelled, her anger contorting her usually pretty features.

Max was right, the woman was vicious. And annoying.

"He's in a meeting," Leyton told her, keeping his voice low.

"He is *not* in a meeting!" she screamed. "I demand that you take me to him right now."

"I'm sorry, ma'am, but that's not possible."

Angelica slammed her hands onto her narrow hips, glaring up at Leyton as though she were trying to figure out how to kill him. Maybe she was, he didn't know. From what he'd seen of her, the woman didn't understand business, nor did she understand just what this arrangement between her and Max truly meant or how it worked.

Leyton had sensed from the beginning that Angelica expected some sort of mafia fairy tale. He'd wanted to tell her a million times that those didn't actually exist. This world… There was nothing sweet and romantic about it, and one day, if she was around long enough, she would figure that out for herself.

"He's not answering my calls, so I want you to get him on the phone," she growled, her lips pursed, her eyes narrowing.

"Again, not possible," Leyton informed her coolly.

"He's *my* fiancé, and I demand to be taken to him."

Lord, have mercy. If only the woman would grow up. Leyton had known the minute Max told him about the *business arrangement* that would allow him to acquire a vast amount of land down along the Mexican border—some prime real estate that would assist in making their lives that much easier—that things weren't going to go as smoothly as they would've hoped.

And the spoiled little political princess was the one who thought the mafia meant expensive clothes, nice restaurants, and protection from the bad guys… Seriously. And here he'd thought they *were* the bad guys.

Yes, she was the reason Leyton wanted to pull out his gun and…

"Damn it. I suggest you remember your place," she snapped. "You're Max's fucking errand boy, which means you're now *my* errand boy. Go. Fetch. Max. Now!"

Fetch him? Seriously?

Okay, so he could deal with quite a bit of shit. Having grown up in Max's world, as his closest friend and now his protector, his right-hand man, the most reliable person in his world, Leyton had seen some crazy shit, done some crazier shit. But this…

This fucking woman took the cake.

Pressing the button on his microphone, Leyton instructed the bouncer at the door to call Ms. Winslow's car around to the back entrance. Taking her by the arm, he turned her toward the rear of the building, keeping to the outer walls to avoid all the people.

"What do you think you're doing?" she exclaimed at the top of her lungs. "Let go! You're hurting me."

He wondered if she was being so loud because of the music or if she thought the shrill sound of her voice actually made people listen. He hoped it wasn't the latter, because … the crazy bitch was delusional.

Once they made it through to the corridor leading to the private exit that they used for celebrities and other VIPs, Leyton released her arm.

"I'm tellin' my grandfather about this!" she screamed as Leyton pushed open the door.

Oh, Lord.

Leyton rolled his eyes. "Very well, ma'am."

"He'll have you fired! He'll have all of you fired!"

Leyton nodded. He'd dealt with Angelica for longer than he cared to.

She turned to face him once again, staring up at him with anger flashing in her blue eyes. "Why is she here?"

"Who?" he asked, pretending not to know who she was referring to.

"That … whore. Why is she here? Why is he talking to her?"

"Ma'am, I don't know what you're talkin' about." Leyton took a step forward, opening the door to the limo when it pulled up. He took a step back and allowed her the opportunity to climb into the car. Of course, she didn't take it, as was his luck.

"You tell Max that I won't stand for this. If he thinks he's powerful, he hasn't seen nothin' yet. That… That bitch. She better stay away from him."

Again, Leyton nodded.

Angelica leaned in closer, her voice lowering somewhat. "I will *not* allow her to interfere with me and Max. She will not interfere, do you understand me?"

Leyton didn't so much as blink.

"Either you make sure she goes away or I will."

Leyton sighed, casting his gaze into the limo, encouraging her to get in. When she did, before she had a chance to yell at him any more, he closed the door and slapped the roof of the car, sending it on its way.

He started toward the door of the club, but it flew open, and Dane stumbled out, blood running down the side of his face.

A lot of fucking blood.

"What the fuck happened to you?" Leyton asked, trying to get a better look at the long gash that ran down the side of Dane's face from his forehead to his jaw.

Holy fuck.

"She's … fuckin'… insane." Dane's knees gave out as he tried to take another step.

Leyton grabbed the big man with one hand, hitting the button on his mic with the other. "I need some assistance at the back entrance. Now!"

Helping Dane to the ground, Leyton squatted near him, turning the man's head to the side and inspecting the skin that was ripped wide open. Was that … bone?

Son of a bitch.

"What the fuck happened to you?" Leyton asked Dane again, this time anger boiling in his gut.

"Angelica… She fucking … cut me."

Goddamn it.

Leyton glanced down the alley, but the limo was long gone.

Either you make sure she goes away or I will.

The crazy bitch's words echoed in his head, the clear threat that she'd made against Courtney.

Shit.

As much of a bitch as he thought Angelica Winslow was, Leyton hadn't quite expected this. He knew that she was as vicious as Max believed her to be, but truthfully, he'd thought it to be more of an act. She came from a world of political power and wealth. In all of her sheltered, overindulged life, she'd probably never heard the word no.

But this… She'd sliced Dane wide fucking open.

"Boss?" Anthony and Rock rushed outside, coming to an abrupt halt when they saw Dane on the ground.

"Get him back inside and call the doc. Get him fixed up."

"Yes, sir," Rock replied, reaching down and practically lifting Dane on his own.

While they helped Dane into the club, Leyton paced.

Fucking shit.

Clearly Angelica was more lethal than he'd given her credit for.

Which meant he did have to relay the threat to Max.

Regardless of whether Angelica intended to follow through, Leyton would not have that one hanging over his head.

He just didn't intend to tell the boss about it tonight. At least not until Max and Courtney had finished … whatever it was they were doing.

■«»■«»■«»■

Angelica's hands were shaking, her chest vibrating from the hatred that filled her. She'd been so fucking pissed at being dismissed she'd lost it, and that asshole Dane had gotten the chance to see her true nature. When he'd attempted to pull her toward the back door after she'd informed him she wouldn't be leaving, she'd been pushed to her limit. It had only taken a second to retrieve the blade from her purse, and when he'd ushered her closer to the exit, she'd turned the tables on him, slashing back at him, not even caring what part of him she hit.

He'd screamed like a little girl when the serrated blade had made contact with his face, and she'd dragged the damn thing down, trying to do as much damage as possible.

She hoped he fucking died, the little prick.

These people truly had no idea who the fuck they were dealing with, and she hated the sweet, innocent act she was forced to play while in their company.

Once the limo started down the road, she pulled her cell phone out of her purse and pressed the number for the one man who would do whatever she wanted.

"Honey, are you all right? It's late," Artemis Winslow asked when he answered the phone.

"She's a problem, Grandpa."

"Who?" he inquired, sounding more awake than he had a second ago.

"That … *whore* of Max's. I want her out of the picture."

"What brought this on, Angel?" he questioned, using the name he'd called her since she was a child growing up in his house after her parents were tragically killed in a freak ice storm that had sent their car off the road and careening over a cliff. Angelica had been three at the time, and she didn't remember a thing about them.

"I went to the club to talk to him about moving up the wedding date tonight and—"

"Why would you want to move it up?" Artemis interrupted, the sleep completely gone from his voice. "We've got the venue set, and the wedding planner is working with that date in mind."

"It doesn't matter. I want her out of the picture."

Silence ensued, and Angelica forced herself to calm down.

"I'm not sure what you want me to do, honey," her grandfather finally said.

"I want her eliminated. Nothing and no one will come between me and Max. Do you understand me? She's not part of the plan. I need this to play out the way we discussed."

"I understand what you're sayin', Ang—"

"No. You don't understand. I'm set to marry him and that … fucking whore… She's a threat. She's a threat to Max; she's a threat to me; she's a threat to the entire plan. This wedding *must* take place. Neither of us can afford for it not to." Angelica had no intention of going into the reasons why. The fact of the matter was, she needed to marry Max, and they couldn't wait. The longer they waited, the harder it would be to…

"Angel, I'll see what I can do."

"Thank you, Grandpa. I'll talk to you tomorrow."

Ending the call, Angelica tossed the phone onto the seat, wrapping her arms around her waist in an attempt to hold herself together. She was quickly losing control, and that was the last thing that needed to happen. She had to keep pushing forward. She had to marry Max, and she couldn't let anyone get in her way. It was the only way to keep from dying at the hands of…

Shit.

If Max only knew what she'd done, what she was capable of doing…

Damn it.

If Marcus Alvarez found her, realized she'd run, ignoring the cartel's orders … she was as good as dead. Although he was merely a distributor, a low man on the totem pole, Angelica knew he was powerful enough to take her out. The only way she could fix this, to keep from being tortured and murdered for her betrayal, was to marry Max, to use him as a safe haven. Marcus wouldn't want to endure Max's wrath. No one wanted to endure that.

By marrying Max, she would be safe. In turn, she'd be able to feed some more information back to Marcus, and maybe he'd forget she ever existed.

Then again, until it was all said and done, Marcus should've been the least of her worries.

Hell, if Max ever found out what she'd done, that she'd already betrayed him in an attempt to establish her own reputation as someone formidable, he'd probably kill her himself. This was her only bargaining chip.

Max could protect her, she knew that much.

Which was why Angelica had to eliminate the one woman who had the power to destroy it all.

Chapter Seventeen

His timing… Quite frankly, it sucked.

While Max moved across the room, Courtney was torn between keeping an eye on him and admiring the beautiful space she was in. His penthouse was … well, it was immaculately decorated, similar to Max's house. Only this felt much more like home, as though she'd been in his thoughts when he'd talked to the designer. She couldn't help but believe that was true, considering there were priceless pictures of Marilyn Monroe on the wall. She didn't think he was much of a fan, but he knew she was.

Glancing over her shoulder, she peered out into the night. The view was amazing as well. She could've easily spent hours sitting there, staring out at downtown Dallas. Especially at night.

Yes, it would be quite easy to get comfortable there.

But that wasn't an option.

"I should go," Courtney said, watching as Max took a seat on the sofa.

"Sit. Down," he insisted.

"But I—"

"Just fucking sit down, Courtney," he growled.

Courtney moved to the opposite sofa, lowering herself as she kept a watchful eye on Max.

"Now just sit there."

She didn't understand what he wanted, but she could feel the heat of his gaze. He didn't move as he watched her, the intensity nearly enough to make her squirm.

God, she'd missed him so damn much. Her chest ached from the lingering pain of knowing he was going to marry another woman, that their time together was officially over. Then again, he'd informed her of that when he'd come to her house the last time. He'd told her things were going to change. She couldn't help but wonder whether she would've made a different choice if she had only known what he'd really meant.

Her gaze drifted to the pictures. Had his future wife been there? Had she seen those pictures? Did she know about Courtney?

Not that any of it mattered now.

"How'd your assignment go?" Max questioned, interrupting the silence that had become nearly unbearable and causing Courtney to turn her attention back to him.

"What assignment?" she countered.

"The rich brat in California. That's where you were, right? Keeping tabs on daddy's little girl. Making sure she didn't do anything stupid."

Courtney hated that Max knew so much about her. He shouldn't have access to that sort of information, but somehow, Max always knew. During all the time they were together, she'd learned so little about his life, but he seemed to have every intimate detail of hers.

"But she did do something stupid, didn't she?" Max asked, drawing Courtney's attention back to his face.

She didn't respond.

"Or was that you, Courtney? Did you set that up? Get her behind the wheel and tip off the cops so they'd take her into custody? Freeing you from the bullshit babysitting job your daddy sent you on?"

The inflection of his voice never changed, not an ounce of emotion in his tone, but every word slammed into her. He knew her too well.

"That's what it was. You were angry. Pissed that he'd given you another bullshit job. You shouldn't have been there, Courtney. But your father sent you away. Making sure that you weren't close enough to keep tabs on what was going on here."

Courtney's eyes widened as she processed his words. Max wasn't just replaying the events of her life for the past couple of months. He was telling her something… That was the way he operated.

"*What?*" Was he saying…?

Max didn't respond.

Courtney slammed her glass down on the table and launched to her feet.

Max followed suit.

They circled one another briefly.

"Did you…?" She came to stand directly in front of him, staring up into those mesmerizing liquid-gold eyes.

"Did I what?"

"Did you have me shipped off? Did *you* set that up?"

Max didn't respond, and the fury ignited in her bloodstream. Before she knew what she was doing, her hand reared back, and she aimed for his face, but Max stopped her. He grabbed her wrist before her open palm made contact with his cheek. In the next breath, she was flush against him, her arms braced against his chest, his face so close she could smell the whiskey on his breath, see the golden flecks in his eyes.

Instead of letting him have the upper hand, she shifted, her knee coming up to take him out, aiming right for the family jewels.

He was faster than she was, moving at the last second, and then she was on her back on the sofa, Max's big body hovering above her, his knee pressed between her legs, his hand encircling her wrists, holding her arms above her head as he stared down at her.

"Why?" she asked, fighting the anger and the hatred. Ignoring the desire that made it difficult to breathe.

"Why what? What is it that you want to know, Courtney?" he growled softly. "Why I showed my hand and called in a favor? Or why I'm gettin' married? Which do you want to know more?"

Courtney swallowed hard, her eyes traveling over his face, taking in every inch of him, reliving every moment they'd ever spent together as it flashed through her mind. It'd always been like this… Their interactions were heated, passionate, and innately sexual underneath it all.

Beautifully brutal, that was how she'd come to think of this thing between them.

And now, as she stared up at him, she wanted him to kiss her. She wanted him to leave her alone. She wanted…

She simply *wanted.*

And she hated herself for it.

"Why would you do it? Why would you have me sent away?" she asked, trying to remember what they'd been talking about.

"Your father sent you away," he responded smoothly.

"Why did you set it up?"

"Does it matter?"

Courtney squirmed, wanting to get closer, needing to get farther away. "Yes! It matters. Okay? It fucking matters."

"*Why?* Why does it matter?"

Courtney's lungs refused to fill with oxygen as she battled the anger, the hurt. The pain. Max had sent her away so that he could get engaged to another woman.

"You made him do it." Her words came out strangled.

It wasn't a question; she already knew.

Nothing. Max didn't say anything in response, and the emotion that bubbled into her throat embarrassed her, made her tear her eyes off his as she stared toward the window overlooking the city. She wasn't going to shed a single tear for him. She couldn't. Not once since the night he'd walked out had she completely given in to the devastating realization that she would never be able to have the only man she'd ever loved. Never had she cried for him.

"Courtney."

She didn't look at him. She didn't want him to see what she knew he'd see in her eyes.

"It's a business arrangement."

Courtney's head snapped back, her eyes slamming into his as rage filled her. "A business arrangement? No, Max," she ground out. "Marriage is *not* a business arrangement. A contract is a business arrangement. A handshake. Hell, access to a front-row parking spot is a business arrangement. Not. Fucking. Marriage. *Why?* Why would you do that? Why would you marry someone you don't love?"

Max locked his gaze with hers, and the silence made her ears ring.

She was breathing hard, waiting for his answer, needing him to tell her. But she never would've expected what he said next.

"Because the woman I do love won't marry me."

Courtney's mouth fell open as she glared up at him. She couldn't believe he'd just said that. Couldn't believe that he had waited until he was engaged to another fucking woman to tell her that he loved her.

"Get. Off. Of. Me," she growled, pushing against him until he rose to his feet.

She sat up, holding her stomach for fear she might throw up, the pain and anger coalescing into a potent mixture of grief that closed off her airway, choking her.

Thankfully, Max retreated to another room, giving her a minute to regain her composure.

Not that she thought it was possible to put all the pieces of her shattered heart back together, but at least he'd had the decency to give her a moment to pretend.

Chapter Eighteen

Letting go… Not easy, no matter how many times he did it.

Max paced the bedroom of his penthouse, trying to erase the image of the pain in Courtney's eyes from his memory. He hated hurting her, but this arrangement—or whatever the hell she wanted to call it—was necessary. And ultimately, she'd pushed him into it. She'd pushed him away, which gave him the right to do whatever he needed to do.

Marrying Angelica wasn't something he looked forward to, but business was business. He had an organization to run, lives that depended on him. And this was merely a means to an end. It wouldn't be forever, or so he continued to remind himself.

Regardless, she had no right to be angry because she'd pushed him this far.

She wouldn't have him.

No matter how much he wished it were possible, Courtney Kogan would never give herself to him completely. And if he couldn't have *all* of her … well, then he couldn't have *any* of her.

"I need to go home."

Max stopped pacing, pausing to look at her as she stood in the doorway to the bedroom he'd had furnished for her. The king-sized bed, the antique dressers, the black silk comforter… It'd all been for her because he'd held out hope, something he'd never done before.

He wanted nothing more than for her to reach out to him, to let him take her in his arms and love her, but he knew that wasn't going to happen.

Not tonight.

Not ever.

He nodded, turning away from her again. "I'll have my driver take you home." Max retrieved his cell phone from his pocket and dialed Leyton, turning his back on Courtney as he moved to the window.

"I need a car for Courtney," he informed the man, ignoring the pain in his chest at the thought of her walking out the door. Again.

"Yes, sir. Uh … we've got a small problem."

"What is it?" Max questioned, recognizing the concern in Leyton's tone.

"I just had a conversation with Angelica. It wasn't pretty, sir."

That wasn't surprising. "What did she say?"

"She saw you with Courtney."

"And?" Max didn't give a shit who Angelica saw him with. It wasn't her fucking business who he talked to.

"Well, when I escorted her out, sir, she made a threat. I didn't think much of it until…"

"Until what?"

Max's body went rigid as he listened to Leyton relay how he'd found Dane slashed from his forehead to his jaw, followed by exactly what Angelica had said to him. "Thank you. Let me know when the car arrives. Make sure there's a detail on the car as well."

"Yes, sir."

The call disconnected, and Max tucked his phone into his pocket. He turned to face Courtney once again. Knowing this would likely be the last time he saw her, he wanted some answers first. And he'd start with the question that had haunted him for so long.

"Why…?" He swallowed hard. "Why couldn't it work with us, Courtney?" Her eyebrows rose, as though he'd surprised her with his question. "Explain it to me. Why did you always run?"

"It never would've worked," she said sadly, moving to the bed and sitting on the edge of the mattress.

Max looked away, returning to the window. "Why? And don't tell me it's because we come from two different worlds. That never stopped you from hopping in my bed."

"If I recall correctly, you coerced me there many times."

Unable to help it, he smiled. She was right. He had. But she'd also come willingly.

"But it wasn't enough, huh?" he inquired.

"It was more than enough," she replied softly. "It just wasn't right."

He knew that arguing with her would get him nowhere. The answer would still be the same, regardless of how he phrased the question. So he went in a different direction. "Why did you come here tonight?" he asked, repeating his initial question that had gotten them to this point as he peered over at her.

"What?" She looked surprised, but he knew her better than that. She was a damn good actress, but he was better at seeing through bullshit than most people.

"Why? Why are you fucking here, Courtney?" he asked, his voice rising, the anger and hurt flooding him.

"Because…"

"Because your client wants information on my upcoming marriage to the senator's granddaughter?" he asked, allowing his frustration to reflect in his tone.

"Yes," she answered bitterly, getting to her feet. "Are you happy now? I came to get dirt on you. Did you actually expect anything else?"

No. *Yes.* Dammit. He hadn't expected anything, but he'd hoped. Clearly he'd lost his fucking mind.

"Why did your father send *you*?" he asked. "You didn't succeed last time. Why not send someone else?"

"Because I'm the only one you'll…"

"The only one I'll what?" he asked, moving closer to her until he was standing mere inches away.

Courtney looked up at him, her expression neutral. "Because I'm the only person you'll trust."

Max swallowed, considering her statement for a moment.

He prepared his next words carefully. As carefully as he could.

When she looked down, Max used one finger to tilt her chin up, forcing her to meet his gaze. "Let's set the record straight right now. I *don't* trust you, Courtney. I've never trusted you." He allowed his eyes to rake down her body. "You're a good fuck, yes. But other than that, you have nothing to offer me."

Courtney sucked in a breath and stumbled backward. Max fought the overwhelming urge to grab her, to pull her into his arms and tell her he had lied. But he couldn't. He needed to push her away. She wasn't going to love him back, she wasn't going to be the woman he could spend the rest of his life with, and that meant she was in danger. She needed to get as far away from him as she possibly could. It was the only way he could keep her safe. And if keeping her alive meant breaking her heart, then so be it.

"I..." The tears that formed in her eyes nearly leveled him, but he didn't budge, didn't allow any emotion to reflect on his face.

"It's time for you to go now, Courtney." A knock sounded on the front door, and Max motioned for her to leave him. "Leyton will bring your friend and ensure you both get to the car."

With that, he turned away from her, his chest burning as though acid filled the space where his heart had once been.

The sound of the door slamming had him closing his eyes. As much as he loved Courtney, as much as he trusted her—because despite knowing better, he *did* trust her—Max knew she would never survive in his world.

Where she thought a fucking parking space was a business arrangement, Max knew better.

In his world, business arrangements came in many forms. A handshake. A threat. Hell, a piece of paper meant nothing, but his word...

His word meant *everything.*

And it was high time he got back to doing what needed to be done.

Chapter Nineteen

Just when you think you know yourself … this happens.

Twenty months ago

"Where are we going?" Courtney demanded when Max led her through the narrow hallway of what appeared to be an abandoned warehouse.

"To have a chat with a friend of yours," he told her brusquely.

Courtney's throat tightened as she processed his words. His tone was lethal, and she'd never seen him quite as angry as he was right then. Considering they didn't have any mutual friends, she knew this wouldn't be good.

When he'd arrived at the Sniper 1 Security office half an hour ago, insisting that she come down to talk, only to instruct his driver to drive when she'd joined him inside the armored Escalade, she'd known something was up. He hadn't said a single word during the entire drive, which had only put her on edge.

And now, as they stopped in front of a steel door manned by a big, beefy guard glaring at her, her heart was racing, and the first trickle of fear dripped into her bloodstream.

"Open the door," Max instructed the guard, his firm grip on her upper arm beginning to hurt.

When the door flew open, Courtney's breath lodged in her throat as Max ushered her inside the ten-by-ten room. It was completely empty except for…

There, strapped naked and bleeding to a metal chair was Weston, one of Max's bodyguards.

"Oh, God," she whispered, taking in all of his injuries.

Weston's head lolled to the side, his eyes swollen shut, his face so battered it was hard to tell who he was. The way he held his arm against his chest, she could only assume it was broken. Even his feet were bloody.

There was no point asking why they'd done this to him.

She knew.

Trying to break free of Max's death grip on her arm, Courtney fought the tears that threatened.

He didn't let her go.

Another man joined them, and then the door closed, sealing them inside the musty room.

Footsteps sounded from behind her, and she saw a tall, bald man with beady eyes and a snarling lip. He looked like the devil himself.

"Do you know why you're here?" Max asked her, releasing her arm.

She swallowed hard but steeled herself. She would not allow Max to see her fear. In her business, fear was a weakness. According to her father, it gave their enemies too much power, something to hold over them. From a young age, she'd been taught to mask that fear, tamp it down, lock it up. It had no place in her world.

"No," she spat. "Why am I here?"

"Do you remember having a conversation with your friend Weston?"

Courtney narrowed her eyes at Max, doing her best not to look at Weston, not to see his battered and bleeding body. God, she didn't even know how he was alive, but based on his appearance, if he even was, it likely wouldn't be for long.

The clank of metal against metal sounded from behind her, and she turned to see the bald guy taking down a thick, heavy chain that had been mounted to the wall.

She turned her full attention to Max and schooled her expression, waiting to hear what he had to say.

"Did you get what you needed from Weston, Courtney?" Max asked, his voice deathly soft.

"I don't know what you're talkin' about," she retorted.

Max grabbed her arm and yanked her forward, practically dragging her until she stood less than a foot away from Weston. The metallic scent of blood drifted toward her, the weak man's shallow breaths all that she heard beyond the erratic beat of her own heart.

"Did you hear that, Weston?" Max asked. "She's not even gonna own up to your death."

Courtney tried to pull away from Max, her heart pounding inside her chest. Max was going to kill Weston. He was going to kill him, and it was all her fault.

She'd met Weston at Max's house, spent a little more than an hour talking to him one morning when Max had disappeared into his office to take a phone call. Sure, she'd been prying, trying to get some information from the younger guy, playing him, flirting with him. It had seemed like a good idea at the time.

At that point, when she'd first started talking to Weston, she'd been with Max for several months, getting deeper and deeper into a relationship with him, but never had she actually gotten any information to take back to her father. Nothing that would take Max down, nothing concrete enough to do any damage to the Southern Boy Mafia, and she'd felt as though she were running out of time.

So, she'd befriended Weston, pretended to like him until she convinced him that she wanted him. And then, she'd gotten his phone number, called him, and invited him to meet with her.

He had.

But the young man hadn't given up any information that would've hurt Max.

"What'd she offer you?" Max asked Weston.

Weston's head shifted, his right eye opened ever so slightly, his tormented gaze meeting hers. She could hardly make out the color of his iris because the lid was so swollen, purple from the bruises that marred his once-handsome face, but she knew his eyes were blue.

"Did she offer her pussy?" Max asked, his tone lethal. "Is that what she offered to give you if you talked?"

"God, no!" Courtney screamed.

She hadn't offered him anything. She'd merely tried to talk to him. Sure, the flirting might've alluded to more, but she'd never intended to do anything with him. She wasn't a whore.

"Then what?" Max demanded, turning his hardened gaze on her. "What reason did you give him to betray me?"

"He didn't..." she uttered, her throat closing around the words. "He didn't betray you."

"No? He met with you in the park, sat with you for two fucking hours, and talked. What'd you talk about? The goddamn weather? If he didn't betray me, what did he do, Courtney? Confess his undying love? Ask you to run away with him? What?"

"I betrayed you," Weston said through swollen lips. "I shouldn't have talked to her."

"He didn't!" Courtney yelled. "He didn't tell me anything."

"But you tried, didn't you?" Max yelled at her directly. "You tried to get him to talk."

Courtney's gaze dropped to the floor as she nodded. She'd tried, but Weston had revealed very little. Not anything that she hadn't already known.

"Anything you have to say to me, Weston?" Max asked.

Lifting her gaze to the broken and battered man in front of her, she wanted to plead for Max to let him go, but she knew better. He was going to die. This was what happened in Max's world. This soulless man was the leader of a dirty underworld where laws didn't apply, the ruler of the darkness that flowed like water through that dismal place she'd found herself living in.

He was the man she'd foolishly fallen for. And she hated that, hated that she'd betrayed herself. Even now, even knowing what was going to happen, she couldn't deny her feelings for Max. He was doing what had to be done. He weeded out the weak links in his organization in order to move forward, just as Leyton had told her he did. It made sense, even if she hated it.

"I'm sorry for betraying you, sir," Weston choked out, but Courtney could tell he wasn't asking for forgiveness. The man had figured out that it wouldn't be forthcoming, but his death certainly would.

Max grabbed Courtney's arm and yanked her toward him, leading her back to the door. She was ready to go, didn't want to see what would inevitably happen next.

"No, sweetheart," Max whispered harshly against her ear. "You're gonna see what happens when someone betrays me. And maybe you'll learn not to dig any deeper."

"Or what?" she snarled, glaring up at him. "Will you have me killed, too?"

Max's eyes went soft, confusing her momentarily. "No. But anyone who dares to talk to you about me will find themselves in Weston's place."

She heard the chains rattle and then found herself pulled up against Max, her back to his front as his arms banded around her, his hand cupping her jaw roughly, forcing her to watch the gory scene.

The bald man worked diligently to attach the chain to a hook that dangled above Weston. Once in place, he held the loop in his thick hands as he stood behind Weston. The man's empty eyes were trained over Courtney's head, and she knew the moment Max gave the signal.

Refusing to look away because she wasn't going to allow Max to win this one, she kept her eyes on Weston, praying for his soul, asking God to forgive him as the asshole took the chain and wrapped it around Weston's neck, then released a lever that slowly hefted Weston into the air.

Weston struggled, cried out, the will to live forcing him to fight against the chains choking the life from him. A tear slid down Courtney's cheek as Weston wailed, pleading for his life until he could no longer speak, his body hanging limp as the bald man kept him suspended by his neck.

She'd known from the beginning that Max was a killer, that he was ruthless and extremely powerful, yet she'd followed this path, and look what had happened.

She'd fallen in love with a killer.

And now, she wasn't much better than him, because Max was right, Weston's death was on her hands. She'd done this to him. It was all her fault.

Chapter Twenty

Respect turns to disgust ...
surprising even him.

Present Day
Sunday morning, April 26th

"Where have you been?"

Max looked up from his desk to see Angelica marching toward him, the heels of her expensive shoes clicking on the hardwood floor. The sun shining in through the windows of his home office bounced off her blonde hair as she moved closer.

"I'm sorry, sir. I tried to stop her," Sal informed him as he ran into the room behind the hurricane that was Angelica.

"It's all right," he told Sal. "Where's Leyton?"

"He had to take a phone call."

Max nodded. "Leave us."

When Sal closed the door, Max turned his attention to Angelica, leaning back in his seat as he studied her. Just looking at her made him want to wrap his hands around her throat and squeeze the life out of her. But he wouldn't allow her to see that anger, that fury because that would give her power over him, and that was the last thing Max would relinquish to the bitch. "What can I help you with?"

"Where have you been?" she repeated, her voice shrill. "I know you weren't home. And I know that you…"

The woman had the good sense to trail off when Max shot to his feet. "I'm not sure how things work in your world, Angelica, but in mine, it's incredibly rude to barge in unannounced. This isn't playtime. I have a job to do, and you're hindering my ability to do it."

"I…"

Max could see that she wanted to argue, but something stopped her. What, he didn't know.

"Have a seat," he instructed sternly, motioning her toward the sofa.

Angelica huffed but walked to the sofa, primly easing down as she kept her knees tightly together, her eyes locked on him.

"Now what can I help you with?" he asked again, taking a seat across from her. "Did you come to offer to pay Dane's medical bills?"

Anger lanced his insides as he thought about what she'd done to one of his longtime friends, a man who'd stood by Max for nearly a decade. Although Dane would live, would eventually recover from the vicious attack, he would forever be scarred.

"What?" Angelica asked, her eyes widening.

"Cut the bullshit," he snapped. Max leaned forward and rested his elbows on his knees. Lowering his voice, he said, "I know what you did. I know you sliced his fucking face wide open. Did you know it took one hundred and seven fucking stitches to sew him back up?"

Angelica didn't say anything, but he could see her seething. She was definitely more malicious than he'd given her credit for.

"Or did you just come to talk about the wedding?" he snarled, leaning back and regarding her with the hatred that filled his gut every time he looked at her.

"Why were you with her?" Angelica hissed.

"With who?"

"Don't you dare play stupid with me, Max. I know you were with … *her*."

Max lifted an eyebrow, waiting for her to continue her rant.

Shockingly, she was silent, but her eyes bored holes in him. He didn't flinch, didn't move as he waited for her to say what she needed to say.

"We're moving the wedding date up," she finally snapped.

Max sighed and got to his feet. "Angelica, I've got shit to do. See yourself out."

"No!" she screamed.

He returned to his desk, ignoring her as she stomped toward him.

He pivoted to face her, took two steps closer, and fisted his hands at his sides. "How would you like to spend some time in prison?" he asked.

Her head snapped back as though he'd hit her. "What are you talking about?"

Max cocked his head to the side. "One hundred and seven fucking stitches, Angelica."

"You wouldn't turn me in," she spat. "My grandfather—"

Max lunged toward her, grabbing both of her arms and jerking her forward. He lowered his face to hers, their noses touching. "Don't ever tell me what I will or will not do. And don't you *ever* fucking try to threaten me. Are we clear? You don't have a motherfucking clue what you've gotten yourself into. You're expecting sunshine and goddamn roses in exchange for protection, and that's the last fucking thing you're gonna get. Cross me one more time, cause any more fucking damage, so much as breathe the wrong way and your grandfather will be making funeral arrangements for his beloved granddaughter. Because I will call Marcus Alvarez myself. Feel me?"

Angelica's eyes opened wider than before. Yeah, he was on to her game. It hadn't taken long for him to find out who she was running from and why.

"You wouldn't," she whispered, her voice hard, cold.

"Don't test me."

Max let her go, taking a deep breath as he returned to his chair and lowered himself into it.

"You don't have a say in this," she ground out. "If you want that land, this will go my way. I've already changed the date. We're getting married next weekend."

This time, Max chose to ignore her.

Before Angelica could get another word in, the door to Max's office opened, causing him to look up. He slowly got to his feet as he watched his father move purposefully across the room.

"Everything okay?" Max asked Samuel.

"We need to talk," his father said, glancing over at Angelica. "I need a minute alone with my son. That'll be all for now."

Max watched as Angelica's big blue eyes grew in disbelief, her disdain evident. Nope, today certainly wasn't her day. And wasn't *that* interesting. And here he'd thought she actually understood the structure of his family. Apparently, being sheltered in the political world had left this woman without the accurate image of what true power really was.

"Now!" Samuel growled.

Angelica jumped, a slight squeak escaping her. With a huff, she turned and stormed out of the room, not bothering to close the door behind her. Thankfully, Sal did the honors, leaving Max alone in his office with his father.

"Sit," Samuel advised, moving closer to Max's desk.

Max adjusted his suit jacket but didn't take a seat. "Something wrong?"

"I received a phone call yesterday."

Max waited for his father to continue.

"From your good friend Artemis Winslow. He was … agitated."

"Did he say why?" Max questioned, not actually giving two shits about Artemis Winslow and his frame of mind.

"Apparently, his granddaughter called him in the middle of the night on Friday, informing him of her future husband's infidelity."

"Before or after she sliced Dane open?" Max retorted, fury igniting in his veins.

"Whose fault was that? He let her get one up on him. He deserved what he got."

Max kept his lips tightly closed, rage coursing through him. That was one of Samuel's downfalls. He'd never truly understood loyalty. According to him, everyone was expendable.

Samuel paced away from him. "Usually, I wouldn't stick my nose in your business, but I'm makin' an exception this time."

Max didn't like the sound of that.

Samuel pivoted on his heel and thrust his hand through his thick black hair. "This," Samuel began, waving his other hand around, "is all yours now. You do what needs to be done. Understand? I won't question your motives, but your head better be in the fuckin' game. If not, I'll rip it all out from under you in a goddamn heartbeat."

Max didn't react.

"That girl… You need to stay away from her."

Max knew exactly which "girl" his father was referring to. He also understood why. Courtney Kogan was part of the organization that had been assigned to get dirt on Max's family. She'd been the one they sent, and Max knew why. Infiltrating his world wasn't easy, but she'd managed to put herself front and center in his life and was likely putting together all of the information she had in order for the feds to take him down. It wasn't the ideal situation, he would agree, but Max hadn't been able to resist her. Hell, he still couldn't. And that made her dangerous.

"She's not a problem," Max told his father.

Samuel thrust his hand through his hair once more, glaring at Max. "Sit down."

This time Max dropped into his desk chair, but he didn't relax the way Samuel did when he took a seat opposite him.

"Did I ever tell you the story about how I met your mother?" Samuel prompted.

Max watched his father cautiously, curious as to where this was headed. It wasn't like Samuel to share details of his life, not even with his own kids.

"The state fair," Max replied, remembering the brief story he'd heard when he was younger.

"True," Samuel said with a malevolent grin. "I met Genny at the state fair. She was thirteen, I was twenty-one."

Although he was well aware of the age difference between his parents, he hadn't known she'd been a child when they'd met. He'd assumed… The thought of a thirteen-year-old wanting anything to do with Max's father sent a chill shuddering through him. That detail had never been part of the story.

"Genny's father, Clyde, was a gamblin' man," Samuel said, his eyes looking far off, as though he were revisiting a different time and place. "Loved the horses, that man. He got himself into a bit of a bind, needed a loan. Your grandfather had done some business with Clyde's old man a time or two, so when Clyde came to him, seeking a loan to help pay off his debt, Floyd felt sorry for him.

"Unfortunately for Clyde, he hadn't made good on that debt, and when I was sent to collect … well, he didn't have the money to repay me."

Max's stomach churned as he predicted where the story was headed. It made sense, explained so much. Still, it left a bitter taste in his mouth.

"Your mother was the repayment for that debt," Samuel said simply, meeting Max's eyes. "Clyde's only child. A beautiful thirteen-year-old virgin who'd thought she had her life in front of her was promised to me. If you want the truth, she was hard to pass up.

"So, needin' to ensure Clyde understood how serious I was, I accepted the offer. Arranged for him to deliver her at the state fair, took possession of her at that time. A few weeks later, I married her, took her virginity. Eventually, years later, knocked her up. Don't get me wrong. I tried tirelessly for years, but she'd pulled one over on me. Damn birth control. It was her fault, really. Apparently she'd had some intrauterine device implanted"—Samuel waved his hand dismissively—"but eventually she had it removed and went to taking a pill."

Max swallowed hard. For the first time in his life, he felt something that didn't even remotely resemble respect for the man. No, this was hatred. His father had doomed his mother to this life because of a debt. And his grandfather. Clyde. How the hell could he simply hand over his daughter to Samuel?

"Oh, don't look so upset," Samuel said dismissively. "She knew the stakes. I gave her two options. She would marry me, spend the rest of her life with me, or I'd kill her father. It was her choice."

Right. Because that was a fucking choice.

"Clyde's still breathin' to this day, and well, you know how it turned out."

Yes, Max knew exactly how that'd turned out. Genevieve hated Samuel, hated her life, and spent most of her time getting fucked by the hired help or drowning herself in booze. But at least her father was breathing. He wondered what Genevieve's mother would've said about it all. The woman had died during childbirth.

Max sighed. "And what's the point of your story?"

Samuel leaned forward, his eyes hard. "What I didn't bother to tell you was that, at the time, your mother had a boyfriend. Nice, well-off young man who'd promised to marry her and give her a perfect life when he got back from the military. He was quite a bit older than she was but younger than me. A bit of a prude if you wanna know the truth. Never touched her."

"She was thirteen!" Max exclaimed. "How old was he?"

"Seventeen or eighteen, I think. Anyway, that doesn't matter because she was mine. But that boy, he wasn't happy that he'd lost her, although he'd started a new life, waitin' for her to grow up, to be old enough for him to claim her. Accordin' to Genny, he was comin' back for her. She used to love throwin' that in my face."

Fuck. Genevieve had been thirteen. What the hell would any fucking grown man want to do with a thirteen-year-old girl?

"Did he?" Max asked, not sure he wanted to know the answer.

"No, he didn't," Samuel snarled. "He didn't come back for her because he made a new life for himself, established a reputation that people respected, fell in love with a good woman."

Max studied his father. "Who was he? What was his name?"

Samuel glared back at him, hatred igniting in his golden eyes. "Casper Kogan."

Max's eyes widened as the shock hit him square in the chest.

Courtney's father?

Genevieve?

Holy. Fucking. Shit.

So it wasn't merely a coincidence, or even just a job. Courtney had been sent there … because of her father?

Samuel got to his feet. "I knew you'd figure it out. And if you know what's good for us all, you'll stay the hell away from that girl. We can deal with a lot of things, Max, but this man has a vendetta against me. He hates me for what he believes I did to Genny, and I'm sure he's out for revenge."

Max couldn't believe it. He didn't know Casper well, but he knew that the man was over the moon for his wife, loved her. But he'd been in love with Genevieve? When they were kids?

"Oh, don't try to figure out the romantic angle," Samuel stated as though reading Max's mind. "It's not always about love, son. Sometimes, it's simply about paying someone back for ruining what they thought they'd had at one point. Casper wears the white fucking hat; he saves people. But he wasn't able to save Genny."

Samuel was referring to Max's mother, admitting what they'd all known. She'd been ruined by him, taken down a path that she clearly hadn't seen coming, and look at her now. She was … damaged.

Samuel took a step closer. "I may be leavin' the decision makin' to you now, but you cross me, boy, and you won't like the consequences."

Max got to his feet, his hands fisted at his sides. "I know what I'm doin'," he told him, shaking off all the images of the story his father had just told him.

"That girl's a problem. She's doin' her daddy's dirty work, and I doubt she even knows it. I've talked to her; your mother has talked to her. She's sneaky, I'll give her that. The only person who put two and two together was your mother."

Which explained the downward spiral Genevieve had been on for the last couple of years. She'd known who Courtney was, known she was Casper's daughter.

"I want that girl out of the picture."

"She's not a problem," Max assured his father, trying to rein in his anger.

"Send her on her way, Max. Do what's right by this family."

"I *said*," Max snarled, "she's not a problem."

"Is that why you spent the weekend fuckin' her in your penthouse?" Samuel snapped.

"For the record, I wasn't with her. Not that I should have to explain myself to you or anyone else," Max hissed, the anger intensifying, threatening to boil over.

It didn't matter how much respect for his father he'd once had, Max didn't appreciate when anyone—fucking *anyone*—questioned him. Not his actions, not his motives. Not a goddamn thing. He knew what the fuck he was doing.

Samuel eyed him suspiciously, and Max didn't move a muscle. "That's not what Artemis told me," Samuel stated roughly.

"And what the fuck does Artemis know?" Max tossed out, letting his father hear his irritation. "He knows exactly what Angelica wants him to know. And what I do is none of her fucking business."

"Maybe not. But you need to keep your fuckin' dick in your pants until after the goddamn wedding. Until then, this can only end badly."

"It's bein' handled," Max assured his father, not intending to go into details as to how.

"Fine." Samuel thrust his hands in his pockets, continuing to glare back at Max. "However, this girl… I don't want her anywhere near this family ever again. I let it go on for far too long, waitin' to see if Casper would play his hand. I'm tired of waitin'. If you can't make that happen, then I will."

Max growled. It was involuntary. Any threat to Courtney, regardless of who was making it, would never sit well with him. There wasn't a man or woman alive who he wouldn't gut and let bleed out if they ever laid a hand on her. His father included. And if Samuel thought for one single minute he could intimidate Max with threats, he'd better think again.

"I see it in your eyes. She means somethin' to you, son. But that's gotta stop. She's not good for this family. And the more she knows, the more of a liability she becomes."

"She's—"

"Don't lie to me, Max," Samuel bit out, his voice low, threatening. "Nothin' you can say will convince me that she ain't important. But I want you to move forward, do what's right. Marry that goddamn bitch," Samuel said, pointing toward the door. "She'll understand her place."

Max wasn't so sure that was the case, but he didn't bother to argue with his father. There was no point.

Without moving an inch, Max watched as Samuel retreated toward the door and left his office.

When Leyton stepped into the room a second later, Max instructed him to close the door.

"Yes, sir?"

"I want eyes on Courtney. No matter what, do not let her out of our sight."

"Yes, sir."

"If so much as a single hair on her head is harmed, I will—"

"No need to clarify, sir," Leyton stated. "I understand."

And with that, Leyton turned and left the room.

Chapter Twenty-One

Weddings… Seemed everyone was planning them these days.

"I'm gettin' married in less than three weeks!" Marissa exclaimed in a harsh whisper, her blue eyes sparkling, her grin wide.

Courtney laughed at her best friend as they sat on Trace's sofa, talking and sharing a bottle of wine. "That you are."

"I still can't believe it, Court."

"Well, you should. You've even got the dress to prove it."

Courtney watched as Marissa's face flushed with happiness. After all that Marissa had been through, it was refreshing to see the other woman so happy. And Courtney was happy for her. In twenty days, when Marissa married Courtney's older brother Trace, Marissa would officially become Courtney's sister-in-law.

Since their fathers were in business together, Courtney had grown up with Marissa. They'd been best friends since birth. They'd made it through school, through their first boyfriends, their first heartbreaks, their first loves… All of it they'd done together.

And when Marissa had nearly been kidnapped, Courtney had vowed to find the bastard who'd dedicated his time and effort to hunting her down. Unfortunately, Courtney had let Marissa down in that regard because she'd refused to go to Max, refused to find out what he knew. If she'd done that, it likely would've been over a long time ago, and Marissa wouldn't have been shipped off to five safe houses in a period of a year.

And Courtney would forever carry that guilt around with her.

"So, tell me about the rich girl."

Courtney smiled. "Not much to tell. She's rich."

"And stupid, apparently."

"That goes without sayin'," Courtney replied. "In her defense, she was raised by the hired help. Her father works twenty-four seven. Her mother is out spending his money as fast as he's makin' it."

"So she has daddy issues?"

"Among others."

"Was she nice?" Marissa inquired.

"Yeah, she was. And when she wasn't rebelling, she was almost tolerable."

"Then you should be happy. She's gonna get the help she needs."

Yes, thanks to Courtney's interference, the girl was spending time in rehab. And hopefully, when she got out, she'd be ready to start over.

Marissa poured more wine and moved back onto the couch. "What's your next assignment?"

Courtney sipped her wine, looking down at the cushion. "Dad wants me here until after the wedding. Then I'm sure Hunter or RT'll find someone else for me to babysit."

She didn't bother to tell her best friend that she was technically on an assignment, that she was once again tasked with trying to dig into Max's world. Nor did she tell her friend that she was doomed to fail because after all they'd been through, after all the shit Courtney had lived through, still finding herself in love with a fucking killer, she had fucked it all up.

Let's set the record straight right now. I don't trust you, Courtney. I've never trusted you. You're a good fuck, yes. But other than that, you have nothing to offer me.

"You need to tell him no," Marissa said, her back stiffening.

Courtney's eyes widened as she tried to process Marissa's words. Surely she hadn't been reading her mind.

"It's time they let you do something you want to do. Your talent's wasted on these snotty little brats whose daddies have more money than sense."

Courtney smiled. She loved how defensive Marissa was of her. They'd always been that way, having one another's backs. Before Courtney could respond, her cell phone rang. She snatched it up from the cushion.

Unknown caller.

Stabbing the screen, Courtney brought the phone to her ear. "Hello?"

Silence.

"Who is this?"

More silence.

"Damn it. If you're gonna keep callin' me, you better find the balls to say something," she snarled, lowering her voice.

When she was met with more silence, Courtney hit the button to end the call.

"What was that about?" Marissa asked, her eyes wide with concern.

"No idea." Courtney glared at the phone. She needed to get Dominic to trace the calls, but she hadn't found the time or energy, not to mention the desire to tell him about what was going on. If word got out that someone was harassing her, Casper would likely assign someone to watch her. And that was the last damn thing she needed.

"How long has that been goin' on?"

Courtney looked up at Marissa. "A couple of days. They never say anything." Ever since the night Max had taken her to his penthouse to talk. Or more accurately, the night Max had shattered her heart with his callous remarks.

"How many times have they called?" Marissa probed.

"Too many," Courtney replied. "I'm sure it's just some kids bein' stupid."

Courtney didn't think that at all, but she couldn't very well tell Marissa that. Despite the fact that Marissa was her best friend, Courtney couldn't bring herself to talk about Max, or anything related to him. Not the assignment she was on—the one she'd failed miserably at on Friday night—and not about the threatening phone calls she'd started receiving in the wee hours of the morning on Saturday. She knew that it wasn't a coincidence, either.

The two times the caller had said something, it had been along the lines of "Leave Max alone," but the caller was using a voice modulator, making it impossible to tell whether it was a man or a woman.

However, Courtney wasn't stupid. She knew of only one person who would want to warn Courtney away from Max. Only one person who would resort to childish bullshit.

His future wife.

Then again, Courtney couldn't blame the woman for being angry. Courtney had battled with the green-eyed monster more than once in the last couple of days herself.

Which was why she'd vowed to stay away from Max at all costs. She was biding her time before she told her father that she couldn't go through with the assignment because she had stupidly come clean with Max the last time she'd seen him.

"Have you told Trace?" Marissa's question interrupted Courtney's thoughts, pulling her back to the moment.

"No. And you won't, either," Courtney said sternly. "I can handle myself. I don't want anyone else involved."

"Is it Max?" Marissa inquired.

Courtney shook her head sadly. "No."

"What happened between the two of you, anyway?"

Taking a deep breath, Courtney faced off with her friend. "I can't say. It's not that I don't want to tell you, but—"

"If you tell me, you'll have to kill me. I know the drill," Marissa said with a snort.

Courtney laughed. "Not exactly what I was gonna say, but sure, let's go with that."

"Fine. Then let's talk about my wedding."

Courtney grinned, grateful that Marissa was willing to change the subject. And though her mood had darkened somewhat, Courtney welcomed the chance to not think about Max.

At least for a little while.

Chapter Twenty-Two

An assignment? Yes, please.

Present day
Tuesday, May 5th

The insistent chirp of her cell phone pulled Courtney from sleep. She knew who it was because she'd assigned ring tones to each member of her family. And based on the noise, she couldn't ignore this call, even if she wanted to. Rolling over, she grabbed her cell phone from the nightstand, forced her eyes open, and peered at the number before hitting the talk button.

"Dad?"

"Hey, baby girl. Sorry to wake you, but this is important. We've got a missin' kid. Need everyone on this one."

Before he was finished with his sentence, Courtney was out of bed and heading to the bathroom. "I can be in the office in forty-five minutes."

"We'll be here," Casper told her quickly, then disconnected the line.

Rushing through her shower after pulling her hair up into a ponytail, Courtney managed to get ready in fifteen minutes. Her outfit of choice was always the same when she was heading out on an op such as this one. Black tank top, black pants, combat boots, and yes, her gun. Not to mention, a backup she kept in an ankle holster beneath her pants.

Without fanfare, she snatched her keys and her cell phone, grabbed a Mountain Dew from the fridge on the way out the door, and as she'd told her father, forty-five minutes after she'd crawled out of bed, she was walking into the main reception area of Sniper 1 Security.

The place looked like a madhouse.

Everyone was there, racing around, talking, yelling…

"They're in the conference room, waitin' for you," Jayden said, looking haggard for the first time in a long time.

Adrenaline crashed through Courtney as she double-timed it down the hall, eager to get to work. It'd been months since she'd been on an assignment such as this one. Most of hers—aside from the special situation with the Adorite family—were limited to bodyguard duty, but she welcomed this more.

The door to the conference room was open, so she walked in, grabbed a folder from the table before taking a seat at the back of the room, beside Z.

RT was at the front of the room going over the details. He merely nodded at her before he continued.

"Fiona Suarez is five years old," RT explained, nodding toward a screen behind him. "Black hair, brown eyes, last doctor's visit shows her at three feet four inches, forty-two pounds. She's on the small side.

"She was last seen by her mother on Friday night when Fiona's father came to pick her up for his weekend visitation. Ricardo Suarez, thirty-eight, stands five feet ten inches, weighs one hundred eighty pounds. He has a day job working in construction, but it's no secret that he's running drugs down near the border. Has ties to one of the cartels in Mexico.

"The little girl lives with her mother in San Antonio, father lives in Laredo. According to the mother, he's always punctual, picking Fiona up every other Friday, delivering her back on Sunday night. The parents' relationship is strained, but he's good to Fiona, loves her."

"Shit," Trace grumbled from beside Courtney.

"My sentiments exactly," RT said. "Based on what I've learned from Mrs. Suarez, it's a real possibility that Ricardo has taken Fiona into Mexico, probably getting protection from the cartel."

Courtney stared at the men around her, then looked back at the picture of the dark-haired little girl in the pink dress, big brown eyes peering back at the camera as though she didn't have a care in the world. Her heart went out to the little girl, as well as the mother. If Fiona's father had taken her and didn't want her to come back, slipping into Mexico was an easy way to do that.

"I've got a couple of contacts in Mexico," Z informed them. "I'll reach out, have them put some feelers out. See if they can find anything."

Courtney didn't say a word as everyone talked over one another, tossing out ideas, coming up with a plan. They would head down to Laredo, talk to Ricardo's boss, his co-workers, what little family he had. They were already at a disadvantage considering Fiona's mother hadn't realized she was missing until two days after she'd been taken—not until Sunday when she should've been returned home. And now … they'd tacked on an additional day because, according to the information in the folder, the police had told Fiona's mother they couldn't do anything since Ricardo had visitation rights. Since Fiona's mother had informed the police that she did not believe her daughter to be in danger, they hadn't issued an Amber Alert. Courtney was inclined to believe it had more to do with the drug cartel that they weren't pursuing her as quickly as they should.

Shit.

This didn't look good for Fiona.

"The police aren't jumpin' on this one," RT continued. "The cartel has a stronghold on the border, and if Ricardo made it across, it's gonna take some work to flush him out."

Listening to the drone of voices filling the room, Courtney's hands fisted in her lap. She knew what she had to do, knew who she had to reach out to. It would likely bring Fiona back to her mother sooner than they could on their own. Sniper 1 was good at what they did, but this… They were up against a timeline that was drastically tilted and not in their favor. Ricardo could have gone to ground at this point, hiding out with the little girl, hoping for enough time to pass that people stopped looking. Or hell, he could very well have disappeared entirely, foregoing Mexico and on his way to … anywhere.

"Court? You okay?" RT asked.

She quickly nodded, leaning forward. "I've got a contact. I'll see if he can give me any information. Regardless, I'll head down to Laredo, do some snooping."

"I'm goin' with you," Z said firmly.

Knowing it wouldn't do any good to say no, Courtney simply nodded. They didn't do these jobs solo, at least not most of the time.

"Ricardo's mother also lives in Laredo," RT explained. "Talk to her first, talk to his friends, the other dealers. See if this was planned. Maybe Ricardo told her what he was gonna do. But be careful."

"Will do," Courtney said, peering over at Z. "I've got an errand to run. Then I need to stop at the house, grab a couple of things. I'll meet you back here in three hours?"

"Roger that," Z answered, his attention quickly turning back to RT.

Not wanting to waste any time, Courtney headed out to her car. Before she went home, she had one stop to make. And hopefully, if things went well, in three hours, a trip to Laredo wouldn't be necessary.

Chapter Twenty-Three

Be careful what you wish for.

Max leaned back in his chair, studying Leyton. Now that he was fully apprised of the situation with one of his distributors, he relaxed somewhat. He still had more questions, but he couldn't seem to concentrate due to the fog that had overcome him in recent days.

"How is she?" Max questioned, referring to Courtney. It'd been ten days since he'd seen her last. Although he'd been the one to send her on her way, Max still thought about her every minute of every day, wondering what she was doing, who she was with … whether or not she was thinking about him. Hell, he'd give anything just to see her, touch her, hold her…

It was official. Courtney Kogan was solely responsible for ruining him.

Leyton's gaze darted to the desk. "Good. She doesn't leave her house much. Just to go to work or visit her folks."

"No new assignments?"

"No," Leyton confirmed. "At least not anything that'll send her off the grid."

Max wasn't sure why he was happy to hear that, but he was.

"What about Angelica?" he asked.

"She's stayin' put for now. I had a chat with her, told her to back off."

Max smirked. "And she listened?"

"Doubtful," Leyton replied with a grin. "But, I laid it out for her, told her to chill with the nonsense. However, she's still workin' on a way to move up the wedding, and she's hell-bent on the sixteenth."

"Of course she is," Max told him. "That's the day Trace and Marissa are gettin' hitched. She doesn't want me there."

"But you're still goin'?" Leyton inquired.

He nodded. Nothing short of a bullet would keep him away. He didn't give a fuck what his father said; this was Max's life, and he fully intended to live it the way he wanted to.

"I don't know what it is with that woman, but I think she's up to somethin'," Leyton relayed.

"Who?" Surely Leyton wasn't talking about Courtney.

"Angelica. I know that the marriage arrangement was her idea because she pissed off Alvarez and she convinced her grandfather to put it in motion, but she's on edge. I think she's worried you'll back out, concerned that you don't need Winslow as much as they need you."

Max agreed. However, Max and Leyton had already put some things in motion that would require the land deal to go through. The blowback, should things not go smoothly, could be painful. "I'm at odds right now. Let's work on a backup plan, though. We can't backtrack now. It'll show weakness. But she's right to be worried."

Leyton nodded.

The door to Max's office opened slowly.

"Sir?" Sal called when he stuck his head inside.

Looking past Leyton toward the door, Max lifted an eyebrow in question.

"Courtney's here to see you."

Max frowned, his eyes darting to the doorway behind Sal.

"They just let her through the main gate."

"She say what she wanted?" he asked, getting to his feet at the same time Leyton did.

"No. Just that it was important."

Fuck.

When he glanced over to Leyton, the man simply shrugged.

It'd been a little over a week since the last time he'd seen or talked to her, and after what he'd said to her, Max hadn't expected her to want to have anything to do with him. That had been the plan, pushing her away, shielding her from the crazy that was Angelica until Max could figure out what needed to be done.

"Send her in," Max told Sal, reaching for the decanter and pouring himself a drink. It was too early in the morning, but if he was expected to come face-to-face with the woman who haunted his dreams and every waking moment, he had to do something.

"I'll work on a backup plan," Leyton told him before leaving him alone.

A few minutes later, as Max stood at the windows overlooking the back of his house, he heard the door open. He didn't turn to face her immediately, steeling himself for seeing her again.

"Max?"

He closed his eyes at the sound of her voice, his gut churning from the pain that had overtaken his world since he'd sent her away from him.

A minute passed, maybe two, before Courtney spoke up again; this time she sounded closer.

"I know you don't want to see me, but…"

Max turned around, his eyes raking over her from head to toe as he tried to catch his breath.

There before him was the sexiest woman he'd ever seen. Her dark hair was pulled back in a ponytail; she had absolutely no makeup on her beautiful face. The black tank top she wore showed off her toned arms, and the baggy black BDUs did little to disguise her sexy body. The black combat boots and the Ruger 9mm holstered on her side made his fucking dick come to life.

He'd seen the woman in everything from an evening gown to absolutely nothing, and he was pretty damn sure he'd never seen her as fucking hot as she was right that moment, looking like a complete badass.

Forcing his gaze away from her, he strolled back to his desk. "What can I do for you, Courtney?"

"I need your help," she told him.

His eyes lifted to meet hers. "With?"

She took a few steps closer, and he noticed her throat work as she swallowed hard. She was nervous, that was clear. "We've got a case. A little girl."

Max waited for her to continue.

"Looks like the father kidnapped her."

"And how do you think I can help?" he questioned curiously.

"Mother lives in San Antonio, father in Laredo…"

Their eyes locked together as she trailed off, and Max knew what she was asking of him. He had plenty of contacts, including some of his own men down there who could very well find what she was looking for within the hour. But he wasn't willing to give in to her quite so easily. After all, he was a businessman. He didn't do favors; he didn't extend his services for free. If she wanted something from him, he wanted something in return.

"When did she disappear?" he inquired.

"Friday night when the father picked her up for his weekend visit. She should've been back Sunday evening. They never came back."

He let his eyes trail over her for a moment, then it hit him. "And what?" he asked, nodding to her choice of clothing. "You're gonna go find her?"

Courtney's head cocked to the side as she glared at him. "It's my job, Max. That's exactly what I'm gonna do."

Shit.

He had known from the day he'd met her that she was in the security business. As sexist as it sounded, he much preferred her on the glorified babysitting jobs that her father and brothers preferred to send her on. Never had he really considered the other jobs she dealt with. In all the time they'd known one another, she'd disappeared on a few occasions, but she hadn't shared the details with him, and truthfully, he'd convinced himself that she'd been… Hell, he'd never given it much thought, refusing to think that she'd put herself in danger at someone else's expense.

Then again, her father had assigned her to him, which, above all else, was likely the most dangerous assignment she'd ever been on.

His gut twisted at the thought of Courtney heading down to Mexico in search of that little girl. He understood her reasons for doing it—no one wanted to see something bad happen to a child, not even him, but…

No, Max didn't like the idea of her being the one sent on that quest.

"Max?"

He met her iridescent gaze once again.

"It wasn't easy to come here," she said, her voice soft. "I know how much you hate me, and I know you never wanted to see me again, but I… I need your help. This little girl needs your help."

Setting the empty tumbler down, Max propped his ass against the front of the desk, crossed his ankles, and stared at her. “And you want a favor?”

Courtney’s chin tilted upward, her back going ramrod straight. “Yes. I’m askin’ for a favor. But not for me. For the little girl.”

Max smirked. “The little girl doesn’t need me, Court,” he told her harshly. “You do. I’m sure your brothers and their friends are off and running, ready to find her on their own. They don’t need me, either. *You* do.”

He could see that she wanted to argue, but he respected the hell out of her right then for managing not to say what was clearly on her mind.

“You know what? Forget it,” she said through gritted teeth. “I don’t need your fuckin’ help. I don’t know why the hell I bothered to ask.”

Courtney pivoted on her heel, but before she could make it to the door, Max was on her. He grabbed her arm, spun her back to face him, and slammed his mouth down on hers. Without waiting for her permission, he thrust his tongue past her lips. She appeared stunned, but only for a second, and the instant she regained her senses, Max knew because she was kissing him back, her arms ringing his neck, her fingernails digging into the back of his head as she moaned into his mouth.

Just as it had always been between them … intense, hot, electric.

Backing her against the wall, he dominated the kiss, never giving her an ounce of control as he inhaled her.

Fuck.

It was impossible for him to resist her. No matter how imperative it was that he stay away from her, he just couldn’t fucking do it.

"Max," she said against his mouth, her teeth nipping his lower lip. "We can't…"

Oh, but they could. If he really wanted to, he could so easily fuck her against the goddamn door, make her scream out his name as she came.

But he didn't.

How he managed to find that sliver of control, that tiny ounce that still remained, he didn't know, but he did. Forcing himself to release her, he jerked away.

"Consider it handled," he told her roughly as he maneuvered to his desk, adjusting himself, doing his damnedest to ignore the throbbing of his dick.

"Max," she said softly.

"I said consider it handled!" he yelled. "Now go. Leyton will call you when it's done."

He heard her sigh. The sound that followed—the click of the door opening and closing—had him inhaling deeply, his chest aching more with every breath he took.

Damn her.

How the fuck had he gotten to this point?

It was a question he didn't really want an answer to.

Because, no matter what, it didn't fucking matter.

Chapter Twenty-Four

Well. Nice to see you, too.

Courtney was pacing the floor of her living room as she waited for a phone call. At that point, she didn't give a shit who called, but she needed the damn phone to ring before she had to head out and meet Z. She'd thought for sure that Max would come through for her … for little Fiona Suarez.

A pounding on her front door had her jumping, her heart slamming against her ribs.

"Open the damn door, Courtney!"

In a rush, Courtney threw open the door, coming face-to-face with RT.

He didn't ask to be invited in, merely pushed his way past her, his hand sliding through his blond hair.

"What the hell did you do?" He confronted her directly, his crystal-blue eyes ablaze with fury as he abruptly came to a stop less than a foot away.

"Good to see you, too," she said snidely, closing the door behind him, never turning her back on him.

"Answer the goddamn question, Courtney."

"I would," she snapped, "if I knew what the fuck you were talkin' about." She hated that her voice didn't come out as strong as she'd anticipated.

"They found her. The little girl."

Her eyes widened as she stared at him. "That's good, right? She's okay?"

"She's fine, not a scratch."

"So why're you yellin' at me?" she questioned, her voice rising.

"You went to him," RT scolded. "You fucking went to *him* for help."

Knowing she wouldn't be able to hide anything from RT, she turned away, heading for the kitchen. She didn't make it far before he had his hand on her arm. For the second time in one day, she was manhandled by a man, and it was starting to piss her off.

Spinning to face him, Courtney shoved RT. Hard. "Don't do that," she snarled.

RT yanked his hand back. "Sorry," he barked. "But you haven't answered me, Courtney. Damn it. Why'd you ask *him* for a favor?"

Feeling the anger rush to her face, she stared back at the man she took her orders from. "Because she was the only thing that mattered. That little girl needed to come home. I'll call in a million favors, RT, if it means savin' some little girl's life. You, of all people, should know that."

And just like that, she felt herself falling apart. A sob erupted from her chest, and tears formed in her eyes.

The next thing Courtney knew, she was in RT's arms, the dam had officially broken, and she was sobbing uncontrollably. Everything in her life was so fucked up. So confusing and she didn't even know where her loyalties were anymore. She hadn't even questioned going to Max, hadn't given it a second thought. She knew he had associates down there, *knew* if anyone could get to that little girl before it was too late, it would be him.

Sure, she recognized that Sniper 1 would've found her, they would've eventually brought her home safe and sound—at least she'd like to believe that was the case—but Max had an unlimited amount of resources. His connections were finite. There were people so loyal to him they'd lay down their lives, and she'd known when he issued the order to bring the girl home safely, that was exactly what would happen.

"Shh. Court. I'm sorry," RT crooned, his muscled arms banded around her, his chin resting on her head. "She's safe. You did good."

"Then why are you pissed at me?" she questioned, holding back a sob and forcing him away from her.

Another knock sounded on her door, and she didn't even have a chance to answer before Z was strolling in, his dark eyes scanning the room, taking in the scene before him.

"You okay?" Z asked her instantly, his gaze bouncing between her and RT.

"Fine," she said, shoving a stray hair out of her eyes as she turned away from them. The last thing she needed was for them to see her cry. She never cried.

"What the fuck, man?" Z questioned. "She saved the girl, and you come give her shit?"

"She fucking went to the Adorites."

Silence descended, and Courtney hesitated before turning back, not wanting to see the anger on Z's face as well.

"Since when do we give a shit how the job gets done?" Z probed, surprising her when she glanced back to see that he was facing off with RT. "She did what any of us would've done had we been in her shoes. She used the resources available to her."

"The fucking Adorites, Z," RT growled. "Their favors don't come free."

Z glanced down at her, his hard features softening. "What does he want in return?"

Courtney shook her head. "Nothin'." Unfortunately, he didn't want a damn thing from her, and she had no idea why that bothered her so much.

"Why the tears, little one?" Z's tone was soothing as he closed the gap between them and pulled her into his arms. The man was a giant at six foot six inches, and she felt dwarfed by him, but she welcomed his strength for a brief moment. "You want me to kick this guy's ass?"

Courtney laughed, as Z probably wanted her to.

The situation was tense, but it wasn't necessarily because RT had stormed into her house and yelled at her. That was settled. But what lingered, the electricity that sparked in the air between the two men… That was potent.

She knew that there was something transpiring between RT and Z, something that would eventually come to a head, and she doubted it would result in a fight, but she knew that it would end in a physical confrontation. Likely a horizontal one.

Squeezing Z briefly, she pulled away. "I'm good. It's just been an emotional day. That's all."

"Someone else's ass I need to kick?" Z asked seriously. "Whisper his name and consider it handled."

Consider it handled.

Those words reverberated in her head, but it was Max's voice she heard saying them. He'd come through for her, as she'd known he would. Relief swamped her, and she planted her ass on the arm of the couch, her legs suddenly too weak to hold her up.

"I wish you hadn't gone to him," RT said, his voice softer, less angry.

"Me, too," she told him truthfully. "But the only thing that mattered was her. I knew he'd be able to get the job done."

"I refuse to be in debt to the fucking mafia," RT told her, his voice rising once again. "Next time you feel the need to go to him, don't. We can handle our own shit, Courtney. No matter what bullshit he's fed you, he's not a good guy. He's not a fucking hero."

Courtney didn't bother to argue because RT was right. Max wasn't a hero, but in the same sense… No, he wasn't a hero.

"You need anything before we go?" Z asked, obviously desperate to put distance between himself and RT.

Courtney shook her head. She needed to fall into bed, to close her eyes and fight the memories of the day, forget what it had felt like when Max had claimed her mouth, his familiar touch combing over her body, the heat and the power she'd felt radiating from him…

She needed to forget him, period.

"I'm good. But…" Courtney looked at Z. "Thanks for comin' over." She turned her gaze to RT. "As for you … you're welcome."

The corners of RT's lips curved slightly, but he didn't allow the smile to form. "Next time…"

"I got it," she retorted. "Now get the hell out."

Z laughed as he and RT headed out, closing her front door behind them.

As she stared at the space the two men had just vacated, Courtney took a deep breath, swallowing the emotion that choked her.

It was the only thing she could do because she damn sure wasn't about to fall apart again.

Once was more than enough.

Chapter Twenty-Five

Just breathe.

"They found the little girl," Leyton explained when he stepped out onto the back porch. "She's on her way back to her mother."

Max nodded but didn't move from the chair he'd been sitting in for the past few hours. He didn't have the energy to do much more than that. As it was, he'd watched the fucking grass grow, trying his best not to think about Courtney, and never had it actually worked. He'd thought of nothing but her.

But the point was, he'd tried.

"She was in Mexico. As they predicted, he was running with her. I had Shark run him down. He brought them back across the border, took them to a safe location before he called it in. We left word with the local police and got word that she's safe."

"Does Courtney know?" Max asked, still gazing out at the lawn.

"I haven't called her. I wanted to see if you wanted to do that. But I will, if you need me to."

Max nodded again. "I'll call her."

He knew he should've left that task to Leyton, allowed him to deal with Courtney, because the last thing Max needed was to hear her voice, but he couldn't seem to pass up the opportunity.

"I'll be in the office if you need me," Leyton told him before leaving him alone once again.

Max retrieved the fifth of whiskey sitting on the ground beside him. Lifting the bottle, he looked at the level and groaned. He'd damn near downed the entire bottle, but still the numbness he'd been seeking hadn't come.

Taking a swig, he retrieved his phone from the table beside him. He scrolled through the contacts until he found her number and punched the button to place the call. His heart lurched when it began to ring.

"Hello?"

Max closed his eyes when he heard her voice again, fighting the emotion that flooded him. He couldn't speak, couldn't get anything past the lump that formed in his throat.

"Max?" she whispered.

"Yeah," he finally said. "It's me."

Neither of them said anything for a few moments, and then before he could come up with something to say, Courtney spoke.

"Thank you," she paused momentarily. "For what you did. RT told me they found her." Another pause before she continued, "So, thank you … for finding the girl."

Max didn't respond, just listened to her breathe, wishing she'd remain on the phone for the rest of his life so he could hear her. It was hard enough that he couldn't be with her, couldn't hold her in his arms. Listening to her breathe would suffice for a little while.

"I should—"

"No, don't go," he said in a tortured whisper. "Don't hang up. Just breathe, Courtney. It's…" He choked back the emotion. "Just breathe. Please."

Courtney didn't respond, nor did she hang up, and he could hear her breathe, which was all he needed as the night descended around him.

If only their time together could've been more like this. Less chaos, more peace.

There was no doubt in his mind that he'd never be content without her, never be able to move on. As it was, he was contemplating calling off the wedding because he couldn't go through with it. Not only because he wasn't willing to walk into a trap—because no matter the angle, the fact of the matter was Angelica had orchestrated this shit—but also because he would never be able to let Courtney go.

Not entirely.

But he also knew he could never have her.

She was stubborn, always pushing him away when the only thing she needed to do was pull him closer. He'd protect her. He'd love her. Hell, he'd give her the fucking moon if she wanted it. There was nothing he wouldn't do for her.

Their relationship had always been rocky. From the very beginning, they'd been thrust into this by outside forces, and as each day passed, Max was closer to figuring out what those were.

Now that he had something to go on, he was working to find out the truth.

He still replayed the conversation he'd had with his father over and over in his head.

And what's the point of your story?

What I didn't bother to tell you was that, at the time, your mother had a boyfriend. Nice, well-off young man who'd promised to marry her and give her a perfect life when he got back from the military. He was quite a bit older than she was, but younger than me. A bit of a prude if you wanna know the truth. Never touched her.

She was thirteen! How old was he?

Seventeen or eighteen, I think. Anyway, that doesn't matter because she was mine. But that boy, he wasn't happy that he'd lost her, although he'd started a new life, waitin' for her to grow up, to be old enough for him to claim her. Accordin' to Genny, he was comin' back for her. She used to love throwin' that in my face.

Did he?

No, he didn't. He didn't come back for her because he made a new life for himself, established a reputation that people respected, fell in love with a good woman.

Who was he? What was his name?

Casper Kogan.

Max focused on Courtney breathing softly into the phone. He wondered if she knew, but he couldn't ask her. He didn't want to know that everything that'd happened between them had been a lie. He was a strong man, but he doubted he could physically survive if he found out she'd played him the entire time.

He needed to believe that she had loved him. Even if that was over, he needed to fool himself into believing at some point it had been true.

Chapter Twenty-Six

Happy birthday, love.

Sixteen months ago

"Where're we goin'?" Courtney asked, laughing as Max dragged her through his house.

He'd hardly given her enough time to get dressed. She'd never seen him quite like this.

"You'll see," he told her. "Now close your eyes."

"What? Why?"

A tingle of trepidation ran through her. He didn't seem upset, but with Max, she never knew what to expect.

"Close them," he insisted, stopping abruptly and turning to face her when they were in the hallway that led out to the garage.

With a heavy sigh, she gave in, closing her eyes as she waited patiently for whatever it was he was going to do.

"Don't hurt me," she said softly.

Even with her eyes closed, she could sense Max's reaction to her words.

"Never," he told her, his warm lips pressing to her mouth. He cupped her face in his hands. "You should know that by now. I'd never hurt you."

For some reason, she believed him, despite the knowledge that she had of him. At this point, she knew who he was, what he did, what he was capable of doing.

And her feelings for him were complicated. She loved him. She feared him.

Sometimes she even hated him. Hated him for the things he'd done, such as making her watch Weston die. But even then, she had understood his reasoning. It didn't make her feel good that she could so coldly shrug off a man's death, but Max had told her that Weston had known what he'd been signing on for when he'd been brought into his world.

It was logical. As logical as anything could be in a world wrought with murder.

Max was smart. He'd admitted to knowing who she was and what she was after, never pretending not to know what she was up to, which made it difficult for her to stay away from him. It gave her an excuse to be with him, an opportunity to get closer, to try to find out something.

Or so she had told herself.

Truth was, she had done the unthinkable and fallen in love with him. Her heart now ruled her actions.

"Keep your eyes closed," he whispered against her mouth.

Courtney nodded and then linked her fingers with his when he took her hand.

A door opened, and she was being pulled behind him. She didn't peek, didn't try to see what he was doing, which spoke of the trust she had in him, despite knowing better.

"You ready?" he asked when they came to a stop.

"Yes."

"Then open your eyes."

Courtney did, glancing around at the garage. It looked the same as always, still held seven … no, make that eight cars.

Wait.

"Holy shit," she said softly. "That's a nice car."

"You like it?" he asked, sounding proud of himself.

"Who wouldn't?" The newest model convertible Corvette Stingray was likely the sexiest car of them all. She'd always had a fondness for sports cars, but she'd never been truly fond of Corvettes. At least not until they'd recently released the Stingray again.

Max stepped in front of her, blocking her view of the car. "Happy birthday."

"How…?" Confused, she studied him. "How did you know?"

"What? That it was your birthday or that you'd want that car?"

Courtney peered around him. "That… That's for me?"

"It is," he told her. "Now go check it out."

Feeling slightly off-kilter, Courtney slowly moved around the car, her gaze darting between Max and the sleek shark-gray metallic car.

"Seriously, Max. This is… Well, it's incredible, but you know I can't take this car."

"Yes, you can," he told her simply.

The top was open, so she peered inside, taking in the sexy, jet-black leather interior. She wondered what it would feel like to sit behind the wheel.

"Get in," he told her as he opened the passenger-side door.

When he slipped into the car, she grinned. What the hell. It wouldn't hurt to take it for a test drive, right?

And then, when they got back, she'd tell him she couldn't keep it. Because falling in love with him was one thing. Accepting a car that likely cost him close to a hundred grand was something entirely different.

□»«□»«□»«□

"Pull over," Max instructed when they were hidden by a copse of trees deep on his land. He'd wanted her to test-drive the Corvette, but admittedly, he'd had something else in mind, as well.

Another birthday present for her.

Courtney stopped the car, frowning when she looked over at him.

"Don't look so upset," he said with a smile. "Now get out."

If he wasn't mistaken, there was a hint of concern in her eyes, but he shrugged it off. He didn't want to think that she'd fear him for any reason. She'd surprised him earlier when she'd muttered for him not to hurt her, and he had to wonder where that was coming from.

Then again, she knew him, knew what he was capable of. But in the same sense, if she ever thought he would hurt her, she didn't know him well at all.

Once she met him at the front of the car, Max turned to her, taking her into his arms and crushing his mouth to hers, his hands trailing down her hips, over her thighs, and then back up beneath the thin fabric that covered her. She'd worn a skirt, which had been his suggestion, and again, he'd had something in mind when he'd made the request. He had to wonder whether she'd figured that out yet or not.

Easing her onto the hood of the car, Max pulled back enough to look at her.

"Kick off your shoes. Wouldn't want you to scratch the paint."

Courtney grinned, and her shoes hit the ground.

"Now for my next gift," he told her.

"And that would be?" she asked.

"An orgasm. On the hood of your car."

"Hmm. I like the sound of that."

Max lifted her legs over his shoulders and bent down, pressing his mouth against her panty-covered mound. He teased her briefly but then slid her panties to the side and drove his tongue through her wet slit.

Courtney moaned, her hands clutching his hair as she pulled him closer. He licked, sucked, tormented her with his tongue while she writhed against the hood of the car. He could sense she was holding back, drawing out her pleasure, and he gave her what she needed. He maintained a slow, sensuous pace, even worked her panties off of her at one point.

When he pushed two fingers inside her, she cried out, her hips bucking as she tried to force him deeper while he sucked her clit firmly between his lips, flicking his tongue over the sensitive bundle of nerves until she couldn't take any more.

"Max! Don't stop!"

He had no intention of stopping, and she should've realized that by now.

Long minutes passed while he feasted on her sweetness, alternating between fucking her slowly with his fingers and driving her mad with his tongue. Fast, slow, fast, slow. He wasn't giving her enough to send her over the edge, wanting to ride this out with her.

When she shifted, putting one hand on the hood of the car, the other gripping the back of his head and jerking him closer, burying his face in her pussy, he laughed, making sure she felt the vibration on her clit.

His dick was hard as steel, eager to seek the warmth of her body, but he wanted to wait, wanted to send her careening into bliss before he turned her over and fucked her right there in the open.

"Max!" The way she growled his name told him she was close.

Adding a third finger, he began fucking her slowly while he flicked his tongue over her clit, circling the little nub until she was once again bucking against him.

"I'm gonna come, Max! Make me come. Please make me come!"

Her body tensed, her thighs gripping his head as she screamed his name over and over, her orgasm rocketing through her.

The instant she relaxed, he pulled her from the car, turned her around, forced her chest down while he shoved his sweatpants down.

"Fuck me," she pleaded. "Fuck me hard."

She sounded desperate and he knew how she felt.

He quickly filled her, thrusting his cock deep into her, the wet warmth of her cunt gripping him. The position made her tight, and the pleasure ignited an inferno in his bloodstream.

Out of control, he pounded into her, fucking her hard, holding her hair in his firm grip. She continued to plead, to beg him for more as she thrust her hips back against him. Within minutes, he was sweating, although the cool breeze should've helped.

It didn't.

Then again, when it came to Courtney, nothing kept his blood from boiling. She made him want, ache, need. She made him hungry, and he never seemed to get his fill.

"Fuck, baby." He groaned. "That's it, squeeze my dick."

He pounded into her again and again while her muscles clenched around him.

"Fuck!" Courtney screamed. "I'm … coming again!"

The beautiful sound of her voice had him letting go, coming hard and deep inside her.

Chapter Twenty-Seven

One order of what they're having, please.

Present Day
Saturday, May 16th

Courtney wiped at a tear that escaped when Marissa said her vows to Trace, hoping the cameras wouldn't catch her emotional battle as she stood behind her best friend, holding her bouquet for her while Marissa pledged her undying, eternal love to the man she would spend the rest of her life with.

It was sweet, there was no doubt about that, but that didn't mean Courtney wasn't counting down the minutes until they were finished. The couple looked so happy, so in love. And though Courtney had already fast-forwarded—at least in her mind—to the part where she could sneak off to a corner and indulge in too much wine for the remainder of the day, she was still happy for her friend and her brother.

"You may now kiss the bride."

Thank God.

Courtney whistled along with the others when Trace planted his lips on his new bride's and dipped her backward, kissing her senseless.

Everyone got to their feet, clapping and whistling, sharing the couple's beautiful moment.

Married.

Trace and Marissa were finally married.

Before the joyful couple could rush back up the aisle, Courtney pressed Marissa's bouquet into her hands and hugged her tightly.

"I'm so happy for you," she whispered, kissing Marissa on the cheek. "Enjoy this day."

"I will," Marissa said, tears in her eyes.

Marissa quickly turned back to Trace, taking his hand before they headed back up the aisle they'd come down just a short time ago.

Courtney remained standing, watching the excitement with her fourteen-year-old niece, Shelby—who'd been a bridesmaid—and watched the mayhem that ensued. Jayden came over to join them, her eyes red from what Courtney assumed had been her own tears. Weddings did that to people.

It was definitely a happy day.

For some.

"You coming inside?" Shelby asked as the young girl stepped forward.

"In a minute," Courtney told her, patting her arm gently. "Go, enjoy yourself. Take Jayden. Keep her in line."

Jayden smirked, then turned to follow Shelby.

Rather than standing out like a sore thumb and inviting questions she didn't have answers to, Courtney blended into the group, smiling and chatting with everyone as they made their way inside the lodge—a fancy hotel-like place that handled everything that the wedding party and guests could possibly need—where the reception would ensue.

Once they'd all made it in, some twenty minutes later, Courtney made a beeline for the bar. As she stood there, considering her options, she decided to forego the wine in lieu of something a little stronger.

"Vodka and seven, please," she told the bartender. "Make it a double."

"Goin' for the hard stuff already?"

Courtney turned at the sound of her father's voice, smiling up at him.

"You okay?"

"Of course," she said in a tone that dared him to challenge her.

Based on the way he watched her, he didn't believe her, but Courtney had no intention of trying to convince him. Today was a good day, one that should be spent celebrating. The last thing she wanted to do was bring anyone down.

"I'm fine," she repeated.

"Good. I'm gonna want you to save a dance for me later." Surprisingly, Casper kissed her on the forehead and sauntered off in the opposite direction, leaving Courtney by herself.

She knew that had been her father's way of telling her to stay put. He wouldn't tell her directly that she couldn't disappear; however, he wasn't above his less-than-subtle request.

Not that Courtney intended to go anywhere. Marissa was her best friend, and Trace was her brother. She wanted to celebrate this moment with them, and she was bound and determined to keep a smile plastered on her face. No matter how hard it was. If only for a few hours, she could do this. She needed to get her mind off everything else. And what better way to do it than spending it with her family and friends, celebrating two people being in love.

Taking the drink the bartender passed over to her, she lifted the glass to her lips and drank deeply. When she'd consumed the entire glass in a less-than-ladylike move, she turned back to him. "Another, please."

His eyebrows lifted slightly, but he turned to get her another.

Maybe if she got shit-faced drunk, some of these people's happiness would seep into her and she wouldn't feel like such a fraud.

And if not, then at least she could hope the alcohol would be enough to numb her.

For eternity.

Chapter Twenty-Eight

Staying away ... no longer an option.
So there's only one way to do this.

"Are you sure you still want to do this?" Ashlynn asked as the limo pulled away from his sister's sprawling estate.

Max smiled. "A little late to ask that now, don't you think?"

Ashlynn laughed, but he didn't sense any humor in the tone.

Of Max's three brothers and two sisters, Ashlynn had always been the one who could read him so well. Although she was three years younger than he was, they were extremely close. Then again, they were a close-knit family. Some families opted to go into medicine together in order to make the world a better place. Some chose politics. Some chose simply to love one another and lead simple, unsuspecting lives. Max's family chose to keep the economy moving along, and they did it together.

Just because they weren't saints didn't mean they didn't care for one another. Sure, they fought, and their arguments sometimes included bullets and certainly threats, but underneath it all, they were there for each other.

Considering how standoffish their parents were, it'd been a means of survival growing up. Samuel and Genevieve weren't what some would consider good role models, and Max wasn't referring to the death and mayhem that shrouded them. Nor had they been overly affectionate toward their kids, and definitely not to one another. As far as relationships went, it was clear that Samuel and Genevieve hated each other. With a fucking passion.

And now, thanks to his father's revelation, Max understood why.

Neither one of them was faithful to the other, yet they'd condemned themselves to the arranged marriage they'd ventured into thirty-nine years before. While Samuel kept time with women who were far too young for him, Genevieve spent hers with a flurry of pool boys, or so she referred to them. It wasn't an ideal marriage, it didn't involve love or even respect, but there was loyalty there—one likely held together with threats. There was no doubt in Max's mind that his parents would be together till death. The question was, would they be the ones to kill each other?

"What is it about this girl that has you so … distracted?" Ashlynn asked, drawing him from his thoughts.

"I don't know," he told her truthfully. There was no sense in lying to her. She'd just see through him and harass him until he finally confessed.

"You love her?" Ashlynn asked, her tone gentle, serious.

Max lifted his head and met his sister's hazel eyes. She looked so much like their mother had when she was younger, it was sometimes eerie. Then again, Ashlynn was a lot like Genevieve in many ways. Although Max's mother remained married to his father, she hadn't spent the past four decades faithful to the man, nor did she try to hide it.

As for Max's sister, Ashlynn had her fair share of suitors over the years, but never once had she claimed to be in love with one of them. She didn't do love, she'd told him once. And he believed her.

"Yes," he finally said. "I love her."

"So why let her walk away?"

"If only it were that simple." Max didn't know how to explain things to her. Hell, he didn't even know how to explain them to himself.

"Seems pretty cut-and-dried to me. You marry the woman you love, send the wicked witch of the west packing, and we all move forward with our lives."

Max grinned. Ashlynn hadn't made any effort to hide her disdain for Angelica. "The wicked witch is no longer in the picture."

Ashlynn's eyes went wide. "You called it off?"

Max nodded.

"What about the land?" she asked. "How will—"

"I don't know yet," he told her directly. "I've got a couple of people diggin' up some dirt on the senator as we speak." And Angelica, but he didn't mention that part.

"Does Samuel know?" Ashlynn asked. She'd always referred to their father by name. Most of them did. The only one in the family who referred to Samuel and Genevieve as Mother and Father was Madison.

Max gave her a *what do you think* smirk.

"I definitely think we can work the angle for the land in another way," Ashlynn continued, obviously not needing Max to contribute to the conversation. "It'll be easy to dig up some dirt on the old man, get him to bend to our will. Or hell, I'm sure we can get somethin' on her. She's a nasty bitch."

Glancing out the window, Max listened to his sister. He'd always appreciated her take on things. She was perceptive, seeing everything and not only what the end goal was. She could be ruthless when necessary, but she always had the family's best interests in mind.

"I've thought it all along—I'm not so sure that Angelica isn't hidin' something. Something that even her grandfather doesn't know."

Max cut his eyes to her once again. "What?"

That was the first he'd heard of Ashlynn's suspicions, and he instantly reflected back on his conversation with Leyton. They'd already figured out what Angelica's angle was, but neither of them had mentioned it to anyone else.

"I heard her on the phone the other day. She'd come over to Samuel's house to talk to Genny about the wedding—you know, all that lovey-dovey bullshit she spouts. When Genny disappeared, probably to fuck Rafe, I don't think Angelica realized anyone else was around, but I'd stopped by to talk to Samuel when I overheard her talking to someone on the phone."

"Who?"

"My guess is her grandfather. She never said his name, but the way she talked to him… Let's just say that if we'd ever dared speak to Samuel like that, we wouldn't have lived to see the light of the next day."

Max chuckled. Ashlynn was right about that. Respect was a big thing in the Adorite family. Growing up, they'd endured plenty of pain, far too many lessons to keep up with, because they'd dared to disrespect Samuel in some way. The man had always had a heavy hand, and none of them had walked away unscathed. But according to Samuel, his methods had worked. They'd learned to respect the family.

"Anyway," Ashlynn continued, peering out the window, "the wicked witch told whoever she was talkin' to that he needed to talk to Samuel. Something about refusin' to wait any longer for the wedding because she was runnin' out of time." Ashlynn looked back at him. "I didn't know she was tryin' to move up the date."

Max nodded. "She'd been tryin' for today. I told her no."

"Well, she apparently didn't listen very well because she'd been pushin' whoever she was talkin' to hard. Obviously she didn't get her way, and yes, I'm ready to celebrate now that you've come to your senses. Just don't do anything stupid. Let me help you off this path of destruction you've found yourself travelin' down."

Max smiled, peering out the window again.

"I guess I can call the dogs off her now," Ashlynn said, a smile in her voice as she retrieved her phone.

"Who? Angelica? You had people watchin' her?"

Ashlynn grinned when Max looked at her. "Big brother, I love you with all my heart, but you haven't been thinkin' clearly. And until you figured out which way was up, I was merely lendin' a hand. If something had come up that you needed to know, I was gonna tell you. And now, since she's out of the picture, my boys will be happy to let her be."

The car came to a stop as Max continued to stare at his sister. She was right, he certainly hadn't been thinking straight. Not for a while now. But tonight, he had every intention of changing that. After a shit load of thinking, Max had finally determined what he wanted, and he knew exactly how he was going to go about getting it.

Sure, it would require some deception, as well as a couple of threats, but that was nothing compared what he truly wanted to do.

"Shall we?" Ashlynn asked when the door opened.

After getting through the security that manned the doors, Max led Ashlynn toward the reception room. The place was filled with people laughing and smiling. It looked as though they'd just finished eating, which was good, because the last thing Max wanted was food.

He scanned the room, looking for the one person he wanted to speak to before he got too engrossed in the party or, more specifically, in finding Courtney. He found Courtney's father standing against the wall, talking to Bryce Trexler—the father of the bride chatting it up with the father of the groom. They were both laughing, slapping one another on the back. He kept his eyes on the pair until it appeared their conversation was coming to a close.

Patting Ashlynn's hand, which was on his arm, he said, "There's someone I want you to meet."

Max approached Casper cautiously when Bryce took his leave, watching the man as his eyes drifted to Ashlynn briefly. There was recognition on his face, and Max had the urge to punch him. Not because he looked at Ashlynn—there wasn't anything sexual about his gaze—but because Casper had allowed Genevieve's life to get so fucked up. Had he been the knight in shining armor he claimed to be today, he would've ridden in on his goddamn white horse and saved her from the villain a long fucking time ago.

Instead, Casper Kogan hadn't made good on his promise to Max's mother. He'd simply moved on with his life, leaving Genevieve to fend for herself.

And Max would never forgive him for that.

"Casper," Max greeted formally. "I'd like you to meet my sister, Ashlynn. Ashlynn, this is Casper Kogan, Courtney's father and one of the founders of Sniper One Security."

Casper did the gentlemanly thing, shaking her hand and smiling when appropriate, but his hardened gaze returned to Max instantly.

"It's very nice to meet you," Ashlynn said politely.

"Can you give us a minute?" Max asked Ashlynn.

She smiled, clearly feeling the tension between him and Casper, then turned to Leyton, who led her over to the bar.

"What are you doin' here?" Casper asked in a harsh whisper.

"I was invited," Max replied with a smile. "And I'm here to see your daughter."

"You shouldn't be here at all," Casper snarled, his voice low so that no other guests could hear.

"We'll have to agree to disagree on that," Max told him, not backing down. "I *should* be here. And I am. Not only do I need to talk to Courtney, but I wanted to let you know that I recently learned some interesting information. It was actually a very disturbing story, if you want to know the truth." Max paused for effect, following with, "From my father."

Casper's eyebrows flew up into his hairline.

"Did you think it'd be a secret forever? Did you think you could manipulate the situation, try to dig into my world, and never be found out?"

Casper didn't respond, so Max continued, lowering his voice as well.

"Whatever good you thought you could do, you can't. You can't undo what's already taken place, and you need to realize that before somethin' bad happens. This white knight syndrome you've got, it won't fix things. She's in too deep, and Samuel will never let her go. So, if you think you can come in and save my mother from the hell she's been in for the last forty years by finding a way to take the rest of us down, you need to think again."

"I don't know what you're talkin' about," Casper retorted harshly.

"I don't doubt that you're good at what you do, but I'm better. *You* sent Courtney to *me*. You thought you could save the day, save my mother from herself, and in the meantime, possibly get some information that would take me down. Am I close?"

Again Casper remained silent.

"It won't happen. And unless you're ready for me to air that dirty laundry, I suggest you back the fuck off."

"Stay away from my daug—"

Max leaned in. "It's too late for that. You should've known in the beginning that I wouldn't be able to let her go, so you've got to own up to it. I love your daughter, and I have no intention of stayin' away from her. No matter what you or anyone else says."

"You'll get her killed," Casper warned.

"You should've thought about that before you sent her to me. Now, I'm all she's got. I'm the only one who can protect her, and you can bet your fucking ass that I'll do that. Even if I have to give my life for hers. But from here on out, you won't interfere. Call her off, and let me handle this thing with her on my own. Goin' forward, I'm no longer a job for her. Sniper One can back the fuck off. You can take *that* to your client." Max took a deep breath. "If there ever was a client to begin with."

Casper's wife, Elizabeth, chose that moment to come over, forcing Max to smile at Casper. He thanked him for the invite and backed away, leaving the man staring after him, likely processing everything Max had just said. He didn't know what Casper would do, but he knew what the man was capable of. He only hoped that he had Courtney's best interest in mind, because if he thought he could keep Max away, he'd soon find out what type of enemy Max could really be.

Half an hour later, after diligently mingling with the bride and groom's friends and family and enduring Casper's death glare from across the room, Max finally located Courtney. He'd had Ashlynn on his arm the entire time, Leyton only a few feet behind them, while they politely smiled and talked, although the only thing he'd wanted to do was seek out Courtney, get her alone and…

Hell, he didn't know what he wanted to do.

He was supposed to be pushing her away, keeping her at a distance. Protecting her. For her sake.

She wasn't safe. Not with Angelica stirring up shit, or his father making threats—idle or not. Now that Max had officially called off the wedding, he figured they'd both be hell-bent on taking him out, which made Courtney all the more vulnerable. Max needed to keep her safe, not dangle her in front of the others, only making her that much more of a target, but he feared, until he worked this out with her, he'd never be able to move forward completely.

He couldn't stay away from her. And he no longer intended to.

"There's your chance," his sister whispered close to his ear.

Max released Ashlynn's arm, allowing her to step away from him as he approached Courtney. Ashlynn had already given him a hard time, informing him that this was not a good idea—at least not here—but Max hadn't listened to her.

Not that she hadn't been speaking the truth. Even he knew that showing up at this wedding, with the sole intention of speaking to one woman in particular, wasn't the smartest move he'd ever made. But that hadn't stopped him from accepting the invite when he'd received it, surprising as it had been.

"Courtney," he said softly as he approached the dark-haired beauty.

He fought the urge to smile when she slowly turned on her heel and glared at him.

"Why did you come?" she asked softly, reaching for his arm and grabbing his jacket, pulling him away from the group she'd been speaking with.

Max offered them a polite smile as he allowed Courtney to drag him away.

"I was invited," he told her when she finally stopped in a dark hallway.

Damn, the things he wanted to do to her right there in that alcove, hidden away from the rest of the people celebrating Trace and Marissa's nuptials. It would be so easy, too.

"I know that," she snapped, her voice low. "That didn't mean you had to accept."

"Of course I did. It would've been rude not to," he countered.

"I'm not doing this with you," Courtney stated bitterly. "You and me… That ain't happenin'."

Max grinned. He knew the flash of teeth was probably predatory, but he couldn't help himself.

"See," he said softly, leaning closer, trapping her between his body and the wall behind her, "that's where you're wrong."

"Damn it, Max."

Courtney's eyes widened as she looked up at him. She might not like him, and Max could accept that, but that didn't mean she didn't want him. She did. It was written plain as day on her beautiful face.

"Tell me you miss me," he ordered, keeping his voice low, his mouth hovering close to her ear.

"I don't miss you," she argued.

Max pulled back enough to look into her eyes. "Liar."

Neither of them moved; neither of them said a word. Max continued to breathe her in, to study her face, waiting for that sign, the one he'd seen before. The one that told him just how hard it was for her to resist him, no matter what she wanted to tell herself.

"We can't do this, Max," she finally said in a harsh whisper.

"Wrong again," he informed her.

"Why, Max? Tell me why."

Trailing his finger down her smooth cheek, he kept his gaze locked with hers. "Because you and me … we've got some unfinished business."

Chapter Twenty-Nine

Unable to resist, that's all there is to it.

Fifteen months ago

Courtney balked at the well-dressed limo driver/bodyguard who'd arrived at the Sniper 1 Security office, waltzed right into the reception area, and requested to speak to her. Luckily, RT had been heading out or she might have never known he was there.

"Dane? What are you doing here?" she questioned.

"Mr. Adorite asked that I bring you to the restaurant," he said simply, as though that made any sense at all.

Glancing around, grateful that Jayden had left for the day, she searched for the clock on the wall. It was…

"Shit," she muttered. "I'll call him. I have to cancel, but…" Courtney trailed off at the look of unwavering fortitude in Dane's dark brown, nearly black, eyes. "What?"

"Mr. Adorite is on the way to the restaurant now. If I don't arrive with you, he'll—"

Courtney lifted her hand, stopping him. "Fine. Give me two minutes."

As much as she wanted to argue, Dane was not the man she needed to have the conversation with. He was merely the messenger, and she had no doubt that if he went back and informed Max that she had decided to blow him off, Dane could very well take a bullet.

She liked Dane. He was a good man, despite his dark side. He'd been friends with Max for a long time, and his loyalty was unwavering. Had he been anyone else, sure, she would've sent him on his way, not caring what happened to him, but she happened to like him. So, today was his lucky day.

Although it didn't seem to be hers.

Rather than waste precious time, Courtney steeled herself for the inevitable while she retrieved her purse, slipped into the restroom to powder her nose and pull her hair up into an unruly—although quite sexy—knot on top of her head.

When she returned, Dane shot her a grateful smile. "Thank you, Ms. Kogan."

Courtney nodded and then followed him to the elevator.

Less than twenty minutes later, she was weaving her way through the tables to the one Max occupied at the very back of the lovely little Italian restaurant that he favored. It was the same place he'd taken her on their first official date.

Max got to his feet to greet her, taking both her hands and pulling her into him so that he could place a kiss on her lips.

"I'm glad you could make it," he said as they both sat, a hint of annoyance ringing in his tone.

"I'm sorry. I've got this thing … it's called a job. I was busy workin' on a case."

Max lifted his wineglass to his mouth as he watched her. "What case is that?"

Courtney knew better than to tell him the details of her work. She was having a difficult enough time trying to find the blurred line she'd been straddling for the last ten months, ever since she'd found herself giving in to the dark side and her lust for this man.

"It doesn't matter," she told him.

The waiter approached, delivering their salads and quietly slipping away.

Great. He'd already ordered for her.

As was the case whenever they went out, unless she requested otherwise, Max would generally order even though he knew she despised being treated like a trophy. Tonight, she suspected he'd done it because he was upset that she'd so blatantly forgotten their dinner date.

Truth was, she hadn't forgotten at all, She'd merely been planning to ignore him entirely.

Not the most mature reaction she'd ever had, but Courtney couldn't seem to disassociate with her logical self, making stupid, reckless decisions in the name of … love. Spending time with him was only making things worse. She was getting in over her head, and she couldn't seem to stop the domino effect that would ultimately lead to his demise, or hers.

Max's silence drew her attention to him, and she glanced up, noticing he was staring at her, his fork held halfway between his food and his mouth. The next thing she knew, the fork had clattered to the plate, her hand was in his, and he'd pulled her from her chair. She stumbled along behind him as he led her through the crowded dining room toward a hall. His palm smacked on the ladies' restroom door before he shoved it open, peering inside.

Luckily, the room was empty. Before he yanked her inside, she noticed Leyton, Max's right-hand man, standing sentry in the hallway.

Without a fraction of a second to think, Courtney found herself pressed against the ornately wall-papered wall, Max's fingers linking with hers as he lifted her arms above her head, his mouth crashing over hers. Whimpering because the need to touch him was too great, Courtney instantly gave in to the kiss, something she found herself doing even when she should've known better.

Whether she was happy, angry, lonely, or pissed, she always wanted him. Sometimes more than she wanted to.

"Why do you push me, Courtney?" Max mumbled against her lips. "Why do you try to fight me every step of the way?"

When he pulled back enough that she could look into his eyes, she told him the truth. "Because I hate you."

Okay, so it was only partial truth. She also loved him, but she damn sure wasn't going to tell him as much. She hated him more. She hated who he was, what he did, what he made her feel. She was supposed to be one of the good guys, and ten months ago, before she'd met Max, she would've sworn that would never change, but now… She'd seen too much, witnessed a side of Max that should've made her sick, but it hadn't.

Max growled. "You don't hate me, Courtney."

"I do," she declared, wishing he'd put his mouth back on hers.

His gaze dropped to her lips, and as she'd hoped he would, Max slammed his mouth back on hers. Courtney sucked his tongue into her mouth. She bit his lip, kissing him hard and trying to physically hurt him the way he'd emotionally hurt her. But he didn't seem to mind the pain because the kiss only got hotter, her body igniting as he crushed himself against her. The friction was brutal and beautiful, and she hated herself as much as she hated him for wanting him despite everything.

"I need to be inside you," he growled against her ear when he pulled his mouth from hers. "Let me, Courtney. Let me fuck you right here, right now."

A broken cry came from her throat, and she knew she was giving in because she knew no other way when it came to Max. She wanted him with a passion that defied logic and reason. An inferno of need flared inside her, scorching her from the inside out as her pussy clenched in anticipation of feeling him inside her.

Max held her wrists with one big hand while he undid his slacks, shoving them down and freeing his cock. He lifted her skirt, yanked her panties down her thighs until she could wriggle out of them, allowing them to drop to her ankles before she kicked them away completely.

And the next thing she knew, he was inside her, filling her, stretching her.

"Yes," Courtney moaned, loving the way it felt when he pushed deep. "God, yes, Max."

When Courtney looked into his golden eyes, she didn't see the frustration or anger that she'd sensed in him earlier, although she knew it was there. It was always there, but she saw what she always saw when their bodies became one—adoration and intense desire. There was no doubt about it, Maximillian Adorite was ruthless and cruel, but when it came to her … there was something intrinsically good in his eyes, something that made her want to be as close as she could to him.

Max's hips thrust forward, his cock jamming into her as her body acclimated to his girth. He was so big, filling her completely, and she wanted more of him.

"Fuck me," she growled. "Fuck me, Max."

Before she could catch her breath, Max pulled out of her, whirling her around so that her palms were on the wall, and that was when she realized there was a mirror in the corner. She watched, fascinated as his big hands gripped her hips before he filled her yet again, eliciting a cry from her. It felt so good.

Max didn't coddle her, and he didn't treat her like she was made of sand and would blow away in the wind at any moment. No, right there in that restroom, Max treated her the way she wanted to be treated. Although he claimed her body, used her for his own pleasure, he gave more than he took, and she found herself craving him. At the same time, she despised him for who he was, for what he did.

"Look at us, Courtney," Max commanded as he fucked her from behind.

Courtney's eyes lifted, raking over their reflections in the mirror. She saw her flushed cheeks, her kiss-swollen mouth as he rammed into her again and again. The tingle in her core was beginning to radiate outward. She didn't want it to ever end, but she knew she couldn't stop it.

"What do you see, Courtney? What do you see in that mirror?"

"You. Me. Fucking," she said, her words punctuated by his powerful thrusts. She knew he hated when she called it that. Max didn't mind her encouraging him to fuck her, to take her harder, faster. But he didn't appreciate her lessening what transpired between them.

She did it to keep her distance from him, because Courtney knew that if she gave in to him completely, she'd lose a part of herself that she would never get back.

Cutting her gaze up to meet his, she begged him to make her come. His lips thinned as he focused on sending her over the edge. She returned her attention to their forms, to the way he so easily controlled her pleasure. It'd been that way since day one, since her first taste of him, and it hadn't lessened in its intensity.

"Come for me, Courtney."

And as though she were waiting for that moment, her mind separated from the intense sensations flooding her body, giving in to the glorious warmth that coiled tightly inside her and radiated outward, overwhelming her until she couldn't hold back any longer.

Courtney screamed as her orgasm ripped through her. Max's hands gripped her hips tighter, and he slammed into her once, twice, and on the third time, he stilled, his cock pulsing deep inside her as he came.

It was in that moment that Courtney felt another piece of herself break off, another piece of herself that she'd given to this man. She knew it wouldn't take long before he'd control her, and she knew there was no way she could ever allow that to happen.

□»«□»«□»«□

After they both got cleaned up, Max returned to the table with Courtney. They finished their meal mostly in silence. He didn't attempt conversation, nor did she. And he was okay with that. Words wouldn't make it any better.

Although she'd willingly given in to the need that plagued them both, he could tell she was pissed at him. Part of him knew he should give a shit; the other part wasn't in the mood. He had too much shit on his mind, too many things going on that he couldn't bring himself to care whether or not she wanted to come to him when he needed her.

She'd started retreating more and more over the last couple of months. He wasn't stupid. She was trying to put distance between them, and he was attempting to keep that from happening. This thing between them was fucked up, even he recognized that.

The majority of the time they spent together, they spent with him buried inside her body. He fucking loved being balls deep inside her. On the sofa when they watched television, in the backseat of the limo before and after they went to dinner, in the shower, the bath, even in the swimming pool. But mostly, he loved having her in his bed, waking up with her in his arms. He had an unhealthy obsession with her that would likely get one or both of them killed if things continued to progress the way they were.

Yet he couldn't stop it.

He'd let down his guard in recent months, allowing her to get closer than he should have. He'd learned his lesson with Weston, having to kill one of his own men because he'd betrayed him. No, Max hadn't lost any sleep over it, but he knew that it'd been his fault. She was getting too close, and he was overlooking her actions, letting her get by with things he knew he shouldn't.

One of these days, she was going to get her hands on something that could ultimately hurt him, his family, his organization, and he didn't doubt that Courtney would try to take him down if the opportunity ever presented itself.

It would be the ultimate betrayal, as far as he was concerned. She wouldn't be allowed to get away with it, but Max couldn't bring himself to think about the consequences for her actions. She'd have to die, and that was something he couldn't fathom.

He needed her to come over to his side, but he wanted her to want him. To want to be with him. To fucking love him.

Not that she would ever allow that to happen.

And that was his biggest problem—one he had no idea how to fix.

Chapter Thirty

Inevitable. Yes, that's the word she'd use to describe it.

Present Day
Saturday

Courtney was prepared to argue with Max right there in the middle of Marissa and Trace's wedding reception, to tell him to go to hell, but the next thing she knew, he was pulling her along behind him as he headed down the long, narrow hall of the lodge.

"Where're you goin'?" she hissed, trying to keep her voice down so that others didn't hear her. She had no idea who was lingering in this part of the spacious resort that did everything from family reunions to weddings, but she didn't want to draw attention to herself if someone was.

"Somewhere private," Max said, his tone cool and calm.

"Max! Damn it," she huffed. Rather than continue to argue, because she knew it was futile, Courtney did her best to keep up with Max's long stride.

After they ascended a set of stairs to the second floor, he ignored several closed doors as they traversed the long hall. She figured he had a destination in mind, or else, knowing him, he would've been looking for any unlocked door. She knew he'd eventually get to where he was going, because that was the way her luck seemed to be going these days, but she remained silent.

When he did stop in front of a door, he slid a key card through the electronic reader, disengaging the lock. "You first," he instructed, turning the knob and pushing the door open.

Glaring up at him, she stepped inside but didn't move farther than the small entry of what appeared to be a room much like any hotel room. "What are you—?"

Courtney didn't get the question out before Max's mouth was on hers, his hands sliding into her hair, holding her head as pleasure-pain ricocheted through her insides.

The first thought was to pull away, but that quickly faded, so she threw her arms around him, desperate to get as close as she could. She couldn't stay away from him, couldn't keep a safe distance, no matter how many times she ridiculed herself for being stupid.

Two and a half painfully long months had gone by since he'd fucked her against the wall of her kitchen, and she still ached for him. Hell, the other night, when he'd asked her to stay on the phone with him just so he could listen to her breathe, it'd taken everything in her not to go to his house, to throw herself into his arms, to beg him to take her back, to give in to this ache that was plaguing her.

"Courtney." Max said her name, the most sensual sound she'd ever heard as he crowded her against the wall.

He continued to kiss her while his hands trailed down to her thighs, where he proceeded to bunch the long skirt of her dress into his hands until Courtney felt cool air caress her legs. The warmth that infused her when his palms met the bare skin of her thighs nearly stole her breath. He pushed her dress up, his hands sliding around to her ass as he jerked her closer.

"Max," she moaned when his lips left hers, leaving a trail of fire along her jaw, her neck.

"I need to feel you, Courtney. All of you."

Despite her mental headshake, Courtney encouraged him, tilting her head to give him better access as she pulled him closer.

Max reversed their positions, backing her over to the bed. After he managed to unzip her dress at the back, Courtney shoved his jacket off his broad shoulders. Long minutes of his mouth trailing fire over her skin, their hands groping one another like desperate teenagers, and then she was completely naked.

It didn't seem to matter how much time drifted by when they weren't together, it always came back to this. A familiarity that wasn't lost with time, a desire that didn't diminish with the passing hours, days, months.

"Lie down," he instructed gruffly as he unhooked the cuff links on his shirt.

Courtney did as he said, her eyes glued to him as she watched him undress before her. With every inch of golden skin he unveiled, her body temperature ratcheted up a notch or two until she was burning from the inside out.

Just when she thought he would join her on the bed, Max surprised her by roughly gripping her hips and jerking her until her ass was on the edge of the mattress.

The move was sexy, determined, and she felt her body flush with more heat, all thought fleeing.

"I have to taste you," he said hurriedly as he went to his knees on the floor, his eyes leaving a heated caress along her skin.

Courtney's back arched at the first feel of his tongue against her sensitive flesh, his fingers separating her labia as he licked her. Slowly.

"Max!" It was so good. Too good.

A flurry of anticipation rocked her, making her head spin. Everything up to that point had happened so fast she could hardly remember how they'd gotten there, but she didn't want him to stop.

She'd missed this, missed the way he could so easily play her body like a finely tuned instrument. For the entire year they'd been together, she'd known his touch so intimately. Hell, she knew more about the way he felt than she did anything else about him, yet she still wanted him, still craved what he could give her.

"You want more?" he asked, pausing.

"God, yes!" She wasn't above begging, but thankfully, she didn't have to.

When his warm breath caressed her slick folds, she sucked oxygen deep into her lungs. And when his wicked tongue slid over her sensitive skin, the air rushed out of her. Her hands went to her breasts, fondling roughly to keep her from giving in too soon to the unprecedented pleasure that only Max knew how to deliver.

"So sweet," he breathed against her skin. "So soft, so wet. I've fucking missed you, Courtney."

Courtney pushed her hips upward, trying to increase the friction of his tongue against her clit, but Max gripped her thighs, holding her legs open wide, making it impossible for her to do anything more than endure the exquisite pleasure as he devoured her pussy, licking, sucking, fucking her with his ruthless tongue.

"Max! I'm gonna come. I can't hold on. Oh, God, Max. Please!" She had no idea what she was asking for, but whatever it was, Max delivered. Two fingers thrust inside her while his lips wrapped around her clit, sending her hurtling into a blissful orgasm that momentarily robbed her of her senses.

Then he was above her, his mouth hovering over hers, his heavy cock resting between her thighs, the crisp hair on his chest scraping deliciously against her nipples. His knees settled between her legs as he guided himself into her. His forearm came to rest beside her face, one hand cradling her head as he pressed his lips to hers and thrust into her without preamble.

Courtney moaned as he penetrated her, his cock filling her until breathing became difficult. She was only focused on him inside her, the way his hips retreated ever so slowly before thrusting forward again, lodging him deeper than before.

There wasn't a rush anymore, at least on his part, but Courtney needed more of him. She needed *all* of him.

When he pulled back, his eyes locking with hers, she gave herself over to him. Her hands trailed to his face, her fingertips stroking his rugged, handsome features. Over his dark brow, down his smooth cheeks, over his lips until his eyes closed and he fucked her ever so slowly.

It was different than the last time. Possibly different than any of the times before.

There was something far deeper, far more intense than their previous encounters. This wasn't just sex. And the worst part…

Courtney had no idea what to do with that knowledge.

Chapter Thirty-One

Will we? Yes. Now the question is how.

Max's eyes closed as Courtney's fingers trailed over his skin. The way she grazed his face, his neck, down the tense muscles of his back, then back up, sliding along his jaw… It sent him soaring, flying higher than he ever had.

When she stopped, he turned his head and kissed her palm as he impaled her slowly, sweetly. He never wanted this moment to end because he feared he would never have it again, and that was no longer acceptable. Being with her, having her in his arms was the only way he saw his life going forward. Spending another minute without her wasn't an option, but he didn't know how to tell her that.

So he figured he'd show her.

Lowering his mouth to hers, Max adjusted his body and managed to roll to his side, taking Courtney with him. When he was on his back, he pushed inside her again, gripping her hips.

"Sit up," he ordered. "I want you to ride my cock while I watch you."

Courtney pushed off him, her hands resting on his chest while she kept her eyes trained on his face, her hair falling over her shoulders, the ends teasing her nipples. She began to gently rock forward and back, the sweet grind against his cock sending shockwaves of pleasure through him.

"So beautiful," he told her, watching as she shifted forward, her eyes closing, her perky breasts with their rosy nipples swaying with her.

He had missed this. Missed her.

But this was different. This was more than he'd anticipated. There was no way he could return to life as normal after this. Not without her. He'd anticipated this moment, being skin to skin with Courtney while he filled her. Not just the rough fucks they'd had in the past. This was more. So fucking much more.

"Damn, baby," he groaned when her inner muscles clamped around his dick. "Fuck me."

Courtney's eyes opened, meeting his as she continued to impale herself on his dick, riding him, using him for her own pleasure. He could see it in the heightened color in her cheeks, the way she bit her bottom lip when she moaned.

She was killing him slowly, and he never wanted it to end.

"I need more," she said on a pleading breath.

Once again, he flipped their positions, driving himself into her in one powerful thrust. Every sensation intensified as that telltale tingle at the base of his spine warned him that the pleasure would overwhelm him soon. He wanted to make her come, make her cry out his name before he filled her.

Increasing the pace, Max shifted his knees, linked his fingers with hers, and lifted her arms above her head as he began fucking her harder, deeper.

"More, Max. Please," Courtney begged, her head tilting back as her hips thrust upward to meet his. "All of you."

Sweat dotted his forehead as he continued to watch the myriad of expressions play across her face. Desire, pleasure, need… It was all there for him to see, and he couldn't look away as he fucked her harder, faster.

Her legs came up, her knees locking around his hips, her ankles digging into his ass as he pumped his hips, buried himself deeper.

"Courtney. Fuck, love." The words came out on a tortured whisper, but he couldn't stop them.

Courtney's hands tightened around his as her body tensed, the sweetest cries of pleasure escaping her as she came.

Max didn't slow, continuing to impale her, to fill her because he couldn't bring himself to stop. And then, his release detonated, sending his head spiraling as his body tightened, his dick pulsing inside her. He slammed into her one final time as he came, harder than he'd ever come before in his entire life.

Several minutes passed, but he refused to move, even as his cock softened inside her. He never wanted to leave the haven of her body, didn't want her to get the idea to run away from him again. When he had no choice but to pull out, he got to his feet and headed for the bathroom. He wet a washcloth, cleaned himself, then, when the water was warmer, he retrieved another.

Returning to the room, he used the cloth to clean Courtney as she lay on the bed, her eyes open, watching him intently.

Relieved that she hadn't tried to get up and get dressed, Max climbed onto the bed beside her, pulling her against him, her head resting on his chest as he wrapped his arm around her, kissing the top of her head.

"We shouldn't have done that," Courtney finally said after a lengthy silence filled the room.

"That's not what I was thinkin'," he responded sharply. He knew she was about to push him away, and he wasn't going to have any of it. Not this time.

It was time for the games to end. Once and for all.

Courtney lifted her head, propping herself up and meeting his gaze. "You're engaged to be married, Max. This was stupid. Reckless. And it can't go any further. You know that as well as I do."

Giving in to the frustration, Max flipped her onto her back, holding himself above her, his nose nearly touching hers as he stared into her eyes. "First, I'm not engaged—"

"Yes, you—"

"Let me finish, goddammit," he growled. "I ended it, Courtney. And if I hadn't, it would've ended the instant I stepped foot in this room. This … *you* … are what I've wanted, Courtney. Accept that." Max swallowed hard. "So, the question is no longer *will we*? The answer to that is yes. The new question, the one that we'll work together to find the answer to, is *how*? We *will* make this work. That's no longer an option."

Courtney shook her head, her eyes drifting closed.

"Open your eyes, Courtney," he commanded. When she did, he turned her chin so that she was looking at him once more, and for the first time, he said the words that he'd felt for so long. "I love you. *Only* you. And I refuse to spend another fucking minute without you."

Chapter Thirty-Two

Was that...? Yes, it was. That strange feeling ... definitely hope. A lot of it.

As much as Courtney wanted to argue with Max, to tell him that this couldn't work, she couldn't bring herself to do it. She'd become so used to pushing him away, even when she didn't want to, that the reaction was instant.

But she fought it.

She was back to that point … back to weighing right versus wrong, and wrong was winning, hands down.

He loved her.

Max *loved* her.

Did she think it would work out? No, she didn't. But that was only because they were from two entirely different worlds. But that didn't mean she didn't love him, because she did. And as she'd learned, staying away from him wasn't working, anyway. They always ended up together, like this.

Touching his face, Courtney blinked past the tears in her eyes, swallowed past the emotion clogging her throat. Max's head lifted, allowing her to see his beautiful face better.

"We'll figure this out, Court. I promise you that."

"But you *are* engaged," she repeated.

"No, I'm not," he said with a huff, dropping onto his back beside her once more.

"What does that mean?" Well, she kind of understood the words, but as of the last time she'd spoken to him, he *had* been engaged.

"I came here for a reason," he told her, peering over at her. "And because I had an ulterior motive—getting you back—I ended things with Angelica."

"What did she say?" God, could she dig herself any deeper? Did she really care what the other woman had said?

"It wasn't pretty." Max sighed. "It's not so much Angelica that I'm worried about, though."

"Who then?"

"My father."

Oh, shit. Courtney knew that she was doomed if Max's father was against the idea of him being with anyone else. She knew that Max had been planning to marry Angelica for a business arrangement. He'd said so himself. Granted, she still wanted to know what the two of them had been scheming because that was her nature.

On top of that, she didn't see Angelica giving up quite so easily. In fact, Courtney was pretty sure that Angelica was still stalking her and harassing her, more so than just the annoying phone calls. Not that she intended to share that with Max. If the other woman had gone that far while she'd been engaged to Max, there was no telling what she was capable of now.

Which meant Courtney would need to be vigilant.

Resting her cheek on his chest once more, she listened to the soothing thump of his heart. She was tired of running from him, from this, tired of kidding herself about what she did and didn't want, but this was a big step, right off of a very steep cliff lined with jagged rocks. There was no way she was going to survive this if things went south, which no doubt they would.

Max's hand slipped through her hair, gently rubbing her head. "Quit thinkin' so hard."

"Easier said than done," she told him.

Max kissed her forehead and sat up, forcing her back to the bed. "I need to get you back to the reception."

Shit. Her best friend and her brother had just gotten married, and here she was, naked, in bed with Max.

Launching up from the mattress now that the ideal-world bubble was officially popped, Courtney proceeded to get dressed, scrounging for her shoes and her panties once she got back into her dress.

"Be still," Max commanded, coming to stand behind her.

The warmth of his hand trailed up her back as he zipped her dress. Courtney shimmied into her panties and located her other shoe. By the time she was dressed—not necessarily presentable—Max looked as cool and collected as always. Certainly not like he'd just fucked her brains out.

"Give me a minute," she told him, rushing into the bathroom and closing the door. She took a deep breath and looked in the mirror.

Not as bad as she thought, but she definitely looked well fucked.

It took a few minutes for her to get her hair under control, and it was a damn good thing she'd opted to keep her hair down or she'd be well and truly screwed.

When she stepped out of the bathroom a minute later, she came face-to-face with Max.

"We can't go out there looking like we're in love," Courtney told him point-blank.

His lips curved into a seductive grin, and a tremor of heat shot through her.

"How do you propose we handle it, then?"

Courtney stood on her toes, meeting his mouth with hers. She placed a gentle kiss on his lips. "You go back to your sister, and I'll go back to doing what I did before you arrived."

"Which was?"

She wasn't about to tell him that she'd been throwing herself a pity party, complete with endless alcohol. "I'll mingle with my family."

"When will I see you again?" he asked.

"I don't know," she told him, looking away.

"Not a good answer," he retorted, his fingers clipping her chin and turning her head so she was forced to look at him again.

"It's the only one I've got," she snapped.

"If I don't hear from you tonight, you'll find me at your front gate," he said roughly.

"That can't happen and you know it. No matter what, we can't let people know about … whatever this is."

"Then you'll make every effort to see me. That or I'll go public."

Courtney grinned. "You wouldn't." There was no way Max Adorite would call attention to a relationship that involved someone within the ranks of Sniper 1 Security. He had a reputation to uphold, a business to run, mobsters to protect.

"Don't test me and we'll never know. But push me on this, Courtney, and I'll show you exactly what I'm capable of."

A shiver ran through her, something dark and ominous and oddly sensual filling that cold spot that had been consuming her for the past year.

Max turned her toward the door. "I'll give you ten minutes, then I'm comin' out. Ashlynn and I will be leavin' when I do."

The euphoric feeling she'd had moments ago was replaced with disappointment when she thought of Max leaving, but she knew it had to happen. Nodding, she turned her back on him and reached for the doorknob.

Before she could get out of the room, she was up against the door, her breasts crushed against the hard wood. She adjusted her head so that her cheek rested against the cool surface. Max's breath was hot against her ear.

"The next time I see you, I plan to have you on your knees while I bury my cock in your sweet fucking mouth. And then, I'm gonna fuck you in every position imaginable. And when we're through, we'll start all over again. In my bed."

Damn, the man had the ability to turn her from cold to hot in a millisecond. That was something else she had missed about him: his dirty mouth. He could practically make her come simply by telling her all that he wanted to do to her, or her to him.

"So keep that in mind, Courtney. Think about that while you're out there, talking to other men. They'll never give you what I can give you."

Courtney already knew that. No man compared to Max, and no man ever would.

Max's big palm cupped her cheek, turning her head back so that her mouth met his, his erection pressing against her ass. She sucked his tongue into her mouth, wishing he wasn't holding her against the door. She suddenly had the urge to climb his body.

"I'll be waitin' for your call."

He was the one to pull away first, his lips pressing against her cheek before he took a step back and released her.

"Oh, and Courtney…?"

She waited for him to continue.

"I love you."

Courtney met his heated gaze once more, nodded, and then stepped out of the room, gently closing the door behind her. Taking a deep breath, she glanced down the hallway, wondering whether or not anyone was looking for her, praying they weren't. Because no matter how put together she appeared now, she was still a jumbled mess on the inside.

And she wasn't sure that was going to change anytime in the near future.

Chapter Thirty-Three

The difference an hour can make.

Max waited the ten minutes he'd promised and then left the room. He returned to the gathering, mingled with the guests, attempting to locate Leyton and Ashlynn but finding neither where he'd left them.

Grabbing his phone, he slipped down an empty corridor and dialed Leyton's number.

He stopped moving at the sound of a phone ringing. He peered down the hall, but no one was there. With the phone still pressed to his ear, he ventured farther until he came to an intersecting hallway, and that was when he saw them.

Pulling his phone away from his ear, he stared in disbelief.

"What. The. Fuck?" Max glared at his sister and Leyton as the two of them jerked away from one another.

Leyton had been practically fucking Max's sister in the goddamn hall, up against the wall.

When Ashlynn started to speak, he scowled at her. "Don't. I don't want to fuckin' hear it. You better be out there in five fuckin' minutes or things are gonna get real nasty. And you," he said to Leyton directly, "I'm gonna cut off your goddamn dick."

Turning, he headed back to the others, straightening his suit and trying his best to erase the mental image of Leyton and Ashlynn. What the fuck were they thinking? His closest friend, the man he trusted with his life, was fucking his sister?

Goddammit.

That shit was over. He didn't give a good goddamn what either of them wanted; there was no fucking way he would tolerate that shit. That was a recipe for disaster, and they had to know that. They were both too important to the organization, and if word got out that the two of them were hooking up, shit would hit the fan. Not to mention, Samuel would likely castrate Leyton and feed him his own fucking balls.

But not if Max did it first.

While he fought the urge to check the time, Max took a flute of champagne from a passing waiter and scanned the crowd. He was looking from one person to another, making mental notes of who was who, but that came to an abrupt halt when he saw…

"Are you ready?" Ashlynn questioned, her tone clipped.

"Is that…?" he began, grabbing Ashlynn's arm before she could storm off.

"What?" Ashlynn replied.

"Is that Dani?" he asked.

He received a mumbled response from Ashlynn before she encouraged him to leave.

Max watched while his cousin Dani made her way across the room toward one of Courtney's brothers. She looked determined, and he wanted to know why the hell she was there. Last he'd heard, she'd been shipped out of the country for school by her father, Max's uncle Nick. No one had been given a reason as to why she'd disappeared so quickly and without reason, other than she was handling some personal issues while also completing her degree. That news had never sat well with Max, and as he watched Dani approach Hunter, he got the unsettling feeling that there was a hell of a lot more to that story.

"Come on," Ashlynn commanded. "We need to go."

Max heard Leyton's footsteps behind him, and when he managed to drag his attention away from his cousin, he couldn't bring himself to look at Leyton or Ashlynn, the memory of what they'd been doing replacing his curiosity over seeing Dani at the Kogan wedding.

"Call the car around," Max demanded, taking Ashlynn's arm and pulling her toward the front door.

She didn't argue, didn't make a scene, but the death rays coming from her eyes practically burned a hole into the side of his face.

Once the limo arrived and Leyton opened the door, he pushed Ashlynn inside and joined her.

"What the fuck was that for?" she snarled when the door closed and they were safely inside.

Max ignored her.

"Let's get one thing straight, Max," Ashlynn hissed. "You might be in charge of the business, but you damn sure aren't in charge of my life. You better get familiar with that concept right fuckin' now."

Max took a deep breath. He was going to fucking kill Leyton. He was going to string him up by his balls and watch him dangle from the ceiling. He wanted to hear the bastard begging for mercy. What the hell was he thinking?

If Samuel found out that Leyton was… Hell no.

"It's over before it starts, little sister," Max barked, meeting Ashlynn's angry stare. "When Samuel finds out about this—"

Ashlynn interrupted, leaning in. "He's not gonna find out about it. If he does, then he'll learn that you're still fuckin' that girl. That you're forsaking the entire business for pussy."

Max growled. It wasn't like that with Courtney, and Ashlynn knew it.

Rather than argue with her, he turned his attention out the window.

No matter what Ashlynn thought, this shit with Leyton was over. There was no way that Max was going to allow them to be together. It was too fucking dangerous.

After they dropped Ashlynn at her house and got her safely inside, Max ordered Leyton into the back of the car with him. He sensed the other man's hesitance, but he didn't detect an ounce of fear.

That was one thing he'd always respected about Leyton. The reason he entrusted the man with his personal safety and his family's safety.

"What the hell were you thinkin'?" he demanded when the car was in motion once again. "No, don't fucking answer that." Max met Leyton's gaze head on. "You will only receive one warnin'. You stay the fuck away from my sister. Do you understand me? If I catch you with her again, I'll saw your fucking nuts off with a rusty butter knife. And then I'll fucking feed them to you. Don't touch her again."

Leyton didn't say a word, but Max felt his anger. It was clear that Leyton wanted to argue, probably wanted to stab Max with the knife he kept sheathed on his side. But he wouldn't. If he cared about living to see another day, he would shut the hell up and do exactly what he was told.

They rode in silence until the limo pulled up to the estate, coming to a stop in front of the house. Max climbed out, still reeling from what he'd seen, still furious that Leyton would think that fucking Max's sister was even allowed.

And that was the reason Max never heard the gunshots, never saw the shooter standing less than ten feet away from him until it was too late.

Chapter Thirty-Four

That's it. I'm done.

Thirteen months, three weeks, and two days ago

"Where are you going?" Max asked as he followed Courtney down the stairs and into the foyer of his house.

"I'm done," she told him.

"Done what*?" he questioned, trying to remain calm as she traipsed through his house, snatching her purse and her car keys from the table near the door.*

"Done with you!" she yelled. "It's over, Max. I can't deal with this shit anymore."

Max stared at her, trying to process her words.

For the first time in three weeks, she'd spent the night in his bed, and when he'd woken up, she had been lying beside him, wide awake, staring at the ceiling. When he'd whispered good morning, she'd lost her shit.

The woman had gone absolutely fucking crazy, and he had no fucking idea why.

When she headed for the door, he grabbed her arm, halting her instantly. She spun around so fast he didn't have time to block the hand that came barreling toward his face. The loud crack of her palm against his cheek echoed in the tiled entryway, but he didn't let her go.

"I'm not doin' this with you anymore, Max. I'm tired of bein' your fuck toy whenever you need a release. You call me over here, expect me to drop everything I'm doin' and come runnin' when you need me. Well, you can find someone else to entertain you because I'm finished."

What the fuck? Had she fucking hit her head or something?

Max swallowed hard, holding on to the anger that surged inside him. Courtney almost sounded convincing, but he knew her better than she thought he did. He knew what she was up to, knew the game she was playing, and he was ready to pull his hair out because of it. Especially since everything she said was bullshit. He damn sure didn't treat her like a fuck toy. Never had. She was coming up with excuses, that was what she was doing.

If she wanted him to believe her, she probably should've waited until she had a reason to be angry at him. As it was, they'd fucked until they were exhausted, and she'd curled up in his arms and fallen asleep. Surely he wasn't supposed to believe she was pissed about that.

For the last few weeks, she'd been threatening the same thing. Telling him how much she hated him, how much she despised him. But she still ended up in his bed, still begging him to fuck her, still looking at him in that way that told him she was a liar.

Oh, he didn't doubt for a second that she hated him. He understood that.

She was pissed because she'd found out the perfect world she'd thought was on the other side of her door wasn't quite so perfect. Those rose-colored glasses she'd shielded herself with all these years had cracked, and what bled through wasn't pretty. Life wasn't what she'd thought it was, and she'd seen the other side.

Not only that, but she hadn't run away. Nope. She'd stayed because she wanted to and simply tried to convince herself that it was his fault.

And here she was, making threats again, and he was tired of dealing with the shit. He had too much on his mind, too many problems to deal with; he had no time to put up with her childish behavior.

So, he made a decision right then and there.

Releasing her arm, he took a step back. "Go."

Her eyes widened, her mouth opened but closed quickly. "I'm never comin' back, Max."

"Good," he told her. His stomach cramped at the thought of her leaving him for good, but he needed her to come to terms with what she really wanted.

"Good?" she railed.

Max took a step closer to her. "You came to me, Courtney. Remember? You came to me a year ago, seeking me out. I was your mission; I was your job. You climbed into my bed; you allowed me to slide into your body. You wanted me just as much as I wanted you. That's on you. If you want to run away, if you want to pretend that you hate me when, in fact, you actually don't hate me, you hate yourself for not hating me, then fine. Go."

When she didn't say anything, he continued.

"You've seen what I'm capable of, Courtney. You know what I do, even if you want to pretend you don't. All this time, you've tried to convince yourself that you don't have enough dirt to take me down, but that's not true, is it? I've got cameras in every inch of this place. I see everything that goes on. I know every move you've made.

"All the information you've found, I've wanted you to find. Never once were you the one in control, Courtney. That doesn't happen in my world. Never underestimate me. You don't get to have control; you don't get to pull one over on me. I've known from the second you stepped through that fucking door what you wanted from me. Did you get it? Did you find what you needed to take me down?"

She swallowed but didn't speak, her eyes never leaving his.

"You wanted to be here. You came back time and time again because you *wanted to be* here. *I didn't beg; I didn't plead. You came on your own because you want me. You need me."*

"I hate you," she whispered.

"I'm sure you do. But that's fine because I hate you just as much. I hate that I want you so goddamn bad; I hate that I can't sleep when you're not here. I hate that you have more control over me than you even know you have and I'm powerless to do anything about it."

"Liar," she snapped.

Max grabbed her arms and jerked her to him. "I'm a lot of things, baby, but I'm not a liar."

Courtney's sharp inhale caused him to release her. Max wasn't going to try to convince her to stay. It wasn't working. She wanted to go, so she should go. And if she took what little knowledge she had and tried to take him down, he'd deal with the consequences. Nothing he hadn't dealt with before.

But if she didn't… If she kept that information to herself, Max would know. He would know exactly how she felt about him, and that gave him a little bit of hope.

"Now go!" he yelled. "Get the fuck out of my house. Take your games and your bullshit and do whatever it is that you do. I'm tired, Courtney. So fucking tired."

Her eyes turned glassy, and he knew she was fighting her emotions. She had wanted him to stop her, but he'd been doing that for the past year. He'd been trying to make her love him, and until she could admit to herself that she did, there wasn't anything more he could do or say to change that.

"I've got shit to do," he told her and turned away, his gut screaming in agony as he forced himself to leave her standing there. "You can see yourself out because I'm done."

Max slipped into his office, shutting the door quietly behind him as he leaned against it, listening. Several minutes passed, but then the front door opened and closed, and he knew she was gone. Likely out of his life forever.

A knock sounded on the door, and he moved away, calling out that it was open.

"Sir? Everything okay?" Leyton asked when he stepped into the room.

"Fine," he grumbled, turning to face him. "I want eyes on her at all times. I want to know every move she makes. I want photos. I want to know every fucking place she goes, who she talks to, what they fucking say."

"Yes, sir."

"And Leyton," Max continued, "I don't want to hear one goddamn word about her. Understood?"

Leyton nodded, then slipped out of the room, leaving Max staring at the door. For the first time in his life, his heart actually hurt. He'd done the unthinkable. He'd fallen in love with the enemy, and now he had to pay for that.

He had to pay by watching her walk away, knowing there wasn't a fucking thing he could do to change it.

Chapter Thirty-Five

No! This isn't happening!

Present day
Saturday night, May 16th

Leyton watched as Max crumpled to the ground, his own blood roaring in his ears. Everything seemed to be happening in slow motion.

Two rounds…

Max's body jerking backward…

Falling…

Falling…

Fuck!

Lifting his gun, Leyton aimed at the blonde woman standing in the shadows, the one he hadn't even noticed when they'd pulled in, the one still pointing her gun at Max's prone body. Without thinking, he fired one round, aiming for her leg, wanting to take her down but not kill her. At least not yet. She would have to pay for what she'd done, and he'd be the one to ensure that happened, but he didn't have time to deal with her.

Angelica screamed as the bullet pierced her thigh, hopefully shattering bone, and the world came back into focus. Leyton ran to Max, rolling him onto his back, checking for a pulse.

There was blood.

So. Much. Fucking. Blood.

Everywhere.

Sal and Dane came running out of the house, and when they saw Max lying on the ground, chaos ensued. Somehow, Leyton managed to keep himself under control as his best fucking friend bled out on the concrete before him. Relying on every ounce of his self-control, he went to work, needing to stop the blood, needing to make the decisions. The ones that would—God willing—save Max's life.

"Call nine-one-one!" Leyton ordered Dane, his voice stronger than he expected it to be. "And get her the fuck out of here. Call Doc, get him over here for her. Don't tell a fucking soul she's here. Got me?"

"Yes, sir," Dane said, phone to his ear as Sal hefted the screaming bitch into his arms and marched her inside, slamming the door behind him.

"You better hang on, boss," Leyton ordered Max, leaning down and listening to the man's labored breaths. One shot had pierced his chest, and the other… Fuck. The other had been a head shot.

Max was bleeding profusely, and for the first time in his entire fucking life, Leyton was terrified of losing the only family he had. Ripping off his jacket, he wadded it in his hands and pressed it against the wound on Max's chest. "You're gonna be fine, boss. If you're not, I hope you know I'm gonna fuck Ashlynn all over your goddamn house. Every room. In your bed. Your shower. Your favorite fucking chair. So you better fucking live through this so you can kill me for doin' it."

Lights flooded his vision as the ambulance pulled into the circular drive. Leyton didn't leave Max's side as the paramedics took over, doing all the shit they did when someone was … dying.

He managed to move out of the way, giving them plenty of room as he supervised the entire thing. He mentally ran down all the things he needed to do, all the people he needed to call while he watched them work on Max.

He prayed to a god he didn't believe in, unwilling to lose Max. Not like this. Fuck. Not like this.

Several minutes later, they had Max loaded into the back of the ambulance. Leyton instructed Dane to follow them in the Escalade because he was going to go with Max. There was no way in hell he was leaving him. Not for a fucking second. But when he tried to climb in the ambulance, the paramedic informed him he couldn't go.

"Wanna bet?" Leyton growled, getting right up in the man's face. "If you don't let me in there with him, you'll need another one to come get you when you're bleedin' all over the goddamn ground. Yeah?"

The man's eyes flared bright, and he took a step back, allowing Leyton inside. No one would keep him away, not a single fucking person.

This was his job… It was *his* job to protect Max.

And he'd failed.

Goddammit, he'd failed!

Chapter Thirty-Six

When they say life comes to a grinding halt ... believe them.

By the time Courtney got home from the reception, she was tired and hungover. Apparently she'd had more alcohol than she'd thought earlier in the evening, and stopping abruptly after Max's arrival had given her one hell of a headache.

Somehow she'd made it through the freakishly long night, although, for the past four hours, she'd wished that Max hadn't left her there alone. She'd been the one to tell him they couldn't act as though they were in love, but she'd actually wanted that. Just for a little while.

Just a little time to pretend her life wasn't as fucked up as it was. To *not* have to pretend that she wasn't in love with a gangster. She simply wanted to be normal. Although she didn't really know what normal was.

Kicking off her shoes, Courtney grabbed the remote and turned on the television. It was nearly two in the morning, and she doubted there was anything worthwhile on, but if she had to be awake, at least it would keep her mind occupied. After all, Max had informed her that if he didn't hear from her tonight, he'd show up.

As much as she wanted that to happen, she knew better. Smiling to herself as she remembered the things he'd said to her before they'd gone their separate ways, Courtney retrieved her cell phone from her clutch and was just about to dial Max's number when she saw an image on the screen that halted the air in her lungs.

It was a breaking news story, a headline scrolling across the bottom of the screen while a dark-haired anchorwoman stared directly into the camera.

"Yes, it's confirmed. We've just been told that Maximillian Adorite, leader of the infamous Southern Boy Mafia, has, in fact, been taken to the hospital. Apparently, Mr. Adorite was shot outside his home several hours ago. An ambulance was called to the scene, and he was transported to the hospital, but we don't have much more information at this time. A suspect has not been named, nor do we have word on his condition, but our very own Tabitha Hornsby is on her way to Baylor Hospital, where she'll give us an update as soon as she has more information."

Courtney's heart was racing, her legs trembling as she stared at the television set, waiting to hear more. Waiting for someone to tell her what was going on. It took her a few seconds to realize the cell phone she was clutching in her hand was ringing.

Glancing down at the screen, she saw it was Max's number, and a broken sob escaped her as she punched the button on the phone.

"Max?"

"No. It's Leyton." The rough voice on the other end of the phone sounded as tortured as Courtney felt.

"What's goin' on? How is he?"

"He's in surgery," Leyton informed her. "I shouldn't be callin' you, but…"

"But what?" Courtney asked, her tone slightly hysterical.

"Samuel will probably kill me, but … Courtney, you need to get down here now. It… Fuck it all. It doesn't look good."

"What happened?" she asked. "Who shot—?"

"You know I can't tell you that on the phone. Just get down here. Now."

The line disconnected, and Courtney stared at the blank screen, tears streaming down her face. Max had been shot.

It doesn't look good.

Leyton's words echoed in her head.

Just get down here. Now.

Oh, God. She needed to get to Max.

Grabbing her keys and her clutch, she snatched her shoes from the floor but didn't put them on as she ran for the door. She hopped in her car and headed for the hospital, all the while praying that Max wouldn't die on her.

Twenty minutes later, she was running down the hall toward the intensive care unit waiting area, where Leyton had instructed her to go via a text message, her shoes in one hand, phone in the other. She came to a jarring halt when she saw Samuel and Genevieve talking to a doctor, Max's brothers and sisters standing beside them. They looked devastated. Her heart broke, pain streaking through her chest as she watched Max's mother crumble, tears running down her face.

"Courtney."

Leyton's deep voice pulled her from her trance, and she turned to see him standing off to the side. He was disheveled, his face creased with what she could only assume was worry mingled with the emotionally crippling pain that people felt when someone close to them was hurt.

"He's…?" God, she didn't want to know. She didn't want to hear, but she had to ask.

"He made it through surgery," Leyton told her, pulling her against him. It was then that she realized her legs had weakened, her knees giving out completely.

"It was touch and go, but he's still alive."

"And…?" She knew there was more, more that he wasn't telling her.

"They don't think he's gonna make it through the night, Courtney," Leyton told her straightforwardly, his mouth inches from her ear as she pressed her face against his shirt, clutching his jacket.

She was suddenly cold. So cold.

Tears poured down her face; sobs wracked her entire body as she tried to process what Leyton was telling her. She had no idea how long they stood there, but it wasn't until Samuel came over that she managed to pull herself together.

"Why is she here?" Samuel asked sternly.

Courtney noticed Ashlynn standing just a few feet away, her face streaked from her tears.

"I called her," Leyton told the old man. "Max is gonna need her."

"No, he's not," Samuel hissed. "He only needs—"

Courtney took a step back from Leyton, staring at Samuel in horror and disbelief. The move happened so fast she nearly got knocked to the ground when Leyton pulled Samuel by his shirt when the older man lunged for her.

"With all due respect, *sir*," Leyton ground out, "Max is gonna need *her*. Not you. Not me. Not his mother or his sisters or his brothers. Max is gonna need *her*. If you want him to pull through this, you need to accept that right now."

Courtney couldn't believe what she was seeing, couldn't grasp what she was hearing. Leyton was manhandling the leader of the Southern Boy Mafia. A man who could end Leyton's life in a heartbeat, and surprisingly, Samuel wasn't fighting him. That meant…

Oh, God. That meant that it was true. They didn't think Max was going to make it.

"He's right. He needs her," Ashlynn said in a tortured whisper.

"Where's…?" Courtney couldn't force the question past her dry lips, but she had to know. "Where's Angelica?"

Leyton released Samuel, and Max's closest friend's hardened gaze slammed into Courtney's. She sucked in a breath. That look. She knew that look.

The hatred that consumed Leyton's usually handsome features told her more than words ever would. She glanced over at Samuel, then Ashlynn. The fury she saw in their eyes confirmed her suspicions. Angelica had shot Max. She had… She had tried to *kill* him.

Courtney had to regain her composure. She had to get to Max. She needed to see him, to touch him, to tell him that he better not fucking die on her or she'd kill him herself.

"When can I see him?" she asked, her voice stronger. She managed to slip on her shoes, wipe the tears from her face as she pulled herself together.

"Only one visitor at a time," Samuel said faintly, more human than Courtney had expected from him. "His mother—"

"*She* goes in first," Leyton stated, his tone leaving no room for argument.

Samuel nodded, shocking Courtney as she watched the older man stroll away, returning to his wife's side.

Courtney didn't know what to say or do, so she allowed Leyton to lead her down the hall. When he stopped in front of a closed door, she looked up at him.

"You need to listen to me clearly," Leyton said softly. "He can't die. Do you understand what I'm tellin' you? He can't fucking die. You go into that room and you make him want to live, Courtney. You're the only one he'll live *for*. So get your ass in there and tell him he can't die." The last words were said on a hoarse whisper, a rough sob erupting from Leyton's chest, and she understood just how much Max meant to him.

Nodding, she turned toward the door. Taking a deep breath, she pushed it open and stepped inside. Leyton closed it behind her, and then she was standing several feet away from Max. Her heart stopped beating; her lungs ceased to work as she stared at the man in the bed.

There were cords and wires and machines everywhere. A nurse was checking the readout on something, standing beside Max's bed. He looked… God, he didn't look like the man she knew, the man she loved. His usually formidable presence was nowhere. In its place…

"Come sit with him," the older woman instructed kindly. "Talk to him, dear."

"Can he hear me?" Courtney whispered.

"We'll never know until you try."

Courtney slowly moved toward the bed, more tears slipping down her cheeks as she stared at the man she'd fallen in love with, the man she resented for being who he was. The very man she would spend the rest of her life loving if he would just wake up.

He had to wake up because she'd never bothered to tell him that she loved him. Not directly.

And in addition to that, the alternative just wasn't acceptable.

Chapter Thirty-Seven

I love you, and now it hurts to breathe.

"I'll be right outside," the older woman said, nodding toward a window, where Courtney noticed there was a desk situated so that the nurse could watch him directly.

When she was alone with Max, Courtney moved to his side, hesitant to touch him as she watched his chest rise and fall evenly. His beautiful eyes were closed; his face reflected more peace than she'd ever seen on him.

She instantly hated it. She wanted to feel his overwhelming presence, see the glimmer in his golden gaze, watch the way his lips quirked slightly when he was amused by her, by something she said, something she did.

"Oh, God," she breathed softly, collapsing into a chair positioned at his side. "Max."

Gently taking his hand, she wrapped her fingers around his, lowering her forehead to her arm. The tears returned, and she couldn't stop them as she closed her eyes and prayed. She had no idea how much time passed, but the nurse had returned twice before Courtney managed to stop the waterworks.

After grabbing a tissue and blotting her eyes, she once again took Max's hand, her eyes raking over his face. The right side of his head was bandaged, as was his chest. His hand was limp but warm, reassuring her that he was still with her. For how long, she didn't know.

As she took in the sight of him, another sob tore from her chest, but the tears didn't come. He was still so … beautiful.

"I love you," she told him, keeping her voice low. "You do know that I'm not lettin' you leave me, Max. It's not an option. You're not the one who can leave. I can't…" Courtney's chest heaved with the emotion viciously ripping her apart from the inside out. "I can't live without you, Max. I can't. I won't survive it."

As she clutched his fingers, listening to the monitors beeping and the monotonous sound of the machines helping him to breathe, Courtney thought back to the first time she'd realized she was in love with him.

Curled up in his arms, Courtney placed her hand on Max's chest, sliding her fingers through the soft hair. She could feel his strong heartbeat beneath her palm. His hand came to rest over hers, lifting it as he placed a gentle kiss to the tips of her fingers.

"I'm glad you're here," he told her. "I'm glad you stayed."

She was, too, although she couldn't tell him that. The past three weeks had been a whirlwind for her. She'd spent her time fighting a war inside herself, trying to figure out when things had gone so horribly wrong. Somewhere along the way, over the course of the last six months, she'd found herself falling for him, deeper and deeper every time she saw him. Until right here, right now, she didn't understand the band that was tightening around her chest.

It was a foreign feeling, this emotion erupting inside her.

A few short hours ago, when Max had brought her back to his house, she'd been ready to flee. Again. Determined to put an end to this because she couldn't see any other way out. He was supposed to be a job. She was supposed to be the one who would take him down, make him pay for his long list of crimes, but instead, Courtney was allowing her heart to make her decisions, and she was powerless to stop the damn thing.

"What're you thinkin' about?" Max asked, his lips brushing her forehead.

Courtney didn't answer him. She couldn't.

There was no way she was going to let him know that she was thinking about love, trying to imagine what a future with him looked like.

"Talk to me, Court," he encouraged her.

Forcing a smile, she lifted her head and peered at him in the dimly lit bedroom. "I need to take a shower."

Without waiting for his response, she slipped out of his bed and padded to the bathroom. There was a wall that split the room in half, and she walked around it to the opposite side, where the showerhead was located. Turning the knob, she stepped out of the way, waiting for the water to warm as she fought the emotion still bubbling in her chest.

She needed to go home. She needed to forget Max, to take what information she had, hand it over to Casper, and move on with her life. She wasn't cut out for this. She wasn't the super spy she'd hoped she was. Infiltrating Max's world had been damn near impossible, and what little she'd learned, she couldn't even bring herself to share with anyone else. It wasn't enough to do any damage. At least not yet, but that didn't seem to matter. The issue she had was that she didn't want to turn it over, didn't want to take him down.

Hard hands slid over her shoulders, and Courtney's breath lodged in her throat as Max moved closer. His body was warm as he pulled her beneath the spray, his arms wrapping around her, forcing her back against him.

"Quit thinkin'," he ordered gently.

"It's hard not to," she told him. It was the truth. She couldn't stop thinking, wondering, dreaming. Trying to figure out where this was headed while ignoring the fiery crash she suspected it would be in the end.

"Not as difficult as you might think," he responded, his lips meeting her neck.

Courtney tilted her head, and he sucked the sensitive skin between his lips. She sighed, enjoying the way his big hands caressed her skin, flattened against her chest and moved downward, over her breasts, her belly, lower…

Max turned her so that she was facing him, his fingers tilting her chin up so that she was forced to look up at him as he maneuvered her against the tiled wall. Clouds of steam filled the oversized shower, drifting around them, concealing them in their own fantasy world for a little while.

"I know what you're feelin'," he told her, his lips brushing hers, his eyes scanning her face as though he was trying to figure her out.

"You don't," she told him. She didn't want him to know what she was feeling.

"I do," he assured her. "The feelin's mutual, love."

No, it wasn't. It couldn't be. There was no way this was happening. Courtney was not falling in love with Max, and he certainly wasn't falling in love with her. They were enemies, from opposite sides of the law. She was one of the good guys; he was one of the bad.

He stole her breath with a deep, sensual kiss, his tongue sliding into her mouth. He was gentle but strong as he shifted her so that his cock rocked against her entrance. Courtney angled her hips, wanting to feel him inside her, to pretend for a little while that being in love with him wasn't wrong. He was evil; she wasn't supposed to love him, but her heart didn't seem to care.

Their bodies slid together, tongues melded, hands roamed.

"Ahh, Court. Baby." He breathed against her mouth as he penetrated her, sliding up inside, deeper, filling her completely.

Her body gripped him, stretching around him as pleasure ignited her nerve endings, leaving her breathless and aching for him.

"This is what it's supposed to feel like," he whispered against her ear as he began to slowly thrust his hips.

Rather than fuck her senseless, he was driving her crazy with his maddeningly slow pace, but it felt so good. Being wrapped in his arms, the steely length of his body against hers as he filled her… Courtney never wanted it to end.

"Max," she pleaded. She needed more, so much more.

"Look at me," he ordered, his tone still tender as he lifted his head.

Her eyes opened, and she met his glistening gold gaze.

His thumb brushed over her lip as he pushed inside her again, retreating ever so slowly.

"Let me love you, Courtney."

Her brain screamed no while her heart grabbed on to his words, pulling them deep inside, holding them there.

Sensation flooded her. Glorious, exquisite sensation that bloomed in her core, radiating outward, filling her with hope although she knew it wasn't real.

Sliding her palms up his chest, she wrapped her hands around his neck, her fingers brushing the stubble along his jaw, her thumbs caressing his lips as they remained locked together with their eyes and their bodies.

He continued to thrust deep, retreating slowly until there was no controlling the pace. Their bodies dictated what they needed, their craving for one another spurring them faster as Max began to impale her deeply.

"Max," she whispered, still battling the emotion.

"Love me, Court. Right here, right now, just love me. That's all you need to do."

Courtney nodded, her head falling back against the tiled wall, eyes closing as she continued to scrape her fingers over his neck and jawline, loving the way he consumed her every sense.

When the pleasure became too much, her breaths rushing in and out of her lungs, she let her hands fall to his shoulders, clutching at him, digging her nails into his skin as she tried to pull him closer, wanting to take him completely inside her body so she'd never have to let him go.

He leaned down, his teeth nipping her earlobe, pleasure-pain jolting her to her core as he fucked her harder, deeper.

"You feel so good, love. Perfect. I could spend the rest of my life just like this. I want to feel your body squeeze me, taking all of me."

Courtney was panting, unable to hold back as he continued to mumble dirty words in her ear, sending her soaring higher, the tingling in her core igniting into an conflagration of sensation, ripping her into pieces as her heart pounded, reaching out to him in ways she knew she would never survive.

"Love me, Courtney," he commanded, his words vibrating through her. "Love me, baby. That's all I need. I fucking need you to love me."

Courtney cried out, her orgasm detonating, shredding her completely. "Max!"

"That's it," he whispered, his hips jerking roughly as he thrust deeper. Shallow and hard, he filled her until his body stilled, his lips crashing down on hers as he groaned into her mouth.

And Courtney knew right then that she would forever be in denial because not *loving him was no longer an option. It was too late for that. She'd fallen for him. Harder than she'd ever expected.*

"Max," Courtney whispered now, clutching his fingers. "You can't leave me. I won't let you. I haven't had enough time with you." Her voice was strangled, the words coming out in a desperate rush. "I love you, Max. I love you, and I can't let you go. You can't leave me. Do you understand me? You. Can't. Leave. Me."

The tears broke free again, and Courtney sobbed until her body ached. Until Leyton came into the room and pulled her into his arms, holding her close, his hand brushing down her hair. She hated falling apart, but the mere thought of losing Max…

She honestly didn't think she'd survive it.

Chapter Thirty-Eight

Trusting someone... What do you do when that's no longer possible?

Three days later
Tuesday

A knock sounded on the closed hospital room door, and Courtney looked up from her iPad. She'd been alternating between reading the news stories regarding Max's shooting and skimming her emails, answering those she could, ignoring others entirely.

Her eyes widened when she saw her mother and father standing there, waiting for her. Putting her tablet down on the table beside Max's bed, she got to her feet, kissed Max's forehead, and then slipped out into the hall.

"What're you doin' here?" she asked, glancing over to see Leyton watching them intently.

Elizabeth moved in, pulling Courtney into a tight hug before taking a step back and holding her shoulders. Her mother was studying her as though Courtney might fall apart at any second. She wasn't far off.

"How's he doin'?" Casper asked, seemingly ignoring the big man mentally documenting their every move.

"Better," she said when her mother released her, glancing over her shoulder and into the room where Max still remained unconscious. "The doctors think he'll wake up any time."

It'd been the greatest news she'd ever received when the doctors had finally agreed that he was improving. There was some swelling on his brain, and they claimed it was a good thing that he wasn't awake. He needed to heal, and this was the fastest way for him to do that.

Courtney just wanted to hear his voice, see his beautiful eyes, but she was taking each minute one at a time. She figured this was Max's way of teaching her some patience.

The thought made her smile, but she wiped it away immediately, turning back to face her parents.

"I got your message," she told her father.

"Let us buy you some lunch," Casper said. "We need to talk."

"I'm not leavin' him," she insisted quietly.

"We'll go to the cafeteria," Liz replied. "You'll call her if anything changes?" Her question was directed to Leyton.

"Yes, ma'am."

Courtney met Leyton's gaze and didn't move until he nodded, assuring her he would call her.

The three of them started down the hall, and she heard footsteps behind her, turned to see Dane following them. "Boss would kill me if I left you unprotected," he told her simply.

Courtney nodded. Security had been beefed up significantly. She didn't go anywhere without a protective detail, and never was Max left alone without at least one person—usually Leyton—guarding him. After what Angelica had done, Courtney understood, although she knew that the woman wasn't going to be a problem. Not for a while, anyway, considering Courtney and Leyton were keeping her stashed away until they decided what to do with her.

Quite frankly, Courtney wanted to put a bullet in her brain, but Leyton didn't think that was a good idea.

Yet.

They kept walking, making their way through the various hallways and buildings that made up the enormous hospital.

Once they'd made it down to the basement, where the cafeteria was, grabbed a couple of sandwiches and drinks, the three of them found a seat while Dane stood guard a few feet away. He wasn't even trying to hide who and what he was, despite the fact the hospital police were keeping close tabs on all of them.

"There's somethin' I need to tell you," Casper said gravely after she'd started picking at her sandwich.

Courtney met her father's gaze, surprised by the somber tone. He appeared almost apologetic.

"I understand," she told him. "I'm not upset that you called off the job." Her assignment, the one that required her to uncover information regarding the guns, drugs, and whatever the involvement was between the senator and Max, had officially been called off.

"It's not…" He took a deep breath, glanced at Liz, then back to her. "No, it's more than that."

Liz's hand slid around Casper's, squeezing it reassuringly while they both watched her.

These people were her parents, and she'd seen them in a variety of different situations. She'd seen them overly excited, desperately grieving, even trembling with anger, but never had she seen them look quite this uncomfortable.

"What's goin' on?" Courtney asked, pushing the sandwich away and giving them her full attention.

Casper inhaled deeply, then met her gaze. "I've done somethin' I'm not proud of, and unfortunately, I put you in the line of fire when I made the decision."

For a moment, Courtney thought her father was going to cry, but she knew that couldn't be real because he never cried. Never.

"When I first put you on this assignment"—he looked away—"to find more information on the Adorites, I did it for selfish reasons. It wasn't just a job."

Courtney's eyebrow lifted, her eyes narrowed as she processed his words.

"There isn't a client who wants information on the Adorites," he said quickly. "*I* want information. For my own personal reasons."

Liz touched Casper's arm.

"Before your mother came into my life, there was another woman. A girl, really. You know where my parents lived. Well, this girl was my next-door neighbor's daughter. They moved in when I was seventeen, a senior in high school. She was thirteen."

"She was a child," Courtney whispered, casting a disbelieving look at her mother, then back at her father.

"Exactly. But love doesn't understand age. And before you look at me like I'm the devil, you should know I never touched her. Never even kissed her. But I still loved her, or thought I did, anyway. When I turned eighteen, I went off to the military, always intending to come back, to find her waiting for me as she'd promised.

"Anyway, I thought I would end up married to her one day. But I gave myself to the Marines, met your mother, realized that I hadn't even understood what true love really was until her."

Casper cast a look at Liz, his love for her evident on his face.

"What's your point?" Courtney asked, knowing there had to be one in there somewhere.

"That girl's name was Genny," Casper explained. "Genevieve Jenkins."

Courtney's gasp caught Dane's attention, but she waved him off. "Are you saying…?"

"Yes," Casper said roughly. "And she's the reason I sent you on that assignment in the beginning. I needed to confirm my suspicions."

"Which were?"

"That Genny had been forced into marrying Samuel Adorite, that she'd been a payment for a debt."

Courtney thought back to all the things she knew about Genevieve. The woman wasn't happy; there was no pretending otherwise. She hadn't had much interaction with Max's parents over the last couple of years, but the few times she'd seen them together, she knew they didn't much care for one another.

"I used you, Courtney," Casper said softly. "And I'm not proud of that."

"Because you what? Loved her? What happened to the whole *best to move on, to forget the past* spiel you gave me?" Anger bubbled in her chest as she realized what he was telling her.

Her own father had used her, put her in this position.

"Did you know?" she asked her mother bluntly.

"Yes," Liz confirmed. "Casper and I talked. He doesn't hide anything from me, honey. You know that."

"And you were okay with that? With him trying to find this girl he claimed to be in love with?" Courtney couldn't believe they were having this conversation.

"Love doesn't always make sense," Liz explained, reaching for Courtney's hand. Before she could touch her, Courtney jerked away.

"Y'all are married. Why would you be okay with him wanting to find her?"

"When he told me his suspicions, I was curious, as well. If this girl had been forced into a world she didn't want to be in, I thought it noble that your father wanted to try and get her help."

"Help? You thought you could help?" Courtney laughed without mirth. "So what? It wasn't enough that you left one girl in the fire? You decided to push me there, too?" Courtney leaned forward, resentment burning in her chest. "And you thought I'd be able to get that information for you? Why? Why'd you pick me? Why not Hunter or Conner? Or even Trace?"

"Because they wouldn't have stood a chance," Casper said, sounding defeated. "I knew that Max would be taken with you."

"You pimped me out for your own gain?" she exclaimed, her voice shrill, bitterness simmering deep in her gut.

"It wasn't like that," Casper growled. "Never like that. I didn't know that you'd…"

"What? You didn't know that I'd fall in love with him?" she snapped.

Casper's face went white. "You're not—"

"Oh, but I am, *Dad.*" Pushing to her feet, she glared at her parents, fighting the tears that threatened. She couldn't believe he'd put her in that position, used her for something that seemed like a betrayal to his own family. And her mother… God, she couldn't believe her mother was sitting there defending his actions.

Without a word, Courtney spun around and marched out of the cafeteria. She didn't want to see her father right then. He'd betrayed her, hurt her, practically pushed her into this world, and she couldn't understand, couldn't fathom how any girl from his childhood would make him do such a thing.

She'd always thought of Casper as the noble one, the good man who'd go to any lengths to save those who needed to be saved, but this…?

Oh, God.

Dane came up beside her, keeping pace with her as she stomped up the stairs and then down the long, winding halls that would take her back to Max. He had the decency not to say anything, and she was grateful. As it was, she was ready to punch something, or someone, and the last person who deserved her wrath was Dane.

When she came to a stop in front of Max's door, she stared through the window at him, wondering if he knew this. If he knew that his mother and her father had been … what? Boyfriend and girlfriend nearly forty years ago? It even sounded absurd.

Taking a deep breath, she glanced over at Leyton and then went into the room, closing the door behind her. For now, she needed to be alone, and the only person she wanted to be with was unconscious and clinging to life.

Funny how, when she needed him most, he was close enough to touch but still not completely available to her. Much as their relationship had always been.

Chapter Thirty-Nine

Let her live … doesn't seem fair.

Two days later
Thursday

Courtney entered the small, dark room when Leyton opened the door for her, stepping inside and then nodding for him to close it behind her.

"Where's Max?"

Courtney glared at the bitch handcuffed to the bed of the safe house where they'd stashed her while they waited for Max to wake up, to tell them what to do with her. Not that she didn't have her own ideas about what to do with Angelica, but Leyton had convinced her that Max deserved to make that decision.

Tamping down the rage that consumed her just by looking at Angelica, Courtney said, "Still in the hospital. Still unconscious, thanks to you."

"Is he gonna…?"

"Is he gonna *what*, Angelica? Live? Die? Which would you prefer?" Courtney spat, fury consuming her once again.

"It shouldn't have happened," Angelica said, looking away from Courtney.

"A little late to feel remorse, don't you think?"

"I loved him," Angelica barked, her head snapping back around, her blue eyes slamming into Courtney's.

"Is that right? Sorry, I forgot that one way to show that is to *shoot the man in the fucking head*!" she yelled, hating that Angelica had the ability to make her so angry.

Then again, she'd been in a constant state of rage ever since her father had told her about what he'd done. She couldn't help but think that if he'd have minded his own business, stayed out of the Adorites' business, they wouldn't be here. Max probably wouldn't be in a coma and … and Courtney wouldn't be staring at the woman responsible for putting him there, ready to strangle her with her bare hands.

"When are you gonna let me go?" Angelica asked.

"Who says I am?" she questioned, moving to the window and pulling the curtains back and peering outside.

"If you were gonna kill me, you'd have done it by now," Angelica said with a heavy sigh.

"True," Courtney stated, dropping the curtain and moving toward Angelica. "I'll be meetin' with your grandfather. Once he hands over the land and the deal is done, I'll give you back."

Angelica's eyes widened.

"And yes, you'll spend the rest of your life watchin' your back, never knowin' if you'll be eating a bullet when you come out of the store, or if someone'll be waiting to pull every single one of your fingernails off before slicing you into little pieces. You'll never feel safe again, and I'll make damn sure of that."

The two of them stared at one another momentarily, the hatred they felt for one another palpable in the small room.

"You only *think* he loves you," Angelica snarled. "But if that were the case, why did he spend night after night fucking me when you were gone? Explain that one."

Without thinking, Courtney pulled her gun from the holster on her hip, released the safety, and pressed it against Angelica's forehead, smiling when Angelica's smug expression was replaced with sheer terror.

"He's a man," Courtney said through gritted teeth. "They sometimes make rash decisions. But tell me this, when he was fucking you, did he look you in the eye? Or did he take you from behind? Did you ever wonder if he was pretending you were me? Huh? *Explain that one.*" Courtney pushed the gun against Angelica's face.

She received all the answers she needed when Angelica looked away. The mere thought of Max with another woman made her want to pull the trigger, to send Angelica to hell, where she belonged, but she managed to refrain.

Barely.

"That's what I thought." Holstering her weapon, Courtney headed for the door. "I'll make sure your grandfather knows you're healin' nicely," she said as she opened the door.

Stepping into the hall, Courtney turned to look back at the woman. "Oh, and one more thing … I might be showin' you some mercy by lettin' you go, but just remember, you made your own bed. And yes, I know about Marcus Alvarez. I'm thinkin' it might be time to have a little chat with him."

Leaving her to chew on that, Courtney slammed the door harder than she had intended and met Leyton in the hallway.

"I need Artemis's phone number," she told him. "I'm ready to set up a meeting. We'll get him to release the land to Max and let her go. It's the only deal he'll get. No money will exchange hands. I don't think she'll be causin' any more problems for him in the future."

Leyton pulled her up short, turning her to face him.

"You don't have to do this," he told her.

"Yes, I do," she assured him, meeting his gaze head on. "I love him, Leyton. He will come back to me, and I will never let him go again. Until then, I'll be handlin' his affairs, keepin' things runnin' until he can."

"And your father? The assignment?"

"It's over," she told him quickly. "Turns out, there never was a client."

Leyton's expression reflected his curiosity. Courtney couldn't tell him the details, not until she was able to tell Max. As much as Max trusted Leyton, Courtney knew better than to go behind his back. If she was going to commit herself to him, she had to do it right. It wouldn't be easy to earn Max's trust, considering who she was and all that they'd been through.

Good thing Courtney was used to working for what she wanted most.

And she'd never wanted anything or anyone as much as she wanted Max. Enough that she was willing to cross that line, the one she'd never be able to cross back over once both feet were firmly in place.

"I'll set up the meeting," Leyton told her, opening the front door, where two armed men were waiting for them.

"I need to talk to Ashlynn," Courtney said. "She and I have some work to do."

He nodded, taking her arm and leading her to the armored Escalade in the driveway.

"I'll call her, too," Leyton stated, his approving smirk not going unnoticed.

Chapter Forty

Loyalty over love ... not an easy choice.

After stopping by the hospital for a few minutes while Courtney visited with Max, Leyton did her bidding, contacting the senator and setting up a meeting for two weeks out. The man seemed overly anxious, which was why Leyton had decided to hold him off for a little while. He fucking deserved to wait after what Angelica had done.

Hell, it was a wonder the bitch was still alive, but he had to thank Courtney's rational decision making for that. They'd both been tempted to put a bullet in her head more than once. If it weren't for the fact he was trying to keep the peace until Max recovered, he'd have capped her the first time he'd gone to visit her in that safe house. He got the feeling Courtney wanted to, as well, but Max's woman was proving to be significantly more sensible than he'd ever given her credit for.

Now, as the Escalade pulled into Max's garage, the bulletproof door closing behind them, he listened to the phone ring, waiting for Ashlynn to answer.

"What can I do you for?" Ashlynn asked, her voice reflecting a hint of a tease.

Leyton was glad to hear her sounding a little better than the last time he'd talked to her. Saturday night had been hell on them all, as had been the following days while they'd waited for some good news from the doctors regarding Max's condition. It seemed that no one had even breathed until they'd been told that his condition had been upgraded from critical to stable.

"Your future sister-in-law would like to meet with you," he said, grinning when Courtney glared at him before she hopped out of the vehicle and went inside, leaving him alone.

"Does she know you've married her off already?" Ashlynn chuckled. "Not that it's a bad thing, mind you. She's proving herself nicely."

"That she is," Leyton said, going on to tell Ashlynn about the visit to the safe house.

"Someone needs to put that bitch out of her misery," Ashlynn said. "It's a good thing y'all are keeping her whereabouts a secret. I'd have put a bullet between her eyes by now."

"I know." Leyton loved listening to Ashlynn's voice. He'd harbored a slight obsession with Max's sister for quite some time. Only recently, and only once, had he given in to those urges. He knew better than to fuck with Ashlynn. She was as dangerous as Max, and she would be the first to say as much.

Didn't mean Leyton didn't crave her. He wanted to strip her naked and fuck her nine ways to Sunday, then start at the beginning and do it all again.

But Max had put a halt to that, and Ashlynn was loyal to her brother.

Not to mention, she had told Leyton that if anything had transpired between them, it would've only been temporary. As in one time.

Ashlynn wasn't known for her relationships with men. She had plenty of men trying to get in her pants, and she liked to make people believe she was far more promiscuous than she actually was. But she seemed to forget that Leyton knew her better than anyone else. He'd been around the longest, had protected her as much as he'd protected Max over the years.

And he would continue do so, even if it was from afar. Beating down the urges he had where she was concerned wasn't as easy as he would've liked, but it was necessary.

"When does she wanna meet?" Ashlynn questioned.

"Today. We're back at the house for now. If you can get here in the next couple of hours, she said she'd like to talk."

"I'll have Jase bring me," she said, referring to her head of security.

"Be careful," he said firmly. "I know Angelica is out of the picture, but with Max out for the time being, the danger is escalating."

"I know," she said softly. "We can trust her, right, Leyton?"

Leyton glanced over at the door where Courtney had disappeared a few minutes before. "Yes," he said affirmatively. "We can definitely trust her."

"I thought so, just wanted to make sure."

"So I can let her know you're comin'?"

Ashlynn's sexy chuckle made his dick harden. "I'm on my way. And let her know I look forward to talkin' to her, as well."

Leyton hung up the phone before he let his thoughts slip to places they shouldn't be. He couldn't have Ashlynn, regardless of how much he wanted her. Loyalty was the most important thing in Leyton's world. Considering Max was the only family he had, he wouldn't jeopardize that. No matter how hard it was to resist her.

Chapter Forty-One

Love... It's why we keep putting one foot in front of the other.

Two weeks later
Wednesday morning

"Good mornin', Ms. Kogan," Sal greeted when Courtney made her way back downstairs.

She'd come back to Max's house early enough to take a shower before her meeting with Artemis, leaving Max at the hospital with Dane and Rock. As each day passed, it was getting more and more difficult to leave him, although she knew that she had to keep moving forward while he was still unconscious. It didn't change the fact that she wanted him to open his eyes, and she wanted to be there when he did.

"Good mornin', Sal. Is Ashlynn here yet?" she asked, allowing him to fall into step with her as she headed to the kitchen for coffee.

For the last two weeks, Courtney's entire world had shifted on its axis. She'd spent every single night at the hospital with Max while Leyton or Dane took the day shift if she had something she needed to do. Although Max hadn't yet woken up, the doctors were holding out hope that he would, and Courtney was inclined to believe them. She wasn't giving up hope, either.

He *would* wake up; she merely wished it was sooner rather than later.

"She's on her way," Sal replied.

"And Leyton?"

"He's on the phone with Samuel. Said he'd meet you in Max's office."

"Perfect. Thank you."

"Ma'am, if you don't mind me sayin', you look … better."

She didn't feel better, but she smiled at him anyway. Since the night of the shooting, she'd gotten little sleep and fueled herself with Mountain Dew and whatever someone brought to her from the cafeteria at the hospital. She hadn't spent any time working out and had actually lost weight, which she didn't consider a good thing. Not like this.

Truth was, she wouldn't feel better until Max was awake and back at home where he belonged. But in the meantime, while he was still in a coma, Courtney had business to attend to.

Max's business.

A knock sounded on the front door, and Sal excused himself. He returned a moment later with Ashlynn in tow.

Without hesitation, Courtney walked over to Max's sister, hugging her tightly.

"How is he?" Ashlynn asked, her voice wary as she clutched Courtney.

"He's gonna wake up any minute," Courtney said cheerfully.

Ashlynn pulled back, a small smile on her lips.

"Dane's with him right now. He promised to call if anything changes."

Ashlynn nodded. "And we're still set to meet with Artemis?"

Courtney nodded, her gaze hardening as she looked back at Max's beautiful sister. "We are. He'll be here in"—Courtney glanced at her phone—"ten minutes if he knows what's good for him. Coffee?"

"Sure."

After pouring coffee into two mugs, Courtney handed one to Ashlynn and then led the other woman into Max's office.

Courtney had been running Max's business with Leyton's and Ashlynn's help. After a lengthy conversation with Leyton on the night Max had been shot, she'd learned that there were things that needed Max's immediate attention, and since he was currently decommissioned, she had no choice but to step in. Otherwise, Samuel would take over, and based on the impression Leyton had given her, confirmed by Ashlynn, that wouldn't be a good thing. Since Brent wasn't in any position to take over, although he would've been the next in line, Courtney had assured them she'd handle things, and Max would be back in power before they knew it.

Because she fully believed Max would wake up at any moment, she had agreed without an ounce of reluctance.

Not that it was easy.

Her brothers and RT were up in arms about her decision to move into Max's house temporarily. They had no idea that she was currently managing his entire world, and she had no intention of letting them know, either. She'd compartmentalized the information Casper had given her, unable to talk to anyone about it yet, so she didn't even have a stable argument. But they'd backed off somewhat, and she figured Casper had told them to.

She hadn't spoken with Casper since that day at the hospital. She'd ignored his calls and his texts. Until she was able to wrap her head around what he'd done, she didn't have anything to say to him. Courtney had decided that this war her father had waged with Max wouldn't ensue until Max was strong enough to fight back. Which also meant that everything she learned during the time she was helping out would be off limits to Sniper 1. Indefinitely.

As with any time she stepped into Max's office, Courtney struggled to breathe. She missed him. She wanted to talk to him, to feel his arms around her. Hell, she'd give anything to argue with him. It'd been too long, and the doctors had told her that there was still a chance he wouldn't remember anything when he did wake up. That was something she couldn't even fathom, so she refused to think about it.

"Mornin'," Leyton greeted, stepping into the room behind them and closing the door.

Courtney turned to look at him, noticing the way his eyes drifted over Ashlynn briefly. There was certainly something going on between those two, but Courtney didn't know what. They appeared to be trying to hide something, from each other or everyone else, she wasn't sure which. But it was something.

Leyton met Courtney's gaze as he pressed the transmitter in his ear and then nodded. "Artemis has arrived."

"Good," Courtney said, making her way around Max's desk and sitting down. "Have him frisked before he comes in."

Leyton smirked and nodded.

She inhaled deeply as she eased into Max's chair, taking in the scent of him that still filled the room. An ache started in her chest, and she attempted to push it back.

Peering up at Leyton, Courtney waited for his instruction.

"Artemis is gonna demand to know where Angelica is," Leyton told her as he moved closer.

"Of course he is," she replied. Not that she had any intention of telling him. The bitch was lucky to be alive. Hell, if Samuel had been allowed to know where she was, the woman would've been six feet under at this point.

"He'll be willin' to make a deal in order to get her back." Leyton nodded to the contract on the desk.

Which was the plan.

Courtney reread the first paragraph, then pushed it away. She knew what it said. It was the transfer of ownership for the land that the Adorites were seeking. More specifically, it was going to give them a route directly into and out of Mexico, not to mention a handful of border patrol agents who were already on Artemis's payroll. In return, Artemis would walk away from the Adorites, forget anything and everything he'd ever learned about them, and get his granddaughter back safely.

If he were to renege on the deal at any time, Angelica would go to prison for the rest of her life. If she lived that long.

A knock sounded on the office door, and Leyton moved around behind Courtney while Ashlynn took a seat across from her.

"Come in," Leyton called out.

The door opened, and Artemis walked in the room looking like death warmed over. His aging face was lined with worry, making him appear decades older than he probably was.

Not that Courtney gave a shit about his well-being. His granddaughter had attempted to kill Max. Shooting him in his own fucking driveway. The mere thought made her want to launch out of Max's chair and strangle the old bastard.

"Where is she?" Artemis asked, fire igniting in his eyes when he looked at Courtney.

"Have a seat, Mr. Winslow," Courtney said firmly, motioning for the chair across from her.

She heard Leyton shift, saw in her peripheral vision as his hand landed on the gun holstered at his side. Figuring what the hell, Courtney checked for hers, watching Artemis's face as she did.

"Sit down, Mr. Winslow!" Courtney snapped when the old man simply stared back at her with hatred in his gaze.

When he finally slipped into the chair, Courtney relaxed against the high back, watching him intently. "As you know, we've got a score to settle with you. We've got something that you want, and you've got something that Max wants."

"Max is in a coma. He doesn't *get* what he wants," Artemis snarled.

"See, that's where you're wrong. Until Max is fully recovered—which, mark my words, will happen—I'm seein' to his affairs. And that means that what Max wants, Max gets."

"Where's Samuel?" Artemis asked, glancing over at Ashlynn, then back to Courtney.

Courtney's phone rang, drawing her attention away from the man. Her hands shook as the screen lit up, Max's name flashing before her. Glancing back at Leyton, she saw his eyes widen. He nodded and Courtney hit the button on the screen.

"Hello?"

"Hey, love," Max croaked, his voice weak and strained. "I just called to listen to the meeting."

Goosebumps broke out over every inch of her skin. He was … awake.

He sounded frail but good. Courtney's heart threatened to explode; her belly churned with nerves as she soaked in the sound of his voice.

"Of course," she told him, hitting the button to put him on speaker and keeping herself together as she stared at Ashlynn, watching a tear slip down Max's sister's cheek.

Artemis's eyes widened. "Where's Samuel?" he repeated. "Clearly he should be handlin' this while Max is…" His words trailed off as he glanced down at the phone.

Courtney lifted her chin, straightened her back, and placed her elbows on the desk, pinning Artemis with a hardened stare. "You're lucky that I'm handlin' Max's affairs until he's home. We figured it was safer for your granddaughter if we kept Samuel in the dark about this one. If you wish to see Angelica alive, it's in your best interest not to reach out to him, either," Courtney explained sternly.

"How do I know she's not already dead?" Artemis asked, his eyes flying to all three faces in the room.

Leyton moved, laying his phone on the desk in front of Courtney, alongside hers. She reached forward, punched a button. After two rings, a gruff male voice answered with a grunt.

"Put her on the phone," Courtney commanded. "Her grandfather would like to speak to her."

Artemis leaned forward, but Leyton growled, forcing the man back into his seat.

"Grandpa? Please help me. Please, Grandpa," Angelica cried. "I want to come home. I don't want to be here anymore. Please."

"Angel? Are you—?" Artemis choked on his words. "Are you okay? Did they hurt you, honey?"

"I…uh… Grandpa? Please do what they want. Give 'em the land. Give 'em whatever the hell they want. I don't wanna go to prison."

"I will, Angel. You'll be home soon. Very soon."

A sob resounded through the phone, and Courtney disconnected the call.

"Now, shall we?" Pushing the paper toward Artemis, she once again leaned back in the chair, her eyes darting down to her phone as though that would allow her to see Max. As it was, she was ready to bolt, run out of the house, and get to the hospital. Swallowing hard, she remembered she still had business to conclude. "It's cut-and-dry. The land belongs to Max. You sign on the dotted line, and one week from today, Angelica will be returned to you in one piece."

"One week?"

"One week," she confirmed, frustration consuming her. "The deal goes through, she's back with you. You pull any bullshit—"

"Did you hurt her?" Artemis growled.

Courtney's face heated from her anger. Leaning forward, she glared at the old man. "Mr. Winslow, your granddaughter shot Max. Twice. Once in the chest, once in the head. He's clinging to life, and you ask whether or not we hurt *her*? What do *you* think?"

"If you laid one finger on—"

Courtney slammed her hand down on the desk, causing the phone to rattle and Ashlynn and Artemis to jump. "You're not in a position to offer threats, Mr. Winslow. Her gunshot wound was tended to. If you do what needs to be done, she's not gonna die, she's not gonna lose her leg. But if you don't sign that goddamn paper, all bets are off. I'll kill her myself!"

Leyton leaned forward, handing Artemis a pen. She watched as he scrawled his name on each of the pages, initialed where required. A few minutes later, Sal escorted him out of the room.

Courtney exhaled sharply as she pushed to her feet, snatching her phone from the desk.

"It's done, Max," she told him. "I'm on my way to you right now."

"Court?" he whispered softly.

"Yes?" she asked, her heart threatening to climb out of her throat.

"I love you."

"I love you, too," she cried, unable to hold back the sob. "I'll be right there."

Chapter Forty-Two

Awake … finally. Not that it changes anything. Yet.

The sound of Courtney's voice as she easily handled Artemis made Max's chest swell with pride. The woman never ceased to amaze him.

He'd woken a few minutes ago to Dane's ugly mug staring back at him, a wide grin splitting the other man's face when Max cleared his throat, trying to get his attention. Before he knew what was happening, the nurse was called in, and things got hectic for a few minutes as they explained to him what had happened, where he was, all the things they'd done to him.

Blah, blah, blah.

He hadn't heard a word they'd said as his brain fizzed from all the information, but he'd pretended to pay attention. They'd told him more than he cared to hear, but not what he wanted to know.

By the time he had croaked out his first words, he'd been anxious for answers.

"Where's Courtney?" he'd managed to force past his dry throat.

"Meetin' with Artemis," Dane had told him abruptly. "I'll get her on the phone right now."

Dane had already been dialing the phone, putting it on speaker, and setting it on the table that hovered over Max's lap.

The instant he had heard her voice, he'd felt light-headed.

According to the chatty nurse, he'd been in a coma for nineteen days, and Dane had told him that Leyton and Courtney were manning the fort, making sure things were taken care of until he came home. Not *if*, he noted. According to Dane, Courtney spent her nights at his side and her days running his business like a champ.

Max wanted to see her. He wanted her to tell him everything that had happened in her own words. It was all he could think about.

"Should I call anyone else while we wait for her?" Dane asked after he disconnected the call with Courtney.

"No," Max rasped. "I'll let Courtney make that decision."

"Yes, sir. Do you need anything?"

"Yes," Max said, peering up at Dane. "I need you to shut up."

Dane grinned again and relief filled his chest. He felt like he'd been run over by a train, perhaps two trains. But he was alive, and that was the only thing that mattered.

He glanced around the room, taking it all in. On the whiteboard on the wall was the nurse's name, a phone number, and a jumble of other shit he could hardly read from that distance, but then he saw it…

Max, if you wake up and I'm not here, I want you to know I love you. ~Courtney

For the first time in his adult life, he thought he just might break down and sob. She loved him.

"Sir? You okay?" Dane questioned.

Max nodded, not trusting his voice not to give him away as he continued to stare at her handwriting.

He must've dozed off, because the next thing he knew, Courtney was at his side, her cool fingers brushing over his cheek, her warm lips pressing against his.

"Max."

He forced his heavy eyelids open, smiling as he looked at her for the first time in what felt like a lifetime.

"I love you," he whispered.

Courtney smiled as a tear slipped down her cheek, lingering on her jaw for a moment before dropping to the blankets. "I love you, too."

He wanted to reach up and touch her, but he was too weak, too tired. He settled on gazing at her, memorizing her every feature.

Neither of them said anything as they stared back at one another for long minutes, until Max could no longer keep his eyes open. When he finally gave in to sleep, as he drifted off into nothingness, he heard Courtney's voice.

"I'm not leavin' your side again. I'll be here until you're ready to go home, Max."

He only hoped she intended to go with him, because he knew there was no way he could do this without her.

He didn't want to.

Chapter Forty-Three

Home … right where he wanted to be.

Three weeks later

"It's about damn time you're up and movin' around. Lazy bastard."

Max rotated at the sound of his brother's voice, grinning. "Me? You're the one sittin' on your ass."

"Damn right I am," Aidan retorted with a gruff laugh. "My legs gave out waitin' on your old ass."

Max chuckled, the move making his chest hurt.

His wince of pain didn't stop Aidan from coming over and hugging him as though he were made of glass and would shatter at any moment.

Max had been out of the hospital for less than twenty-four hours, had just spent the first night in his own bed after nearly an entire month flat on his back in the damn hospital. Hell, if his mother had anything to say about it, he'd still be in there, enduring the wicked wrath of that physical therapist, but luckily, Courtney had taken charge, ensuring Max was taken care of in every way. And now he was home, feeling significantly stronger, yet still working on his stamina.

"You need a haircut," Max told his younger brother as he ventured into the kitchen.

"Why? You wanna borrow some?"

Max laughed. His head had been shaved for the surgery when the bullet had grazed his skull. Luckily, it'd been minor, as minor as head shots could be, anyway. As for the slug he'd taken to the chest … that one had been a different story. The bullet had missed his heart, but it had punctured his lung. Had it not been for Leyton's quick thinking that night, Max likely would've died.

But what most of them didn't know, before the bullets had hit him, Max had already had a reason to live. Courtney. As far as he was concerned, leaving her had never been an option. And according to her, he'd taken his own sweet time coming back to her in order to relay that information.

"Mornin', sir," Walter greeted as soon as Max stepped into the overly bright room.

"Mornin'," he replied.

Aidan maneuvered onto a barstool while Max eased into a chair, both of them watching as Walter moved efficiently around the kitchen, preparing food.

"Is Miss Kogan joinin' you?" Walter questioned.

"She's in the shower," Max told him.

"And you're down here?" Aidan snorted. "Damn. I think that head tap might've done more damage than they thought."

Max grinned at Aidan, taking him in. His younger brother looked good. Not quite as pissed off as he usually was, although Max did notice the storm clouds brewing in Aidan's eyes. Seemed those never disappeared completely.

Aidan wasn't Max's biological brother, and that was apparent in his appearance. While Max and the others had dark hair and olive skin, Aidan was blond, brown-eyed, and tan. Samuel and Genevieve had adopted Aidan when he was just a few weeks old. The story behind that had never been revealed to any of them, which Max figured was part of the reason for Aidan's anger.

Ashlynn had been only a month old when Aidan had come into their lives, making the two of them practically twins if it weren't for the fact they didn't come from the same parents. But for all intents and purposes, Aidan was as much blood as anyone could be. At least as far as they were all concerned.

"Vic's on his way over. So is Brent," Aidan told him, referring to his other brothers.

Max nodded. He'd seen Victor and Brent and both of his sisters while he'd been in the hospital. They'd hovered over him like a bunch of fucking babysitters, making sure he did what he was supposed to do, when he was supposed to do it. All while he ordered them to leave him alone.

They never did listen. But that wasn't unusual.

"Where's Madison?" Max asked, referring to his baby sister.

"She's with Ashlynn. They're takin' care of somethin' for Courtney. Leyton's with them."

Max knew that meant they were handling business. From what he'd gathered from Courtney, Leyton had been stoic during the entire ordeal, making sure everything was managed effectively, all the meetings were kept, the clubs were maintained, the deals were completed. According to Leyton, Courtney had been the one keeping them all together. She'd run his world as though she'd been born into it.

He was still torn about that, not sure how he felt about Courtney knowing so much. When he'd regained some semblance of his strength, he'd looked to Leyton for reassurance. He knew Courtney was no longer on assignment, no longer working for Sniper 1 Security; however, she was still loyal to her family.

Something had happened, though, between her and her father, and Max had an idea what that was, but he'd yet to broach the subject with Courtney. He figured when she was ready to talk to him about it, she'd come to him.

Leyton had told him he had nothing to worry about. Courtney had been the one to go to Leyton, told him that she would be handling Max's affairs until he was back on his feet. She'd never doubted that he would live, spent the first few days after he'd been shot in the hospital with him, never leaving his side.

Hell, she'd single-handedly brought Artemis to his knees, forcing his hand after they'd hidden Angelica away, letting her heal from the gunshot wound Leyton had inflicted on her after she'd shot Max. Had it been Max's decision, Angelica would've been dead, but as it was, Courtney had ensured the woman's life was forever altered.

Then again, when it came to Marcus Alvarez and Angelica's involvement with him, Max had to wonder if she'd end up dead anyway. He hadn't yet spoken with the man, needing to gain back more of his strength before he took that one on, but he fully intended to.

"Hey, Aidan. You're here."

Max heard Courtney's voice before he saw her. He looked up to see her heading toward his brother, her smile widening when she looked over at Max. The love that shone in her eyes made him instantly stronger. She was the reason he was healing so fast. She gave him the strength to push forward even when the pain was vicious, threatening to suck the life right out of him. He'd kicked the pills, not willing to give in to a weakness. He'd seen what that shit did to people, and he wasn't a fucking idiot.

"There she is." Aidan grinned stupidly, hugging her back.

Courtney walked over, kissed Max quickly on the lips, and then worked her way to the refrigerator, chatting with Walter and helping him to get things together.

Max felt as though he were in a dream, watching as the woman he loved moved around his kitchen easily, interacting with his brother. She talked to Aidan and Walter, laughing and joking with them. And when Vic and Brent arrived, she talked to them, too, after hugging them both.

"She's different now."

Max jerked his head at the sound of Leyton's voice. The chair scraped on the hardwood as Leyton took a seat beside him.

"How so?" he asked, his gaze returning to Courtney as she greeted Ashlynn and Madison.

"I can't put my finger on it."

"Good or bad?"

Leyton cocked his head to the side. "Is there anything good in our world?"

Yeah, Max thought to himself. *Her.* She was the good in his world.

"She's a natural," Leyton said. "And I'll be honest, I'm not sure I've ever met anyone as loyal to you as she is."

That didn't mean she wouldn't turn on him, Max knew. They came from different worlds, and she'd been thrust into his, living it daily. He figured once she felt the sun on her face again, realized how dark it was with him, she'd bolt.

But as he watched her face light up again, he chose to ignore that fear.

"Come eat," Courtney announced.

Getting to his feet was easier than it'd been for weeks, but the tightness was still there, a hint of pain stealing his breath. Not wanting to show weakness, Max masked his expression and headed to the dining room with the others.

Taking his seat at the head of the table, he watched his brothers and sisters, smiled at Courtney, and kept his eye on Leyton, making sure the man didn't so much as wink at Ashlynn.

"So…" Victor said between bites. "Care to tell us what really went down?"

They'd all agreed not to share the details of the shooting until he was out of the hospital and Angelica was out of the picture. He knew his brothers would want revenge, and likely his sisters, too, but Max needed for that part of his life to be over. Getting Angelica out of the picture was a priority for moving on with his life.

Max nodded to Leyton.

Leyton cleared his throat, then relayed the details of the night of the shooting. Max still had a difficult time hearing it, knowing that his life had nearly been ended.

When that part of the story was concluded, Brent spoke up.

"While you were out of it, Samuel called a meeting."

That got Max's attention.

"He met with all of us," Brent continued.

"Not me, he didn't," Ashlynn said harshly. "Why the fuck didn't I know about this?"

Brent cast a quick glance at Victor as though they were trying to decide who would talk.

Victor was the one who spoke up. "Samuel wanted you on the outside. Said you were in too deep with Courtney."

"What the fuck?" Ashlynn reacted angrily, slamming her fork down on her plate.

"Let him speak," Max said, his voice still not as strong as he'd wanted it to be.

"Samuel confided in us, did his level best to convince us that Courtney was the enemy."

Max reached for her hand, needing to feel her touch.

"It was more of a vent session, really," Madison added. "He rambled on and on about nonsense. Wanted us to corner her, try to get some information from her."

"What information?" Courtney inquired.

"To be honest," Brent said with a grin, "I don't fuckin' know. Like Mad said, he was ramblin'. Somethin' about the past bein' the past, live and let live, movin' on. That sort of nonsense."

Max glanced at Courtney. When she met his gaze, he knew that she knew.

She sighed heavily, then put down her fork and picked up her coffee. "There's a story behind that one."

All eyes turned to her, and Max squeezed her hand gently. It was her story to tell, although his brothers and sisters might think otherwise.

"I'll tell you," Courtney said, addressing them all. "But I'm warnin' you, I don't think you'll like what you hear."

Knowing she didn't know the other side of that story—Samuel's side—Max interrupted. "Can I?"

Courtney nodded at him, then glanced down at the table.

"Our paths didn't cross just because of who we are and what we do. Courtney wasn't sent here simply to dig into our organization. There was a deeper reason behind it, one that we could've never guessed." Max went on to relay the story as his father had told it, in all its gory detail.

By the time he was finished, Ashlynn and Madison were teary-eyed while Brent and Victor looked as though they were ready to tear Samuel's head off.

"My father was in love with Genny when he was younger," Courtney relayed. "Of course, he could've never known what would happen to her when he went off to the military. Apparently, though, he'd never let it go. Unbeknownst to me, he wanted more detail, wanted to know specifically how Genny was doing."

"But you weren't looking into her," Leyton said simply.

"No, I wasn't," Courtney confirmed. "I had no idea."

Victor sat up straight and narrowed his eyes at Courtney. "Tell us this…"

Max felt her hand tense beneath his.

"How much did you learn?"

"Enough," Courtney said, her eyes darting from each person at the table. "Enough to do some damage, and that was before I helped out while Max was in the hospital."

"So why didn't you share that information?" Brent questioned.

Courtney didn't respond right away, and Max squeezed her hand. He knew why. The same reason she'd vacated her own life to take over his while he'd been in the hospital. The same reason she came back time after time.

"I love him," she finally said. "I've always loved him."

"So you protected him?" Madison asked.

"Not necessarily," Courtney retorted. "I just didn't feel it necessary to divulge the information I had. I didn't feel as though anyone needed to know."

"You pretended not to know anything," Ashlynn said. It wasn't a question.

"Correct."

"So what happens now?" Victor asked. "Clearly Samuel is up in arms. Doesn't like that Courtney's involved, and if her father is really trying to save Genny, then it makes sense."

"Nothing happens now," Max stated. "We get back to normal. Run the businesses the way they were meant to be run."

"And if Samuel interferes?" Brent asked.

"Then we'll deal with it when the time comes," Max stated firmly. "By doing whatever is necessary."

Part of him hoped it never came to that, but Max would never underestimate his own father.

It would likely end up getting him killed if he did.

Chapter Forty-Four

Life as they knew it...
Yeah, that's over now.

After breakfast was finished and the dishes taken care of, Courtney helped Max get settled in his office before going outside to call her father. Casper had left her several messages, those messages increasing in volume in the last few days, and she knew that avoiding him forever wasn't an option. Now that Max was home, she felt a little safer calling him. As though talking to Casper wasn't like a betrayal to Max.

Especially since it was clear Max had known what had happened. She'd been appalled at the story he'd relayed, about the callous way Samuel had spoken about Genevieve. Their mother had never been a person to Samuel. She'd been a payment, something he owned. The thought still gave her chills.

"Baby girl," Casper greeted on the third ring. "Where are you?"

"Not now, Dad," she told him. "I just wanted to call and check in."

"I heard he's out of the hospital," Casper stated gruffly. "So I take it he lived."

"Don't," she hissed, anger slicing through her.

Silence descended, and Courtney wished she'd have resisted the urge to call. Too much had happened, and she'd managed to separate herself from her family for this very reason. They wouldn't understand why she'd turned her back on doing the right thing and ended up on the other side. Hell, sometimes she didn't understand.

But she did love Max. And as the story always went, love was love. That was the simplest and most complicated definition. It couldn't be defined by gender, age, religion, or class. And in Courtney and Max's case, it couldn't be defined by morality, either.

"We need you back at work, Court. The assignment is over."

"There never *was* an assignment," she snarled, lowering her voice. "Don't forget, this was all you."

"Court…"

"No, Dad. I don't wanna hear it. You've said what you needed to say. And when I'm ready to talk, I'll come to you."

"You can't hate me forever," he retorted.

"I don't hate you," she retorted. Lowering her voice, she continued, "I could never hate you. But I'm … angry. You used me. You *hurt* me."

Silence fell around her, and Courtney was tempted to hang up.

"How is she?" Casper finally asked.

"Oh, my God. I can't believe you're askin' me that."

Casper didn't respond.

Courtney stared out into the yard, trying to calm herself.

"She's not happy," she finally admitted. "But I think you knew that."

Casper grunted.

"But it isn't your place to interfere in their life," she told him frankly. "The decisions they make are theirs to deal with. You can't interfere just because you don't understand them."

"He forced her to marry him," Casper growled.

"And how is that any of your business?" she replied. "They have children together. They've survived forty years without you stickin' your nose in their business. Why now? Why did you have to do this now?"

"There are people in this world who you never forget," Casper replied quietly. "You wonder how they are, what they're doing. Not knowing… You're right, it's been a long time, but Genny's been on my mind. I can't explain why, exactly. I just needed to know that the life she's leading is the one she wants."

"Dad! That's not your place. You're not her white knight. Do you not get that?"

"Why are you still there?" he asked, ignoring her question and tossing out his own. "What is it that you're tryin' to do? Get intel?"

"You know it's not like that, Dad," she said softly. "I… I'm not his enemy anymore."

"So, what? You're his partner now? His business associate? You're gonna get yourself killed."

"I'm not involved in Max's affairs. He doesn't let me that close." It was a lie, but one she intended to maintain for the time being. "And he'll keep me safe. You of all people should understand that."

"You love him."

It wasn't a question. Her father already knew, as did the rest of her family, and she was no longer willing to deny it. Only once in all the time Max had been in the hospital had she thought about going to her parents despite their betrayal. But she hadn't. Instead, she'd called Marissa. Courtney had broken down, desperate for someone to make things better, for someone to save Max, because the thought of moving through life without him had become unbearable. Her best friend had been there for her, supporting her and promising she always would.

But through it all, Courtney had still felt alone. She'd felt as though she had abandoned her family, let them down, even though technically it was the other way around. Her father had thrown her to the wolves, used her because he felt guilty. And she had no one to talk to about it. She couldn't even talk with Marissa about it, couldn't share her innermost fears with her best friend, because despite Marissa's insistence to the contrary, she wouldn't understand. Not to mention, Marissa was married to Courtney's brother.

Some of the things Courtney had done over the last two months, some of the things she'd seen... There were days she wondered how she would live with herself as the darkness continued to grow inside her.

"Baby girl, we want you to come home," Casper said softly. "It won't be easy, but it's the right thing to do."

"I'm not leavin' him, Dad."

"So, what? You plan to stay with him forever? Then what? One day I'll be assignin' someone to sneak their way into *your* world? To find dirt that'll help put you away? Is that what you want, Courtney?"

Courtney closed her eyes and took a deep breath. "Dad, you always told me that sometimes we had to do things that didn't make sense to everyone else."

Casper didn't respond, but she could practically feel his anger. And his guilt. She knew him, knew he was taking responsibility for her actions because he'd sent her into this situation. But he wasn't entirely at fault. He'd set it in motion, sure, but the rest… It was all on her.

And until she knew which path was the right one—for her—she had to stay the course.

"I've gotta go, Dad. Love you."

Without waiting for him to respond, Courtney hung up the phone and rested her arms on the railing around the veranda.

"Are you okay?"

Spinning around, she came face-to-face with Max standing just a few feet away. Her hand landed over her heart as the damn thing threatened to come out of her chest.

Max moved closer, close enough for her to inhale his intoxicating scent, to get lost in the warmth of his body.

"You heard that?" she asked.

"I did," he told her, pulling her against him, allowing her to rest her face on his chest. She was careful not to touch the still-healing wound. "I won't lie to you," Max said, "I need you. Not to take care of me. I *need* you."

Pulling back and looking up into his face, she told him the truth. "I don't know how long I can do this."

"This?" he asked.

"Us," she answered softly. "I love you, I can't deny that. I know I shouldn't, but I do. It's ruining me, making me into someone I don't recognize, someone I don't want to be. But I can't change how I feel about you."

Max watched her but didn't say anything.

"How long did you know?" she asked, the words suddenly out of her mouth before she could call them back.

Max's eyebrow lifted slightly, but he didn't ask what she was referring to.

"When did Samuel tell you about my father and Genevieve?"

He sighed, releasing her from his hold and moving over to the railing. "It was the same weekend I showed you the penthouse for the first time."

Courtney mentally traveled back in time, trying to recall what'd happened.

"After you left that night, I didn't come home, and my father automatically assumed you and I had been together. He broke the disturbing news to me then."

Disturbing? It was more than disturbing.

Turning to face her, Max gripped the railing. "Without censoring his true feelings, Samuel told me the story, about how Genevieve's father had been in debt, needed a way out. My grandfather loaned him the money, and when he couldn't repay it, Samuel was sent to retrieve it. Her father offered his thirteen-year-old daughter as payment."

She didn't move a muscle. He'd relayed the same information to his brothers and sisters, but it was as though she were hearing it for the first time. It sickened her all over again.

"Apparently, the fact that your father and my mother were childhood sweethearts isn't something Samuel's dealing with. At least not well, anyway."

"Do they love each other? Your parents?" she asked, already knowing the answer.

"No," he said quickly. "But she won't leave him."

"Because he'd kill her?" Courtney inquired.

"I wouldn't doubt that he would, but that's not why she stays. At least I don't think so."

"Then why? Why would she stay with him?"

"Loyalty. Sometimes it's the warped thoughts that drive us to do things we wouldn't normally do. Kind of like your father's need to rescue her."

"I still don't understand why he'd do it."

"It no longer matters," Max told her. "I confronted Casper at your brother's wedding. Told him to back off because I loved you. Because I wasn't willing to stay away from you any longer."

How had she not known about that? Casper had never told her that.

Max pushed off the rail and came to stand in front of her. "I know it's hard to understand why he'd do that to you, but I'm not sorry he did," he told her, his hands cupping her face. "He brought you to me, gave me something to live for." Max's lips brushed hers lightly. "I love you, Courtney. And I'm selfish. I'm not gonna let you go."

Courtney knew that was the truth. He wouldn't willingly let her go, and for now, she was okay with that. From here on out, they would figure out how to make this work, or they'd have to agree that it wouldn't. Either way, she wasn't running anymore.

"I need to rest," he told her softly. "Come upstairs with me."

Courtney smiled. "I know you, Max. If I come upstairs with you, you won't get any rest."

"I'm okay with that." His smile hit her right in the chest.

Taking his hand, she led him inside.

Chapter Forty-Five

This side of Max...
Yes, this she could deal with.

One month later

Courtney stood in the shadows, watching the people who'd come out to Devil's Playground for the evening. From where she stood, she could see Leyton eyeing the ever-growing crowd, making his rounds. Near the doors that led up to Max's office, Rock looked very much as his name implied. Dane was at the front entrance behind her, keeping an eye on the newcomers, while Darius played the role of bouncer at the door.

She'd arrived earlier in the day with Max and their security detail but had left him in his office while she'd gone to the penthouse for a bit. They'd resorted to staying at the penthouse more and more these days, especially on the weekends, mainly to stay off his father's radar. Samuel had gone into a rage when Max had informed him that she was there to stay.

Not that Courtney blamed him, considering how she'd been thrust into their world by her own father, who'd thought he'd been doing a good deed, trying to save Genevieve from whatever he believed she needed to be saved from. Samuel didn't seem to be able to overlook that fact, though, which worried both Max and Leyton. In turn, it made her a little leery of the man. However, when she'd tried telling Casper that he might want to watch his own back, he'd shrugged it off, more worried about her than anything.

Strong hands landed on her hips, pulling her up against a hard body, and Courtney instantly melted into him, knowing exactly who was behind her. Considering he was still breathing, it could only be one man. Anyone else who'd dared to touch her like that would've been dead on the floor from multiple bullets.

"You look lonely," Max said against her ear, loud enough that she could hear him over the thumping bass.

"Do I?" she asked, tilting her head to the side when his lips met her sensitive skin.

That was one thing she'd noticed about Max since the shooting. Or more accurately, since he'd regained enough of his strength and stamina to keep up with her. He was feisty. Much more so than before. She'd also noticed that he didn't seem to have any qualms about where they had sex these days. Public sex had become a fascination of his recently, and Courtney couldn't say she was bothered by it. The man knew how to keep things interesting, that was for sure.

"What're you wearin' beneath this skirt?" he asked, his teeth nipping her earlobe.

"Why don't you find out for yourself," she dared him.

Max's hand trailed down her thigh, then ventured back up, beneath the hem of her short skirt.

"Damn," he growled at the same time she moaned.

Nope, she wasn't wearing anything beneath the skirt. Just for him.

"Put your hands on the rail," he instructed.

Courtney reached forward and gripped the metal bar that separated them from the dance floor. People were dancing and grinding against one another less than three feet away. The only privacy they had was the shadow that fell on that particular area, but it wasn't enough to keep them hidden if someone cared enough to watch.

Using his fingers, he teased her ruthlessly for several minutes, pressing her clit lightly, then sliding his finger lower, dipping inside. Repeating the process over and over until she was breathing hard, desperate for more. The way he held her, she couldn't move easily, couldn't get him to go deeper with his finger, so she took what he offered. Then his fingers disappeared altogether.

Max's warm hands gripped her hips beneath her skirt. He forced her legs apart with his foot, and the next thing she knew, his cock was sliding into her from behind. One muscular arm banded around her waist, holding her against him as he leaned forward, his mouth against her ear.

"You're wet for me. You like this, don't you? You like when I take you like this? Wherever and whenever I want."

Knowing he wouldn't hear her over the thunderous music, she nodded, shifting her hips backward, taking more of his cock deeper into her body.

"You wouldn't even care if they all turned around and watched, would you?"

Courtney shook her head. At the moment, she didn't give a shit about anything or anyone. Max filling her was the only thing she could focus on.

"You know what they'd see if they turned around?" he mumbled against her ear, pulling back and slamming into her. "They'd see me owning your body, claiming you, making you mine."

Courtney turned her head, her lips meeting his cheek. "Always yours."

Max drove into her over and over, his mouth brushing hers briefly. When his lips trailed over her jaw, she glanced out into the crowd, noticing there were a couple of people watching them. A sexy redhead was grinding against a tall blond man behind her. He was holding the woman the same way Max was holding Courtney, but unlike her and Max, the other couple's clothes hindered their ability to go any further.

"You like them watching you?" Max's warm breath caressed her ear, his cock tunneling in and out of her at a maddeningly slow pace. "Knowing that I've got my cock buried in your sweet pussy though they can't actually see. It turns you on, doesn't it?"

Courtney nodded.

Max released her body and put his hands over hers, forcing her to lean forward. He then began to drive himself deep, igniting nerve endings, making her knees weak and her body burn. Clenching her inner muscles, Courtney pushed her hips back against him, forcing him deeper until he was impaling her roughly, fucking her hard while she kept her eyes on the couple still watching them.

There was no disguising what they were doing. It was clear by the way his hips thrust forward that Max was fucking her, but Courtney didn't care. She honestly didn't care who watched.

When her orgasm crested, she tossed her head back against his shoulder and cried out, the sound muffled by the music and the conversation. Max's body stilled, lodged deep inside her. She felt his dick pulse as he came, his hands gripping hers tightly while he pressed his cheek against hers.

With the show over, the couple turned away and slipped into the crowd, causing Courtney to smile.

Yeah, she definitely liked this new side of Max.

A lot.

Chapter Forty-Six

Some things are unforgivable.

Max returned to the penthouse with Courtney after their little episode in the club. He'd nearly taken her again in the elevator on the way up, finding it damn difficult to keep his hands off her these days.

Maybe it was the near-death experience, dealing with his own mortality, or simply because she was finally his… He didn't know what it was, but he found her so damn irresistible. And that was saying something considering he'd always been drawn to her.

While he poured two fingers of whiskey into a glass, Courtney kissed him lightly. "I'm gonna take a bath."

He smiled at her, noticing the invitation in her white-gray eyes.

"I've got somethin' to deal with," he informed her, hating that he couldn't join her.

She nodded, then smiled as she left him standing there watching the seductive sway of her hips.

Before he could act on the lust that had reignited in his veins, there was a knock on the door. With drink in hand, he went to the door, opening it and allowing Leyton to come inside.

"Drink?" he offered.

"Sure," Leyton said, making his way to the sofa and dropping down on it.

Max poured Leyton's drink and handed the glass over before moving to the sofa across from him.

"How'd it go?" Max inquired.

"The deal's done. Guns were delivered."

They'd been expecting the first shipment via the new channel they'd established after taking possession of the land that Artemis had handed over. Max had partially expected things to go south, so he was happy to hear they hadn't. It had been in Artemis's best interest that this shit run smoothly.

"And my father?" Max asked, watching Leyton closely.

Leyton took a long swallow and then glanced out the window, frowning. "He's entertaining a couple of people."

Max drained his glass and leaned forward, placing it on the table. "That's a problem."

"I know," Leyton confirmed, meeting his gaze once again.

"What do you think I should do about it?" Max asked, seeking his friend's input.

Leyton crossed one ankle over the opposite knee. "I wish it could be different," Leyton said grimly, meeting his gaze. "Unfortunately, your father's become a liability."

"He's become more than that," Max told him firmly.

"If you want to protect her, you don't have a choice," Leyton said, confirming what Max had already determined. "Even if he doesn't go through with it now, there's always a chance he'll try again. And next time, we may not be notified ahead of time."

"But he's still in the talking phase?"

"Seems that way. We'll know more in a few hours after the meeting takes place."

Max got to his feet and moved to the windows. He'd never thought his life would come to this. Never thought his own father would turn on him, but it appeared Samuel was heading down a path that he would never come back from.

"Does she know yet?" Leyton questioned.

"Not yet. I'd planned to tell her tonight."

"You need to. Despite the loose ends she still has with her family, Courtney's in this with you, Max. She loves you."

"And I love her," he muttered. "She's my life, my very reason for breathing."

"She'll understand," Leyton told him.

"I doubt that," Max stated, turning to face his longtime friend. "But I don't have a choice. If my father goes through with this, if he gives the go-ahead and orders a hit on Courtney, he's a dead man. And I'll be the one to take him out." Sighing, he headed for the bar, retrieving his empty glass on the way. "I want to know the instant Ace gets back with you."

Ace was a well-known mercenary they'd done business with in the past. No one knew what his real name was; they simply called him Ace due to the fact he could take out a person—any person—with one shot, nothing more. Ace had been the one to contact Leyton when Samuel had reached out to him, agreeing that he would make Samuel an offer he couldn't refuse and would relay the details back once he had them.

Leyton got to his feet, tossed back the remaining liquid in his glass, and then set it on the bar. "Will do, boss."

"Hey," Max called out as Leyton reached for the door handle, "Thanks."

Leyton nodded, then left Max to stare after him, contemplating what it was going to do to his mental stability when he had to kill his own father. Truth was, he'd never thought it would come to this, but there was no way he could allow Samuel to get away with ordering a hit on someone important to him. If he did, then others would think they could get away with it, as well.

So, Max was left without a choice. The only way to prove that those he loved were untouchable was to take out one of his own.

The thought still made him sick.

Chapter Forty-Seven

Trust me when I tell you …
I understand.

Courtney awoke to the sound of Max's hushed voice. A quick glimpse at the clock told her they'd only been in bed for a couple of hours and the sun wouldn't be up for several more.

"Yeah?" There was a lengthy pause, followed by, "Thanks."

Max's heavy sigh worried her, and when he crawled up behind her, pulling her tight to his body, her heart started a heavy thump in her chest.

"What's wrong?" she asked, keeping her voice calm.

Max didn't reply.

Turning in his arms, she tried to see him in the dim light of the room but could only make out his profile. "Max?"

"It's okay, baby," he said softly, pulling her head down to his chest, his arms winding tightly around her.

She fought him, refusing to allow him to shut her out. After all they'd been through, Courtney couldn't stand the thought of him keeping something from her. They'd made it through the last two years, fighting their desire for one another, giving in to them, and now, they'd settled into something that was as peaceful as she'd imagined it could be. All things considered.

There was still danger lurking, still things about Max that she would never understand or condone, but she'd finally figured out where she belonged. And if she could overcome her own demons and finally resign herself to loving him for the rest of her life, she deserved to carry his burdens as well.

"Talk to me," she insisted, her voice low. "Who was that?"

"Leyton," he told her, pressing his lips to hers as he cupped the back of her head and pulled her closer.

Courtney knew what he was doing, could feel his need to change the subject, and he intended to do that by making love to her. As much as she wanted that, she needed this more. For a solid year, they'd used sex as a way to keep distance between them. And ever since he'd been shot, that hadn't been the case. The sex was still potent, not to mention frequent, but there was something deeper when they came together. Even tonight when he'd fucked her in the middle of the club, it'd been different.

"What did he say?" she asked, pulling her mouth from his and placing her hands on his chest, keeping some space between them but not enough that she couldn't feel his heartbeat or his warmth.

"He confirmed what I'd already suspected," Max said roughly, sitting up abruptly, forcing her off of him.

The lamp came on, and she blinked until her eyes adjusted to the golden glow filling the space. Max grabbed his jeans and yanked them on. When he left the room, she reached for his shirt, pulled it on, and began buttoning it as she followed him into the living room. She found him pouring a drink, and as she rolled up the sleeves so that her hands were free, he moved to the floor-to-ceiling windows, staring out at downtown.

"You can talk to me," she told him, making her voice stronger than she felt. She hated seeing him like this. Something was obviously wrong. What, she didn't know, but she wanted to be there when he needed someone to lean on.

"I wish that were true," he snapped, tossing back his drink.

"What does that mean?" she countered hotly, feeling her face flame with anger. "Why can't you? You don't trust me, Max? After all the shit I've done for you, you don't fucking trust me?"

Max spun around, pinning her with his eyes. "It's not about trust, Courtney. I *do* trust you. I've always trusted you. That's not the problem."

That revelation did wonders to subdue the anger. He'd once told her in that very same penthouse that he'd never trusted her. Although she'd suspected he'd only been trying to hurt her with his words, there'd been a lingering doubt left behind.

"Then what is?"

"I don't want you to hate me," he declared, shocking her with the statement.

She studied him briefly, then said, "I could never hate you."

"No? What if I had to kill someone else, Courtney? Someone close to me. Would you hate me then?"

Courtney squared her shoulders. "No, I wouldn't. Not if it meant doing what needs to be done."

She was shocked at the conviction behind her words, scared more because they were the truth. She didn't like the idea of Max having to kill someone, but she understood it. Never in her life had she been so callous to think that she could take a life without hating herself for it, but then Angelica had done the unthinkable, and Courtney had considered it.

Hell, she still weighed her options from time to time.

Like when she watched Max having breakfast, smiling and talking to Leyton. Or when he spent time with his brothers and sisters, laughing in a way that made her heart swell. When he sat at his desk, reading whatever had captured his attention… Those were the moments when she knew that she could so easily take a life if it meant protecting him. And she doubted she would even flinch.

Max moved closer, lifted her chin, and forced her to look at him. "And if I had to kill my own father?"

Her gasp was the only sound, other than the pounding of her heart.

"Why? Why would you do that?" she asked, suddenly not understanding anymore.

"Sometimes things have to be done. Horrible things, Courtney. If it means protecting the people who mean the most to us, we do it without regret."

"Samuel?" *Oh, God.* She didn't want to know what Max's father had done that would earn him death. Sure, the guy was pure evil and likely deserved to die for a countless number of things he'd done in his life, but not at Max's hand. "What did he do?"

"The worst thing he could possibly do," Max said harshly.

"Which is?"

Max's eyes caressed her face briefly before he locked them with hers once again. "He ordered a hit."

Courtney's stomach churned. "On who? My father?" She knew that Samuel hated Casper for what he'd done, for interfering, for sending Courtney into their world. But to kill him, that didn't make sense. It would only bring some powerful people down on him.

"Not your father," Max whispered, the words sounding tortured. "Samuel ordered a hit on … you."

Chapter Forty-Eight

Love me for eternity.
That's all I need.

Max watched as Courtney's eyes glazed over, and he thought she was going to pass out. He wrapped his arms around her, but she didn't lean into him, didn't hold him, didn't so much as move.

"Why?" she asked, the word muffled as she pressed her face against his chest.

Max kissed the top of her head and then pulled away from her. "As payback to your father. He wants to hurt Casper, to show him that no one interferes with his family."

"That'd do it," Courtney said, her tone light. Too light.

She moved away from him, grasping the back of the sofa as though attempting to keep her legs beneath her.

"It'll never come down to that," he assured her. "Courtney, I'll never let him hurt you."

"You can't kill your own father," she declared, whirling around, her eyes wide, glassy with unshed tears.

"I can," he told her sharply. "And I will. That bastard sealed his fate when he ordered the hit. I knew what he'd been plannin', so I sent someone in. Someone who would agree to take your life but has no intention of following through."

He could sense her confusion, and he wanted to tell her it would be all right, but he couldn't. Those reassurances didn't mean shit in his world. Death was inevitable.

And she'd seen firsthand what he was capable of, but there was so much more she would never know because he didn't want to see the light completely dim in her eyes. As it was, over the last weeks, she'd become colder in many ways. Except when it came to him.

She was embracing his world, effortlessly moving in, and eventually, she'd be so involved there'd be no way out. That was the way things worked. Once in, always in. Death was the only way out. Not that he intended to let her go, nor would he let anyone hurt her. He'd die before he allowed that to happen.

"There has to be another way." Courtney's eyes lifted to his.

Max shook his head. Unfortunately, this was the way of the world. When word got out that the Adorite boss had ordered a hit on the woman Max loved, he'd be expected to avenge her. And the only way to do that was to take out the threat.

If he wanted to prove himself as the future boss, he had no choice but to follow through.

Which he fully intended to do.

Reaching for her, Max dragged her over to the sofa. Sitting, he pulled her into his lap, forcing her to straddle him. Sliding his hands beneath the shirt—his shirt—he caressed smooth, warm skin. She had nothing on beneath, and the urge to see more of her was too much. With his eyes locked on hers, he proceeded to release the few buttons she'd hooked, then opened the shirt, giving him a front-row view of her beautiful body.

"Max," she whispered, her eyes never leaving his.

"I need to feel you, Courtney," he told her, running his hands over her skin again. Over her hips, her waist, her ribs, then cupping her beautiful breasts, bringing one to his mouth. He licked her nipple until she moaned.

"Inside me," she insisted.

Max released her from his mouth so that he could remove his jeans. Courtney shifted, allowing him room to lift his hips and push the denim down his legs and then off completely. With that task accomplished, he resumed his feast. And when Courtney took his rigid cock into her body, impaling herself, he groaned.

She was so warm, so wet… It didn't matter when, where, or how, but when Max was inside her, he was in heaven. Nothing or no one would ever take that away from him. Hell was a way of life, something he trudged through every single day because this was the life he'd been born into, the life he'd ultimately chosen. But her… Courtney was light and energy and good. He craved that little sliver in his world, feeding off her goodness, knowing it would never help but needing it all the same.

"Max," Courtney breathed against his ear, her hand cupping his jaw as she rode him slowly.

Max grazed his fingers over her skin, teasing her nipple, caressing her body while he lost himself to her. Cupping her face, he rested his forehead against hers while pleasure snared him.

"I love you," he whispered as her hips continued to rock forward and back, his cock buried deep inside her body. Her muscles clamped down on him, sending awareness rippling through his balls, the beginning urges to come tingling in his spine.

"I love you, too," she said on a rough moan.

"Marry me, Courtney," he said, holding her hips, guiding her body as he slowly penetrated her.

A small smile formed on her lips. "Always tryin' to distract me."

"Not this time," he told her truthfully. "I want you to marry me. To spend the rest of your life with me. It's all I want, all I need. I can't breathe without you."

Courtney rocked forward and back, sensation after sensation rocketing through him while he waited for her answer.

"Yes," she said, her lips brushing his lightly. "I'll marry you, Max."

Max rocked her faster against him while he thrust up into her, increasing the friction. He slid his thumb over her clit, circling it, pressing down until she was gasping and moaning, her nails biting into his shoulders.

Before she came, Courtney leaned down, crushing her mouth to his, and Max let go, time standing still as her pussy gripped him, milking him dry. He didn't stop kissing her, unable to let her go. He wanted to stay right there forever, to forget the bullshit that had invaded his world, but he knew he couldn't.

Dawn would be there soon enough, and when it arrived, Max had some final decisions to make.

Some that would ultimately alter the course of his entire life.

Chapter Forty-Nine

That's not how this is supposed to work, you know.

The next day

The following morning, Courtney convinced Leyton to accompany her to the store so she could pick up a few things. It had actually taken longer to convince him than to actually get to the store because he'd been hell-bent on keeping her locked up, just in case Samuel did something stupid. In the end, Courtney had won that argument, but Leyton hadn't been happy with her. After last night and that morning, Max had officially worn her out, and she was starving, yet there wasn't anything in the penthouse to cook. So, she'd decided to rectify that while Max showered.

Now, as she and Leyton emerged from the elevator, her cell phone rang. Rummaging for it at the same time she grabbed her key, she hit the talk button and crammed the phone between her ear and her shoulder.

"Hello?" Courtney fumbled with the key to the penthouse, trying to jam it in the lock but missing on both attempts while Leyton chuckled from behind her.

Before she could unlock the door, it opened, and she came face-to-face with Max.

The voice on the phone sounded. "Courtney? It's RT. We've got a problem."

"And what? You need my help?" she asked, hating that she sounded a little perturbed.

Fact was, she was *extremely* pissed at RT and the rest of the Sniper 1 crew for the way they'd treated her. Although her reasons for not continuing to work for her father hadn't been shared—at least not by her—she had still expected them to be a little more understanding, perhaps wanting to get her side of the story. Instead, they'd all jumped to their own conclusions, assuming she'd left because of Max.

"Yeah, we do. Considering who we're dealin' with."

That captured Courtney's interest, and she stopped, setting her purse down on the coffee table.

"Who is it?" she questioned RT.

"Angelica Winslow is missing."

Courtney spun around and looked at Max, then Leyton. They were watching her curiously, but not saying a word.

"Angelica is missing? Did someone hire you to find her?"

"Her grandfather. He seems to think that Max had somethin' to do with it, but he won't say why," RT explained.

"He's not involved," she assured him.

Max's head tilted sideways, and Courtney covered the phone with her hand. "Artemis Winslow hired Sniper One to find his granddaughter. It seems she's missing."

Without a word, Max spun around, his attention on Leyton as they moved into the other room. "Do we still have eyes on Angelica?"

She couldn't hear what Leyton was saying, so she turned her attention back to RT. "I'll see what I can find out, but I'm tellin' you, Max isn't involved. He's lookin' into it now."

"I hope you're right about this, Court. Heads are gonna roll if he kidnapped the senator's granddaughter."

"Trust me," she said through clenched teeth. "It wasn't him."

"I'll be waitin' for your call," RT said and then disconnected the line.

When Max returned with Leyton in tow, Courtney asked the first thing that came to mind. "Do you think this has to do with Marcus Alvarez?"

Courtney had talked to Max about Angelica's involvement with the South Texas drug cartel that'd sprouted sometime in the last decade. They were merely distributors for one of the Mexican cartels that routed drugs into Texas from Mexico, but were working to make a name for themselves. As it turned out, Angelica had been introduced to Marcus by chance, wound up screwing the guy only to realize how deep she'd gotten. By then it'd been too late. And that had been how she'd been turned on to Max, thanks to her manipulation of her grandfather.

"I doubt it," Max said simply. "Doesn't seem his style. She's nothin' in the grand scheme. To him, anyway. She believes she's more than that, but I've talked to Alvarez. He agreed to let it go after I explained what she'd done to me."

"Could he have lied to you?"

Max shared a look with Leyton and then shrugged.

"What does that mean?"

"Anything's possible," Max told her.

"Okay, if it's not him, then any ideas who *might* have her?"

Max's eyes narrowed. "My father."

"What? Why?"

"Knowin' him, he's bringin' you forward by drawin' out your family."

"Shit." There was no way Courtney was going to allow that to happen. She would not let that crazy bastard hurt her family.

Grabbing her purse from the table, she made it three steps before Max pulled her up short. Leyton moved to stand in front of the door, as though he was going to keep her from leaving.

"No. You're not goin' after him," Max ordered.

"He's gonna kill my family, Max. I'm not just gonna sit back and watch it happen."

"You won't have to," he informed her, but she didn't like his tone. He was going to exclude her from the plan; she could feel it.

"I'm meeting with my father," Max told her. "You're gonna stay here with Leyton. I'll take Rock with me."

"No!" she exclaimed. "You're not gonna kill him, Max." Courtney still couldn't wrap her mind around Max killing his own flesh and blood. No matter how ruthless the guy was.

Max gripped her arms, yanking her toward him, his face serious. "This isn't open for discussion. Either you stay here with Leyton or I'll tie you to the goddamn bed myself."

Courtney glared at him, jerking out of his grasp. "Fuck you. I'm not some little girl you can order around, Max. I know what the fuck I'm doing."

"And so do I," Max told her.

Her stomach twisted when she thought about the night Max had been shot, the days she'd spent praying he'd wake up, the weeks of rehabilitation that had followed. She couldn't do it again. She wouldn't allow him to do this. Not for her.

"I can't lose you," she told him, her voice strained. "I'm not willin' to risk it."

"Nothin's gonna happen to me," he said, stepping closer, his hand sliding into his pocket. When he pulled out a ring, her eyes nearly bugged out of her head.

"You agreed to marry me, right?"

She couldn't speak, the words dying in her throat as she took in the size of the rock. There was no way she could wear that thing.

Max obviously didn't agree with her because he took her hand and slipped it onto her finger.

"I'm comin' back to you, Courtney. I swear to you. You promised to marry me, and I'm gonna hold you to that."

She shook her head. No matter what he said, no matter how much charm he oozed, she wasn't going to let him do this alone.

Dropping her purse on the sofa, she grabbed her phone.

"Who're you callin'?" he questioned.

"I need to call RT. The least I can do is send them somewhere else. I'll tell 'em about Marcus. That'll deter them for a bit."

Max watched her skeptically. But then he slammed his mouth on hers in a kiss so hungry, so devastating it nearly knocked her off her feet. Unfortunately that didn't last long. He pulled away and stormed out the door before she got a chance to catch her breath.

Or argue with him.

Chapter Fifty

Time to face the music.

"Keep her in there!" Max ordered Dane as he slipped into the elevator. "Leyton's with her, but if she pulls one over on him, under no circumstance does she get out of this building. Understand?"

"Yes, sir," Dane agreed, a confused expression on his face as the elevator doors closed between them.

Max grabbed his cell phone. By the time the doors opened on the first floor, he'd sent off a text to his brothers and sisters, instructing them to meet him at Samuel and Genevieve's. As he was climbing into his Charger with Rock in the passenger seat, his phone rang. He quickly punched the talk button.

"What's goin' on?" Ashlynn asked. "And yes, before you grill me, I'm on my way now. But I want a heads up."

Max proceeded to inform Ashlynn of the situation, and was, yes, met with the exact response he had expected from her.

"Get it done. I'm behind you all the way."

With that, they disconnected.

Max had known he could rely on Ashlynn to have his back. As for the others, he wasn't so sure.

"Care to share what's goin' on?" Rock inquired as they drove.

"Angelica's missin'. If I'm right, my father has her."

Rock frowned.

"What? What the hell is it?" Max questioned.

"I don't know if that's the case."

Max waited for him to continue.

"Last night, Angelica attempted to get into the club. Said she needed to talk to you. Somethin' about a drug cartel or some shit. We sent her away, figured it was bullshit."

"Fuck," Max growled.

It was too late to turn back now. His brothers and sisters were already on the way, and he needed to address this issue with Samuel, anyway. Figuring he'd get this done and over with, he told Rock to contact Leyton.

By the time they pulled up to his parents' house, it appeared everyone else had arrived. Rock didn't allow Max out of the vehicle until they'd determined the coast was clear. With two of Ashlynn's bodyguards standing outside the door, along with his own three-man team, two of which had been in the car behind them, Max made his way inside.

And prepared for the inevitable.

Chapter Fifty-One

The shit hits the fan. A lot of it, too.

Courtney hated herself for what she was about to do, but she had no choice.

Opening the front door, she saw Dane standing in the hall, his gaze sliding over to her, a frown replacing his neutral expression.

He glanced over her shoulder as if he expected Leyton to come out. She could've told him that Leyton was otherwise occupied, but what fun would that be? Knowing Leyton, he'd be able to get out of the closet she'd locked him in within minutes, which meant she had no time to waste.

"You know the boss'll kill me if you leave that penthouse."

Courtney smirked.

"Well…" She stepped into the hall, closing the door behind her.

When Dane turned her way, she pulled her gun, aiming it directly at him.

"I have somethin' to handle. I know he gave you an order, but I'm not stayin'."

"Goddammit, woman," Dane grumbled. "Why the hell can't you make it easy on me? Haven't I been through enough shit lately?"

Courtney felt bad for him. He'd healed from Angelica's vicious attack, but the scar that ran down his entire face was a brutal reminder of how things could go bad so easily. She had no intention of hurting him, but she would if he didn't let her go.

With her gun aimed at him, she inched toward the elevator and punched the button to go down.

"I'm just gonna call Darius. He'll stop you on the first floor," Dane said with a resigned sigh.

She smiled at him and pulled her other hand from her pocket. "As much as I appreciate you lookin' out for me, Max is more important."

Dane's eyes widened briefly.

And then she tased him. She didn't use enough juice to do much damage but enough to take him to the ground. While he was still twitching, she hopped in the elevator and stabbed the button for the first floor. Slipping out of the building was simple, making it to her car equally so. Only when she was flooring it out of the parking garage did she dial Darius, informing him to check on Dane. And Leyton.

He cursed a blue streak when he realized what she'd done, but Courtney didn't stay on the line long enough to hear the most creative words he came up with.

The next call she made was to Marcus Alvarez. She'd stolen his number from Angelica's phone, in case she needed it in the future. And what do you know? It came in handy.

"Who the fuck is this?" the gruff voice sounded.

"Where is she?" Courtney demanded.

"Who the fuck you talkin' about, *chica*?"

Courtney rolled her eyes. "Where's Angelica Winslow?"

"Ahh, you're lookin' for the double-crossing *puta*."

"Where is she, Marcus?"

"My guess is that *hijo de puta loca* has her. *Loco bastardo*."

"Who?" she questioned, getting irritated with his rambling.

"Adorite."

Fuck. Max had been right.

Hitting the button to end the call, she cursed.

Half an hour later, Courtney pulled into Samuel and Genevieve's estate. Stopping the car abruptly at the gate, she hopped out quickly, making a big scene until the guard on duty came running out toward her. As soon as he was close enough, she disabled him, taking him to the ground and knocking him unconscious with a quick blow to the head. Hitting the button to open the gate, she was back in her car, speeding up the driveway.

The sheer number of cars parked in front of the house wasn't surprising. If Max was willing to take out his own father, he'd give his brothers and sisters a warning beforehand. Sad part was, she didn't think any of them would care, because their loyalties—from what she'd seen over the last two years—weren't to their parents but to one another.

Peering around, she was surprised to see that there wasn't any security outside. She doubted the same could be said if she were to simply walk in unannounced, so she figured coming in from the back would be a better idea. Slipping around to the side of the house, she peeked in what windows she could, not seeing anyone.

By the time she reached the back of the house, she could hear muffled voices. Based on the volume, there was quite a bit of heated conversation taking place inside.

Within a minute, she was inside the house, shaking her head at the security measures in place. The sliding glass door at the back had been left unlocked, making it incredibly easy to get inside.

She remained close to the wall, peeking around corners, looking for the bodyguards, but saw none. And when she slipped into the hallway that led to the main family room, she understood why.

"Talk!" Max yelled.

"Nothin' to talk about," Samuel retorted casually, although his wide eyes said he wasn't as calm on the inside as he was attempting to project. "As far as I'm concerned, you've got two choices."

Courtney crept closer, glancing into the room to see Samuel standing behind a chair while holding a gun on Angelica, pressing it against her temple. Circling them was Aidan, Brent, Victor, Ashlynn, Madison, Max, and Rock.

Damn. Maybe she should've brought Leyton. He'd likely know exactly what to do.

Knowing there was no time to think about that, she focused her attention on where everyone was in the room.

It seemed the only two people talking were Max and his father. The only person wielding a gun was Samuel. At least from what she could tell from her vantage point.

"And they would be…?" Max probed.

"Own up to your mistake, son. I'll take out Courtney, and we can all move on with our lives."

"Or…?"

"The hit stands, and she'll need to watch her back because she will die. One way or the other. Either way, this one"—Samuel nudged Angelica's head with the gun—"needs to die. She knows too much."

"There is no hit," Max declared loudly. "You were set up, old man. I knew what you were plannin'. And Ace… He's one of mine. So your plan has a few holes in it."

Courtney kept quiet, focusing on her breathing despite the anger that soared through her. It was hard to believe this man could be so cold as to kill her because her father had wanted to reassure himself that Genevieve was all right. It'd been a stupid move on Casper's part, sure, but killing someone in the name of revenge just didn't make sense. What would it benefit? With her out of the picture, Casper—as well as her own brothers—would merely go to the ends of the earth hunting him down.

There was a crash at the front of the house, but Courtney couldn't see what it was.

"Does it?" Samuel asked, laughing mockingly.

Courtney's heart leaped into her throat when she saw Casper, RT, Trace, and Conner step into the room, guns blazing.

"Son of a bitch," Max ground out.

Samuel shifted, retrieving another gun and aiming it directly at her father.

"Put it down," Max demanded, rage unlike anything she'd ever witnessed reverberating from those three words.

"Or what? You actually give a shit about this bitch?" Samuel scolded. "She tried to kill you." Samuel nodded toward Casper. "And him? He's too fuckin' nosey for his own good. Thought he could best me by sendin' his only daughter in to infiltrate my world. To save my *wife*." The crazy laugh that followed had the hair on the back of Courtney's neck standing on end.

As silently as she could, Courtney unlatched the safety on her gun, keeping it trained on Samuel. She wouldn't get a kill shot from where she stood, but it'd do enough damage to take Samuel down.

Angelica was shaking like a leaf, her chest heaving, tears streaming down her face, and yet Courtney couldn't muster an ounce of fucking sympathy for her. She'd shot Max. Twice. Tried to kill him, and now that the tables were turned, she couldn't handle the pressure.

The bitch never would've lasted in Max's world.

As Courtney shifted, attempting to get a better bead on Samuel, she wondered when she'd become one of them. Sure, she knew she'd been dangling over the edge for a while now, but she didn't remember falling. That moment—when she'd decided that not all lives were worth saving—had apparently come and gone. Clearly, she'd moved on, accepted the fact that sometimes people couldn't be saved.

Damn it!

Leyton came scrambling through the front door, his eyes wide as he glanced from one person to another. RT turned, pointing his gun at Leyton while Casper and Trace remained focused on Samuel, Conner keeping his attention on Max.

"Put the gun down," Casper bellowed at Samuel, his voice deep and authoritative. "Hand over the girl, and we'll leave you to handle your own family shit."

"Is that right?" Samuel snarled. "Now you're willin' to back out of my life? To stop snoopin'? Why's that? Why the fucking change of heart, Kogan?"

"Where's Courtney?" Max demanded, glaring at Leyton.

"She got away from me," Leyton said, his gun aimed directly at RT.

It was a standoff.

Courtney knew the shit was about to hit the fan, but barging in would likely cause someone to get shot, and she couldn't bear the thought of any one of these people going down for her. And Max would likely go crazy not knowing where she was, so she decided to chance it.

"Hand her over," Courtney called out, stepping out into the open. "Hand her over and you can have me. That's what you want, right?"

"Son of a bitch!" Max roared, and her good deed went completely unheeded. The next thing she knew, Samuel's gun—the one he had aimed at Angelica's head—shifted. But he didn't point it at her; instead, he did what she'd feared all along.

Samuel turned the gun on Max, but Max's back was turned to his father as he watched her, a crazy glimmer in the old man's eyes. A shot rang out, someone yelled, then Max went down, and Courtney was pretty sure her heart stopped beating in her chest.

Chapter Fifty-Two

Fuck.
(The only word that comes to mind.)

"Fuck!" Max yelled, shoving Leyton away. "Get the fuck off me."

He was on his feet, scrambling to get Courtney while chaos ensued, people yelling, screaming, someone crying. The only thing he could focus on was her. She was on the ground, eyes closed, and he was sure his life had come to an end right there in his parents' living room.

"No! Goddammit, no!" he roared, pulling her to him.

"Where's she hit?" Leyton asked, moving in closer while Courtney's father attempted to force Max away.

Max grabbed his gun and aimed it directly at Casper's face. "Move back!"

A hand pulled at his arm, and he glanced down to see Courtney's eyes open. She reached for the back of her head, rubbing as she looked around, seemingly confused.

"I'm not hit," she said. "Someone pushed me."

"Put the gun down!" RT barked.

All eyes turned to see…

Samuel was lying on the ground, blood pooling around him, his eyes closed. He was dead. There was no doubt about it based on the single bullet wound straight through the center of his forehead. Angelica had fallen to the floor, curled up in a ball as she sobbed uncontrollably. The last person Max gave a shit about was her.

"Fuck." Max helped Courtney to her feet, holding her against him as he watched in horror as his mother held a gun to her own head.

"I'm sorry," Genevieve cried softly.

"Genny, don't do this," Casper stated softly.

"I won't go to jail," she said, her green eyes shifting toward Casper. "I've spent my entire life in this prison. I won't survive."

"You won't go to jail," Casper assured her. "You're finally free."

Max couldn't believe his ears. He glanced toward RT and Courtney's two brothers. One nod from Casper and the three men turned and retreated from the house.

"Put the gun down, Genny. It's over. It's over, honey," Casper pleaded, his tone calm.

"Please, Mom," Ashlynn called out. "Put down the gun. It's over. He's dead."

Max watched as Ashlynn slowly approached Genevieve, her voice soft as she continued to talk her down. A minute later, Casper had Genevieve's gun in hand.

Victor and Madison were at her side, helping her into a chair.

Having lost at least ten years off his life, Max turned around and pulled Courtney into his arms. And that's when he saw him.

"Fuck!"

Releasing Courtney, Max ran to Dane's side. He was lying in the hallway, blood pooling around him. He'd been shot. His eyes were rolling back as he held his shoulder.

Voices grew louder as the others realized what had happened.

Courtney dropped to her knees beside him, slapping a cloth over the bullet wound on Dane's upper arm.

"You crazy asshole," she mumbled to him. "You're the one who pushed me down. Why'd you go and do that?"

Dane smiled. It was weak, but it was a smile. "Boss woulda killed me if I didn't protect you."

Shit. Dane had taken a bullet. One that had been meant for Courtney.

"Rock! Victor! Clean up!" Max ordered, glancing over his shoulder at the others standing in the living room.

Leyton retrieved the gun from Casper's hand, ordering Courtney's father out of the house.

They had to get Samuel's body out of there. They could only do so much to keep the police away, and a gunshot wound meant police. They had plenty of people in their pocket, but this would be the second cover-up, not something the good boys in blue were going to like doing.

Not that Max gave a shit. He'd do what needed to be done.

But with the Sniper 1 guys there, Max didn't see this ending well.

"I said move out of the fuckin' way."

Max pulled his gun when Courtney's brother pushed his way through. Aiming at Conner's head, Max watched as the big man squatted beside Dane. Ignoring Dane's echoing howl of pain, Conner ripped Dane's T-shirt from collar to sleeve, then roughly turned him onto his side.

"It's clean. Went straight through. He'll live."

Conner let Dane drop back to the floor.

"Mad, get the doctor over here," Max demanded. "Rock, Victor, I still want that body out of here."

They had to get the house cleaned up, and someone needed to deal with Genevieve.

Taking Courtney's hand, he helped her to her feet, then crushed her body to his, burying his face in her neck. Her fingers slid into his hair as she held him. He would've never forgiven himself if something had happened to her.

When he managed to gather some semblance of control, he pulled back from her, cupping her face in his hands. "Are you all right?"

She nodded. Smiled. Then she pulled his head back down and whispered in his ear. "But I think Dane needs a raise."

Max laughed, shocked by the sound. Everyone else appeared to be as well because all eyes turned to him. He ignored them. There'd be a lot of conversations taking place now that this was over, but for the moment, Max didn't want to talk. He simply wanted to hold Courtney in his arms and never let her go.

Glancing across the room, he noticed Rock helping Angelica to her feet. In his hand… Holy hell. Rock was holding a gun… Was that the gun his mother had used to kill Samuel? What the hell was he…?

Right before his eyes, Rock took the gun and placed it in Angelica's hand, placing her prints on the butt of the gun.

"If I had to guess," Rock told her, "you'll be walking outta here on your own. Just remember, if you decide to talk, decide to tell anyone anything about what you saw today, you'll be the one the cops come for. Between you and me, orange ain't gonna look good on you, neither."

Angelica's eyes widened as she stared up at the big enforcer who'd just done what no one had thought to do. He'd placed the murder weapon in Angelica's hand, effectively arming them with something that was sure to keep her quiet going forward.

"He's a smart one," Courtney said softly, causing Max to peer down at her.

"That he is."

"Maybe he needs a raise, too."

Max smiled.

"Is your mother gonna be okay?" she asked.

Max looked over at Genevieve, who still appeared to be in shock. "Eventually," he told Courtney. "Now that it's over, I'm sure she'll figure it all out eventually."

At least he hoped that was the case.

Two hours later, Max was sitting at his mother's dining room table with Genevieve. Courtney was in the kitchen making coffee for the three of them. Everyone else had left a short time ago, but Max hadn't been ready to leave his mother alone. She was doing better, or so it seemed, but he was still worried about her. Enough that he intended to leave one of his enforcers there to keep a close eye on her, even though he knew she would try and refuse him.

"Here you go," Courtney said softly, delivering Genevieve a steaming mug of coffee.

"Thank you, dear," Genevieve responded politely.

Courtney disappeared and then returned with two more mugs before joining them both at the table.

"You don't need to babysit me," Genevieve stated, glancing from Max to Courtney. "I promise, I'll be fine."

"Will you?" Max questioned disbelievingly.

Genevieve's gaze slid toward the doorway to the living room. There was no trace of what had happened earlier. Victor and Rock had cleaned the scene while Madison assisted. It wasn't the first time they'd had to sanitize a room, so it hadn't taken them long.

"Do you want me to handle the funeral preparations?" Max offered, watching his mother closely.

Genevieve simply nodded, her attention quickly turning to Courtney. "Your father looks well."

"He told me that he knew you when y'all were kids," Courtney prompted, clearly curious as to the story there.

Max knew that Courtney had heard her father's version, and he'd heard Samuel's, but as of yet, no one had heard Genevieve's account of events. He was just as interested as Courtney was in understanding what had prompted her to stay with a man like Samuel for four decades.

"He feels guilty," Courtney said when Genevieve didn't respond.

Genevieve offered a small smile. "He shouldn't. I never blamed him."

"Maybe you should have," Courtney replied.

Genevieve looked up, meeting Courtney's gaze directly while Max studied the two women.

"No. It was never Casper's fault. We were young. And I was definitely too young for him at the time. I knew when he went off to the military that he wouldn't be coming back. Not for me, anyway."

"According to him, that had been the plan," Courtney interjected.

"Maybe in the beginning, sure," Genevieve replied. "But my life had been mapped out for me long before that time would've ever come." Genevieve looked away, her eyes clouding as though she were remembering that life. "My father didn't make the best decisions. And then Samuel came into our world, and my father was scared. Actually, terrified was probably a better way to explain it. I remember talking to him after Samuel came to collect the debt the first time. He'd given my father one week to come up with the money. I knew that wasn't possible. We didn't have any money. My mother was already gone, and my father was still grieving, all those years later.

"Despite what Samuel believed, he didn't bully my father into using me as payment for the debt. It was actually my idea. I knew how boys looked at me, and I'd seen that disgusting praise in Samuel's eyes the first time I saw him. I told my father that he needed to offer me as payment, so he did."

"Why would a father do that?" Courtney asked, anger apparent in her tone.

"It wasn't an easy decision," Genevieve explained, meeting Courtney's gaze before glancing over at Max.

In that moment, Max saw all of the anguish he'd never seen before on his mother's face. She'd spent forty years with a man she hated, but she'd followed through with her promise. She'd married him, had his children, and ultimately stayed by his side. The fact that she'd been the one to take his life was only fitting considering the hell she'd lived through because of him.

"My father tried to argue with me, but I played up the guilt. He was all I had. My mother died giving birth to me. I didn't have any brothers or sisters, no aunts or uncles. My grandfather, Clyde's father, wasn't exactly the doting type. So, I refused to lose the only person who'd ever loved me.

"We played it off as though it were Clyde's idea, which seemed to appease Samuel. I don't know if it was the idea of taking a thirteen-year-old virgin that appealed to him or simply taking Clyde's only daughter away, but either way, he agreed. In fact, he made a big spectacle of it all, and in the end, everyone believed Samuel had been the one to bully Clyde into handing over his only daughter."

Courtney leaned forward. "What about my father? Did he know?"

"No," Genevieve confirmed. "I didn't want him to know. I made my father swear not to tell him. Casper deserved so much more than me," Genevieve said sadly. "I used to use him as a way to piss off Samuel, telling him that Casper would come back for me although I knew that would never happen. Only because Casper didn't know what had happened."

"He suspected," Courtney relayed.

"Of course he did. He knew my father and my grandfather, knew the types of people they were involved with because of their gambling problems. People like Samuel had been coming to the house plenty over the years. In fact, Casper was always the one to protect me from them. We'd hide out in his tree house until they left. Truth was, Casper was more like a big brother than anything else. Sure, I thought I loved him. I was young and he was handsome, charming, smart. And very protective. Casper is a good man."

"Why'd you stay with him?" Max questioned.

"So he didn't kill my father. He used to throw that in my face all the time, telling me he could off Clyde in a heartbeat. I was scared of him at first."

"And then…?"

"I had always planned to leave him. The older I got, the more opportunity I thought I had. We'd been together for nearly thirteen years when I got pregnant with you," Genevieve said, looking directly at Max. "I had been on birth control for a long time, hiding it from him. Then, I had some problems, and the doctor removed the implant and put me on the pills. I was twenty-six. I knew it wouldn't be long before Samuel found them. He wanted me pregnant. When he discovered them, he…"

"He what?" Max asked, knowing what the answer was.

"He beat me. Then he threw away the pills. The next thing I knew, I was pregnant with you. After that, leaving him wasn't an option. He stopped threatening to kill my father because he had something else to hold over my head."

Genevieve glanced down at her mug.

"He started threatening to take you away from me. And then when Brent was born, it got worse. He told me if I ever left, he'd kill you both. At that point, I knew there was no way out."

Silence filled the room. Courtney placed her hand on Genevieve's. "I'm so sorry."

"It was no one's fault. Not your father's, not my father's. I made the choice to stay. And now…"

"Now you're free," Max told his mother. "You're free to do whatever it is you want to do."

"I want to support my children," Genevieve said softly. "It's all I've ever wanted."

Max didn't say anything to that. He'd been born into this life, and there was no turning back. Regardless of what decisions had paved the way, this was where he was, who he was. And he didn't plan to turn back now. The question that he still needed to answer was how it worked without his father in the picture. Unlike in the movies, Samuel Adorite wasn't the Godfather, he wasn't the one who'd garnered respect and established the relationships. That had fallen on Max, so even with Samuel out of the picture, their businesses wouldn't be affected.

But how he handled things in the coming days would likely make all the difference in the world.

And Max simply had to figure out what he needed to do.

And then he needed to do it.

Chapter Fifty-Three

Loyalty. It's a requirement.

Three and a half weeks later
Friday

"Where do you think you're goin'?" Max asked Courtney when she attempted to slip out of bed. It was too early to get up, as far as he was concerned. However, it was never too early to…

She smiled back at him, a mischievous smirk that made his body harden instantly.

"Don't think I'm lettin' you out of this bed just yet," he told her as he rolled onto his back and watched as she sat up, the sheet shielding his view of her stunning breasts.

"Well, I thought maybe you'd want to…" Her grin widened. "Oh, never mind."

Max laughed, then pulled her back down on top of him. "Thought I'd want to what?" he asked, burying his face in her neck and inhaling her sweet scent. "Thought I'd want to do *this*?"

Adjusting his position, Max slid one finger into her pussy. Yep, she was already wet, but he'd expected that since he'd spent the last half hour teasing her while she slept, or pretended to sleep, which he figured was more likely.

Courtney moaned, her hand sliding over his rigid cock, stroking him until his breath lodged in his throat.

"No," she told him, breathless. "I was thinkin' of somethin' more like this."

She slid down his body until her mouth hovered inches above his dick. Her breath fanned the engorged head, and he couldn't look away. Her little pink tongue darted out, caressing the tip. He sucked in a breath, his hands gripping the sheet beneath him.

"I like your way of thinkin'," he told her. "Go ahead, suck me. I'll watch."

Courtney's sexy lips wrapped around the head of his cock, her teeth scraping sensually. Her eyelids lowered as she laved him with her tongue, the delicate rasp along the underside making his dick pulse in her mouth.

"Don't stop," he told her. "Take all of me."

Placing his hands behind his head, he propped himself up so he could watch her, feigning a casualness he didn't feel as she blew his mind right along with his dick. For long minutes, he held himself in check, enjoying the warmth and suction of her mouth, the exquisite feel of her tongue curling around him… When she hummed, his hips thrust upward, driving his cock into her mouth. She wrapped one hand around the base, stroking in time with her mouth as she bobbed up and down on him.

"Damn," he muttered harshly. "You're gonna make me come. Is that what you want? You want me to come in your mouth?"

Her eyes slid up to meet his, and she nodded, increasing the suction of her mouth.

Reaching for her, he twined his fingers in her silky hair and pulled her head down, controlling the pace as his climax threatened.

"That's it, baby. Suck me," he growled. "Fuck."

He kept his eyes trained on her, on his dick fucking her mouth until he couldn't take any more. His hips bucked, his cock pulsing as he allowed his release to overcome him. Her eyes met his as she swallowed, her tongue darting out to lick him clean. It was the sexiest fucking thing he'd ever seen.

Then again, everything about Courtney—everything she said, everything she did, every fucking breath she took—was sexy.

Pulling her up his body, he wrapped her in his arms and kissed her hard, tasting himself on her tongue. He lingered, stroking her tongue with his while he got his breathing under control.

"What're we gonna do today?" he asked, leaning back enough to see her face.

Courtney smiled. "It's Ashlynn's birthday," she said sweetly. "We're gonna party like rock stars. And later tonight…" She kissed his mouth. "You can return that favor."

"In the club?" he inquired, loving the feisty side of his soon-to-be wife.

"If that's what you want."

"Oh, it definitely is," he whispered, licking his way into her mouth once more. "More than anything."

Twenty minutes later, Max was in his office while Courtney showered. He had business to attend to before they let loose for the night. And more importantly, he needed to have a conversation with Leyton.

As it was, they'd had to increase security tenfold. Now that he'd taken over the Southern Boy Mafia, moving into the role his father had held for years, things were changing.

Drastically.

Strangely, they were getting stronger, more powerful, garnering more respect. It was almost as though Samuel had been holding them back, which, no doubt, he probably had been. The man hadn't been in his right mind for quite some time, and although Max understood Samuel's overall objective, the way in which he'd gone about getting things done left something to be desired.

For instance, taking a thirteen-year-old as a bride for a payment of a debt.

Sitting in his desk chair, Max pulled out a folder he kept locked in the bottom drawer of his desk. It contained all of the information regarding every member of the Southern Boy Mafia. Not their personal information, though. Those details were locked in another safe, one that no one except for Max and his second-in-command knew. Which, at that point, was no one.

That was the reason for the meeting he'd scheduled with Leyton. He needed Leyton's input on who would take over as underboss now that Max was boss. It wasn't an easy decision.

"Mornin', sir," Leyton called when he came into the room.

"Mornin'. Have a seat," Max stated, nodding toward the chair across from his desk.

Leyton kept his eyes firmly on Max.

Max hadn't informed Leyton why he was calling him into his office so early on a Friday morning, but the other man clearly knew it was important. After closing the door behind him, Leyton took a seat, his eyes never straying from Max.

Leaning back in his chair, he ordered his thoughts.

"I need your opinion," Max began. "I've given a lot of thought to the organization and the direction it needs to go."

Leyton nodded.

"The leadership of the Adorite family, or Southern Boy Mafia"—Max grinned—"whichever you prefer to call it, has always remained within the family. We've always instated the next in line, which technically means that Brent would move into my previous role, however…"

Leyton lifted an eyebrow, but he didn't speak.

"I'm not sure Brent's ready, or even willing, for that matter, to take over that position. He's got little initiative."

"Have you talked to him?" Leyton inquired.

Max leaned forward, resting his forearms on his desk. "At length, yes. He informed me that he's not ready, but I'm inclined to believe that he's never had the intention of taking over. He just never out-and-out admitted that part."

"I'd have to agree," Leyton stated, crossing his ankle over his knee and resting his hands on his stomach. "He's content with the day-to-day, but as far as decision making, I don't think he's interested."

"I know someone who is, someone I think would be able to handle the position brilliantly."

"Ashlynn?" Leyton inquired.

Max had actually given plenty of thought to that. "I spoke with my sister," Max told him frankly. "She was flattered, but she turned me down flat. However, she wasn't my first choice, either."

Leyton's eyes narrowed on him, and Max knew he was trying to figure out what direction he was headed. So he decided to enlighten him. "I met with my brothers and sisters yesterday, as you know. And we came to a decision."

"Which is?"

"My first choice for second-in-command has always been you."

Watching his friend closely, Max fought the urge to smile when Leyton's eyes widened, his jaw hanging open.

"Me? But I'm not…"

"Not what? Family?"

"Yes," Leyton said firmly.

"We tend to disagree. Technically, no, you're not family. There's no Adorite blood in your family line, but that's not the definition of family. At least not as far as I'm concerned."

"What did they say when you suggested it?" Leyton's eyes were still wide, but his cool demeanor had returned, as though their feedback wasn't important. Max knew better.

"It was unanimous." Leaning back in his chair once again, Max smiled. "So, that means if you're willin', then we're offerin' you the position. Just remember, with that power comes responsibility. And once in, never out."

Leyton's lips curved upward. "I've been in this from the beginning. You of all people should know that."

"I know you have, which is the reason for my choice. You've never let me down."

"What about Courtney? What did she say?"

Max smiled. "Courtney only had one concern, of course. She's always the voice of reason."

"And that was?"

"My safety. According to her, without you, I'm vulnerable." Max had actually found their conversation amusing, but he'd understood her point. If Leyton were to move into the role, it left a hole in his own security, and with the position he was taking over, that was a serious aspect they couldn't overlook.

"She's a very smart woman," Leyton replied. As he sat up straight, Leyton's expression turned serious. "Who'll take over my position?"

"I know who I'd suggest, but I'm gonna ask you to answer that one," Max told him frankly.

"Dane," Leyton stated without thought.

Max nodded. He'd been thinking the same thing, but he wanted Leyton to elaborate.

"The man took a bullet for your fiancée," Leyton continued. "He's proven his loyalty time and time again. Aside from Rock, he's the only one I would trust with your life."

"And what about you?" Max inquired. "Who'll step into that position for you?"

Max could sense that Leyton didn't think it was necessary, but there were precautions that had to be taken. In their world, the police were out to get them as much as anyone else, so expecting the good guys in blue to ride in and save the day was never an option. And as Courtney had said, they were vulnerable, even if they didn't want to admit it.

"Can I have some time to think about it?" Leyton asked.

"Think about what? Taking over the position? Or who'll be watchin' your back?"

Leyton grinned. "You should always know that I'll do whatever you need me to do, and I'll do it to the best of my abilities, boss. If you trust me to help run this organization, I don't have any questions. As for someone watchin' my back, I'll need to weigh my options. I'm not willin' to take your security from you, which means I'll have to get creative."

"Will one of Ashlynn's boys work?" Max knew that Ashlynn had more than they all did when it came to her security, but due to her position within the company and her visibility, that was necessary.

"No," Leyton stated adamantly. "Those boys are right where they need to be. I trust them with her life, and that's all that matters."

Max considered that statement for a moment. His thoughts drifted back to the time he'd caught Leyton and Ashlynn making out in the hallway, and he wondered whether that had escalated. Surely he'd have known because he saw everything. If it had, they'd hidden it well. Then again, Max knew that not only was Leyton loyal to him but he was loyal to the entire family, which meant he'd go to all lengths necessary to ensure that Ashlynn was protected. Regardless of what his underlying reasons were, or if they were more personal than business.

"Oh, and one more thing..." Max watched as Leyton's eyebrows lifted in question. "Second-in-command or not, I better not ever catch you fuckin' my sister anywhere. Certainly not in my bed or my favorite fucking chair, or anywhere else in my goddamn house. Got it?"

Leyton's confused expression amused Max. Yes, he'd heard that entire tirade the night he'd been shot and Leyton had saved his life. He'd never forgotten that, either.

When Leyton didn't say anything, Max laughed. "We good?"

"Yeah," Leyton said with a chuckle. "Whatever you say, boss."

"Then it's settled?" Max focused on Leyton again. "Effective immediately. We'll announce tonight."

"And my first assignment?" Leyton asked, getting to his feet.

"You can start by moving the fuck out of my house," Max joked. "Check your account. You'll find more than enough to get your own place."

Leyton laughed, as Max had thought he would.

"My pleasure. It ain't easy to sleep with all that moanin' and groanin' goin' on in your room."

Max smirked. “Trust me, that won’t be stoppin’ anytime in the near future. At least not if I have anything to say about it.”

Reaching out, Max waited for Leyton to shake his hand.

Leyton looked down, then placed his palm against Max’s. “You’ve always been like a brother to me. It’s an honor, boss. Truly.”

“Give it time.” Max chuckled. “The first time you’re shot, you probably won’t feel that way.”

“True. Very true.”

Chapter Fifty-Four

It was never a question ... until her. Until them.

Leyton made his way through the crowded club. He felt different, and he didn't need to wonder why that was. The announcement had been made tonight, which hadn't been done at the club the way Max had said it would be; instead, it had been handled over dinner, where all of the Adorites, including Courtney, had come together. Max's future wife had felt that something more official needed to take place rather than just a speech at the club where they'd be celebrating Ashlynn's twenty-sixth birthday.

The day had been surreal.

Many people wouldn't understand, but for him, this was an honor. Maybe being imbedded in a mob family didn't appeal to everyone, but for Leyton, it was more than a career choice. They were family. Regardless of the job or the end result, ultimately, he had a place he belonged.

That hadn't always been the case for him.

Word was spreading quickly through the club with the others, and Leyton found himself shaking hands a lot. He'd already run into a few associates who informed him that they'd like to speak to him at the first available opportunity.

That was business, so he'd informed them to reach out next week. He'd meet then.

Tonight was about having a good time.

After nodding to Courtney and Max, who were sitting at the bar smiling at one another like no one else was there, Leyton took the stairs up to the VIP section, looking for one person in particular. The guest of honor.

She'd disappeared nearly half an hour ago, and he was just making sure she was all right. Or so he told himself.

The sound of a woman moaning had him slowing. He didn't know who was beyond that curtain—at least not for sure—but the sensual moans were familiar.

His breath lodged in his throat when he turned the corner to find…

Ashlynn.

Lord have mercy.

Unable to look away, Leyton remained glued to the floor, his eyes traveling over the sleek lines of her body hidden behind the black silk of her dress. It should've turned him off to see the woman who'd invaded his deepest, darkest fantasies as of late in such a position, but it didn't. In fact, his dick instantly hardened as he took in the scene.

Ashlynn was impaled on the dick of her head of security, Jase Malone, riding him like a woman obsessed.

"That's it, baby," Jase groaned. "Ride my dick. Are you thinkin' about him right now?"

Leyton's eyes widened when he heard the question. Who? Who the hell was he talking about?

"God, yes," she cried out.

"Are you thinkin' how good it'd feel if Leyton's big dick was fillin' your ass?"

"Yes," she affirmed, breathless.

"You want him fucking your sweet ass while I'm plowin' this pretty pussy?"

"Both of you," she confirmed. "I want to feel you both."

Leyton's eyes slid down to where the two were connected, watching as Jase's dick slid in and out of Ashlynn while the man's big, bronze hands gripped her ass cheeks, separating them as his finger explored her asshole.

"Tell me what else you want, baby," Jase encouraged.

Ashlynn continued to ride him, impaling herself on Jase's thick cock. Leyton's body was rock hard as he took them in. He could so easily make all their fantasies come true simply by moving into the room, releasing his dick, and filling her ass. It was tempting; there was no doubt about that.

Then again, he didn't want to die, and Max had already threatened him. But did Max know about this…? About Jase?

"I want to feel your mouth on my pussy," Ashlynn said between cries of pleasure. "I want you to bury your tongue deep." Ashlynn sucked Jase's tongue into her mouth as though showing him what she wanted. "And I want to watch Leyton's dick slide in and out of your ass. I want to see him fuck you, take you, make you fucking beg."

It was Jase's turn to groan. Or fuck, maybe that'd been him, Leyton didn't know, but the erotic scene flashed in his head.

How the fuck had she known? He'd always been careful to hide his bisexuality. From everyone. So, did she know? Or was that just a fantasy?

"Fuck yes," Jase growled. "I want to feel his dick in my ass, fucking me hard and fast while I lick your pussy."

They were both breathless.

"I need more," Ashlynn pleaded.

"Turn around for me," Jase instructed.

Leyton took a step back, hiding in the shadows, not wanting them to know he was there.

Jase's cock slipped from Ashlynn's cunt as she stood. When she was facing the other way, Jase got to his feet and ordered her to bend over the arm of the sofa. She did as instructed, her skirt hiked up, Jase's slacks around his thighs.

Leyton had always had a thing for Ashlynn. The woman was sexy as fuck and wild as all get out. Although he hadn't quite known she was *this* wild. His own sexual proclivities had kept him from pursuing her fully—before he'd known that Max would saw his balls off and feed them to him if he did—but clearly he'd had no reason to worry where she was concerned. Ashlynn Adorite could clearly handle anything Leyton would want from her.

Jase filled Ashlynn's pussy from behind in one fluid move, his thick cock going deep.

"Fuck me, Jase. Fuck me the way you'd fuck Leyton. The way you've told me you want to."

Holy shit.

That wasn't expected. Not at all.

And now, Leyton couldn't take his eyes off Jase, admiring the man's lean, muscular form as he slammed his hips against Ashlynn. The man was sexy as fuck, there was no doubt about that. He was a couple of inches shorter than Leyton, definitely not as broad, but there wasn't a damn thing small about him. His blond hair was kept short, his aquamarine eyes glowed, and he had a smirk that'd caught Leyton's attention before.

Yep, the guy was pure sin, and the two of them together were a temptation not easy to resist, but somehow Leyton managed.

When Jase shoved two fingers into Ashlynn's ass, making her beg for more, Leyton thought he would come in his pants.

But when Ashlynn's head turned and her sparkling hazel eyes met his, a seductive smile tipping her lips, Leyton knew… She'd wanted him to find them. She'd set this up.

And fuck if he didn't want to join in, but he knew better.

Loyalty was everything in Leyton's world. And he was nothing if not loyal to Max. If Ashlynn's brother found out that Leyton and Jase were making her a filling in their heated sex sandwich, there was no doubt that they'd both lose their lives.

Or worse.

Their balls.

Chapter Fifty-Five

Whatever you want ...
you just have to ask.

By three o'clock in the morning, Devil's Playground had cleared out.

Since Max hadn't opened the club to the public that night, it hadn't taken long to make sure it was empty, and while Dane and the others did that, Max sat with Courtney at the main bar, watching her intently.

"Did you have a good time tonight?" he asked when she finished her drink and turned her full attention back to him.

"I did. I think everyone did."

Leaning in, he couldn't resist running his lips along her jaw, then down her neck. "I still owe you something."

"You do," Courtney agreed. "And I'm ready to take you up on it."

Max pulled back, looking her in the eyes. "Here?"

"Why not?" she asked.

The next thing he knew, she had hopped up onto the bar, sliding down so that she was sitting in front of him, her legs spread wide. Without having to say a word, Courtney pulled her skirt up to her hips, baring her pussy to his hungry gaze. She was grinning down at him, clearly eager.

He'd known she hadn't been wearing panties. He'd figured that out when they'd been dancing and his hand had not-so-innocently traveled up her inner thighs. She'd been slick and warm, just as she was now.

"Spread your legs wider," he ordered, pushing the stool away when he got to his feet.

Courtney's eyes sparkled as she did as he instructed, widening her legs for him.

Starving for the taste of her, Max placed his hands beneath her knees and hefted her legs up and open, giving him better access. The position spread her wide as he swiped his tongue over her heated flesh, licking her slowly.

"You taste so fucking good." Max continued to eat her, devouring her with his tongue, fucking into her and circling her clit before sucking it into his mouth.

Courtney's hands clutched his head, her fingers pulling his hair as she pulled him closer, fucking his face as intently as he was thrusting into her. He continued, relentlessly bringing her as much pleasure as he could right there in the empty club. If he had any patience whatsoever, he'd have stopped long enough to find some booze to pour over her, just so he could lap it up from between her thighs.

But he didn't. Rather than waste a second, he fucked her with his tongue, thrusting it into her over and over as she bucked her hips against him, her fingers tightening in his hair as she yanked his head closer.

"Max," she said breathlessly. "Fuck yes. I'm gonna come. Don't stop. Never stop. Oh, God!"

Courtney's release was his only goal; making her come against his mouth was the only thing he could think about.

He held out, teasing her slow, then fast, repeating over and over until she was begging, pleading for him to make her come. Only then did he give in, focusing all of his attention on her needy little clit until she was screaming loudly enough to surely alert the men who were standing guard around all the entrances.

Not that he cared.

This woman… She was all that mattered. Her pleasure, her love, her very soul was all that he needed, and now that he had it, Max knew that their lives were just beginning.

And he was looking forward to the ride.

Courtney hopped down from the bar, nearly toppling him when she practically fell on him. "I think it's time you take me up to the penthouse," she whispered. "And since you've got nothing else to do tonight—except for me—I think we should start with a bath."

"And then?" he inquired, wrapping his arms around her and kissing her when her lips glided against his.

"And then … we'll just take it one step at a time."

"Have I told you that I love you lately?" he asked.

Courtney smiled. "Yes, but I'm happy to hear you say it over and over again…" Her smile widened. "While you're buried to the hilt inside me."

"I can do that," he told her. "I can certainly do that."

That's exactly what Max did.

Until the sun came up.

And then he started all over again.

One step at a time, just like Courtney said.

Epilogue

Beautifully brutal ... even then there's a happy ending.

One month later

Courtney sat at the table in the dimly lit Italian restaurant beside Max while they waited for her parents to arrive.

"Nervous?" Max inquired, smiling over at her.

"Me? I'm married to a mob boss. Why on earth would I be nervous?"

Max laughed, a full, hearty sound that made her body tingle.

For the past few weeks, they'd been getting through one day at a time, moving forward, figuring out how this thing between them worked.

Was it easy?

Hardly.

But that didn't mean she wasn't happy, because she was. At least as far as her love life was concerned.

She and Max had gotten married in a very simple ceremony. In Vegas. Where the only witnesses had been Dane and Leyton. They hadn't told anyone else about it, but that was something they'd both wanted. As far as Courtney was concerned, marriage was a piece of paper that did little to reflect what their relationship truly meant. They'd been to hell and back, suffered for so long that getting to this point had seemed nearly impossible at one point.

Yet they'd made it.

The only obstacle left to hurdle was the one that had put a strain on her relationship with her family. As much as Courtney wished she could shrug it off and pretend it didn't gut her from the inside out, she couldn't. And making amends with them was important. Even Max had recognized that, and that was the very reason they were at a restaurant, preparing to have dinner with her parents.

When her father and mother arrived, Courtney's heart fluttered in her chest. She was so happy to see them, even if the feeling might not be mutual.

The second her mother met her gaze, Courtney saw relief, and in turn, she released the breath she hadn't realized she'd been holding.

Once they approached the table, Max stood, offering his hand to Casper. Courtney's father glared down at it but finally returned the gesture. Courtney's mother leaned down and hugged her tightly, sending another surge of emotion through her.

"Thanks for coming," Courtney told them.

"Did you doubt we would?" Casper inquired, glancing between her and Max.

Courtney shrugged.

Casper sighed.

"I'm sorry," Casper told her directly. "I know I've been a little difficult to get along with lately, but I hope you understand my position. It's not every day that I find out my only daughter has run off and gotten married. Without telling anyone."

Casper glared at Max.

"It wasn't his fault," Courtney explained. "Fact was, I didn't want anyone there. We've…" Courtney glanced at Max briefly. "We've been through a lot in the last few months. And we know, no matter how we slice it up, there will always be a difference between what you do and what he does. I'm no longer questioning that. It's just the way it is now."

"Don't feel bad," Max said roughly, "my sisters weren't too thrilled, either."

Liz chuckled. "Her brothers had a few choice words to say as well. Not to mention Marissa."

"I really wanted y'all to come tonight so we could…" Courtney wasn't quite sure how to phrase it, but she needed to change the subject.

"Call a truce?" Casper asked when she didn't finish her statement.

"Yes," she said with a smile. "That works. Can we call a truce?"

Casper looked at Max, then back at her. "I think it's possible. Under one condition."

Great. Leave it to her father to make this into some sort of business arrangement.

Liz touched Casper's arm, giving it a gentle squeeze.

"What's that?" Courtney asked, not sure she wanted to hear it.

"I need you to help out at Sniper 1," he told her.

Courtney instantly shook her head. "That's not a good idea."

"Hear him out." Those words, out of Max's mouth, surprised her.

"I'm not askin' you to babysit anyone, but you're a valuable part of the company. Your expertise, your skill... They don't come along every day. You can call the shots on what you help with. I'm not askin' you to make a choice here. I know what your choice is. I'm just not ready to let you go from my life completely."

Tears clouded her vision as she listened to her father's heartfelt words. He was saying so much more than his words did. And she loved him for that. Didn't mean she'd take him up on the offer, but she would definitely consider it.

"So, from this moment forward, let's start over. We're always gonna be your parents, and we're always gonna worry about you and question your choices." Casper grinned slyly. "But we also know that we raised a smart woman. And just because we don't necessarily agree with all your decisions, we understand why you made them."

"What your father's having a hard time saying," Liz interrupted, "is that we love you. That'll never change. In the long run, we only want to make sure you're happy and safe."

Max's arm came around her shoulder. "Thank you," she told them, relief swamping her.

Casper's gaze darted over to Max's once again. "Don't thank me yet. You've yet to join us for a family dinner."

Max laughed. "Don't worry, when that time comes, I'll be sure to double my security."

Casper's grin widened. "You do that. Just remember, you're up against the best in the business."

Courtney looked at Max, grinning when he peered down at her. "Trust me," Max said with a smile, "that's not something I'll ever forget."

Acknowledgments

I have to thank my family first, for putting up with my craziness. From my sudden outbursts when I think of something that needs to be added or when I question why one of the characters did what they did, to the strange hours that I keep and the days on end when I'm MIA because I'm under deadline or just engrossed in a story… Y'all are incredibly tolerant of me and for that, I am forever grateful. I love you with all that I am.

My street team – The Naughty & Nice Posse. Ladies, your daily pimping and support fills my heart with so much love. You are a blessing to me, each and every one of you.

My beta readers, Chancy and Denise. Ladies, I'm not sure thanks will ever be enough. However, not only are you the ones who catch the weird things and ask the bigger questions, you've both become my friends and you keep me going.

My copyeditor, Amy. Punctuation and grammar… well, that's not my strong suit. But it is yours and you are truly remarkable at what you do. You simply amaze me and I am so glad that I found you.

Nicole Nation 2.0 for the constant support and love. This group of ladies has kept me going for so long, I'm not sure I'd know what to do without them.

And, of course, YOU, the reader. Your emails, messages, posts, comments, tweets… they mean more to me than you can imagine. I thrive on hearing from you, knowing that my characters and my stories have touched you in some way keeps me going. I've been known to shed a tear or two when reading an email because you simply bring so much joy to my life with your support. I thank you for that.

♥▫▫▫▫♥▫▫▫▫♥

I hope you enjoyed Max and Courtney's story. Beautifully Brutal is the first book in the Southern Boy Mafia series, which is a spin-off from the Sniper 1 Security series. You can read more about Courtney's family (the good guys) by checking them out on my website.

Want to see some fun stuff related to the Sniper 1 Security series, you can find extras on my website. Or how about what's coming next? I keep my website updated with the books I'm working on, including the writing progression of what's coming up for the Southern Boy Mafia series. www.NicoleEdwardsAuthor.com

If you're interested in keeping up to date on the Adorites as well as receiving updates on all that I'm working on, you can sign up for my monthly newsletter.

Want a simple, *fast* way to get updates on new releases? You can also sign up for text messaging on my website. I promise not to spam your phone. This is just my way of letting you know what's happening because I know you're busy, but if you're anything like me, you always have your phone on you.

And last but certainly not least, if you want to see what's going on with me each week, sign up for my weekly Hot Sheet! It's a short, entertaining weekly update of things going on in my life and that of the team that supports me. We're a little crazy at times and this is a firsthand account of our antics.

♥····♥····♥

About Nicole

New York Times and *USA Today* bestselling author Nicole Edwards lives in Austin, Texas with her husband, their three kids, and four rambunctious dogs. When she's not writing about sexy alpha males, Nicole can often be found with her Kindle in hand or making an attempt to keep the dogs happy. You can find her hanging out on Facebook and interacting with her readers - even when she's supposed to be writing.

Nicole also writes contemporary/new adult romance as Timberlyn Scott.

Website

www.NicoleEdwardsAuthor.com

Facebook

www.facebook.com/Author.Nicole.Edwards

Twitter

@NicoleEAuthor

Also by Nicole Edwards

The Alluring Indulgence Series

Kaleb

Zane

Travis

Holidays with the Walker Brothers

Ethan

Braydon

Sawyer

Brendon

The Club Destiny Series

Conviction

Temptation

Addicted

Seduction

Infatuation

Captivated

Devotion

Perception

Entrusted

Adored

The Dead Heat Ranch Series

Boots Optional

Betting on Grace

Overnight Love

The Devil's Bend Series

Chasing Dreams

Vanishing Dreams

Also by Nicole Edwards (cont.)

Sniper 1 Security
Wait for Morning

Southern Boy Mafia
Beautifully Brutal

Standalone Novels
A Million Tiny Pieces

Writing as Timberlyn Scott
Unhinged

Unraveling

Chaos